"With his recent work, Brian Stableford has assumed the seer's cloak of the late Olaf Stapledon, writing future history with both gripping intellectual content and heart. Don't miss *The Fountains of Youth*."

—Michael Bishop

"A coolly dazzling exploration of the potentials of humanity. If all SF is really about Now, Stableford's Now is the biggest imaginable."

—Ian MacLeod

"Stableford leaves behind the detective stories of his earlier future histories . . . to expound at length on the questions posed by immortality. The result is a much slower paced book that will still please fans of broadly imagined, speculative civilizations."

—*Booklist*

"A grand meditation on the state of human mortality. Thoughtful without being grim, this leisurely tale of one man's lifelong quest belongs in most SF collections."

—*Library Journal*

"Despite its two prequels, this book stands on its own as a work of philosophically satisfying SF."

—*Netsurfer Digest*

"Stableford presents a viewpoint from which our most common assumptions about life and death appear archaic, suggesting that biotechnology might eventually change our fundamental conception of what's 'natural.'"

—*American Scientist*

Tor Books by Brian Stableford

Inherit the Earth
Architects of Emortality
The Fountains of Youth
The Cassandra Complex

The Fountains
of Youth

BRIAN STABLEFORD

TOR®

A Tom Doherty Associates Book • New York

THE FOUNTAINS OF YOUTH

Copyright © 2000 by Brian Stableford

This book is printed on acid-free paper.

Edited by David G. Hartwell

A Tor Book
Published by Tom Doherty Associates, LLC
175 Fifth Avenue
New York, NY 10010

www.tor.com

Tor® is a registered trademark of Tom Doherty Associates, LLC.

Library of Congress Cataloging-in-Publication Data

Stableford, Brian M.
    The fountains of youth / Brian Stableford.
        p. cm.
    "A Tom Doherty Associates book."
    ISBN 0-312-87206-2 (hc)
    ISBN 0-312-87534-7 (pbk)
    1. Immortalism—Fiction. I. Title
PR6069.T17 F68 2000
823'.914—dc21   00-025598

First Hardcover Edition: May 2000
First Trade Paperback Edition: October 2001

Printed in the United States of America

0 9 8 7 6 5 4 3 2 1

For Jane, and everyone engaged in the serious
business of learning to live in the future

Acknowledgments

A much shorter and substantially different version of this novel was published in the April 1995 issue of *Asimov's Science Fiction*. I am very grateful to Gardner Dozois for publishing that novella and reprinting it in his annual collection of the *Year's Best Science Fiction*. In the course of researching Mortimer Gray's *History of Death* I consulted numerous academic studies of attitudes to death, of which the most useful proved to be *Man's Concern with Death* by Arnold Toynbee, A. Keith Mant, Ninian Smart, John Hinton, Simon Yudkin, Eric Rhode, Rosalind Heywood, and H. H. Price (London: Hodder & Stoughton, 1968); *The Hour of Our Death* by Philippe Ariès (London: Allen Lane, 1981); and *Death, Ritual, and Belief: The Rhetoric of Funeral Rites* by Douglas J. Davies (London: Cassell, 1997). I should also like to thank David Langford for his invaluable contributions to the collaborative future history we first set out in *The Third Millennium* (1985), much of which is reconfigured herein; Jane Stableford for proofreading services and helpful commentary; and David Hartwell for helping to keep the flickering flame alight.

The Fountains of Youth

Preface

A nyone who has chosen to read this autobiography must be hoping to gain some insight into the same question that led me to write it: Why did Mortimer Gray write *The History of Death*?

The easy answer is, of course, that somebody had to do it, and once I had published my first volume I had staked a claim that others were bound to respect, no matter how impatient they became with my slowness or the thrust of my arguments. It would, however, be disingenuous to pretend that anyone else's history of death would have been exactly the same as mine. The question would still remain: Why did *Mortimer Gray* write the particular history that bears his name? What experiences shaped him and cast their shadow upon his history?

It would, I suppose, be possible to begin the search for an explanation with the Great Coral Sea Catastrophe, which provided my first near-death experience as well as my first meeting with Emily Marchant, but it would not be right. I was Mortimer Gray long before I set sail on the ill-fated *Genesis*, and there is a sense in which the historian of death was already in the making before the Decimation. At the risk of telling my readers rather more than they need or desire to know, therefore, I feel that I must start at the very beginning of my own story, with an account of my unusual childhood. There, I hope, it will be possible to locate the seed of the individual that I became and the work that eventually made me famous.

PART ONE
Childhood

Mortal humans had no alternative but to live in the present. They woke up every morning knowing that disaster might strike them down before evening in any of a hundred different ways, and they knew that even if they were to survive, still they were ephemera bound to Earth for a mere moment of its history. Our parents and grandparents hoped that they would be different and that they would have the opportunity of living in the future, but their hopes were dashed;no sooner had they reached the crossroads of their burgeoning careers than they learned the sad truth. Ours is the first generation of humans to have the privilege of knowing that we really can live in the future; ours is, therefore, the first generation to have the responsibility and the duty of discovering how that might and ought to be done.

—Mortimer Gray
Introduction to Part One of *The History of Death*, 2614

ONE

I was born in 2520, an unexceptional child of the twenty-sixth century. Like my contemporaries, I was the beneficiary of a version of the Zaman transformation, which differs hardly at all from the one most commonly used today. By comparison with the children of previous centuries, however—excepting a minority of those born in the latter decades of the twenty-fifth century—I and all my kind were new. We were the first true emortals, immune to all disease and further aging.

This does not mean, of course, that I shall never die. There are a thousand ways in which the life of an emortal might be ended by accident or misadventure. In any case, future generations may well regard it as a major discourtesy for any earthbound person to postpone voluntary extinction too long—and those who choose not to remain earthbound multiply the risk of eventual death by accident or misadventure at least a hundredfold.

Given that all my readers are in exactly the same condition as myself, it may seem unnecessary even to record these facts and rather ridiculous to make so much of commonplace circumstance. If I am exceptional in any way at all, however—and why, otherwise, should I take the trouble actually to write my autobiography?—then I am exceptional because I have tried as hard as I can during these last five hundred years to make my fellow human beings conscious of the privileges and responsibilities of the emortal condition.

My own transformation was carried out at Naburn Hatchery in the county of York in the Defederated States of Europe, but as soon as I was decanted my foster parents removed me to a remote valley in the Nepalese Himalayas, where they planned to raise me to early adulthood. In those days, every team of mortal co-parents had to formulate its own theory as to the best way to bring up an authentically emortal child. Such decisions seemed uniquely problematic, because my co-parents and others like them knew that their children would be the last to see their parents die and that theirs was the duty of supervising humankind's last great evolutionary leap. Previous generations of parents had, of course, had some cause to hope that they were mere mortals entrusted with the care of emortal children, but my foster parents had every reason to believe that I was a member of a different species: the one that would inherit Earth as their own species surrendered to extinction. Such longevity as my parents had was contrived by nanotechnological repair, requiring periodic "deep tissue rejuvenations" that were hazardous in themselves and left their recipients horribly vulnerable to the kind of mental erasure that had been known for six centuries as "the Miller Effect." None of my fosterers was a ZT, but they all understood well enough how different ZTs were from their own fate-betrayed kind.

Although the first, still-imperfect, ZTs had been born seventy-five years earlier it was still rare in 2520 for any company of parents to include a ZT. People in their seventies were generally considered too young to be contemplating parenthood even though few beneficiaries of nanotech repair lived significantly longer than two hundred years. It was not until 2560, at the earliest, that ZT children were likely to have even a minority of ZT parents; even then it was considered a matter of course as well as courtesy that mortals—or "false emortals," as they were still commonly called—were given priority when applications for parenthood were submitted to the Population Agency. They were the ones under pressure of time, the ones whose needs and desires were urgent.

I take the trouble to recall all this not merely to stress that mine was the common lot of my unique generation but also to justify the seeming eccentricity of my foster parents' approach to child rearing. They took their chosen task so seriously that they could not simply accept commonplace assumptions about the best way to bring up a child; they felt that they had to approach every decision anew, to reexamine all assumptions and reevaluate all conclusions.

There was a time when I thought my parents slightly mad, especially when I was still able to eavesdrop on their interminable arguments and recriminations, but I do not think it now, even though no modern newborn spends his childhood as I spent mine. My parents took me to the remotest part of Nepal as soon as I was born because they thought that it would be good for me. Papa Domenico thought that it would be good for me because it would prove to me that there was no place on Earth so bare of resources that its doors did not open directly into his beloved Universe Without Limits, while Mama Siorane thought that it would be good for me because it would put me much more closely in touch with "brute reality," but it does not matter which of these apparently contradictory theses was closer to the truth. Although I never became what Papa Domenico would have called a "dedicated virtualist" I have been an assiduous explorer of the Universe Without Limits, and I have certainly had my share of bruising contacts with brute reality, so I suppose they were both right in their different ways.

This autobiography will have little or nothing to say about virtualist Utopianism and a great deal about realist Utopianism, but that does not mean that Mama Siorane was any more of a mother to me than Papa Domenico was a father. I had eight parents, and that—in association with the efficiency of VE education—is generally conceded to be perfectly sufficient to make every modern child the son or daughter of the entire human race. That is what I am, as are we all. That is why my personal history is, in a sense, the personal history of everyone who is potentially able to live in the future.

TWO

The ages of my fosterers varied from 102 to 165. They were humble enough not to think of themselves as all-wise but vain enough to think of themselves as competent in the art of parenting as well as brave. They were confident that they were fully qualified to swim against the tide of convention. I suppose that they were able to agree that I should be raised in one of the remotest areas of the world, in spite of their very different notions of why it was a good idea, because they had all lived through the heyday of the Decivilization Movement. Even those among them who had not been sympathetic to its nebulous ideals had strong feelings about the unsuitability of cities as environments for the very young.

Had it not been for the relocation of the UN bureaucracy to Antarctica my parents might well have chosen the Ellsworth Mountains over the Himalayas despite their modest elevation, but the intensive redevelopment of the Continent Without Nations influenced their choice. Their selection of a specific location was heavily influenced by the absurd competition undertaken by the "supporters" of Mount Manaslu, who were then augmenting the peak for the third time in order to claw back the title of "the highest mountain in the world" from the Everestians and Kanchenjungans.

The valley where my co-parents established their hometree was approximately midway between Everest and Kanchenjunga. Its only other inhabitants—or so my fosterers believed when they rented the land and planted the tree—were members of a religious community, some two dozen strong, who lived in a stone-gantzed complex at its southern extremity. There was another stone edifice high on the slope above their own site, but my parents were assured that although it had been the home of another religious community, it was now unoccupied.

Modern readers, who have been taught that all religion had been virtually extinct for three hundred years in 2520, will be more surprised by the proximity to my hometree of a living community of monks than a seemingly dead one, but retreatist sects carrying forward versions of Buddhism and Hinduism had shown far greater resilience than the followers of other traditions, and such communities had their own reasons for preferring locations remote from civilization. My foster parents found no particular cause for astonishment in that they were to become neighbors of one active monastery and one derelict one. Nor did this detract, in their eyes, from the supposed remoteness of the site.

The valley where I was brought up bears little resemblance now to the state it was in when I lived there. It fell victim to one of the less contentious projects of the Continental Engineers. Its climate is almost Mediterranean now, thanks to the dome and all its subsidiary facilities, and it is only an hour from Kathmandu by tube train. The Hindu community at the southern end of the valley is long gone—its stone-gantzed harshness replaced by luxuriant hometrees—but the stone edifice my parents nicknamed Shangri-La is still standing. When the cloud lifts it presents much the same appearance to the valley dwellers as it presented to me in earliest childhood. Because it remains outside the protective shell it must seem to young children, as it once seemed to me, to be shrouded in mystery.

Because I only lived with my foster parents for twenty years—a mere 4 percent of my life to date—and because much of that time was spent in a state of infantile obliviousness, I find it difficult to write about them as a coherent collective. I got to know them much better as disparate individuals once the collective had broken up, and that probably has as much to do with my impression that they were always quarreling as my earliest memories. I now suspect that they were happier together than I was ever able to believe while they were alive, and I am sure that they were better parents than I ever gave them credit for while I still had to listen to their homilies and complaints.

As a dutiful historian—even one who has stooped so low as to resurrect the dubious genre of spiritual autobiography—I suppose that I ought to make a proper record of my origins. My foster parents were Domenico Corato, born 2345; Laurent Holderness, born 2349; Eulalie Neqael, born 2377; Nahum Turkhan, born 2379; Meta Khaled, born 2384; Siorane Wolf, born 2392; Sajda Ajdal, born 2402; and Ezra Derhan, born 2418. The ovum that they withdrew from a North American bank to initiate my development had been deposited there in 2170, having been taken from the womb of one Diana Caisson, born 2168. The sperm used to fertilize it after the Zamaners had done their preliminary work had been deposited in 2365 by Evander Gray (2347–2517).

I have been unable to discover any more about Diana Caisson's history. The sectors of the Labyrinth hosting the relevant data were devastated by the viral shrapnel of an early twenty-third-century logic bomb, and I have never been able to discover any hard-copy reference. Evander Gray was a longtime gantzing engineer who had spent the greater part of his working life on the moon, although he had done three tours of duty in the asteroid belt; he had died in an orbital settlement.

In Mama Siorane's and Mama Meta's eyes, Evander Gray must have qualified as a pioneer, although Papa Domenico would doubtless have pointed out to them that there had been "space pioneers" as long ago as the twentieth century. At any rate, the three years separating notification of Evander Gray's death from the exercise of his right of replacement testifies to the fact that although no one was in a tearing hurry to perpetuate his heritage, he was considered a reasonably good catch. He was reckoned good enough, at any rate, for my parents not to hesitate long over the selection of my surname. If Papa Dom disapproved, he did not think it worth exercising his power of veto.

I do not know why I was given the first name Mortimer, although I did ask several of my foster parents.

"We liked it," was all the answer Papa Domenico offered.

"It sounded serious," was Mama Eulalie's contribution. "We wanted a serious child."

"It seemed to flow well in association with the surname," Mama Meta said. "People who have to wear their names for centuries will need names that flow well. Mine never did. I always envied Laurent his."

"The name originally belonged to a crusader associated with the Dead Sea," Mama Sajda informed me, in the overscrupulous manner that I was often said by her co-parents to have inherited. "It's a corruption of the Latin *de mortuo mari*—but that had absolutely nothing to do with our decision. So far as I remember, it got the vote because it was the only leading candidate to which no one had any strong objection."

That sounded only too likely at the time; it still does.

Unlike my donor father, none of my foster parents had restricted themselves to a single vocation. Five of them had already served terms as civil servants when they married, and two more were to do so afterward. Four had already worked as research scientists, and one more was subsequently to be added to that number. Three had been structural engineers, and three more were to dabble in that art. Three had done stints as retail managers, two as Labyrinth navigators, and two as VE techs—although the last two figures were doubled by endeavors subsequent to parenthood.

Five of my co-parents had constructed hypertextual mandalas of one kind or another before they had charge of me, although none had worked in the field of history. I cannot single any one of them out as a key influence on the development of my own career. If I am as pedantic as some people say, I suppose I might be reckoned to be more Mama Sajda's son than anyone else's, but she was essentially an *organizer* whose genius lay in the delicate social art of managing VE conferences. I don't recall feeling closer to her than to any of my other mothers.

At the time of my birth Papa Laurent had probably built the most considerable public reputation, as an Earth-based xenobiologist, but his quantum of fame was subsequently to be exceeded by Mama Siorane and Papa Ezra, both of whom moved to extraterrestrial frontiers, where celebrity could be more cheaply obtained. Mama Siorane contrived an interesting and newsworthy death on Titan in 2650 and Papa Ezra made a significant contribution to the modification of the Zaman transformation for application to fabers.

In spite of the relative bleakness of my early surroundings and the arguments my fosterers always seemed to be having, I received the customary superabundance of love, affection, and admiration from my parents. In claiming their own rations of "personal time" with my infant self my devoted mamas and papas subjected me to a veritable deluge of stimulation and amusement. Their determination to familiarize me with the vicissitudes of a harsh natural environment and the delights of a multitude of virtual ones never extended so far as to leave me exposed to the merciless elements without a supremely competent suitskin, or to place me in danger of addiction to synthetic pleasures. I was not allowed to play unattended in the snow until I was twelve, and I was not allowed to indulge in the most seductive virtual experiences until I was several years older than that.

In sum, with the aid of excellent role models, careful biofeedback training, and thoroughly competent internal technologies, I grew up as reasonable, as charitable, as self-controlled, and as intensely serious of mind as all my city-bound contemporaries.

THREE

The majority of the children I met and played with in the homelier kinds of VEs spoke of "real life" in terms of cityscapes: crowds, buildings, and carefully designed parks. The minority who had contact with wilderness mostly thought of it in terms of forests, oceans, and the Antarctic ice cap. Only a couple lived in close proximity with mountain slopes, and even they thought my own situation peculiar, partly because no one was busy sculpting the mountain that loomed over my valley and partly because my only near neighbors were monks.

When I was very young my VE-linked friends had not the slightest idea what a "monk" was. Nor had I. The members of the accessible community at the north end of the valley communicated among themselves in a language that was either archaic or private, and although I did not entirely trust my parents' word that the community high on the mountain slope was extinct, I had no solid grounds for thinking otherwise. The cloud so rarely exposed the buildings to view, despite the winds that kept them continually astir, that such brief periods of clarity as did occur only served to intensify the mystery of their nature.

To tell the truth, the actual monks seemed to me to be the least interesting feature of my environment when I was eight or nine years old. I was much more entranced by the storms and the peculiar transactions of the snow, by the abrupt changes of temperature and texture to which the air was subject whenever I passed out of the safe interior of the hometree, and by the precarious meltwater ecology of the valley floor. My friends, however, were not at all interested in weather reports; they wanted to know about the mysterious mystics and sages who had once occupied the edifice on the mountain and still practiced their arcane rituals in the southern part of the valley. It was not that my friends could not imagine precipitous slopes, or snow, or hectic atmospheric conditions; the problem was that I had no way to persuade them that my actual experience of such phenomena was very different from their virtual experiences.

"Yes," Pyotr would say, "*of course* I know what cold feels like. We have cold in Moscow too. But we don't have monks."

"*Of course* I can imagine thin air," Marianna would assure me. "It's just a matter of barometric pressure. But I can't imagine religion."

They were wrong about being able to imagine what Himalayan cold and Himalayan air felt like, but there was no way to prove it. I thought they were equally mistaken in their assumption that the monks and their beliefs were interesting, given that the few I saw in the distance always seemed so utterly mundane, but I couldn't prove that either and soon capitulated with inevitability by ceasing to try.

The continued curiosity of my friends eventually compelled me to find better answers to their questions, but throughout my formative years—from six to sixteen, say—even the "better" answers were wholly invented. I made up different tales at different times, and my accounts became far more elaborate as my sources of inspiration expanded in number and quality, but it was all fantasy. I knew little or nothing about what my allegedly Hindu neighbors believed or did, and nothing at all about what might once have gone on in the allegedly Buddhist community set so high on the looming slope as to be beyond reach.

None of my co-parents ever visited the complex at the far end of the valley, nor did any of them attempt to learn the language spoken by its inhabitants. None of them would ever have dreamed of trying to climb the mountain that separated them from the place they called Shangri-La, for want of any better name. They had brought their child to remotest Nepal so that he might live in the presence of magnificent strangeness, not that he might penetrate its secrets. By the time I left the valley I understood, vaguely, that they had installed me there because they thought that the valley might teach me to be humble in my humanity, to show me the last vestiges of the untamed earth that had shaped my ancestors, and to give me a proper sense of the value of my emortality. While I was actually there, however, it was simply the place I was in, monks and all. My view of it was conditioned by the knowledge that all the other people of my own age with whom I was encouraged to socialize in VEs had anchorages in reality that seemed more desirable to me because they lay far closer to the heart of human society. I was never lonely as a child, but I knew that I lived in a lonely place, fit only for mad monks, and that I had been put there on purpose.

"But it's not a lonely place," Papa Domenico assured me, on one of the rare occasions when I actually complained. "There are no lonely places any more. Wherever humans go, they take the virtual universe with them. We can hold infinity in the palms of our hands, although we've grown so accustomed to the miracle that we no longer seem to be capable of grasping the wonder of it. As long as you're connected to human society, the Universe Without Limits is yours, the best part of your heritage. Even the monks have that."

Papa Laurent told a different story. "One day, Morty," he said, "the feeling of loneliness will be precious to you. You'll be glad that it formed such an important part of your sentimental education. The UN may make a big song and dance about keeping Earth's population stable and using emigration to the moon and the microworlds as a safety valve, but the simple fact is that now that your generation really can live forever the population of the Earthbound will creep up and up and up. The future you'll have to live in will be so desperately crowded that there won't be any lonely places left—and you'll have something to look back on that all your contemporaries will envy. You'll have an understanding that they'll never be able to cultivate—although the monks will hang on to it, if they ever manage to recruit any true emortals."

They were both talking nonsense, of course, but not for the reasons that occurred to me as a child.

Perhaps, in the end, my parents' plan did achieve most of what it was intended to achieve, even though they could never agree as to exactly what that was—but while I was actually living in the parental hometree I could not help but see things differently. I found some delight in the ruggedness of the terrain, but I also felt a good deal of resentment against the continual assertiveness of wind, water, and biting cold—and my curiosity about the perverse people who had chosen to live here, not merely for a while but indefinitely, grew along with that resentment. Even at the age of eight, I knew that I would never take the trouble to learn a new language in order to communicate with the enigmatic people who lived at the other end of the valley, but I knew that there would come a day when I was big enough, strong enough, and brave enough to climb the mountain that separated me from Shangri-La.

I did not expect that I would be able to talk to its inhabitants, even if they turned out not to be extinct, but that was not the point of the imagined endeavor. The point was to confirm that Shangri-La was indeed a *place*, not a phantom of the cloud and a mirage of the sunlight—and to prove that I was the kind of person who could go wherever he wanted to go, despite the vicissitudes of the weather.

y failed attempts to climb the mountain that loomed so large over my childhood home resulted in a few bruising falls. I listened patiently to the lectures all emortal children must endure regarding the magnitude of every risk they take, but I also learned by slow degrees how to use an ice ax and how to make the most of toeholds. My parents decided soon enough that in view of our having chosen to live among mountains it would be ridiculous to suppress my ambition to climb, so they began investing in smart suitskins with all kinds of extra safety features. By the time I was ten my augmented limbs had the clinging power of a fly's, and if I rolled myself up into a ball I could bounce for miles.

I took more risks than the average child of my kind, but the falls I survived didn't lull me into a false sense of security. My suitskins were exceedingly clever and my internal technology was state of the art, but when I fell I experienced a full measure of terror, and more than enough pain to function as a warning. I was, however, determined to master that slope some day, to find out exactly how the reality of Shangri-La differed from the fantasies I made up for my VE-linked friends.

I was twelve before I accidentally discovered the source from which my co-parents had borrowed the name Shangri-La. It was, I found, the name of a mythical monastery established above an imaginary valley, whose inhabitants lived to be several hundred years old in an era when that was simply not possible. In the original twentieth-century folktale the monastery had been fitted out with a library so that it might serve as a haven of rest and place of refuge for those few civilized men who were wise enough to realize that their civilization was both precarious and irredeemably sick. Neither the first author of the tale nor its subsequent embellishers had been able to witness the twenty-first-century collapse of their sick civilization, nor had they had imagination enough to envisage its rebuilding by the first people who claimed to be members of a new human race, but I could hardly help thinking that the myth was precious as well as prescient. It colored my own private fantasies as deeply as it colored the fantasies I made up for my friends—which became gradually more plausible as I took advantage of my researches in the Labyrinth.

"Monks aren't much interested in emortality," I explained to Pyotr when I was thirteen. "They all believe that life goes on forever unless you can find a way of getting out—which isn't easy. They do have internal nanotech, but that's because they think the extending of a life span from seventy to two or three hundred years is a matter of small concern. They don't think of themselves as separate entities but as pieces of the world's soul. The people who used to live on the mountain thought a human lifetime, no matter what difference IT or gene swapping might make, is just a step on the way to eternity, and what they ought to be aiming at is the annihilation of feeling, because feeling is suffering. Monks think life is intrinsically unsatisfying and that nirvana is better, but they put off their own salvation in order to make a gift of some of their accumulated spiritual credit to the rest of us."

It's surprising what can pass for wisdom among thirteen year olds—but it's not entirely surprising that even its fantasies contain seeds of enlightenment. Much later in life, when I came to consider the great religions as strategies in the great psychological war against death, I had cause to remember my fantasies about the phantom monks of Shangri-La.

As to the reality . . .

It was in the summer of 2535 that I first contrived to climb all the way up the sheer slope that separated my hometree from the stone building. My objective was visible all the way and the rocks were dry; the sun was shining brightly. Given the conditions, it was not a terribly difficult or dangerous climb.

Had the weather changed suddenly—and the weather in those parts *could* change with astonishing rapidity from fair to atrocious before the Continental Engineers stuck their oar in—I might have gotten into trouble, but as things were I hardly bruised my suitskin. I was out of breath and my hands were grazed, but I had only to pause on the threshold of the edifice for twenty minutes to regain my composure.

While I sat there, with my back to the valley, I was able to look through an archway into a courtyard, where there was a statue of Buddha, exactly as I had expected—but there was no sign of anyone walking in the cloister and no sound of any activity within the walls. The place seemed as dead and desolate as I had been assured it was.

It was not until I raised myself to my feet and wandered through the archway that my presence elicited any response.

The courtyard was rectangular, and all its inner faces were as smoothly gray as the external face it presented to the valley. There were no visible doors or windows. When I paused in front of the Buddha I had settled for the conclusion that the edifice was now no more than an unmanned shrine—but then a man in a black suitskin stepped out from behind the Buddha. His skin was as dark as his suitskin—darker than that of any living individual I had seen on TV or met in VE. He was obviously not of local descent, and his suitskin was tailored in a very workmanlike fashion. He didn't look like any kind of monk I had ever seen or imagined.

"Can I help you, Mister Gray?" he said, in exactly the same kind of media-smoothed English that all my foster parents employed. Save for his unfashionably dark and cosmetically unembellished skin he looked and sounded markedly less exotic than many of my VE friends. It was impossible to tell how old he was, but I guessed that he was a true emortal.

"How do you know my name?" I asked.

"We like to know who our neighbors are," he said, mildly. "We don't pry, but we're slightly sensitive to the possibility that others might."

"I'm not prying," I retorted.

"Yes you are," he said. "But that's understandable. We don't really mind. We stopped worrying about your parents a long time ago. We know that they're exactly what they seem to be."

"You're not," I said.

"I don't seem to be anything I'm not," he replied, arching his eyebrows in surprise—but then he figured out that I had meant the comment more generally. "*We* don't seem to be anything at all," he added. "Your parents decided to call this place Shangri-La on their own initiative, and if you decided to elaborate the fantasy . . ."

He left the sentence dangling, implying that he knew more about the tales I'd spun than he had any right to.

Perhaps he would have preferred it if I'd turned around and started climbing back down again, but he must have already accepted that I wouldn't be content to come all the way up the mountain for nothing.

"What is this place, then?" I asked. "If it's not a monastery . . ."

"You can come in if you want to," he said. "But you might find it less interesting than you'd always hoped. I'm Julius Ngomi, by the way."

He smiled as he said it. He didn't really mean what he said about my finding the place less interesting than I'd always hoped—but even after all this time, I still can't quite make up my mind whether he was right or not.

FIVE

There was no obvious sign of a doorway behind the Buddha, but when part of the gray wall drew away at Ngomi's touch I realized that the featurelessness of the edifice might be an illusion.

"We generally use the door on the far side of the mountain," my companion said, waving his hand vaguely in order to suggest that the zigzagging corridor was far more extensive than the eye could see. "There's a helipad there, although it's only usable one day in four."

By the time we had turned three corners and descended two stairways I had lost my sense of direction, but I had begun to realize how extensively the mountain had been hollowed out. There didn't seem to be many people about, but there was no shortage of closed doors, which no one had bothered to hide.

"What's inside them?" I asked, vaguely.

"The litter that dare not speak its name," he replied, gnomically. "Archaeological specimens. Ancient artifacts. Lots and lots of paper. Things that have no present utility at all but somehow seem to warrant preservation nevertheless. We've become very reluctant to throw things away these last few hundred years. The way the history books tell it is that our pre-Crash ancestors—the *old* Old Human Race—became deeply penitent about their habit of trashing everything they owned in wars and began to set up permanent archives at about the same time they built the first genetic Arks. Then, so the conventional history goes, our more recent forefathers became exceedingly paranoid about the perishability of electronic information during the Virtual Terror. That kicked off a new wave of archive building and archive stuffing."

Because he was still talking he paused at the unconcealed door we were about to enter, with his hand hovering a centimeter short of a clearly marked pressure pad. If I'd nodded my head he would presumably have touched it, but I didn't.

"Are you saying that the history books have got it wrong?" I asked, instead. It didn't seem to be an important question as I phrased it, but I never forgot the answer I received, and I never lost sight of its implications.

"Not exactly," said Julius Ngomi. "But all history is fantasy, and there are always different ways of coming at a question. The cynical version is that after Leon Gantz and his nephews had developed a ridiculously cheap way to hollow out mountains, their heirs had to figure out a reason for doing it. So they said, *Hey, let's start filing our litter away for the benefit of future archaeologists. I bet we could devise an archiving system so complicated and so all-encompassing that it would keep a whole battalion of maze architects occupied for centuries and make work for thousands of caretakers. It won't be as much fun as hollowing out asteroids to make gigantic spaceships, but that plan's on hold for the time being, and this one's a hell of a lot more convenient.* So here we are, in the twenty-sixth century—proud possessors of at least ninety-nine mountains whose bowels are constipated by megatons of carefully sorted and painstakingly indexed shit."

As he pronounced the final word, Julius Ngomi finally found the impetus to brush the pressure pad with his fingertips, and the door opened. I had just begun to visualize a tide of sewage flooding out into the corridor when I perceived that it was a perfectly normal circular room. Its perimeter wall was rimmed by a series of flatscreens, alternated with perfectly normal VE hoods. Only two of the six hoods were occupied, but there was a third person positioned at the center of the room, apparently engaged in the impossible task of monitoring all six flatscreens simultaneously. This was a gray-haired woman, whose features were so comprehensively time ravaged that I immediately jumped to the conclusion that she was a bicentenarian spinning out the legacy of her third full rejuve as far as it would go.

"Who's this, Julie?" she asked, mildly, as her pale eyes scanned me from head to toe with what seemed to me to be a practiced sweep. The people under the hoods—one man and one woman, to judge by the contours of their suitskins—didn't bother to peep out to see what was happening.

"Mortimer Gray," said Ngomi. "The kid from the valley. Today's the day he finally grew big enough to complete the climb. About time, considering the number of times he got halfway and chickened out." The insult was uncalled for, and not entirely defused by the levity of the black man's tone.

"Congratulations," said the woman.

"This is Sara Saul," Ngomi said. "She's the boss."

"The chief archivist, you mean?" I said, trying to show that I was on the ball.

They both laughed. "We're just lodgers," Ngomi said. "We don't actually look after the cesspit. To tell you the truth, the cesspit pretty much looks after itself, now that the store is deemed to be full up. Historians crawl over it and scratch its surface now and again, but nobody else pays it much heed. We just rent a few of the leftover nooks and crannies."

"But you're not monks," I said, uncertainly, "are you?"

Mercifully, they didn't laugh at that.

"After a fashion, we are," said Sara Saul. "We're not given to prayer, like the people at the far end of the valley, and we're not what used to be called chipmonks—VE obsessives, that is—but you *could* say that we're in retreat, living ascetically for the sake of our vocation. It *is* a vocation, isn't it, Julie?"

"Definitely," said Julius Ngomi.

I knew that they were teasing me, but I had to ask. "What vocation?"

"We're running the world." It was Sara Saul who answered.

"I thought that was all done in Antarctica," I said, lightly. I was determined not to be taken in, although I knew how far out of my intellectual depth I was.

"There's running and *running*," Julius Ngomi informed me, unhelpfully. "The UN takes care of all the superficial bureaucracy, and they do a damn fine job. We work at a slightly deeper level—no pun intended. We help control the ebb and flow of the world's money. You might think of us as one of the fingers of the Invisible Hand."

Even at the age of fifteen, I knew what the Invisible Hand was.

"I thought the Invisible Hand was supposed to work on its own," I said.

"That's the official story," Julius Ngomi agreed, "but economics is even more fantastic than history. Back in Adam Smith's time the invisible hand was supposed to be a mere statistical aggregation of the demand generated by the separate pursuit of individual interest by billions of would-be consumers and the supply generated by attempts to meet that demand profitably, but it was never as simple as that. The difference didn't matter much when even the wealth of nations was beyond the reach of effective management, because no one had the ability actually to calculate the sum and keep track of all its changing terms—but things have changed.

"The only way the economy could be planned in the days of the old Old Human Race was by the exercise of political brute force to override and channel individual interest. Then the supercomputer happened along, and the workings of spontaneous individual interest became something not merely measurable on a day-to-day basis but futuristically calculable. Demand could already be influenced, of course, in all kinds of clever ways, but the influences were as separate and spontaneous as the interests themselves until it became possible to weigh them and balance them and build them into patterns. So the twenty-first century's best and bravest put their wise heads together and said, *Hey, let's buy up the world and usher in the Golden Age of Planned Capitalism. If we're clever enough, I bet we could organize the stock market crash to end all stock market crashes and come out of it with enough corners in genemod primary produce to obtain effective commercial control of two-thirds of the world's surface—and then we can reel in the other third at our leisure, as long as we never let anyone mention the unholy word* Trust. *It won't be as much fun as conquering the universe, but that plan's on hold for the time being, and this one'll be a hell of a lot more convenient.* So here we are, in the twenty-sixth century, with the effective ownership of the real world in the hands of half a dozen intricately interlinked megacorps, each one dominated by half a dozen major shareholders. Those dominant shareholders have charged their directors and managers with the duty of keeping the economic lifeblood of humankind pumping in an orderly and healthy fashion while its multitudinous heads dream on in the heady clouds of the Universe Without Limits. So that's what we do."

"Oh," I said, while I was trying desperately to think of a question that would sound sufficiently intelligent. All I could think of, in the end, was "Why here? Why not a nice plush officetree in Moscow or Vienna?"

"They're nice places to work and play," Ngomi agreed, "but they're no place to bring up a child. Too many distractions. Even the UN bureaucrats recognize that serious business requires a certain strategic isolation and manifest austerity. You should be grateful that we take our vocation so seriously. It's *your* inheritance, as well as mine, we're keeping in good order. Think of us as fosterers of your entire generation, of the new New Human Race itself. Even those of us who are only false emortals accept the responsibility of making sure that they hand the world over to the true emortals in the best possible condition. That's a hell of a lot more than the old Old Human Race did for our grandfathers—a *hell* of a lot more. Sara and I don't actually *live* here, of course. We just serve our tours of duty once or twice a year. It's a stressful job, and we need our rest—and it's also the kind of job that can get awkwardly addictive, so it's best to spread the work around. Megalomania is *so* unbecoming."

His tone was never less than pleasant, but he wasn't really sharing a joke with me, or even pretending to. He wasn't testing me to see how much of what he said I could follow. He was just amusing *himself*: taking the edge off his monkish exile. If anything had showed on the flatscreens Sara Saul was watching from the corners of her eyes that required her finger of the Invisible Hand to twitch, they'd have bundled me out—but for the moment, the finger was poised above the pressure pad, waiting without any sense of urgency. So two bored adults were taking time out to play with the kid from next door.

Even the people who run the world sometimes pause for play—although rumor has it that dear old Julius hasn't had much free time of late.

"Can I tell my parents what's really here?" I asked. It seemed only polite to ask the question, even though I knew full well that they couldn't stop me.

"Why would you want to do that?" the still-young Julius Ngomi asked me. "I bet this is the first real secret you've ever had. Why give it away? Everyone ought to have a piggy-bank full of secrets. You *can* tell anyone you want—but you'd run the risk that they wouldn't even be interested and that their disinterest would devalue your informational capital. It really is best to plan these things, Mortimer. Today could be an important step in the making of your secret self, the shaping of your unique identity. None of your co-parents is ever going to climb up here to check your story no matter what you tell them, so why not invent your own Shangri-La? Truth is whatever you can get away with."

"Don't lead the boy astray, Julie," said Sara Saul. "Tell your parents what you like, Mortimer. We're not working in secret—we just don't advertise our private addresses. Everybody knows we're somewhere. They'd probably be amused to think of us renting space in a junk mountain—except that it's not really junk. You have to be careful about taking Julie's way of telling things too seriously. What's stored in all these chambers is the real substance of history; the myths spun out in the Labyrinth are just its ghost."

"A library," I said, suddenly remembering the original Shangri-La. "A library that would survive even if the Labyrinth got wiped out by the Doomsday Virus."

"That's right," said Sara Saul.

Julius Ngomi laughed. "All civilizations have to live in the ruins of their predecessors," he said. "Even the ones that never get hit by the Ultimate Weapon. We true emortals are luckier than most, but we'll still be handing down our garbage as well as our gold."

"How far down does it go?" I asked, wondering whether the entire Himalayan plateau might be hollowed out to receive the artifacts that the econosphere no longer required—while the rock that was removed to make room for them was, of course, shaped into new artifacts.

"Not far," said Sara Saul. "We've barely scratched Earth's crust. My kind will have to leave it to true emortals like you and Julie to excavate the mantle and the core and move the planet's insides to the outside as skyscrapers of steel. The asteroid rebuilders are just practicing—the real architects are yet to come. If you can restrain your impulse to scale dangerous heights, Mortimer, you might see the beginnings of the metamorphosis. If you care to join the Type-2 Crusade, you might well play a part in it."

"But it would be silly to exercise too much restraint," Julius Ngomi observed. "It would be foolish to miss out in the present for the sake of seeing a little more of the future unfold. I think you're one of nature's climbers, Mortimer. I think you're the kind of person who'll always be prepared to dice with death, provided that the dice are suitably loaded."

I wasn't sure about that, even then, but I didn't say so. I was fifteen, and I had scaled a dangerous slope. I hadn't found what I'd expected to find—but wasn't that the whole point of scaling dangerous heights? What on Earth would be the point of hollowing out the world if you didn't put the matter you removed to profitable use?

"Can I come back again?" I asked.

"If you like," said Sara Saul. "But there's nothing more to see. Just us, or others like us, laboring patiently."

"Nothing except garbage," said Julius Ngomi. "More garbage than you could ever find the time to look at, even if you lived ten thousand years."

did go back to Shangri-La—not often, and not for any particular purpose, but I did go. The climbing did me good. Keeping the secret of the true nature of the edifice from my incurious parents, at least for a little while, also did me good. Secrets make it easier for children to grow apart from their families.

It wasn't until 2544, when I read the obituaries, that I actually realized who Sara Saul was and what it was that was dying with her. She was a lineal descendant and material heir of Leon Gantz, the inventor of "biological cementation"—and, of course, its converse, "biological deconstruction." She had been born from a Helier womb just like everybody else, but her co-parents really had been a *real family* engaged in the business of protecting the most fabulous fortune ever accumulated by a single human family.

Sara Saul, I eventually discovered, was one of a double handful of people who really did own and run the world while she was alive—but she'd still shriveled like a decaying fruit, and the color had drained out of her along with the life. She'd had more temporal power than any Hindu god, but she'd been mortal. All she had been able to do with what she had, in the end, was protect it for a while and then pass it on. To her credit, she really had seen that as a vocation and had tried to do it as best she could.

She was the first person with whom I was personally acquainted to die. I knew that she would not be the last—but I also knew that the number would be finite. I understood, too, those of us who came after her would have to learn to redefine the concept of "vocation," wherever we figured in the hierarchy of Earth's stewardship; we could no longer rely on mortality to set its limits for us.

It wasn't long after my first success in mountain climbing that the time came for me to leave my loving family, although five years seemed a great deal longer then than it does now. At the time, I was impatient to depart, hardly able to wait for the moment when I would be able to leave my Nepalese hometree to enter a community of my peers. Although the fracture lines of their little community stood out sharp and clear I think all my parents were dismayed by my impatience. Papa Laurent wasn't the only one who strove with all his might to convince me that I ought to treasure the years of my adolescence, to look sideways as well as forward, and to take stock of what I already had as carefully as I counted the freedom that would soon be mine.

"You shouldn't be in such a hurry," Mama Eulalie told me. "Looking back, I have to admit that I must seem to have been in a hurry all my life, but I'm Old Human Race and even I could have benefited from slowing down a little. You're New Human Race, and you can certainly afford to take things easier."

"Every boy-child longs to be free of his parents," Papa Nahum told me, "and every boy-child regrets it later. You'll have a long time to regret it when we're gone—and we shall be going, Morty, sooner than you think. I'm the youngest, and even I'm halfway to the grave. Get the most out of us while you can."

I didn't listen. What child ever does?

There was no fixed period to the business of co-parenthood even in those historically transitional days, but there still seems to be a natural term to the time that any group of people can remain together as an effective team. After twenty years, frayed relationships generally reach breaking point. Not all relationships fray at the same rate, and a few have the strength to resist fracture for far longer, but each of my eight foster parents had to maintain seven different relationships with his or her partners, so the enterprise involved a total of twenty-eight distinct pair-bonds. According to the conventional theory of microsocial dynamics, a collective cannot be sustained once half of its subsidiary pair-bonds have fallen into irredeemable disrepair, and when I remember my co-parents—however fondly—I find it difficult to imagine that one pair-bond in five could ever have been in a healthy state. Even so, they were sorry to part, and not *just* for my sake.

I understand now that my parents were good and tolerant people. I understand how it was that they quarreled so much and yet never descended to hatred, or even to mute hostility. The nucleus of their common interest in my maturation could not exert sufficient attractive power to keep them in their orbits indefinitely, but they weren't glad to be sent hurtling apart at so many different tangents. As soon as I had no further need of their all being together the whole system flew apart, but it seemed to them to be a sad moment, and that I was so delighted to be going must have hurt them all. It was left to me to decide exactly when I would depart for a different community, thus setting the date on which my loving co-parents scattered to the ends of the earth and beyond, and I seized the opportunity without having any idea of the value of that which I was casually shattering. They remained my parents, ever willing to serve as home providers, friends, mentors, and supporters, but after I took my leave, they were no longer marriage partners. After I left I never saw more than three of them together, but it wasn't until most of them were dead that I began to feel the force of that loss.

Once it was determined that I would go to Adelaide, in Australia, to attend university it was soon settled that Papa Dom would go to Antarctica, Papa Laurent to France, Mama Eulalie to the Peruvian Andes, Papa Nahum to Alaska, Mama Meta and Mama Siorane to the moon, Mama Sajda to Central Africa, and Papa Ezra to New Zealand, but we continued to keep in touch. Papa Dom was, after all, absolutely right: in the Virtual World, everywhere within lunar orbit is close at hand, and even Jupiter and Saturn aren't so very far away when they're on the same side of the sun as Earth.

SEVEN

Although my memories of the period are understandably hazy I feel sure that I had begun to see the *fascination* of history long before the crucial event that determined my path in life. I'm sure that I took the kernel of that fascination with me from the valley, and I'm fairly sure that I had it even before I climbed the mountain to Shangri-La for the first time. I must have, or the meeting in the mountain could not have had such a powerful effect.

I have, of course, reproduced the details of my first conversation with Julius Ngomi and Sara Saul with the aid of records made at the time, but I do *remember*, even to this day, the impression left on me by Ngomi's careful heresies. There was already something within me that responded to the mantra, "All history is fantasy," and to the idea of a mountain whose bowels were constipated with the archival detritus of past ages.

In the context of my university studies history seemed—in stark contrast to the disciplined coherency of mathematics or the sciences—to be magnificent in its hugeness, amazingly abundant in its data, and charmingly disorganized. I thought of myself as a very orderly and organized person and looked to the study of history to loosen me up a little—but I looked forward even then to the day when I might be able to impose a little of my own orderliness and organization upon the hectic muddle of the past. I was determined from the very beginning that *my* vocation was to enhance understanding by negotiating between different accounts of how and why and by calming the waters of dissent. If, as Julius Ngomi had suggested, truth was what I could get away with, I wanted to get away with something virtuous as well as grandiose—but I arrived at Adelaide without having the least idea of exactly what that might be.

The last thing Julius Ngomi said to me before I left the valley—the last thing he was to say to me for more than three hundred years, as things turned out—was, "History is okay for amateurs, kid, but it's no work for real people. Historians have only interpreted the world and its revolutions—the point is to change it, carefully, constructively, and without any more revolutions."

I didn't realize at the time that he was quoting or that the quote was deeply ironic. Nor did I realize that his parting shot and Mama Siorane's reflected fundamentally dissonant views about the way the future would and ought to be shaped.

"Forget what Papa Dom says about the Universe Without Limits," she said. "He thinks that the imagination has no boundaries, but it keeps running into the most important boundary of all: the boundary of *action*. History is a good subject to study because it's all about the waves of hopeful imagination breaking on the rocks of effective action. History will teach you that the future of humankind can't be a matter of designing ever-more-comfortable VEs. History will teach you that if you don't actually *do* it, you haven't achieved anything at all—and when you've learned that, you'll be a doer too, not a mere dreamer."

All Papa Domenico added to that was a rude observation about Mama Siorane being as full of shit as the mountain—by that time, alas, my secret had crept out. If Papa Dom could have foreseen that Mama Siorane would die on Titan, gloriously doing instead of merely dreaming, he might have modified his opinion—but he might not. They both deserve full credit for practicing what they preached—Papa Dom went to Antarctica to work for the UN and cultivate the delicious sensations of self-sufficiency, and he died in his VE hood exactly as he would have wished.

The ostensible purpose of a university is to constitute a community of scholars in the interests of further education, but its real purpose is to constitute a community of actual bodies in the interests of further real-space interaction. It would, I think, be too great a wrench were young people to go straight from the flesh-intensive microcosm of a parental home to the adult world, where almost all relationships are conducted almost exclusively in virtual space.

I had, of course, been interacting with other children of my own age in virtual space throughout my time in my parents' hometree, but I had not met a single one in the flesh until I went to Adelaide. I felt that this put me at something of a disadvantage because almost all my contemporaries had been able to arrange occasional real-space encounters, and those who were city-bred were already used to actual crowds. On the other hand, that I had been reared in a remote mountain valley gave me a hint of exoticism that few of the other new arrivals possessed. I didn't make friends easily, but no one did. I was exhilarated by those I did make, but I felt even as I made them that they would be temporary. The accident of contemporaneity hardly seemed to be a sound foundation for lasting intimacy. Perhaps I made too much, secretly as well as overtly, of my having climbed precipitous mountain slopes and seen things that normally remained hidden. Perhaps my fascination with history was magnified so rapidly partly in order to provide me with an excuse for solitary study and private preoccupation. In any case, I was less sociable than the average, but was not at all distressed by it.

It was during my second year of study, in 2542, that the defining event of my life occurred: the event that took my magnified fascination and gave it a precise shape that was never significantly modified thereafter. Before I boarded the sailing-ship *Genesis* in March of that year, I was a dilettante historian pecking here and there at the whole broad sweep of social evolution; when I finally came safely to shore, I was a man with a mission, a man with a destiny.

EIGHT

*G*enesis was a cruise ship providing tours of the Creationist Islands of the Coral Sea. Many of the islands were natural, but the majority were artificial. Two centuries before, the first new islands raised from the seabed had been regarded as daring experiments paving the way for the more extravagant adventures of the Continental Engineers, but the business had soon been routinized. Custom-designed islands had been easy enough to sell or rent out during the twenty-fifth century, to provide bases for large-scale commercial endeavors in Liquid Artificial Photosynthesis and sea farming or to host the artistic ventures in ecosystem construction that gave the islands their familiar name. The latter market had weakened somewhat in the wake of the Moreau scandal, when the UN insisted on instituting much tighter controls and much more careful monitoring of the Creationists' endeavors, but the longest-established islands remained significant arenas of ecological research as well as popular tourist attractions.

Children reared in less unconventional environments than the one chosen by my foster parents were often taken on educational voyages like the one offered by *Genesis*. I had never believed Papa Domenico's assurances that the habit was an obsolete and functionless vestige left over from more primitive times—like any child denied anything, I had instead formed the determination that as soon as I was my own master, I would make good on my parents' omission. I had already toured the Blooming Outback and the reforested Nullarbor, the former by bus and the latter by hot-air balloon; the *Genesis* cruise seemed a logical next step.

It was not only the series of destinations visited by *Genesis* that was held to be valuable but the experience of being under sail. *Genesis* was powered by wind alone, and its silver-controlled system of sails was represented by its owners as a marvel in its own right. The control of a sailing ship was said to be one of the most challenging of all the tasks given to artificial intelligence because of the complexity and unpredictability of the forces that had to be met and transformed into smooth directional travel. So, at least, Captain Christopher Cardigan—who insisted on referring to his own vessel's AI as "Long John"—assured the party of twenty that boarded the *Genesis* in Brisbane on 22 March 2542.

"No matter what so-called weather controllers may say," Captain Cardigan assured us, "the winds answer to no man. They can be mean and they can be furious—but Long John can take anything they throw at us and turn it to our advantage."

I suppose he had every right to be proud and confident, and he certainly didn't deserve to die, but I find it difficult to think of him as anything but a smug fool.

The majority of my fellow passengers was made up by the family of an eight-year-old girl named Emily Marchant. She was traveling with all twelve of her parents, and I remember churlishly thinking that they must be a far more coherent and generous team than my own had ever been. Six more passenger berths were taken by couples a little older than myself, undertaking early experiments in the awkward social art of pairbonding.

On many occasions the ship might have had to set sail with its last remaining slot unfilled, because there were not many people likely to undertake such an expedition solo, but I was determined to make up at least some of the experience lost to me while I was raised in the shadow of Shangri-La. I was not intimidated by the thought of being an outsider in such a company. Captain Cardigan and his crew—which included a chef-programmer as well as the customary service staff—added a further eight to our number.

I was looking forward to the Creationist Islands, especially Marsupial Glory, Dragon Island, and the most famous of all those in the southern hemisphere: Oscar Wilde's Orgy of Perfumes. I had visited the first two as a virtual tourist, but there is something slightly absurd about VE reproductions of scent and taste, and I knew that Wilde's Creation would have to be experienced in the flesh if it were to mean anything at all.

I expected to spend the days that elapsed before we reached the islands sunning myself on the deck and reveling in the unusual experience of having nothing at all to do. Unfortunately, I was struck down by seasickness as soon as we left port. I had, of course, been on several virtual sea journeys without ever suffering a single qualm, but the movement of the actual ocean proved to be brutally different from its VE analogues.

Seasickness, by virtue of being partly psychosomatic, is one of the very few diseases with which modern internal technology is sometimes impotent to deal, and I was miserably confined to my cabin while I waited for my body and mind to make the necessary adaptive compact. I was bitterly ashamed of myself, for I alone out of the twenty-eight people on board had fallen prey to the atavistic malaise.

I was ill throughout the night of the twenty-second and the following day. There was to be a lavish deck party on the night of the twenty-third, which was forecast to be calm and bright, and I convinced myself for all of five minutes that I might be well enough to attend. As soon as I had gotten to my feet, however, my stomach rebelled and my legs turned to jelly. I was forced to return to my bed in abject misery. While my traveling companions—to whom I had barely been introduced as we waited to board the vessel—were enjoying themselves hugely beneath the glorious light of the tropic stars, I lay in my bunk, half-delirious with discomfort and lack of sleep.

I thought myself the unluckiest man in the world—although it turned out that I was, in fact, one of the luckiest.

The combined resources of my internal nanotech and my solicitous suitskin could not make me well, but they could and did contrive to put me to sleep. I have a vague memory of disturbing dreams, but I am reasonably certain that I did not actually awake until I was hurled from my bed on to the floor of my cabin. From that moment on, however, my memory is crystal clear, even after all this time. Although this is the only passage in my autobiography for which I have no objective record to serve as a crutch, I am quite certain of its accuracy.

nine

I thought at first that I had simply fallen—that I had been tossing and turning in consequence of my illness, which had thus contrived to inflict one more ignominy upon me. When I couldn't recover my former position after spending long minutes fruitlessly groping about amid all kinds of mysterious debris, my first assumption was that I must be confused. When I couldn't open the door of my cabin even though I had the handle in my hand, I took it for granted that my failure was the result of clumsiness. When I finally got out into the corridor, and found myself crawling in shallow water with the artificial bioluminescent strip beneath instead of above me, I thought I must be mad.

One of the things Captain Cardigan had proudly told us as we were about to embark was that his pride and joy was absolutely guaranteed to be unsinkable. Even if Long John were to crash, he assured us, *Genesis* was so cleverly designed and constructed that it was physically impossible for her to be holed or overturned. I had taken note of his assurance because, having been raised in a high valley whose only source of water was melting snow, I had never learned to swim. When I finally worked out, therefore, that the boat seemed to be upside down, I could not quite believe the evidence of my eyes and my reason. When I also worked out that the hectic motion I was feeling really was the motion of the upturned boat and not a subjective churning of my guts, I was seized by the absurd notion that my seasickness had somehow infected the hull of the craft. No matter what mental gymnastics I performed, however, I could not find any other explanation for being on my hands and knees, fighting to keep my balance, and that my palms and kneecaps were pressed to a strip light that had definitely been situated on the ceiling of the corridor when I had gone into my cabin. What was more, both my forearms and my thighs were immersed in ten or twelve centimeters of hot water.

There must be a second strip light in the floor, I told myself, uncertainly, *which has now come on while the other has gone off. Somebody*

*must have been running a bath, and the bath has overflowed. Perhaps
the water has shorted out Long John's circuits.*

Then the little girl spoke to me, saying, "Mister Mortimer? Is that
you, Mister Mortimer?"

I thought for an instant that the voice was a delusion and that I was
lost in a nightmare. It wasn't until she touched me and tried to drag me
upright with her tiny, frail hands that I was finally able to focus my
thoughts and admit to myself that something was horribly, *horribly*
wrong.

"You have to get up, Mister Mortimer," said Emily Marchant. "The
boat's upside down."

She was only eight years old, but she spoke quite calmly and reasonably, even though she had to support herself against the wall in order to
save herself from falling over as the boat rocked and lurched.

"That's impossible," I told her, stupidly. "*Genesis* is unsinkable.
There's no way it could turn upside down. Captain Cardigan said . . ."

"But it *is* upside down," she insisted—unnecessarily, given that I had
conceded the point as my assurances trailed off into silence. "The water's
coming in."

"Yes," I said, raising myself up to a less ignominious kneeling position and reaching out a hand to brace myself against the wall. "Yes, it is.
But why is it hot?"

I put my free hand to my lips and tasted the water on my fingers. It
was salty. The water that fed our bathrooms was supposed to be desali-
nated, and this flood was far too copious in any case.

Emily was right. *Genesis* had turned upside down and was letting in
water.

"I don't know why it's hot," she said, "but we have to get out. We
have to get to the stairs and swim."

The light put out by the ceiling strip was no dimmer than usual, but
the rippling water overlaying it made it seem faint and uncertain. The
girl's little face, lit from below, seemed terribly serious within the frame
of her dark and curly hair. She was looking up at me; even though I was
on my knees, she wasn't as tall as I was.

I was thinking clearly enough to see the implications of having to
"get to the stairs." The stairs had led up to the deck—but now they led

down, into the ocean depths. Above us, there was nothing but the machine deck and the boat's unbreachable hull.

"I can't swim," I said, flatly.

Emily Marchant looked at me as if I were insane.

"I mean it," I said. "I can't swim."

"You have to," she said. "It's not hard."

My reflexive response was to change the subject. "Where's everyone else gone to?" I asked. The boat lurched more violently as I spoke, and the little girl reached out to me for support. I took my hand away from the wall and clasped both of her hands in mine.

"Mama Janine put me to bed," Emily said. "Then she went back to the party. Everyone was at the party. There's only us, Mister Mortimer. We have to get out. No one will come, Mister Mortimer."

Like me, Emily Marchant had been raised contented and well adjusted, and she was as wise and level-headed as any eight year old in all the world. Her IT and her suitskin were both tuned to compensate for panic, but she was not immune to fear. Fear, like pain, is universally recognized to be necessary and healthy, *in moderation*. She was free to feel fear, if not sheer, stark, paralyzing terror. So was I. *No one will come, Mister Mortimer*, she had said, packing all the tragedy of the moment into those few, almost dispassionate, words. She was afraid, as I was—and we had every reason to be afraid.

Everyone but the two of us had been on deck at the party—all twenty-six of them. Whatever impossibility had flipped *Genesis* onto her back had thrown every last one of them into the sea: the impossibly warm and impossibly violent sea.

scrambled to my feet. While I held Emily fast in my right hand I put
out my left to steady myself against the upside-down wall. The water
was knee-deep and still rising—not very quickly, but inexorably. The
upturned boat was rocking from side to side, but it also seemed to be
trying to spin around. I could hear the rumble of waves breaking on the
outside of the hull. The noise wasn't loud, but I knew that the hull must
be muffling the sound.

"My name's Emily, Mister Mortimer," the little girl told me. "I'm
frightened."

I resisted the temptation to say *So am I*. Somewhere in the corridor,
I knew, there were lockers containing emergency equipment: not merely
life jackets but "survival pods," whose shells were self-inflating plastic
life rafts. There was light enough to find them, if I could only adjust my
mind to the fact that everything was upside down. Once we had one, we
still had to get it out, and I still couldn't swim—but how hard could it
be, if I could get into a life jacket?

"This way," I said, as soon as I had figured out which way the emergency locker was. Unsurprisingly, it was in the logical place, next to the
stairs, which now descended into angry darkness. I marveled at my being
able to speak so soberly and marveled even more that I no longer felt seasick. My body had been shocked back to sanity, if not to normality.

As we moved along the corridor, I couldn't shake the horror of the
thought that Emily Marchant's *entire family* might have been wiped out
at a single stroke and that she might now be that rarest of all rare beings,
an *orphan*. It was barely imaginable. What possible catastrophe, I wondered, could have done that? And what other atrocities must that same
catastrophe have perpetrated?

"Do you have any idea what happened, Emily?" I asked, as I wres-
tled with the handle of the locker. It was easy enough to turn it the
"wrong" way, but not so easy to drag the door open against the increasing pressure of the water.

"I don't know," she said. "Are we going to die?" The word *too* hung unspoken at the end of the sentence. She was only eight, but she understood the implications of the fact that everyone else had been on deck when the boat flipped over, defying every precaution taken by its careful designers.

"No," I told her. "If we can just get these life jackets on and take this pod with us. . . ."

"It's very big," she said, dubiously—but I knew that if it had been designed to be carried up the stairs it would certainly go down them.

Despite the rocking of the boat, I contrived to get one of the life jackets over Emily's shoulders. "Don't pull it yet," I said, showing her where the ring pull was but firmly setting her hand away from it. "We have to get clear of the boat first. You have to swim as hard as you can— *that* way. Understand? Swim as hard as you can, and don't pull until you're sure you're no longer under the boat. Then you'll pop up to the surface. I'll bring the life-raft pod."

"I've been a good girl," she told me, with just a hint of bleakness in her awful sobriety. "I've never told a lie."

It couldn't have been literally true, but I knew exactly what she meant. She was eight years old and she had every right to expect to live till she was eight hundred. She didn't *deserve* to die. It wasn't fair that she should. It wasn't fair that she should lose her parents either but one misfortune didn't license the other. I knew full well that fairness didn't really come into it, and I expect she knew it too, even if my fellow historians and social commentators were wrong about the abolition of the primary artifices of childhood. I knew in my heart, though, that what she said was *right*, and that insofar as the imperious laws of nature ruled her observation irrelevant, the *universe* was wrong. It *wasn't* fair. She *had* been a good girl. If she died, it would be a monstrous injustice.

Perhaps it was merely a kind of psychological defense mechanism that helped me to displace my own mortal anxieties, but the horror running through me was exclusively focused on her. At that moment, her plight—not *our* plight, but *hers*—seemed to be the only thing that mattered. It was as if her dignified protest and her placid courage somehow contained the essence of New Human existence, the purest product of progress.

Perhaps it was only my cowardly mind's refusal to contemplate anything else, but the only thing I could think of while I tried to figure out what to do was the awfulness of what Emily Marchant was saying. As that awfulness possessed me it was magnified a thousandfold, and it seemed to me that in her lone and tiny voice there was a much greater voice speaking for multitudes: for all the human children that had ever died before achieving maturity; all the *good* children who had died without ever having the chance to *deserve to die.*

"I can't hold your hand, Emily," I told her, as my own life jacket settled itself snugly about my torso. "It would make it too difficult for us to get away."

"You're the one who can't swim," she reminded me.

"I'll be all right," I assured her. "If you see the life-raft pack before you see me, the trigger's *here.* Okay?"

"Okay," she said. We were both looking down into the hole in what had once been the ceiling of the corridor.

"Don't try to hold on to the ladder," I advised her. "Just dive, as deep as you can. Then go sideways, until you can't hold your breath any more. Then pull the ring. It'll carry you up to the surface. I'll be right behind you." I was talking as much for my own benefit as hers. As she said, I was the one whose knowledge of swimming was purely theoretical. I was the one who would have to improvise.

She didn't move. She was paralyzed by apprehension.

"I don't think any more water can get in," she said, with a slight tremor in her voice, "but there's only so much air. If we stay here too long, we'll suffocate."

She was trying to convince herself. She was eight years old and hoped to live to be eight hundred, and she was absolutely right. The air wouldn't last forever. Hours maybe, but not forever.

"The survival pod will keep us alive for a week," she added. She had obviously paid close attention to Captain Cardigan's welcoming speech. She was probably the only passenger who'd actually bothered to plug the safety chips they'd handed out to all of us into her trusty handbook, like the good girl she was.

"We can both fit into the pod," I assured her, "but we have to get it out of the boat before we inflate it. It's too big for you to carry."

"You can't swim," she reminded me.

"It's not hard," I reminded her. "All I have to do is hold my breath and kick myself away from the boat. But you have to go first. I'll get you aboard the life raft, Emily. Trust me."

"I do," she said.

I stared at her. There was no cause for wonder in the fact that she could be so calm and so controlled and yet not be able to hurl herself into that black airless void—but I had to get her out before I got out myself. I couldn't show her the way because I couldn't leave her alone.

"Listen to the water on the outside," she whispered. "Feel the rocking. It must have been a hurricane that overturned the boat . . . but we have to go, don't we, Mister Mortimer? We have to get out."

"Yes," I said. "The pod's bright orange and it has a distress beacon. We should be picked up within twenty-four hours, but there'll be supplies for a week." I had every confidence that our suitskins and our internal technology could sustain us for a month, if necessary. Even having to drink a little seawater if our recycling gel clotted would only qualify as a minor inconvenience—but drowning was another matter. Drowning is one of the elementary terrors of emortality, along with a smashed skull, a fall from a great height and a close encounter with a bomb.

"It's okay, Mister Mortimer," Emily said, putting her reassuring hand in mine for one more precious moment, so that we could both take strength from the touch. "We can do it. It'll be all right."

And so saying, she leaped into the pool of darkness.

ELEVEN

I knew that I couldn't afford to be paralyzed by apprehension, for Emily's sake. I also knew—and am convinced of it to this very day—that if Emily hadn't been there to create the absolute necessity, I would not have been able to lower myself through that hole. I would have waited, cravenly, until there was no more air left to breathe. While I waited, I might have been injured by the buffeting of the rigid-hulled boat, or the boat might have taken on water enough to go down, but I would have waited, alone and horribly afraid.

I couldn't swim.

In the early twenty-sixth century, it was taken for granted that all members of the New Human Race were perfectly sane. Madness, like war and vandalism, was supposed to be something that our forefathers had put away, with other childish things, when they came to understand how close the old Old Human Race had come to destroying themselves and taking the entire ecosphere with them. It was, I suppose, true. Ali Zaman's firstborns were, indeed, perfectly sane from the age of eight until eighty, and we lived in contentedly uninteresting times until 23 March 2542. We always knew what counted as the reasonable thing to do, and it was always available to us—but even we New Humans couldn't and didn't always do it. As sane as we undoubtedly were, we were still capable of failing to act in our own best interests. Sometimes, we needed an extra reason even to do what we knew full well we *had* to do—and I needed the responsibility of taking care of Emily Marchant to make me jump into the hot and seething sea, even though I could not swim, and trade the falsely unsinkable *Genesis* for an authentically unsinkable life raft.

But Emily was right. We *could* do it, together, and we did.

It was the most terrifying and most horrible experience of my young life, but it had to be done, and as soon as Emily had had time to get clear I filled my lungs with air and hurled myself into the same alien void. I had the handgrip of the life-raft pod tightly held in my right hand, but I hugged it to my chest nevertheless as I kicked with all my might, scissoring my legs.

Much later, of course, I realized that if I had only followed Captain Cardigan's instructions and read the safety manual, I would have known where to find breathing apparatus as well as a life raft. That would have done wonders for my confidence, although it would not have made my feeble imitation of swimming any more realistic. I have no way of knowing, but I suspect that it was pure luck and the seething of the sea that carried me far enough away from the boat to ensure that when I yanked the ring to inflate my life jacket I did indeed bob up to the surface.

The surface of the sea was chaotically agitated, and the stars that should have shone so brightly were invisible behind a pall of cloud. I started screaming Emily's name as soon as I had refilled my lungs. I had sufficient presence of mind to hang on to the pod's handgrip while I pulled the trigger that would inflate the life raft. There was nothing explosive about its expansion, but it grew with remarkable rapidity, reducing me to a mere parasite hanging on to the side of what felt like a huge rubbery jellyfish. It was as blackly dark as everything else until the process reached its terminus, at which point the eye lights came on and exposed its garish orange color.

I was still yelling, "Emily!"

No sooner was I struck by the horrid thought that getting into the body of the life raft might not be easy than I found out something else I would have known had I read the safety manual. The activated life raft was at least sloth-smart, and it had urgent instincts built into its biosystems. It grabbed me and sucked me in as if it were a synthowhale harvesting a plankton crop. Then it went after Emily, who was close enough to be glaringly obvious to its primitive senses.

While the raft fought the demonic waves I was rolled helplessly back and forth within its softly lit stomachlike interior, and I could tell that it was no easy chase, but the creature was programmed for tenacity. Although it seemed like a long time to me it could not have been more than three minutes before it swallowed Emily and deposited her alongside me. I grabbed hold of her while we continued to rock and roll, so that we wouldn't be bumping into one another with bruising effect, but it took only another two minutes for me to find the handholds, which allowed me to stabilize my position and to find Emily a coign of vantage of her own.

She spat out some water, but she was fine.

The movement of the boat became somewhat less violent now that its muscles could be wholly devoted to the task of smoothing out the worst excesses of the madcap ride. For a moment I was glad, and then I realized what it meant. If there had been any other human being within detection range, the raft would have chased them.

"Did you read the safety manual, Emily?" I asked.

"Yes, Mister Mortimer," she said, in the wary kind of voice that children use when expecting admonition—but nothing was further from my mind than checking up on her.

"Can you remember whether there were any pods like this on the outside of the boat? Pods that would detach automatically in an emergency?"

"I don't know," she said. "I don't think so."

I kept on hoping, but I was almost sure that she was right. The *Genesis* was supposedly unsinkable, so the only kind of emergency its designers had provided for was the kind where the crew might have to throw a life raft to a swimmer in trouble. There had been no rafts to go to the aid of the people swept overboard when the *Genesis* had first been rudely upturned by the boiling sea.

TWELVE

I t didn't take long to find the teats that secreted fresh water and other kinds of liquid nourishment. By the time I'd sucked in enough to take the taste of brine away, my suitskin had gotten rid of all the surplus water it had accumulated during the escape from *Genesis*. The interior surface of the life raft was suitskin-smart too, so there was no water sloshing around. The only significant discomfort was the heat. The life raft was well equipped to warm its inhabitants up if they were hypothermic, but no one had anticipated that it might need equally clever facilities to cool them down if they'd just had a hot bath and were still floating on top of one.

"How long will it be?" Emily asked.

"I don't know," I said.

"What happened?" she asked.

I didn't know that either, but I had already formed two suspicions regarding what seemed at the time to be the most likely not-quite-impossibilities.

"Something must have fallen out of the sky," I said. "It must have hit the sea very violently, as well as being very hot itself. If it were a comet or an asteroid fragment the satellite ring would have given adequate warning, but if it were actually one of the satellites—maybe even a station . . ."

"Or a bomb," she said, neatly filling in the not-quite-impossibility that I'd considered unmentionable. "It could have been a bomb."

Theoretically, there were no nuclear weapons anywhere in the world—but I'd seen the inside of a mountain that had been hollowed out by gantzers in order to serve as a repository for all the artifacts that the world no longer considered *necessary*—the litter that dared not speak its name. I'd even poked around in a few of the storerooms. I knew that some of what the New Human Race had put away with other childish things really had been merely *put away*.

Theoretically, of course, there should have been no one anywhere in the world insane enough to use a nuclear weapon even if one still existed, but even in the long interval of apparent near-universal sanity that separated the Moreau murders from the rebirth of Thanaticism we New Humans were not *entirely* convinced that our theories were reliable in their account of the limits of Old Human irresponsibility.

"I don't think it was a bomb," I told the little girl. "If anyone was going to start throwing multimegaton bombs around, they wouldn't aim one at the Coral Sea. They certainly wouldn't aim one at *Genesis*—and whatever happened, we must have been very close to the point of impact."

We were both wrong, alas, as any passably conscientious student of history will have known ever since I specified the date on which *Genesis* set sail. Had I been in a clearer frame of mind I would undoubtedly have realized that our hypotheses had only covered two of the three relevant dimensions (up and sideways), but I was still ill. I had stopped noticing it, but my seasickness hadn't actually been *cured*. I didn't suppose that I would be able to complete the reconciliation of my head and my guts while the raft kept on lurching, and I was right.

"They are going to come for us, aren't they?" Emily said. She was putting on a brave face, but the excessive warmth of the raft's interior hadn't brought any significant color to her cheeks.

"Absolutely," I said. "The raft's lit up outside like a firework display, and its systems will be transmitting a mayday on the emergency wavelength that will be audible all the way from Australia to geosynchronous orbit. If they can't redirect a ship to pick us up they'll send a helicopter as soon as it's safe to fly—but the weather's pretty filthy. Anything that can turn the sea into a Jacuzzi is likely to stir the atmosphere up a bit."

"If it was a bomb," she said, "there might be nobody . . ."

"It wasn't a bomb, Emily," I told her, firmly. "They didn't even use big bombs in World War Three or World War Four. It has to be space junk falling back to Earth: an accident in orbit. We happened to be right next to ground zero—a million-to-one chance. They'll send a copter from Gladstone or Rockhampton when they can."

"But if someone had heard the mayday," she pointed out, with deadly accuracy, "they'd have replied, wouldn't they?"

She was right. The raft had to have a voice facility. A hyperspecialized sloth wouldn't be able to hold a conversation with us, but it would be able to tell us what was happening if anything *were* happening. If no one was replying to our mayday one of two things must be true. Either there was no one able to reply, or there were so many maydays filling the airwaves that we were effectively on hold, waiting in a *very* long line.

I realized that if it were a very large space station that had come down, the subsequent tidal wave might have taken out Gladstone and Rockhampton as easily as it had taken out *Genesis*—and flooded every single natural and artificial island west of Vanuatu and south of the Solomons. That was as big a disaster as I could seriously contemplate at the time, but the silence said that even those limits might be elastic.

"They're all dead, aren't they?" Emily said, at last. "All of them."

She meant all twelve of her parents. The three couples and Captain Cardigan's crew were gone too, but she couldn't think about them while her own personal tragedy was so immense.

"We don't know that," I said. "There must have been other pods. They all have good suitskins and first-rate IT. People are surprisingly hard to kill." But I knew as I said it that whatever had tipped *Genesis* over had been more than *surprising*; it had been unprecedented, and well-nigh unimaginable. I didn't have to look out to know that the sea was still seething, and the clouds that had risen from it to blot out the stars were still impenetrable.

THIRTEEN

The sea did not become calm that night. When I was sure that the sun had risen I did take an opportunity to peek out, but the cloud was so thick as to be hardly penetrable, and rain was falling more densely than I had ever seen it before—and there are summer days in the Himalayas, even in these days of supposed climate control, when thirty centimeters of rain can fall in a matter of hours. It was no longer hot inside the raft, although the sea was still ten or fifteen degrees warmer than the falling rain.

I managed to take a little liquid nourishment from the teat, but my IT had not yet managed to get the upper hand in the argument with my subconscious, and I still felt nauseous. It was not until noon that the raft's voice facility finally kicked in and announced that its mayday had been acknowledged.

"Please wait," the raft said, in the curiously plaintive fashion typical of the most limited sloths. "Help will come. Please wait." Clearly, it was talking to another AI no brighter than itself—and if it had taken twelve hours even to cement *that* link, I thought, how much longer would it be before our plight became a matter of urgent concern for a high-grade silver or a human being?

I asked what was happening, of course, and begged to be put into contact with a more intelligent entity, but I couldn't evoke any response other than a simple repetition. I tried to remember how many islands there were in the Coral Sea and Micronesia and how many people lived along the coastal strips of Queensland and New Guinea, but I had no real idea. The only thing of which I could be sure was that the number of people needing help must be at least as many millions as the number of people able to render it—and that most of them would be aggregated in larger and more easily reachable groups than our minuscule microcosm.

"It's not fair," Emily whispered, when it became clear that night was going to fall without anyone coming to our aid, "is it, Mister Mortimer?"

I knew what she meant, but I had a slightly pedantic mind-set even then. "Mortimer's my first name, Emily, not my second," I told her, "and the one thing we can be certain of is that whatever's going on now *is* fair. All the maydays will be feeding into a ganglion somewhere in the Labyrinth, and a supersilver triage system will make sure that the help goes wherever it's most urgently needed. Everything will be done in such a way as to ensure the greatest good of the greatest number. They must know that we're not in any real danger—that the life raft will keep us alive for as long as necessary. They'll come for us when they can."

"But they're not even *talking* to us," she said. "How bad can things be?"

For an eight year old, she was extremely sharp. I figured she deserved an honest answer. "Very, very bad indeed," I admitted. "Whatever it is, it has to be the worst disaster in human history."

"Worse than the Crash?" she queried.

"Worse than the Black Death," I told her, bleakly. "Worse than the last Ice Age, and a hell of a lot quicker. At least as bad as the last big extinction event, if not the one that finally killed off the dinosaurs." I realized as I said it that even the biggest station in near-Earth orbit couldn't have caused that big a splash. One of the L-5 cylinders might have—but what could have moved it all the way from lunar orbit *without any warning*?

"How many people do you think it killed?" she asked, carefully raising her sights above the level of her own family. "Millions?"

"Perhaps millions," I agreed, sadly.

"Like the Crash," she said.

She was eight years old, and I didn't dare ask her exactly what she meant by that. I was prepared to assume that she was only talking about numbers—but I was already a fledgling historian. I knew that the Crash had not been entirely a matter of accident and misadventure. At least some of the viruses that had sterilized the Old Human Race had been deliberately crafted for that purpose, by people who thought of themselves as the midwives and parents of a New Human Race. I couldn't help but wonder whether Emily might, after all, have been right about that bomb, and whether some member of the *real* New Human Race—*our* New Human Race—might have wearied of the slowness with which the world was being handed over to our control.

It was absurd, of course. No *sane* member of the New Human Race could possibly have been as impatient as that, let alone as frankly evil-minded as that, but when you're afloat in a life raft on an impossibly turbulent sea, having never had a chance to recover from seasickness, you can entertain thoughts that you would never entertain at any other time. The fact remained that whatever had caused this disaster *would* hasten the disappearance of the Old Human Race, at least in Australasia and Oceania.

That, in itself, was a sobering thought.

By the time night fell again we had become sufficiently well adapted to the pitching and tossing of the boat to sleep. My slumber was fitful and full of dreams, but Emily slept better and longer, only jerking awake once or twice when her reflexive grip on the handholds weakened and she felt herself moving too far too fast.

While we were awake throughout our second day afloat, we talked about anything and everything except our parents.

I told Emily about the valley in the Himalayas, and the Hindu monks, and the genetically engineered yaks, and the secrets of Shangri-La. She told me about her own hometree in the middle of what had been the outback before the Continental Engineers had constructed the largest of all their irrigation schemes and made it bloom again.

I told her everything I had learned about the hollow mountains full of the world's dross. She told me everything she knew about the Black Mountains of the Northern Territory, whose hollow interiors were vast factories converting the energetic produce of the SAP forests to every conceivable purpose.

We talked about the latest news from Mars and the Oort Halo and the fact that the so-called kalpa probes would soon be overtaking the first-generation Arks, launched in the early years of the Crash by megacorp men half-convinced that Earthbound man was not going to make it through the crisis. We agreed that when the people those Arks were carrying in SusAn finally emerged from the freezer, they would be pig sick at the thought of having been overtaken as well as having missed out on the last four hundred years of technological progress. We talked about the possibility that human beings would eventually colonize the entire galaxy, terraforming every planet that seemed capable of sustaining an ecosphere, and the possibility that one or other of the kalpa probes would soon encounter other intelligent species already engaged with that task.

We also talked about the Type-2 crusaders who wanted to start transporting mass from the outer system to Earth's orbit as preliminary steps on the way to making use of the sun's entire energy output, although I don't recall either of us taking a particular interest in that topic.

"When I grow up," Emily said, "I want to go into space."

"Me too," I said. "There are wonderful sights to see once you get outside the atmosphere—and virtual reproductions can't do them justice any more than they could do justice to Wilde's Creation." I felt a pang of regret as I said it for the loss of Wilde's orgiastic Creation.

"I don't just want to *see* things," Emily assured me. "I want to make things. New worlds." She didn't mention Wilde's island specifically, or any of its neighbors, but I think she had a better sense than I had of their irrelevance to a world in which one could really think in terms of making new *worlds*.

"I don't know about going into space permanently," I said. "No matter how clever our suitskins and IT become, we were shaped by evolution to live at the surface of the earth. It's the only place we'll ever really be at home, unless and until the Type-2 brigade can build and terraform Earth 2 on the far side of the sun. I left my old hometree readily enough, but I'm not sure I could leave a world as easily. It'll be a long time before the Exodus really picks up pace, especially now. . . ." I cut myself off before adding that if the disaster in which we had been caught up really had killed millions, the UN's propaganda in favor of using extraterrestrial emigration as a population safety-valve was bound to be laid to rest, at least for a while.

"Perhaps you're right," Emily said, politely. I can't remember whether it was the last time she ever spoke those words to me, even with the benefit of a tentative *perhaps*, but it might well have been. It speaks volumes for the quality of our friendship that it never needed reinforcement by agreement. No difference in the world could have separated us after what we went through together on *Genesis* and the life raft.

FOURTEEN

Emily and I took all the subjects we discussed aboard the raft very seriously, but we always knew that we were filling in time, trying to make the long wait bearable. When the time came for us to sleep again we were both relieved that the necessity of talking had been temporarily relaxed.

We had been afloat for three storm-tossed days when we finally heard a human voice. There are no words to express the relief that we felt as we realized that the ordeal was over.

"Calling *Genesis* life raft," the voice said, sounding almost laconic through the raft's elementary parrot mike. "This is Steve Willowitch, Air Rescue Mombasa, temporarily reassigned to Canberra. Can you confirm two passengers, alive and uninjured."

The raft's sloth had told him that much. I stabbed the icon controlling the voice transmitter with indecent haste and force. "Yes!" I said. "Mortimer Gray and Emily Marchant. Alive and uninjured."

"Good. I'll be with you in twenty minutes, Mister Gray."

"What the hell *happened*?" I demanded, fearing that he might cut the connection and leave us in suspense for twenty more minutes. "The onboard sloth is too stupid even to pick up broadcasts." I was only then absorbing the import of what he'd said. Air Rescue *Mombasa*? I thought. Reassigned to *Canberra*?

"Sorry for the delay, Mister Gray, Miss Marchant," said Steve Willowitch. "Very bad business—major crust fracture. Seabed came open like a zipper south of Guadalcanal, extended for more than a hundred klicks. Seismologists got no warning from tectonic movements—the primary event must have been way down in the mantle, although the plates started shaking fit to burst thereafter. Hell of a blast—like a hundred Krakatoas, mostly a couple of hundred fathoms deep."

"How many people died?" Emily asked, tentatively.

"Don't know yet," said the air rescue man. "More than three hundred million but we hope maybe less than five. Queensland took the worst but, the waves trashed New Zealand, the Philippines, and what was left of Japan and the western seaboard of the Americas after the first sequence of quakes had finished. And the islands, of course. Eight thousand of them."

Eight thousand of them was the statistic that reverberated in my head, because I hadn't quite grasped the fact that 10 percent of the population of Earth was already feared dead, with more to come. I should, of course, have remembered immediately that Papa Ezra was in New Zealand, but I didn't.

"You were lucky," the pilot told us. "Must be tens of thousands of life rafts still floating, but millions didn't even have a chance to get to a pod."

I looked at Emily Marchant. Her tiny face had always seemed wan in the subdued interior lighting of the raft, and mine must have seemed just as bad, so the mute signal we exchanged through our mutual gaze had no further margin of horror in it, nor any additional sorrow for the hundreds of millions whose deaths we hadn't dared anticipate.

"Thanks, Steve," I said. "Get here when you can—we're okay."

This time, my finger was far gentler as it closed the transmitter. There was no point in leaving the channel open; it couldn't be easy flying a copter through all the filth that was still clogging and stirring the lower atmosphere.

It occurred to me almost immediately that an event of the kind that Willowitch had described would have done far worse damage had it happened five hundred years earlier, but I said nothing to Emily. She didn't seem to mind the silence, so I let my own thoughts run on unchecked.

I knew that if such a crust fissure had opened up while the world was the sole province of the *old* Old Human Race—the pre-Crash mortals—it would almost certainly have killed fifty or sixty percent instead of ten and might have done so much damage to the ecosphere that even the survivors would have been precipitated into a downward spiral to extinction. *Homo sapiens sapiens* had evolved about a million years ago, on the plains of Africa, so five hundred years was only 0.05 of the life span of the species. Had we not renewed ourselves so comprehensively within that geological eyeblink, we would never have had the chance. Thanks to IT and suitskins, Solid and Liquid Artificial Photosynthesis, and our near-total technical control of the ecosphere, Earthbound humanity could and would bounce back, with what might have to be reckoned as minor casualties. We had reached the life-raft pod in time. We were *all* lucky—except for those of us who had perished.

Not that the casualties could possibly seem "minor" to Emily Marchant, I remembered, as I applied a gentle brake to the train of thought. She had lost all twelve of her parents at a single stroke. I was later to discover that I had not lost a single one—Papa Ezra had been high in the mountains—and would gladly have made her a gift of all eight had they been mine to give, but that could not have healed the breach in her circumstances. There would be no shortage of willing fosterers eager to adopt her, even in a world that had lost 300 million people, but it would not be the same. Her personal history had been rudely snapped in two, and she would be marked by her loss forever—but that moment could not bear sole responsibility for what became of her, and more than it was solely responsible for what became of me. I was already a historian; she had already declared that she wanted to join the Exodus and leave the homeworld behind.

"I'm sorry," I said to Emily. "I'm *so* sorry."

She looked at me very gravely, having made her own computation of the scale of the disaster and her own tiny role within it. "If you hadn't been seasick," she said, contemplatively, "I wouldn't have been able to get the pod out."

"If you hadn't been there, neither would I," I told her.

She didn't believe it, but she knew that I wasn't lying—that I honestly meant what I said.

Emily was still hanging on to the inner surface of the wave-tossed raft, but she released her right hand so that she could reach out to me. Solemnly, I took it in mine, and we shook hands for all the world like two businessmen who'd just been introduced.

"Thanks," I said.

"You too," she said. Then—and only then—she broke down and began to weep, helplessly and endlessly.

She was still weeping when the helicopter arrived, but she stopped when she realized how difficult it was going to be to winch us aboard. We had to concentrate and cooperate fully with Steve Willowitch's heroic endeavors.

"It'll be okay, Mortimer," she assured me, as the hawser came down from the hovering aircraft, which seemed so very tiny against the vast dark backcloth of the continuing storm. "It'll be fine."

"Sure," I said, as I lifted her up toward the blindly groping cable. "How difficult can it possibly be, for hardened survivors like us?"

FIFTEEN

Emily was by no means the only child in the world to lose an entire set of parents, and I still shudder to think of the number of parents who lost their only children. There was, as I had anticipated, no shortage of people willing to forge themselves into teams of adopters for the sake of the orphaned children, and all of those deprived of parenthood retained the right to return to the banks. The broken links in the chain of inheritance were mended. Tears were shed in abundance and then were set aside.

The cities devastated by tsunamis were rebuilt, and the agricultural lands around them reclaimed. Even at the time it seemed to happen with bewildering rapidity, fueled by an astonishing determination to reassert the dominion of humankind. There had been talk of Garden Earth for centuries, but our capacity to shape and manage the ecosphere had never been subjected to any severe test. After the Coral Sea Disaster, our gantzers and macrobiotechnologists had both the opportunity and the responsibility to demonstrate that they could deal with *real* Decivilization—and they met the challenge with awesome efficiency. The Continental Engineers were revitalized, if not actually reborn, in those years, and so were the continents themselves.

There is, I suppose, a certain wretched irony in the fact that all our paranoia regarding the precariousness of life on Earth had been directed outward for hundreds of years. We had thousands of artificial eyes scanning every part of the sky for incoming debris, but none looking down. Pride in our accomplishments had caused us to look upward and outward, and it wasn't merely the promoters of the Exodus who had fallen into the habit of thinking of future history in terms of the kind of calculated expansion into the galaxy and appropriation of other worlds that Emily and I had discussed so earnestly while we were adrift. The breadth of our accomplishments and the height of our ambitions had made us forget how little we knew of the violent core of our own world.

Ever since the dutiful seismologists of the twenty-second century had sown the deep probes that measured tectonic stresses and moni-tored volcanoes, giving polite and timely warning of impending earth-quakes and eruptions, we had fallen into the habit of thinking of the planet itself, not merely the ecosphere, as something *tame*. We had taken the effective constancy of the world's interior for granted, to the extent that the silvers guiding our best moleminers had been left to themselves, bearing sole responsibility for the work of descending to the underworld of liquid rocks in search of all manner of motherlodes. We simply had not realized that there were forces at work down there that were easily capable of cracking the fragile biosphere like a bird's egg, to release a fire-breathing dragon capable of devouring everything alive. The limits of AI are such that because we did not think of it, our silvers did not consider it either. If the moleminers' senses picked up any indication of mysterious mantle events akin to that which caused the Coral Sea Cata-strophe, they paid them no heed.

Many people must have made calculations like mine, realizing that we had survived a disaster that might have been an extinction event only a few centuries earlier. There were not so many who made the further calculation that although there had never been an event that destroyed 400 million people within a week, the ordinary processes of mortality had killed that number during every decade of the twentieth and twenty-first centuries. The Old Human Race had not needed the world to be split apart in order to produce and sustain that kind of attrition rate; dis-ease and old age had done it effortlessly, routinely, and *contemptuously*. That, to a young and impressionable historian, was a prospect even more mind-boggling than the consequence of a literally world-shattering event—but it did not calm my view of the Coral Sea Disaster. Perhaps perversely, it seemed to broaden and exaggerate my existential unease.

The deaths that occurred in the Coral Sea Disaster seemed to me to be understandable—direly unfortunate and vilely ominous, but under-standable. Given the magnitude of the cause, the appalling effect was only to be expected, and my subsequent discomfiture accommodated that awareness. The result of my statistical comparisons was not to end that discomfiture, but to generate a new discomfiture in the contempla-tion of days long past.

My attempt to gain a proper perspective shone new light on the knowledge I had always had, but never brought fully to mind, that in 2001—the year that began the millennium in which I lived—the world had contained more than six billion people, *every single one of whom* was condemned to die within a mere hundred years or so: a catastrophe on the same scale as the Coral Sea Disaster every time the last two digits of the date worked their inexorable way round to zero.

And yet the people who lived in those times had accepted that burden as the common toll of nature, philosophically and almost without complaint!

Perhaps I would have done what I eventually set out to do anyway. Perhaps the Coral Sea Catastrophe would have affected me in much the same way even if I had been on the other side of the world, cocooned in the safety of a hometree or an apartment in one of those crystal cities that felt no more than a slight earth tremor and greeted the sun again after three weeks of minor inconvenience. Even if I had written the same history, however, I am not at all sure that I would have written the same fantasy. It was because I was at the very center of things, because my life was literally turned upside down by the disaster, because I was pathetically sick to my stomach, and because eight-year-old Emily Marchant was there to save my life with her common sense and her composure, that the project which would occupy the first few centuries of my life took such a powerful hold over my imagination. I still contend that it did not become an obsession, but I do admit that it became capable of generating a unique passion in my heart and mind.

I did all kinds of other things; I lived as full a life as any of the other survivors of the Decimation. I did my share of Reconstruction work. I was not diminished in any way by the legacy of my experience—but from that moment on, my interest in the history of death could not be dispassionate, let alone disinterested—and it was very soon after being delivered safely back to what was left of Adelaide that I determined to write a definitive history of death.

From the very moment of that history's conception, I intended not merely to collate and organize the dull facts of mankind's longest and hardest war, but to discover, analyze, and celebrate the real meaning and significance of every charge in every battle and every bloodied meter of territory gained.

PART TWO
Apprenticeship

Man is born free but is everywhere enchained by the fetters of death. In all times past, men have been truly equal in one respect and one only: they have all borne the burden of age and decay. The day must soon dawn when this burden can be set aside; there will be a new freedom, and with this freedom must come a new equality. No man has the right to escape the prison of death while his fellows remain shackled within.

—The New Charter of Human Rights
(published 2219; adopted 2248)

SIXTEEN

I visited Emily Marchant a dozen times in the three years which followed the Decimation, but we always met in virtual environments far steadier and more brightly lit than the hectic and claustrophobic space we had shared when the world had come apart and we did not know why. I fully intended to keep close contact with her at least until she was grown, but such resolutions always weaken. She was changing as rapidly as any child, and by the time she was twelve she was no longer the same little girl that had saved my life. Our calls grew less frequent and eventually fell into the category of things perennially intended but never actually done—but we didn't forget one another. We always intended to renew our relationship when a suitable opportunity arose.

Emily told me that she was as happy with her new foster parents as it was possible to be but that she would never forget the twelve who wanted to take her on a journey of discovery through the petty Creations of the greatest genetic artists of the late twenty-fourth and early twenty-fifth centuries. Those destinations had perished in the Flood too; the world was again devoid of dragons and marsupials, temporarily at least, and there would never be another orgy of perfumes as finely balanced as Oscar Wilde's flamboyant tribute to the mythical Jean Des Esseintes.

My own co-parents never gathered in the same place again. Three came together in the flesh at Papa Domenico's funeral in 2547, and three at Papa Laurent's in 2549, but Mama Meta and Mama Siorane were not the only ones who lent their virtual presence to each occasion, even though they were the only ones off-planet. After Papa Laurent's death a full half-century passed before another of them died—that was Papa Nahum, in 2601—and by that time the directions of their lives had diversified to the point at which none of them felt the need to attend even by technological means. It would have been impossible, in any case, for Mama Siorane or Papa Ezra to take any meaningful part in Papa Nahum's farewell, given the time-lapse involved in communication with the outer system; Mama Siorane was on Titan by then, and Papa Ezra had taken his work on the adaptation of Zaman transformations to faber anatomy to the microworlds.

Papa Domenico's funeral in Amundsen City provided my first opportunity to visit the Continent Without Nations and to view the beating heart of the Utopian Bureaucracy. The architects who had built the new United Nations Complex had taken great pride in their ability to make the city blend in with the "natural" landscape, sheathing every building in glittering ice, and their efforts seemed spectacular to eyes that had not yet beheld a real ice palace. They had, at any rate, succeeded in providing the complex with the perfect image of icy objectivity. The funeral was easily accommodated to the same pattern; it was a solemn and businesslike affair, far less lavish than any I had seen on TV.

Not unnaturally, given that it was only five years after the Decimation, the conversation of the mourners was dominated by the trading of disaster stories. My fosterers demanded that I repeat my own tale for the benefit of dozens of their more distant acquaintances, and as I did so, over and over again, the account absorbed something of the spirit of the place and became colder and more impersonal even in my own reckoning.

"This new project of yours isn't a good idea, Morty," Papa Laurent told me. "I don't say it's not worth doing, but it's not the sort of thing that should occupy a *young* man." He was not yet two hundred, but his second rejuve had not taken as well as it should, and he knew that he had not long to live—which inevitably led him to think of himself as very old.

"On the contrary," I told him. "It's work that only a young man can do. It will take decades, perhaps centuries, if it's to be done properly— and I do mean to do it *properly*. The Labyrinth is so vast that the task of building hypertextual bridges to encompass a subject as broad as mine is more than Herculean. Nothing like it has been attempted before because it wasn't the kind of project that a mortal scholar could seriously contemplate. If I don't start now, the task might even prove beyond someone like me. The Decimation cost us a vast amount of historical information as well as four hundred million human lives and thousands of living species—which is, admittedly, trivial by comparison but serves as a timely reminder that the past becomes less accessible with every day that passes."

"But the essential data will all be there," Papa Laurent objected, "even if the bridges remain unbuilt—and we're already on the threshold of an age when that kind of data navigation can be entirely delegated to silvers. Surely they'll be the historians of the future."

"Silvers are very poor commentators," I reminded him, "and they only build bridges to connect preexisting highways. I want to make new connections, to build a huge picture of a kind that we've almost stopped producing. We've become too easily content to let the trees hide the wood, and I want to see the entire forest—but no one will accept my grand overview if I can't demonstrate that I've done all the detailed work. A historian has to pay his dues. My history will take at least two hundred years to complete. I hope to issue it in installments, but the preliminary work will take a long time."

"Don't let it get on top of you," my aged parent persisted. "You can't put off the business of living."

"I won't," I promised—and tried with all my might to keep the promise.

"A history of death is too *morbid* a preoccupation for a young man," he insisted, revealing the extent to which his own mind had lost its ability to move on. "You've always been a little too serious. I always knew that the balance of the team was wrong. We needed lighter hearts than Nahum's or Siorane's or even mine."

"The members of every team of fosterers look back on their work and think they got the balance wrong," I assured him. "I think you got the balance just right. Trust me, Papa Laurent."

Mama Sajda also told me that she'd always known that the team was out of kilter, although it wasn't lighter hearts that she'd thought lacking. "Too many people with their eyes on the stars or Dom's ridiculous Universe Without Horizons," she told me. "I thought it was enough to set the hometree down in a quintessentially real place, but we still couldn't keep our feet on the ground. We should have chosen Africa—the veldt, or the fringes of the rain forest. We were too *detached*."

Mama Meta and Mama Siorane, speaking across the void, were now united in the opinion that I ought to have been raised on the moon or in one of the L-5 habitats, but Papa Nahum—who was also speaking via VE space—was more contented, and so was Mama Eulalie. "Don't listen to them, Mortimer," Mama Eulalie advised me. "Go your own way. Any parents who bring up a child capable of going his own way have done their job."

The similarly detached Papa Ezra, mercifully, was content to talk more about his own work than mine and take the decisions of the past for granted. "We're all going the same way as Dom, Morty," he reminded me. "One by one, we'll desert you. Try to remember Dom kindly—the practice will do you good. You're the only one who'll have to say good-bye to all eight of us."

Papa Laurent's funeral was completely different from Papa Domenico's. Paris did not have the distinction of being one of the most ancient cities in the world, and it had not escaped the Decimation unscathed, but its inhabitants had contrived nevertheless to retain a sense of cultural superiority and calculated decadence left over from the eighteenth and nineteenth centuries. Most Parisians would have put their own city and the UN's ice-clad metropolis at opposite ends of a spectrum of existential sensitivity, and anyone who judged them by appearances would probably have agreed. Our farewell to Papa Laurent was, in consequence, much gaudier, much warmer, and somewhat more tearful than our farewell to Papa Domenico, although I did not feel his loss any less sharply.

"I'm the oldest now," Mama Eulalie said to me, "but I'm damned if I intend to be the next to go. I'll give the others a race." So she did, sur-viving Papa Nahum by thirty-three years and Mama Meta by seventeen—although both of them might have argued as they lay upon their deathbeds that she had accomplished less by virtue of her unwillingness to take risks that many people regarded as routine.

This time, it was Mama Siorane who took me most sternly to task over my vocation. "It's stupid to immerse yourself in the mire of the past, Mortimer," she informed me, sternly. "Laurent wasn't right about many things, but he was right about that. We should have abolished his-tory along with the Old Human Race. I may be just a false emortal stitched together by nanotech, halfway to robothood, but I'm working for the future. The future is where you're going to have to live your life, Mortimer, and it's the future you should be focused on. Leave Earth to the old, and come out here to the real world. The planet's served its pur-pose in giving birth to us, and it's a foolish and cowardly young man who clings fast to his cradle. One day you'll leave, and it would be better sooner than later. One day, all of your generation will have to leave, if only to make room for the next. The Decimation might have taken the pressure off, but it'll return soon enough. It's not good for you to be obsessed with the dead."

"If I ever leave Earth for good," I told her, "I want to come away with a proper sense of progress. I don't think we should expand into the galaxy mindlessly just because up seems to be the only way to go and we're too restless as a race to stand still. I'm as committed as you are to the ethic of permanent growth, but I think we need a better sense of what we intend to *do* in the more distant reaches of galactic space, and we can only get that by cultivating a better sense of *who we are*. We can't do that if we don't fully understand what our ancestors were."

"Utter rubbish," she opined. "Our ancestors were worms and fish, and you can't embrace human aspirations by understanding the blindness of worms and the stupidity of fish. You have to look forward, Mortimer, or you're half-dead even in your emortality."

"Don't take any notice," Mama Eulalie advised, again. "That bitch was always preaching when she was on Earth, and now she's in heaven she's impossible. Some leaders never look behind them, but the wise ones always do."

In a way, I said good-bye to all of them on the day I said my final good-bye to Papa Laurent. It wasn't just that we never gathered together again, even in a VE; we had all moved on into new phases of our existence. We were not the people we had been when we shared a hometree; our collective identity had been shattered. We had been broken down into atoms and dissipated in the flow of history. As with Emily Marchant, my calls to them grew farther and farther apart, as did their calls to me. We never actually *lost* touch, but our touch became tenuous. New acquaintances gradually displaced them to the margins of my life.

SEVENTEEN

B y 2550 I was working fairly assiduously on the introductory tract of what I then planned as a seven-knot work. It was the hardest part of the job, partly because I had to learn to navigate the Labyrinth properly and partly because I was determined not to limit myself to the Labyrinth's resources.

Even in those days many historians worked exclusively with electronic data, but I had been brought up in the shadow of a mountain archive. I think that I had a better sense of the value of what was buried therein than my city-bred peers, and I certainly had a better sense of what had been lost from such repositories during the Decimation. The Himalyan stores had not been affected, but those in Australia, Japan, and Indonesia had suffered considerable losses in collapses caused by earthquakes. Everyone who ever worked in the stores tended to refer to what they were doing as "mining," but in the wake of the quakes the artifacts in more than one in five of the subterranean repositories really did require laborious and skillful excavation.

The physical and electronic relics of mortal men have always seemed to me to be equally vulnerable to the erosions of time and the corrosions of misfortune. That the world has suffered no major geological upheavals since the Coral Sea split and no major outbreak of software sabotage has made me slightly more complacent, but in the twenty-sixth century experience combined with youth to subject my research to the spurs of a sharp sense of urgency. Despite the oft-expressed anxieties of my surviving foster parents, however, I did not neglect the other aspects of my life. In the course of my travels I met a great many people face-to-face, and I was careful to cultivate a good range of VE friendships, some of which had survived since childhood.

While *The Prehistory of Death* was still far from ready for release into the Labyrinth I contracted my first marriage. Unlike most first marriages it was not a pair-bond, although I had made the usual tentative experiments in one-to-one intimacy. It was a non-parental-group contract with an aggregate consisting of three other men and four women, signed and sealed in 2555. Sociologists nowadays insist on referring to such arrangements as "pseudoparental practice groups," implying that the only possible reason for their formation is training for future parenthood, but my partners and I never thought of it in that way. It was a straightforward exploration of the practicalities of living in close association with others.

The Decimation had fractured so many close-knit groups of every kind that it had sent a wave of panic through the survivors, and for at least half a century thereafter everyone's mind seemed to be focused on the problems of forming, maintaining, and surviving the breakage of intimate relationships. Ours was one of many such experiments. Although we were not precise contemporaries we were all far too young to be contemplating parenthood even during a temporary baby boom. Mine was the median age of the group, and my oldest partner was only ten years my senior.

I was introduced into the group by Keir McAllister and Eve Chin shortly after its core had begun to entertain the marriage plan. They were in executive control of a fleet of silvers monitoring and modifying the ecological impact of the hastily rebuilt cities east of Nairobi. I first encountered them during investigations of newly exposed sites from which paleontological evidence of humankind's origins might be excavated, whose presence added yet another complicating factor to their work. Because I was as neutral as anyone available, I became a middleman in the negotiations between the local paleontologists and the ecological redevelopers and found both Keir and Eve refreshingly easy to deal with by comparison with older people. They obviously felt the same and always introduced me to their close friends and co-workers as a kindred spirit.

None of my spouses was a historian. Although they welcomed me as someone who would broaden the range of the group's interests, they all thought my vocation slightly quaint. They were all involved in post-Decimation reconstruction, although none was a gantzer; they usually spoke of their business as "re-greening" even when they were dealing with city folk. Axel Surt, Jodocus Danette, and Minna Peake were all hydrological engineers specializing in evaporation and precipitation.

While Axel, Jodocus, and Minna worked to ensure that future rain would fall where the Continental Engineers thought best and Keir and Eve negotiated its redistribution once it had fallen—among many other equally touchy matters—Camilla Thorburn and Grizel Bielak labored as biologists to deliver a healthy and abundant fauna to the re-greened land from the gene banks contained in the Earthbound Arks. Axel, Jodocus, and Minna liked to describe themselves, lightheartedly, as the Lamu Rainmakers; the rest of us inevitably became known within the family and to its satellite acquaintances as the Rainmakers-in-Law.

Climate control had, of course, been more carefully reinstituted once the great storm caused by the Coral Sea Disaster had abated, and the utter ruination of vast tracts of coastal land had given a new lease on life to the UN's Land Development Agency. The Agency had resolved to remedy many alleged mistakes made by Ancient Nature, which had been carried forward into the post-Crash era by mere historical momentum. All of my marriage partners except Grizel—who worked for the Ark Consortium—were salaried employees of the LDA. Collectively, therefore, we were relatively well-off, although I contributed far less than my companions to the household purse. What little credit I earned to add to my Allocation was earned by assisting my partners in various humble ways, although I hoped that my own work would eventually begin to generate net-access fees.

We established a hometree in the town that the Rainmakers already used as a base: Lamu, on the coast of Kenya. Mama Sajda was living less than three hundred miles away, and she was the only one of my parents who took the trouble to travel to the ceremony. All of them expressed their delight, though, and I had no cause to suspect any of them of insincerity. They all thought that marriage would be better for me than my long honeymoon with the history of death, and I daresay that they were right.

"Don't take it too seriously, though," Mama Sajda warned me. "I've been married five times, and although I hate to generalize from such a small sample I think it's safe to say that even though two isn't usually company enough, eight is definitely a crowd. Don't expect an easy ride, and don't stick at it too long when the wheels fall off."

"Everything will be fine," I assured her. "We don't have excessive expectations. We've all had the opportunity to observe family life, and we know how stormy the emotional weather can get. I don't say we're unsinkable, but I'm sure that we've got enough life rafts handy, just in case."

"You don't know the half of if it," she assured me, "but you'll learn."

I did learn. We all did. That was the whole point of the exercise.

EIGHTEEN

Although we had formed our marriage for general purposes of companionship rather than preparing for parenthood, we didn't go in for overmuch fleshsex in the early years. We were still finding our various ways through the maze of erotic virtuality and had not yet come to terms, even provisionally, with our own eroto-aesthetic priorities. We did eventually take the time to explore most of the subsidiary combinations contained within the marriage, but we were careful—perhaps too careful—to keep the experiments casual lest petty jealousies should threaten the integrity of the whole. Tacitly, at least, we all accepted the conventional wisdom that the young ought to discover spice in variety and delight in many flavors. Whatever suspicions we retained of our various foster parents and the cultural norms that we inherited, we were content to heed the advice that a broad range of experience is the only secure foundation for a gradual refinement of taste.

The marriage was not conspicuously unhappy for any of us, and such quarrels as we had were muted. This may seem to be damning the whole enterprise with faint praise, but we had not expected it to be life defining. We were not in search of perfection but merely of a better understanding of the many modes and causes of social synergy and interpersonal friction. We went in for a good deal of sportive competition and those kinds of tourism that are best indulged in a group. We visited the other continents from time to time, but most of our adventures merely took us back and forth across Africa.

We all became equally familiar with the trials and tribulations of camping out in the rain forest and the difficulty of keeping sunburn at bay in tropical cities gantzed out of yellow and roseate stone. Axel and Minna always wore suitskins that enclosed every part of their bodies, but the rest of us tended to follow convention by leaving our heads and hands naked. Camilla's skin and bald head were heavily ornamented with ceramic inlays, but they did not protect her from the extremes of temperature, brightness, and humidity that frequently stretched the resources of our IT. I was tempted more than once to darken my skin to the same hue as Julius Ngomi's, but I always settled for a less assertive shade of brown.

"This is nothing," Axel would say, from the safety of his biotech cocoon, whenever anyone complained about the violence of the sun. "Imagine what it must have been like in the days when the Sahara stretched from one side of Africa to the other and smart dress hadn't been invented." He was only slightly less annoying at such times than Grizel and Camilla were when they began to lament the almost total loss of what they insisted on misnaming "the first generation rain forest" and its accompanying biota. No matter how many bothersome flies and biting bugs their patient efforts restored to the forests and grasslands they always protested that the originals must have been far more interesting by virtue of the rich cargoes of infectious diseases they had carried and transmitted.

"Biodiversity is one thing," Jodocus said to Grizel, on one occasion, "but defending the rights of killer parasites is something else. Only a lawyer would sink to that."

I believe that her reply—supported by Keir as well as Camilla—included derisory references to "the bowdlerization of the biosphere," "estate agent ecology," and "niche fascism." Such phrases were not meant entirely for comic effect.

To begin with, I had a considerable affection for all the other members of my new family, but as time went by the usual accretion of petty irritations built up. Several proposals were made between 2565 and 2575 to make additions to the group's personnel, but none received the necessary majority. It was, of course, much easier to arrange exits than negotiate new admissions, and the only modification that actually came about was Keir's departure in 2578, as a result of an irreconcilable breakdown of his relationship with Eve.

Eve disapproved of Keir's political activities on behalf of a faction of the Gaean Liberationists, who were bitterly disappointed by the UN's decision to return the population of the Earthbound to its pre-Decimation level in a matter of decades. Eve was a committed Garden Earther herself, but she never wavered in her conviction that the Garden had to be run for the benefit of humankind, whereas Keir became increasingly strident in his advocacy of population reduction with a view to restoring the empire of natural selection to continentwide wilderness reservations. Their ideological differences made it so difficult for Keir and Eve to work together, let alone live together, that one or the other of them had to leave the group.

Keir intended to keep in touch with the rest of us, and we with him, but the resolution faded; although I had known him for some years before the marriage was made, it proved impossible simply to revert to the terms of our earlier relationship. After 2580 more than a hundred years passed before I heard from him again.

Had things continued the way they were, I suppose I would have been the second deserter. Research for the second volume of my history—which I had begun while I was still constructing the first—drew me more and more frequently to Egypt and to Greece in the 2580s and early 2590s. The Rainmakers pointed out that I had no real need actually to travel in order to do the relevant research, but I disagreed.

I explained as best I could that the parts of my project dealing with the remotest eras of antiquity had to be based on the evidence of artifacts rather than texts, and that one could not obtain a proper sense of the significance of artifacts from secondhand accounts and virtual experiences, but my partners were unimpressed. It was not that I did not trust the webs of information distributed through the Labyrinth, but I did not trust their *sufficiency*—and I was as passionate about sufficiency in those days as I was about urgency.

Africa had been a uniquely valuable base for my study of the prehistory of death, but as soon as I moved on to history per se the pressure to find a base in Europe began to build. I would probably have obtained a formal divorce before the turn of the century, even though I knew that it would give my surviving parents more cause to disapprove of my chosen project, but I was spared the slight ignominy of an individual departure from a continuing group by a comprehensive breakup.

Unfortunately, that tiny advantage was far outweighed by the shock and grief of the event that caused the general dissolution: Grizel's death in 2594, at the age of seventy.

Grizel died as most of the people lost in the Decimation had died, by drowning, but the circumstances were very different. From my point of view, though, there was one important point of similarity and one of distinction. I was with her, just as I had been with Emily Marchant on 23 March 2542, but I could not save her.

NINETEEN

Axel, Jodocus, and Minna were required by their work to range across the entire equatorial belt and often took trips to Nigeria. In spite of their constant complaints about the trips I took, the Rainmakers could not be content with secondhand information collected and collated by silvers regarding patterns of rainfall. They did not doubt its reliability, but they doubted its sufficiency.

"You see, Mortimer," Axel explained to me, totally ignoring that I had offered very similar explanations of my own endeavors, "there's no substitute for taking a plane and flying over the territory so that you can see the whole thing as a piece. Statistical data is invaluable, of course, but a broad sweep of the eye can pick up on things that a whole legion of silvers could never pick out of the data drizzle."

It was entirely usual for some or all of the remaining marriage partners to accompany the Rainmakers on these trips. Anyone who felt in need of a change of scene was likely to regard it as a good opportunity. On the trip that led to tragedy, Grizel and I went with Axel and Minna to study the floodplain of the newly rerouted Kwarra. While Axel and Minna did so with all due scientific dispassion, from the air, Grizel and I "investigated" the flow of the river in a more lighthearted spirit, at ground level.

I had not only learned to swim after so nearly losing my life in the Coral Sea but had become rather fanatical about it. It was not that I enjoyed it, particularly—although I certainly found it great fun if my mood and the circumstances were right—but that I had come to think of it as one of the most essential accomplishments of a New Human. Given that drowning was one of the few ways in which a New Human could perish with relative ease, it seemed to me to be necessary for every member of that race to make sure that he or she could fight such a fate with all his—or her—might.

Grizel knew my opinion, and did not mock me for it, but she could not take the matter quite so seriously. She enjoyed swimming in a pool, but she saw no need to make strenuous efforts to learn to counter all the vagaries and treacheries of fast-flowing water. To her, I suppose, the seemingly slow-moving Kwarra must have appeared to be merely a big pool, which held no particular hazards.

To tell the truth, when we went down to the water on the fateful day, even I had not the least inkling of any danger. The day was clear and windless and the surface of the river seemed utterly docile, despite that its level was higher than normal. Axel and Minna had flown off to survey the eastern tributaries, which descended from the Adamouwa Plateau, in the hope of gaining some insight into the reasons for the slightly excessive flow.

As Grizel and I hid from the heat and the bright sun in the shaded shallows, our conversation was all to do with the lack of natural hazards in the immediate vicinity. Grizel, who always described herself as an "ecological purist," thought the policies of the LDA, and Camilla's department in particular, rather pusillanimous. She didn't really want to see the return of such awkward water-borne parasites as bilharzia and the guinea worm, but she was entirely serious about wanting to restock the New Kwarra with crocodiles.

"Crocodiles were around far longer than the other once-extinct species we've brought back," she argued. "If any large-size species had security of tenure, it was them. They'd really proved their evolutionary worth, until we came along and upset the whole applecart. Anyway, they're essentially lazy. They wouldn't bother chasing *people*. Like most so-called predators they prefer carrion."

I didn't bother trying to challenge her admittedly eccentric view of ecological aesthetics; I'd learned from long acquaintance that it was much safer to stick to practical matters. "They could still bite," I pointed out, "and I doubt if they'd be particular if anyone strayed too close to their favorite lurking places. They were somewhat given to lurking, weren't they?"

"Nonsense," she said. "You're a historian and should know better. If you care to consult the figures, you'll see that far more old humans were crushed by hippos than were ever chewed by crocodiles—but we *love* our hippos, don't we? The hippopotamus was one of the first species we brought back out of the banks when we started rebuilding African river ecologies."

I pointed out that we hadn't brought the hippos back because they were harmless—after all, we'd also brought back lions, leopards, and cheetahs in the first wave of ecological readjustments—but because such danger as they posed was clearly manifest and easily avoidable. She wasn't impressed.

"It's just puerile mammalian chauvinism," she said. "Childish fur fetishism. Putting crocodiles at the bottom of the list is just antireptilian prejudice."

I didn't bother to argue that the New Human fondness for birds gave the lie to the charge of mammalian chauvinism, because she'd simply have added feather fetishism to her list of psychological absurdities. Instead, I pointed out that we had been only too willing to resurrect cobras and black mambas. She was, alas, as happy as ever to shift her ground. "Once we were safely immune to their bites," she scoffed. "Snakes are so much *sexier* than crocodiles—according to phallocentric fools."

She didn't say in so many words that the category of phallocentric fools was one to which I belonged, but the implication was there. It wasn't that which drew us apart, though; we were just drifting. As ever, she was happy to shift her ground as a matter of routine, even in the water. I let her go. I didn't want to continue the verbal contest, and I let her go.

On this occasion, she shifted and drifted too far. Although the surface seemed perfectly placid, the midriver current was quite powerful; once in its grip, even the strongest swimmer wouldn't have found it easy to get out again.

When Grizel found that the current was bearing her away she could have called for help, but she didn't. She assumed that the worst that could happen to her was that she'd be carried a few hundred meters downstream before she could get back to the shallows. Ninety-nine times out of a hundred she would have been right, but not this time. As well as being more powerful than it seemed, the midriver current was carrying more than its fair share of debris—including waterlogged branches and whole tree trunks that might have traveled all the way from Adamouwa.

When I became aware that Grizel was no longer near me she was still clearly in view. When I shouted after her, she just waved, as if to reassure me that all was well and that she'd rejoin me soon enough. I set out after her regardless. I didn't have any kind of premonition—I just didn't have enough confidence in the power of her arms and legs. I thought she might need my help to get back to the bank.

I never saw the piece of wood that hit her. I don't suppose she did either; it must have slid upon her as quietly and as insidiously as a crocodile. Logs in water are weightless, but they pack an enormous amount of momentum, and if a swimmer is trying with all her might to go sideways. . . .

I didn't even see her go down.

It can't have been more than three or four seconds afterward when I realized that she was no longer visible, but even with the current to help me it took a further fifteen to get to the point at which I'd last seen her. I dived, but the water was very murky, clouded with fine silt.

I ducked under again and again, moving southward all the time, but I calculated later that she was probably fifty or a hundred meters ahead of me and that I hadn't made enough allowance for the velocity of the current. At the time, I was in the grip of a panicky haste. I was madly active, but I achieved nothing. I just kept ducking under, hoping to catch sight of her in time to drag her head out of the water, but I was always in the wrong place. It was like a nightmare.

In the end, I had to give up, or exhaustion might have made it impossible for me to beat the undertow. I had sanity enough to save myself from sharing Grizel's fate—and I felt guilty about that for years.

TWENTY

Grizel's body was eventually washed up at Onitsha, twenty kilometers downriver. There was a sharp bend there, left over from the days when the old Kwarra had been called the Niger, and the current couldn't carry her around it.

Her limbs had been chewed by something—not a crocodile, of course—and they'd been broken by rocks she'd encountered when she drifted briefly into white water. All that had happened after she was dead, though; she hadn't been conscious of the mutilation.

The postmortem confirmed that the branch had struck her on the temple, probably knocking her out instantaneously. Her dutiful IT had stopped the bleeding and protected her brain from the possibility of long-term damage, but it hadn't been able to lift her head above the surface to let her breathe.

Many people can't immediately take in news of the death of someone they love. The event defies belief and generates reflexive denial. I didn't react that way, although some of the others did. We all had mortal parents—and we had all lost at least some of them—but Grizel had been a ZT like us, capable of living for centuries, and perhaps millennia. Camilla's reaction was the most perverse; even after seeing the body she simply couldn't get her head around the idea that Grizel was dead and wouldn't hear the words spoken. The three Rainmakers admitted the fact readily enough but shrugged it off with set features and ready clichés.

With me, on the other hand, it was not merely belief that was instantaneous. I immediately gave way under its pressure. When I was told that her body had been found and the last vestige of hope disappeared I literally fell over, because my legs wouldn't support me. It was another psychosomatic failure about which my internal machinery could do nothing, just like the seasickness that had saved me from the backflip of the *Genesis*.

I wept uncontrollably. None of the others did—not even Axel, who'd been closer to Grizel than anyone else, including Camilla. They were sympathetic at first, but it wasn't long before a note of annoyance began to creep into their reassurances. I was disturbing them, putting a strain on their own coping strategies.

"Come on, Morty," Eve said, voicing the thought the rest of them were too diplomatic to let out. "You know more about death than any of us. If it doesn't help you to get a grip when you're confronted with the reality, what good has all that research done you?"

She was right, after a fashion, but also very wrong. Jodocus and Minna had often tried to suggest, albeit delicately, that mine was an essentially unhealthy fascination, and now they felt vindicated. Unlike Camilla and Axel, who kept conspicuously quiet because they were having their own acute problems dealing with upwelling grief, they weighed in with Eve, presumably attempting to get over their own reflexive denial by criticizing my acceptance.

"If you'd actually bothered to read my commentary-in-progress, Evie," I retorted, "you'd know that it has nothing complimentary to say about the philosophical acceptance of death. It sees a sharp awareness of mortality and the capacity to feel the horror of death so keenly as key forces driving early human evolution. If *Homo erectus* hadn't felt and fought the knowledge of his own mortality with such desperation and courage, *sapiens* might never have emerged."

"But you don't have to act it out so flamboyantly," Jodocus came back, ineptly using cruelty to conceal and assuage his own misery. "We've evolved beyond *sapiens* now, let alone *erectus*. We've gotten past the tyranny of primitive emotion. We've matured." Jodocus was the oldest of us, and he had lately begun to seem much older than ten years my senior, although he was still some way short of his first century. Had he been a falsie he'd have been booking a date for his first rejuve, and the rhythms of social tradition seemed to be producing some kind of weird existential echo in his being.

"It's what I feel," I told him, retreating into uncompromising assertion. "I can't help it. Grizel's dead, and I couldn't save her. She might have told a few lies in her time, but she didn't deserve to die. I'm entitled to cry."

"We *all* loved her," Eve reminded me. "We'll all miss her. Nobody deserves to die, but sometimes it happens, even to people like us. You're not *proving* anything, Morty."

What she meant was that I wasn't proving anything except my own instability, but she spoke more accurately than she thought. I wasn't proving anything at all. I was just reacting—atavistically, perhaps, but with crude honesty and authentically childlike innocence. But I *had* laid the theoretical groundwork for that reaction in the still-unpublished *Prehistory of Death*. I *had* argued that my reaction was the kind of reaction that had propelled the Old Human Race out of apehood and into wisdom, and I was damned if I was going to be told by a bunch of amateurs who were still in denial that I ought to put on a braver face.

"We have to pull together now," Camilla put in, "for Grizel's sake."

If only it had been that easy. In fact, we all flew apart with remarkable rapidity. Our little knot in the fabric of neohuman society dissolved into the warp and weft, almost as if it had never been—or so it seemed at the time. Much later, I came to realize that it had made a much deeper and more indelible mark on me than I knew; I suspect that it was the same for the others in spite of all their stiff-jawed self-control.

It's not obvious why a death in the family almost always leads to divorce in childless marriages, but that's the way it works. Camilla wasn't being foolish—such a loss *does* force the survivors to pull together—but the process of pulling together usually serves only to emphasize the fragility and incompleteness of the unit.

We all went our separate ways before the century ended, even the three Rainmakers. From then on, they worked on the management of separate storms.

TWENTY-ONE

The first edition of the introductory section of my *History of Death*, entitled *The Prehistory of Death*, was launched into the Labyrinth in 21 January 2614.

As with any modern work of scholarship, the greater part of *The Prehistory of Death* was designed as an *aleph*: a tiny point whose radiants shone in every direction and spread into the vast multidimensional edifice of the web to connect up billions of data into a new and hopefully interesting pattern. Many contemporary works did no more than that, and there was a zealous school of thought which insisted that a true historian ought not to attempt any more than that. A *scientific* historian, these zealots claimed, ought not to dabble in commentary at all; his task was merely to organize the data in such a way that they could best speak for themselves. In this view, any historian who supplied a commentary was superimposing on the data a narrative of his own, which was at best superfluous and at worst distortive.

My response to that argument was identical to Julius Ngomi's: *all* history is fantasy.

I do not mean by this that history is devoid of brute facts or that historians ought not to aim for accuracy in the accumulation and cross-correlation of those facts. The facts of history are, however, documents and artifacts of human manufacture; they cannot be understood in any terms other than the motives of their makers. There is a tiny minority of documents whose purpose is to provide an impersonal, accurate, and objective record of events, but there is a wealth of complication even in the notion of a record whose purpose is accuracy, and anyone who doubts that the compilers of supposedly objective accounts might sometimes have deceptive motives need only ask themselves whether it really is possible for economic historians to obtain a full and true picture of the financial transactions of the past by examining account books prepared to meet the requirements of tax assessment.

In order for a historian to understand the motives that lie behind the documents and artifacts that the people of the past have handed down to us it is always necessary to perform an act of imaginative identification. The historian must place himself, as it were, in the shoes of the maker: to participate as best he can in the *act of making*.

Without this leap of the imagination, no understanding is possible, but every honest historian will admit that any such leap is a leap in the dark, and that the conclusions at which he arrives—no matter how confident he may feel of their certainty—are the products of his own fantasy. A good historian is a scrupulous fantasist, but he is a fantasist nevertheless.

The zealots among my peers argue that if this is the case, then history is impossible and that everything sheltering under that name is false. They point out that the historians of the present do not belong to the same species as the people of the past and that our existential situation is radically different from theirs. I have heard this said many times in connection with my *History of Death*. Its least sympathetic critics have always argued that insofar as my work attempted to go beyond the collation of statistics it was bound to fail, for the simple reason that I, a true emortal, could not possibly perform the mental gymnastics that would be required to allow me to see the world as a mortal would have done.

According to skeptics of this stripe, the people of today cannot possibly hope to understand their ancestors, whose mental processes are and will always remain utterly mysterious to us. All we can sensibly do, such skeptics proclaim, is collate the facts of their brief existence and lay them away in the bowels of metaphorical mountains, heavily armored against our interest and involvement.

Clearly, I have never agreed with this assessment. Nor could I side with those pusillanimous historians who took refuge in the commonplace observation that people had begun talking about a New Human Race in the early part of the twenty-second century and that we could legitimately identify with those of our ancestors who merely believed—or at least hoped—that true emortality was within their grasp. It would be a poor sort of history that derived its authority from the fact that its objects were deluded—and an even poorer sort that attempted to extend its claims deeper into the past by suggesting that the people who lived in the midst of death for thousands of years did so in a state of perpetual denial, never able to accept the all-too-obvious fact that each and every one of them was bound to die, sooner rather than later.

My belief, simply stated, is that we who have drunk of the authentic fountain of youth *do* still have the ability—if we care to exercise it—to imagine what it was like to live with the inevitability of death. I believe that we need only to exercise our own powers of imagination cleverly enough to be able to put ourselves in the shoes of people faced with the prospect of a life span no more than a hundred years in duration, most of which would be spent in a state of decrepitude.

Not only do I believe that this is possible, but I believe that it is highly desirable. How can we understand the world that our ancestors made if we cannot understand the motives and processes of its making? It seems to me that if the pessimists were right about the impossibility of our being able to understand the existential predicament of our ances- tors, then they would have to be just as dubious about our ability to understand one another. We have to learn to be human, and the first generation who laid legitimate claim to the title of the New Human Race still had to learn from their mortal predecessors. Today's children are raised to adulthood by their own kind, but emortals of my antiquity were raised—almost without exception—by foster parents who knew that their own useful hopes had been dashed and that only individuals equipped with the best possible Zaman transformations could have any realistic hope of living for more than two hundred and fifty years, or of sustaining their continuity of self indefinitely.

Like every other individual in history, we pioneers of true New Humanity first learned to see ourselves as others saw us, and no matter what we have learned since then, we carry that legacy within us. While we still have that gift, we still have the ability to see those others as they saw themselves. However New we may be, we are still *the* Human Race, and if we are properly to understand ourselves we must set ourselves to understand those who came before us.

Like history, autobiography is a kind of fantasy, but each and every one of us is permanently involved in constructing the story of his or her own life, and even those of us who are perfectly content to act without recording remain creatures of fantasy. Those of us who record as well as acting are attempting to grasp the substance of our personal fantasies and to be as precise as possible in their construction as well as their interpretation.

For those reasons, therefore, *The Prehistory of Death* carried an elaborate commentary that did not even try hard to be dispassionate. So far as I was concerned, in fact, the commentary *was*—and is—the book. The elaborate hypertextual links forging Labyrinthine pathways through the vast mass of accumulated data were, in my estimation, mere footnotes.

To anyone who still labors under the delusion that such an assertion is heresy against the scientific method I can only say: "I cannot help it. That is what I feel. That is the foundation on which my life and work have been based."

TWENTY-TWO

The commentary attached to *The Prehistory of Death* summarized everything that was known about early hominid lifestyles and developed an elaborate argument about the effects of natural selection on the patterns of mortality in humankind's ancestor species. It gave special attention to the evolution of parental care as a genetic strategy.

Earlier species of man, I observed, had raised parental care to a level of efficiency that permitted the human infant to be born at a much earlier stage in its development than any other, maximizing its opportunity to be shaped by nurture and learning. From the very beginning, I proposed, protohuman species were *actively* at war with death. The evolutionary success of genus *Homo* was based in the collaborative activities of parents in protecting, cherishing, and preserving the lives of children: activities that extended beyond immediate family groups as reciprocal altruism made it advantageous for humans to form tribes rather than mere families.

In these circumstances, I argued, it was entirely natural that the remotest origins of consciousness and culture should be intimately bound up with a keen awareness of the war against death. I asserted that the first great task of the human imagination was to carry forward that war.

It was entirely understandable, I said, that early paleontologists, having discovered the mutilated bones of Neanderthal humans in apparent graves, with the remains of primitive garlands of flowers, should instantly have felt an intimate kinship with them; there could be no more persuasive evidence of full humanity than the attachment of ceremony to the idea and the fact of death. I went on to wax lyrical about the importance of ritual as a symbolization of opposition and enmity to death. I refuted the proposition that such rituals were of no practical value, a mere window dressing of culture. My claim was that there was no activity more practical than this expressive recognition of the *value* of life, this imposition of a moral order on the fact of human mortality.

Paleontologists and anthropologists had argued for centuries about the precise nexus of selective pressures that had created humanity. It was universally recognized that a positive feedback loop had been set up by the early use of tools: that the combination of a deft hand, a keen eye, and a clever brain had facilitated the development of axes, knives, and levers, whose rewards had then exerted even stronger pressure on the development of the hand, eye, and brain. Protohumans made tools, so the story went, and tools made true humans.

Some theorists emphasized technology as a means of making humans powerful, equipping them to hunt and fight; others emphasized its role in making them sociable, facilitating the development of language, and hence of abstract thought. Some saw the domestication of fire—the first great technological revolution—as the origin of metallurgy, others as the origin of the culinary art. None of them were wrong, but none of their accounts were complete. None of them had ever stood back far enough to see the whole picture or identified with their subjects with sufficient intimacy to grasp the aleph that bound the complex picture into a unity.

My contention was that the prehistory of humankind could best be understood with reference to the most elementary aspect of existential awareness: the consciousness of death. Protohumans began to be human not when they became aware of their own mortality but when they did not immediately retreat into denial. Protohumans began to be humans when they decided to use whatever means they had to keep that awareness and thrive in spite of it: to fight death instead of refusing to see it. Of course the domestication of fire was the beginning of cooking and of metallurgy, but its first and foremost purpose was to illuminate: to rage against the dying of the light. Even warmth was secondary to that. Fire was enlightenment, literally and symbolically, and the fundamental purpose of that light was to allow the first humans to see and face the fact of death and to take arms against it.

Humankind's second great technological leap—the birth of agriculture—had previously been interpreted by many archaeologists as *the* key event in human prehistory. Human beings had lived for nearly a million years as hunter-gatherers before beginning to settle down, but once they were finally and firmly settled down, after tens of thousands of years of apparent prevarication, their condition had begun to change with remarkable rapidity. If the Crash could be regarded as its first terminus the process of civilization had been completed in a mere ten or fifteen thousand years.

Most commentators had seen agriculture as a triumphant discovery, but I took a greater interest in the minority who had seen it as a desperate move unhappily forced upon hunter-gatherers whose more subtle management of their environment had been far too successful, generating a population explosion. This minority argued that farming, and the backbreaking labor that went with it, had been a reluctant adaptation to evil circumstance, whose tragic dimension was clearly reflected in multitudinous myths of an Edenic or Arcadian Golden Age.

I had more sympathy with this minority than their traditional adversaries ever had, but I refused to take it for granted that it was *solely* the need to secure food supplies that had caused and controlled the development of settlements. I argued that although the sophistication of food production undoubtedly met a need, it ought not be reckoned the main motivating force for settlement.

I proposed that it was the practice of burying the dead with ceremony and the ritualization of mourning that had first given humans a motive to settle, and that the planting of crops and domestication of animals had been forced upon them as much by that desire as by the environmental pressures of "protofarming." This was, inevitably, a highly contentious claim—but such discussion as it engendered was initially confined to the ranks of vocational historians.

The original version of the *The Prehistory of Death* attracted little immediate attention outside the ranks of dedicated academicians. The traffic through its aleph was by no means heavy during the first few years of its presence in the Labyrinth—but I was not unduly disappointed by that. It was, after all, merely an introduction. I had several more layers to build before my admittedly speculative "whole picture" of the origins of humanity was transformed into what I hoped would be an utterly compelling "whole picture" of the entire human project.

TWENTY-THREE

For ten years after the disintegration of my first marriage I lived alone. I did not think it would be difficult, and in 2995 I had rather looked forward to life in a cozy private realm undisrupted by continual arguments, where I could make final preparations for the launch of *The Prehistory of Death* in peace. I had not realized that the disruption of long-standing routine would be as deeply unsettling as it was. Nor had I realized that solitude requires long practice before it becomes comfortable. Nor had I been fully conscious of the extent to which I had been economically dependent on the Lamu collective.

None of my seven partners had made large amounts of money from their employment. Labors devoted to the General Good are not conspicuously well rewarded—but there is all the difference in the world between a household supported by seven steady incomes and a household devoid of any. Such extra-allowance income as I had generated during the marriage had been trivial and sporadic, and all of it had been secondhand, in the sense that it was work subcontracted to me by my marriage partners. That vanished along with their direct support.

I did manage to pick up a little paid work in the ten years leading up to the launch of the *Prehistory*, most of it derived from work on the teaching programs used by my alma mater. A percentage of the unused credit accumulated by Papa Domenico and Papa Laurent had been transferred to my account shortly before the marriage, but the greater part of it had been reabsorbed into the Social Fund, and almost nothing remained by 2595. For the next ten years I was, in effect, totally dependent on the Allocation I received merely by virtue of being alive.

I could have obtained better-paid work easily enough—the LDA still had plenty to go around, given that the Coral Sea Disaster had set its best laid plans back by more than a century—but I did not want to take time away from my true vocation, at least until the *Prehistory* was launched. Once the first part of my project had been launched into the Labyrinth, I thought, its use would generate an income—which would facilitate work on the second part, whose publication would generate more income, and so on. I was hopeful that the process would build up sufficient economic momentum to be self-sustaining, if only I could get the snowball rolling.

It sounded easy enough when I formulated the plan, and it should have been easier than it was. I obtained an elementary apartment in a capstack in Alexandria, and if I had only managed to play the monkish scholar all the way down the line, focusing my attention *entirely* on the introductory section of my work, I would have had ample credit to draw everything I needed out of the Labyrinth and to eat as lavishly as I desired. Unfortunately, I had grown used to interleaving my Lab-work with more relaxed and more expensive real-space researches laying the groundwork for the second section, and I found it very difficult to break that habit—especially now that I was more conveniently based for excursions to Greece, Kurdistan, Israel, and New Mesopotamia.

Things became difficult even before the release of *The Prehistory of Death*; afterward, they became far worse. The income it generated was not nearly enough to clear the debts I had accumulated in anticipation, and as interest was piled on interest my situation began to deteriorate.

In addition to the other temptations to which I had fallen prey, I had felt compelled to reconstruct and repair the network of virtual relationships that I had allowed to slip away while I was living in close physical proximity with my partners. Some of the people with whom I restored regular contact would have been willing and able to offer me charity, but I was extremely reluctant to take it. It would have seemed that I had only repaired my relationships with them in order to obtain a financial advantage. In any case, I had my pride—and all charity carries a price.

My surviving parents, as might have been expected, quietly relished the opportunities offered by my parlous situation. They had always been enthusiastic to exercise subtle leverage upon the direction of my life, and fate had delivered me into their hands.

"You should have left Earth fifty years ago," Mama Meta informed me, stopping barely a centimeter short of saying *I told you so*. "Gravity holds people down and holds people back. It attaches people to the past instead of the future. I'm not saying that history is worthless, but it's not the sort of career to which anyone should give a hundred percent of their time and effort. The Labyrinth is here too, Morty. General Good work isn't just plentiful on the moon, it's twice as well paid as the same work on Earth—and zero-gee work is triple or quadruple, if you're prepared to learn the tricks of the trade. You'll have plenty of time for hobbies— but you have to move fast. In thirty or forty years the fabers will have a virtual monopoly on zero-gee work, and they'll still have first choice of lunatic work. By 2650 you won't be able to find *decent* work this side of Mars, but if you strike while the iron's hot you can make some real money."

In Mama Meta's reckoning, "decent" work had to be work for the General Good, which also paid at least three times what the Allocation provided. In her view, that ruled out almost everything available on Earth. Mama Siorane's pioneering endeavors among the outer satellites were thoroughly decent, as were Papa Ezra's adventures in genetic engineering, but in Mama Meta's view, Mama Eulalie and Mama Sajda were "harlots of commerce." They earned good money, but they were both employed in Production Management—and that, in Mama Meta's view, was only one short step from the Ent end of EdEnt. "EdEnt is an oxymoron," Mama Meta had assured me, in the long-gone days before I climbed the mountain. "Education is self-improvement, but Entertainment is self-wastage." Mercifully, none of her partners had agreed with her on that one—and even Mama Siorane would have stopped short of describing workers in the commercial sector as harlots. That did not mean, alas, that my other fosterers were willing to side with me in the dispute that inevitably developed between myself and Mama Meta.

"I know I've always advised you to be yourself," Mama Eulalie said, on one occasion when I had complained a little too self-pityingly about Mama Meta's hectoring, "but it wouldn't do you any harm to spread yourself around a bit. It wouldn't actually dirty your hands to get involved in commerce. The people who actually keep the big wheels turning might think it necessary to lock themselves away inside mountains, but the people who do the little jobs lead perfectly normal lives. The MegaMall has plenty of single-skill VE-based work available these days—they actually find it hard to attract young people, and we mortals have an inconvenient habit of retiring long before we're likely to drop dead."

The last remark was a reference to Papa Nahum, who was a lot closer to dropping dead than he or I realized. Like Mama Eulalie and Mama Sajda, he'd spent his life laboring in relatively menial capacities for what they both, in their quaintly old-fashioned way, insisted on calling the "MegaMall." His advice, at least, had no undercurrent of censure.

"When I was young," he said, "I worked very hard. When I reached an age at which the end was in sight, I slacked off. When I was sure I had enough to see me through to the end, I stopped. Work never hurt me but I never learned to like it. I'm Old Human through and through. You're not. If I'd known that I had to work forever, or as near as damn it, I'd have looked at things a different way. We can't tell you how to go about that. Better keep in mind, though, that forever is a hell of a long time to be poor, even in today's world. Taking advantage of unlimited opportunity needs funds as well as endurance."

"If my history is definitive," I told him, trying not to sound boastful, "it'll make money. Not soon, and not a fortune, but it *will* make money. It'll make my name too. When people mention Mortimer Gray's *History of Death*, other people will know what they're talking about."

"Your choice," Papa Nahum said, graciously. "Sorry I won't be around to share the celebration. I want genuine Oscar Wildes at my funeral, mind—none of that cheap rubbish. I don't care how poor you are."

When he died, at the dawn of the twenty-seventh century, I brought genuine Oscar Wildes to his funeral even though I couldn't afford them. Mama Meta ordered Rappaccinis that had been out of fashion for a century, but she didn't mean any insult. She lived on the moon, where flowers were a good deal rarer than people with legs, and anything with petals counted as a wonder.

TWENTY-FOUR

Oddly enough, the most generous moral support I received in the wake of the *Prehistory*'s publication—along with the most generous offers of charitable assistance—came from Emily Marchant, who was now richer than both my families put together.

Emily's replacement foster parents, operating in the capacity of trustees, had reinvested the twelvefold inheritance she had received from her original fosterers in shamir development. It had been the most obvious thing to do, given that the cities smashed by the tidal waves of 2542 would all need rebuilding, but the obvious sometimes pays unexpected dividends. The shamirs designed for the patient and elegant regenerative work that had been the world's lip service to Decivilization had not been well adapted to the task of repairing rude devastation. Gantzing biotech had been stuck in a rut for two hundred years while the Zamaners had taken all the funds and all the glory, but coping with the debris of the tidal waves had given its evolution a new impetus.

It was hardly surprising that Emily had gone into the business herself, cleverly reapplying the lessons learned in the design of new and better shamirs to the improvement of the deconstructors and reconstructors that had been set to work in the interior spaces of Io and Ganymede, building subsurface colonies far more sophisticated than those clustered around the lunar poles. In 2615, however, Emily had not yet formed a powerful desire to go out to the outer system herself. Like me, she was still contentedly Earthbound.

"You really ought to take the money, Mortimer," she said to me, after I had refused for the ninth or tenth time. "It grows so much faster than I can spend it that I keep running into the hypertax bracket, at which point it all gets gobbled up by the Social Fund and redirected to the General Good. I know it's antisocial to regret that, but I can't help thinking that I'd prefer to select my own deserving causes."

"I can't," I said. "It would feel wrong."

"Why? Because you happened to save my life once upon a time? It's not payment, Mortimer. It doesn't alter what you did or make it any less heroic."

"It could hardly have been any less heroic than it was," I told her, mournfully. "Anyway, it's nothing to do with that. It would feel wrong because it would mean that I wasn't doing it *myself*."

"You take the Allocation, don't you?"

"That's different."

"Why?"

I wasn't entirely sure why, but I felt that it was. The allowance awarded to every member of the race was a guarantee of food, shelter, and basic access to the Labyrinth; I tended to think of it as a modest advance payment for the work I was doing on my *History*, even though that would never be officially recognized as work for the General Good. If I had taken Emily's money, and spent it on travel to Athens, Jerusalem, and Babylon, I would have been incurring a debt of a different kind. She couldn't see that—or perhaps she just refused to see it. Either way, it made a difference to me.

"I won't be this badly off for very long," I assured her. "It'll be good for me to struggle for a while. I'll enjoy it all the more when things get better."

"Did it ever occur to you that you might have a masochistic streak, Mister Mortimer?" she asked, reverting to the form of my name that she alone employed, inconsistently, in order to emphasize that she didn't really mean what she was saying.

"Of course it has," I said. "I'm the historian of death—the man whose self-appointed task it is to remind New Humankind of all the fear and pain that went into its making. I'm probably the last of the truly great masochists." I had no inkling at that time of the appalling magnitude of the masochism that was yet to visit the world, whose emortal exponents would outshine me as easily as the sun outshines a candle.

"Well," Emily said, reprovingly, "you know the money's there whenever you need it. You can always change your mind."

I probably would have, eventually. As things turned out, though, I found another solution to my straitened circumstances—or had another solution thrust upon me. Putting it that way makes it sound crudely materialistic, but in reality it was anything but that. When I got married for the second time it wasn't for convenience, or even for companion-ship, and it certainly wasn't for money, although setting up another joint household did solve my financial problems. I married for love, carried away on a tide of passion.

I should, of course, have been immune to such disruptions by the age of eighty-five, but I had contrived to skip that stage of my sentimen-tal education by going straight into a group marriage without bothering with the conventional pair-bond experiments. When I should have been getting the capacity for infatuation out of my system I was busy with other things, like the Great Coral Sea Disaster.

It was, of course, seasickness rather than the fact that I had boarded the *Genesis* as a singleton that had saved my life, but my singleton status had certainly saved me from the sharpest pangs of grief. Had I been part of a couple, I would almost certainly have lost a lover. That had had no *conscious* effect on my continued wariness of pair-bonding experiments, but I have to admit, in retrospect, that it might well have had a subcon-scious effect. At any rate, I had never suffered the legendary tempests of swift passion in adolescence or earliest adulthood and had been safely insulated from them for nearly forty years while I had been a relatively contented Rainmaker-in-Law.

Perhaps I had been storing up trouble all the while I had lived in Lamu, and swift passion had always been within me, waiting patiently for its fuse to be lit so that it might explode at last. If so, the match applied to that fuse by Sharane Fereday was one that caught almost instantly. I was greatly taken with her from the very first time I caught sight of her, although attraction did not blossom into something more elaborate until we had talked for seven hours—by which time it seemed that we had everything in common and that all our emotional well-springs had flowed together into a common sea.

Had I let my poverty restrict me more tightly we would never have met, for it was on one of my most self-indulgent excursions that Sharane and I were thrust together, and as passengers on the bus from Eden to Nod that we were able to converse for seven hours at a stretch.

The early twenty-sixth century had had no shortage of so-called Edens. The tidal waves of the Decimation had obliterated no less than twelve, ten of them Creationist islands. The Eden that I visited on the shore of Lake Van was widely reckoned to be one more folly in the same vein, although its makers had claimed that they were merely remaking the "original" Eden of ancient Hebrew myth on the site where a vanished Elder race had played a godly role in raising the ancestors of the heroes to fully human status.

I was interested in the myth in question—which had survived all the religions that had temporarily appropriated it—because it could be interpreted in a way that linked it to my own theories of the origin of humanity. One way of reading it was to infer that the knowledge which had been allegedly imparted there to the first true humans was the knowledge that they must die.

The other tourists gathered at Lake Van at the time of my visit were interested in the garden that had first been planted there some two hundred years earlier and subsequently embellished by some of the most famous Creationist engineers. Even Oscar Wilde, late in his career, had forsaken his beloved flowers in order to collaborate in the design of the Tree of Knowledge—a much more impressive individual than the Tree of the Knowledge of Good and Evil that an earlier generation of genetic engineers had supplied.

Given that the evidence the archaeologists had found of early human habitation had not yet produced the slightest indication of the preexistence of godlike Elders, Watchers, or oversize Nephilim, I expected to find myself alone in preferring to interest myself in the digs that were still in progress, but I was not. Sharane Fereday was in the museum dome when I arrived, grubbing about in the slit trench with a magnifying glass the size of a dinner plate.

"Hello," she said, smiling. "Have you come to distract me?"

"I've come to work," I told her, hesitating only for a moment before adding: "The risk is that you'll distract me, whether you intend to or not."

She hesitated too, but only for an instant, before saying: "Oh, I intend to. I'm bored already—I'll just have to hope that even though you're not, you'll consent to be distracted, at least for a little while."

Even if I had not found her physically attractive, Sharane and I would still have fallen into conversation, and I would probably have decided before the day was out to join her on the bus to Nod, on the shore of Lake Urmia, following the alleged route of the very first human to be consciously aware that he had committed murder.

I did find her unusually attractive, perhaps because rather than in spite of the fact that she did not resemble any of my foster mothers, but that would not have been enough in itself to excite passion. What excited passion was the fervent interest she took in matters that had not previously interested any of my closest acquaintances.

I soon discovered, of course, that the nature of Sharane's interest in Eden and its significance was markedly different from mine, but that did not seem to matter at all. Given that I had been married for forty years to a company of ecological engineers, the similarities between my notion of history and hers seemed far more important than the differences. Even the differences seemed exciting and productive—if we had been in perfect harmony, our conversations could not have been deeply engaging or so lively.

TWENTY-FIVE

The long conversation that Sharane and I had on the bus to Nod was not the best of the many we shared, but it remains the most precious in my memory because it was the one most sharply edged and focused by gathering emotion. That seems a little absurd now, given that my response to the gathering in question was to become even more intense and pompous than was my habit, but I would be a poor historian were I to deny or conceal it.

"The awareness of death inevitably gives rise to many corollaries," I told Sharane, having explained my own interest in the Lake Van sites and my own need to make actual physical contact with the faint traces of the remote past. "One of them—perhaps the most important, from the point of view of the New Humans—was the notion that killing required some kind of *justification*, in terms of both meaning and morality. Even if the leap to death consciousness didn't occur until protohumans had spread out of Africa, at least as far as ancient Mesopotamia and what is now Kurdistan—in which case it must have been made more than once, in several different places—one can hardly blame myth makers for insisting on a single point of origin and a psychologically satisfying first cause. Having conflated a whole community of primal humans into the parental couple of Adam and Eve, it made perfect sense to make one of their sons the first murderer and the other the first murder victim."

"But the story clearly symbolizes the ancient conflict between nomadic herdsmen and settled agriculturalists," Sharane objected, assertively but not aggressively. Her eyes seemed to sparkle like gemstones when she was assertive—I was to discover soon enough that they seemed to flash like lightning when she was aggressive.

"Possibly," I admitted, "but I suspect that the conflict in question had more to do with different ways of revering the dead than any material conflict of interest. Anyway, the awareness that the act of killing requires special justification must precede the attachment of a particular justification. The idea of a fundamental social conflict between the settled and the unsettled must have been powerful because it was the first root cause of war, which was subsequently to be the principal occupation of that time which organized communities did not need to devote to mere survival."

"That's a cynical way of looking at it," she objected, lifting her slender chin and lowering her dark eyebrows in the slightest possible gesture of censure.

"It's not cynical, it's realistic," I riposted. "Anyway, the particular meaning attached to killing by the Eden myth was selected from an already available set that also included legal execution, human sacrifice, and self-defense—as can easily be seen if the linear sequence of Hebrew myths is tracked a little further. All the other meanings and justifications are there, leading inexorably to the establishment of the crucial commandment: *Thou shalt do no murder.*"

"Isn't it *Thou shalt not kill?*"

"No. That's a much later and rather sloppy translation. The whole point of the commandment is to forbid *illegitimate* killing."

"I suppose you've even got a better explanation for the serpent," she said, without undue sarcasm. She meant, of course, a better explanation than the one poor Grizel had carelessly trotted out in her reference to phallocentric fools rather than the Christian reinterpretation, which had imported an evil anti-God into the older myth.

"Another immediate corollary of death awareness," I pointed out, "is the notion of *poison*. Snakebite must have been the first example to spring to mind, closely associated with bad food. That the serpent proffers fruit is probably an homage to warning coloration. Sometimes, with all due respect to the complexities of symbolism and metaphor, a serpent is just a snake, and a bad apple is just something that tastes nasty and does you no good."

"That's quite brilliant," she said, with a smile like life itself. "Mortimer Gray, you're by far the most interesting person I've met in ages."

"The feeling's mutual, Sharane Fereday," I assured her. "My friends call me Mort, or Morty."

She smiled broadly at that too, perhaps having seen the meaning accidentally contained within the short form of my name.

"So shall I," she informed me.

Sharane's love for the ancient past was even more intense than mine, but it was very different in kind. She was forty years older than I and had already passed through half a dozen pair-bond marriages. She was a moderately successful writer, but her writings were far less dispassionate than those of a true historian—even a narrative historian who took it for granted that all history is fantasy.

Sharane's writings tended to the lyrical rather than the factual, even when she was not writing manifest fiction. Her most popular works were scripts for "dramatic reconstructions," most of which were performed in VE by widely scattered casts of thousands. Some of them were actually acted out in real space with the aid of artful costumes, clever machines, and deft psychotropic biotech. She was the veteran of a hundred battles and a thousand rituals.

On the bus to Nod, Sharane told me that she could never be content merely to *know* about the past; she wanted to re-create it. Even the designing of VE adventures wasn't enough for her, although she had started out that way. She had always wanted to make her creations more solid, so that they had to be actively improvised rather than passively experienced. She was eagerly and flamboyantly old-fashioned in almost everything that she did. She was dressed in an ordinary suitskin when I first encountered her in Eden, but that was because she was traveling. When I first saw her at home, the passion that I had already conceived and nurtured was further inflamed.

In the privacy of her own home Sharane loved to dress in gaudy pastiches of costumes represented in ancient art. She had a particular fondness for Greek and Egyptian designs, and she programed her wallscreens to produce decor to match her moods. She was widely considered to be a garish eccentric, and I suppose I surrendered far too rapidly to that consensus when we eventually split up, but in the beginning I saw her very differently, as a defiant individualist and a true artist.

When I introduced her to my four surviving parents—whose number had only just been diminished by the loss of Mama Meta, sixteen years after the death of Papa Nahum—their recently reinforced disapproval of my lifestyle was quickly redoubled. They were instantly affrighted by her taste in telephone-VEs, and the more they learned about her the more their worst suspicions were confirmed.

"Morty," Mama Siorane told me, in one of her rare transmissions from the vicinity of Saturn, "that woman is quite mad. I have long thought that your fascination with the past had slowed down your own intellectual development, but that woman is so retarded as to be infantile."

When I passed these comments on to my beloved, suitably edited for diplomacy, she merely smiled, saying: "What can you expect from someone who can't even spell her own name?"

I had expected Mama Eulalie to be the only one who might approve, but even she was distinctly puzzled. "She's hardly your *type*, Morty," she said. "Not that I'm accusing you of being boring, of course, but you have always kept company with *serious* people. Are you sure you're ready for this?"

"I'm ready," I assured her.

The only person who wished me well wholeheartedly was Emily Marchant, although the good wishes of my previous spouses were undoubtedly sincere and only fell short of wholeheartedness by that margin which inevitably moderates the enthusiasm of an ex-partner contemplating a replacement relationship.

TWENTY-SIX

I moved into Sharane's hometree on the island of Crete in September 2619 and we married in March 2621. Even though we had been living together very happily for some months, many of our mutual friends were mildly astonished that we actually formalized the arrangement. The difference in our personalities seemed glaring to others but was quite irrelevant to us.

Solitude, poverty, and intensity of purpose had begun to weigh rather heavily upon me before we met, and my carefully cultivated calm of mind had threatened to become a kind of toiling inertia. Sharane brought a welcome breath of air into an existence that had threatened to become rather stuffy. I always knew, I suppose, that from her point of view I was merely one more amusing distraction in a long sequence, but for her the very essence of life was play. She was not in the least disposed to hide that fact or to be ashamed of it.

"Work is only the means to an end," she told me. "Play *is* the end. Life is a game, because there isn't anything else it can be—certainly not a job or a mission or even a vocation. Without rules, life has no structure, but if the rules become laws, life loses its freedom and becomes a sentence; they have to be *rules of play*. People like that mother of yours who can't spell her name think play is silly, but that's because they've made their own rules too rigid and unforgiving. Play is very serious, especially the kind of play that involves dressing up and pretending. The ancients understood that—that's why they had exotic costumes and special scripts for use in their most solemn religious ceremonies and sternest legal rituals. The past is an intellectual playground, just like the Labyrinth, and you and I are just happy children delighting in its use and transformation."

She was certainly unconventional, but she was *magnificently* unconventional, and I loved her for it. The fact that she funded much of the research I put into the second part of my *History*, and funded it lavishly, did not figure in my calculations at all. I would have married her if she had been as poor as I was—although she, admittedly, would not have married me had those been our circumstances.

I found in Sharane a precious wildness that was unfailingly amusing in spite of the fact that it wasn't truly spontaneous. Her attempts to put herself imaginatively in touch with the past—*literally* to stand in the shoes of long-gone members of the Old Human Race—had a very casual attitude to matters of accuracy and authenticity, but they were bold and exhilarating. For a while, at least, I was glad occasionally to be a part of them, and when I was content to remain on the sidelines I enjoyed the spectacle just as much.

From her point of view, I suppose I was useful in two ways. On the one hand, I was a font of information and inspiration, offering her a constant flow of new perspectives. Thanks to me, she was able to revisit old exploits with a new eye, so that she could remake them in interesting ways. On the other hand, I provided a kind of existential anchorage whose solidity and mundanity prevented her from losing herself in the flights of her imagination. Neither of those roles was infinitely extendable, but they were valuable while they lasted, and she loved me for the style as well as the efficiency of the manner in which I fulfilled them.

It would have been convenient if we had both come to the end of our infatuation at exactly the same time, but even the best pair-bonds rarely split as neatly and as gently as that. As things turned out, I was the one who suffered the disappointment of losing a love that I still felt very keenly, after a mere twenty years of acquaintance and eighteen of formal marriage.

Sharane and I talked for a while, as even young married people do, about the possibility of recruiting half a dozen more partners so that we might apply to raise a child. It would not have been impossible, or even particularly unusual, given that the Decimation had made licenses much more freely available. We settled, however, for filing our deposits in the local gamete bank with a polite recommendation that some future group of co-parents more than a thousand years hence might consider them appropriate for combination. It was the romantic option—and when we split up, neither of us hated the other enough to rescind the recommendation.

What eventually drove us apart was, I suppose, the same thing that had brought us together. The opposite tendencies of our characters fused for a while into a healthy whole, which seemed greater than the sum of its parts—but the robust tautness of the combination eventually decayed into stress and strain.

"You're too serious," Sharane complained, as the breaking point approached, echoing Mama Eulalie's anxieties about my suitability for alliance with such a mercurial creature. "You work too hard, and you're too hung up on details. Historical research should be a joyful voyage of discovery, not an obsession."

"I'm not against joy," I replied, a trifle defensively and more than a trifle resentfully, "but I'm a serious historian. Unlike you, I have to discriminate between discovery and invention."

"All history is fantasy," she quoted at me. "Truth is what you can get away with."

"The fact that all history is fantasy doesn't mean you can just *make it up*," I insisted. "It means that even at its most accurate and authoritative, history has an irreducible element of creativity and imagination. Julius Ngomi might have taken that as a license to propagandize, but I'm a real historian. I have to search for the truth that stands up to skepticism and doesn't simply fold up into a pack of feeble pretenses."

"You're such a *pedant*," she riposted, exasperatedly. "You go on and on about farming being a reluctant and degrading response to ecological disaster, but you're a farmer through and through. Most people think backbreaking labor is a thoroughly good thing—motor of progress and all that—but you know perfectly well that people were a lot better off when they hunted and gathered for six or seven hours a week and spent the rest of their time sitting under the acacia tree telling one another tall stories. You know it, but you don't *do* it. That's not merely stupid, Morty, it's *perverse*."

I tried to resist, but her eyes were flashing.

"To see hard work for what it really is and then to devote your life to it anyway is protracted suicide," she went on. "Unless the New Human Race can rediscover the delights of play and throw away its whips and spurs we'll never be able to adapt to emortality. I'll say one thing for your late Mama Meta: at least she knew that the work ethic belonged in outer space. Okay, so we had to rebuild after the tidal waves—but we've done that now, thanks to your little friend's shamirs. Now, it's time to get back to the Garden, to begin the Golden Age again. *Homo faber* is essentially a spacefaring species; those of us who are keeping our legs should accept that we're *Homo ludens.*"

"I'm not sure about that," I countered, reassuming my usual palliative tone. "I was never happy about those war-addicted fools hijacking the label *Homo sapiens.* We're the ones who have the opportunity to be true sapients, and I think we ought to take it. Play is great, but it can't be the be-all and end-all of emortal existence. Those legs that the fabers are discarding are the price we pay for the luxury of keeping our feet on the ground."

"You think I need *you* to keep my feet on the ground," Sharane came back, "but I don't. I need somebody who doesn't think that keeping our feet on the ground is a *luxury.*"

"Touché," I conceded. "But . . ."

I knew that the break between us had been completed and rendered irreparable when she wouldn't even hear my rebuttal. "I've been weighed down long enough," she said, callously. "I need to soar for a while, to spread my wings. You're holding me back, Morty."

TWENTY-SEVEN

My first divorce had come about because a cruel accident had ripped apart the delicate fabric of my life, but my second—or so it seemed to me—was itself a horrid rent that shredded my very being. It seemed so vilely unnecessary, so achingly unreasonable, so treasonously uncaused. It hurt.

I hope that I tried with all my might not to blame Sharane, but how could I avoid it? And how could she not resent my overt and covert accusations, my veiled and naked resentments? Once the break became irrevocable, the relationship was rapidly poisoned.

"Your problem, Mortimer," Sharane said to me, when her brief lachrymose phase had given way to incandescent anger, "is that you're a deeply morbid man. There's a special fear in you: an altogether exceptional horror that feeds upon your spirit day and night and makes you grotesquely vulnerable to occurrences that normal people can take in their stride, and which ill befit a self-styled Epicurean. If you want my advice, you should abandon that history you're writing and devote yourself to something much brighter and more vigorous." She knew, of course, that the last thing I wanted at that particular moment was her advice.

"Death is my life," I informed her, speaking metaphorically, and not entirely without irony. "It always will be, until and including the end."

I remember saying that. The rest is vague, and I've had to consult objective records in order to put the quotes in place, but I really do *remember* saying exactly those words.

I won't say that Sharane and I had been uniquely happy while we were together, but I had come to depend on her closeness and her affection, and the asperity of our last few conversations couldn't cancel that dependency. The day that I found myself alone again in a capstack apartment in Alexandria, virtually identical to the one I had formerly occupied, seemed to me to be the darkest of my life so far—far darker in its mute and empty desolation than the feverish day when Emily Marchant and I had been trapped in the wreck of the *Genesis*. It didn't mark me as deeply or as permanently—how could it?—but it upset me badly enough to make it difficult for me to work.

"Twenty years is a long time even for an emortal when you're more than a hundred years old, Mort," Mama Sajda told me, when I turned to her for comfort. "It's time for you to move on." I would of course have turned to Mama Eulalie had my options not narrowed when she died in 2634.

"That's what Sharane said," I told Mama Sajda, in a slightly accusatory tone. "She was being sternly reasonable at the time. I thought that the sternness would crumble if I put it to the test, and I thought that her resolve would crumble with it, but it didn't."

"I can't say I'm surprised," she replied, tersely.

Had I been in a less fragile mood, I wouldn't have been able to say that I was surprised either, but that wasn't the point, as I tried hard to explain. I was convinced, perhaps foolishly, that Mama Eulalie would have understood.

"I'm truly sorry," Mama Sajda said, when I was eventually reduced to tears.

"She said that too," I was quick to point out, not caring that I was piling up evidence to back Sharane's claim that I had an innately obsessive frame of mind. "She said that she had to do it. She said that she hated hurting me, but she would say that, wouldn't she?"

Now that forgetfulness has blotted out the greater part of that phase of my life—including, I presume, the worst of it—I don't really know why I was so devastated by Sharane's decision or why it should have filled me with such black despair. Had I cultivated a dependence so absolute that it seemed irreplaceable, or was it only my pride that had suffered a sickening blow? Was it the imagined consequences of the rejection or merely the rejection itself that hurt me so badly?

Mama Sajda wanted to help, but only for a week or two. Mama Eulalie had added injury to Sharane's insult by dying mere years before I had the greatest need of her. She had been 257 years old and had outlasted not only Papa Nahum, who had been born two years after her, but also Mama Meta, who had been seven years younger. Even so, she had not lasted long *enough*. None of my other co-parents had come to Mama

Eulalie's funeral. Their association with her was too far in the past. Raising me had ceased to be a defining experience for them. I didn't hold it against them. I figured that none of them was likely to be around for another twenty years, although I'd never have guessed that Mama Siorane would be the last to go, frozen on the crest of a Titanian mountain, looking up at the rings of Saturn. She was the only one who didn't actually have a funeral, but even I didn't go to Papa Ezra's. I was still Earthbound, reluctant to lose what people like Mama Siorane had begun to refer to as my "gravirginity."

When I said my last good-bye to Mama Sajda in 2647, too close for spiritual comfort to the place at which I'd failed to save Grizel from drowning in the treacherous Kwarra, I said my last good-bye to that whole phase in my life: to the tattered remnants of childhood, the bitter legacies of first love, and the patiently accepted hardships of apprenticeship. The second part of my *History of Death* was launched the following year, and I was possessed by a strong sense of beginning a new phase of my existence—but I was wrong about that.

I was maturing by degrees, but I still had not served the full term of my apprenticeship.

TWENTY-EIGHT

The second part of *The History of Death* was entitled *Death in the Ancient World*. It plotted a convoluted but not particularly original trail through the Labyrinth, collating a wealth of data regarding burial practices and patterns of mortality in Egypt, the Kingdoms of Sumer and Akkad, the Indus civilizations of Harappa and Mohenjo-Daro, the Yangshao and Lungshan cultures of the Far East, the cultures of the Olmecs and Zapotecs, and so on. It extended as far as Greece before and after Alexander and the beginnings of the Roman Empire, but its treatment of later matters was admittedly slight and prefatory, and it was direly neglectful of the Far Eastern cultures—omissions that I repaired by slow degrees during the next two centuries.

The commentary I provided for *Death in the Ancient World* was far more extensive than the commentary I had superimposed on the first volume. It offered an unprecedentedly elaborate analysis of the mythologies of life after death developed by the cultures under consideration. Although I have revised the commentary several times over and extended it considerably, I think the original version offered valuable insights into the eschatology of the Egyptians, rendered with a certain eloquence. I spared no effort in my descriptions and discussions of tomb texts, the *Book of the Dead*, the Hall of Double Justice, Anubis and Osiris, the custom of mummification, and the building of pyramid tombs. I refused to consider such elaborate efforts made by the living on behalf of the dead to be foolish or unduly lavish.

Whereas some historians had insisted on seeing pyramid building as a wasteful expression of the appalling vanity of the world's first tyrant-dictators, I saw it as an entirely appropriate recognition of the appalling impotence of all humans in the face of death. In my view, the building of the pyramids should not be explained away as a kind of gigantic folly or as a way to dispose of the energies of the peasants when they were not required in harvesting the bounty of the fertile Nile; such heroic endeavor could only be accounted for if one accepted that pyramid building was the most useful of all labors. It was work directed at the glorious imposition of human endeavor upon the natural landscape. The placing of a royal mummy, with all its accoutrements, in a fabulous geometric edifice of stone was a loud, confident, and entirely appropriate statement of humanity's invasion of the empire of death.

I did not see the pharaohs as usurpers of misery, elevating the importance of their own extinction far above that of their subjects but rather as vessels for the horror of the entire community. I saw a pharaoh's temporal power not as a successful example of the exercise of brute force but as a symbol of the fact that no privilege a human society could extend or create could insulate its beneficiaries from mortality and mortality's faithful handmaidens, disease and pain. The pyramids, I contended, had not been built for the pharaohs alone but for everyone who toiled in their construction or in support of the constructors; what was interred within a pyramid was no mere bag of bones absurdly decked with useless possessions but the collective impotence of a race, properly attended by symbolic expressions of fear, anger, and hope.

I still think that there was much merit in the elaborate comparisons that I made between late Egyptian and late Greek accounts of the "death adventure," measuring both the common and distinctive phases of cultural development in the narrative complication and anxiety that infected their burgeoning but crisis-ridden civilizations. I am still proud of my careful decoding of the conceptual geography of the Greek Underworld and the characters associated with it as judges, guardians, functionaries, and misfortunate victims of hubris.

I disagreed, of course, with those analysts who thought hubris a bad thing and argued for the inherent and conscious irony of its description as a sin. Those who disputed the rights of the immortal gods, and paid the price, were in my estimation the true heroes of myth, and it was in that context that I offered my own account of the meaning and significance of the crucial notion of tragedy. My accounts of the myth of Persephone, the descent of Orpheus, and the punishments inflicted upon the likes of Sisyphus, Ixion, and Tantalus hailed those inventions as magnificent early triumphs of the creative imagination.

The core argument of *Death in the Ancient World* was that the early evolution of myth making and storytelling had been subject to a rigorous process of natural selection, by virtue of the fact that myth and narrative were vital weapons in the war against death. That war had still to be fought entirely in the mind of man because there was little yet to be accomplished by defiance of death's claims upon the body. The great contribution of Hippocrates to the science of medicine—which I refused to despise or diminish for its apparent slightness—was that the wise doctor would usually do nothing at all, admitting that the vast majority of attempted treatments only made matters worse.

In the absence of an effective medical science—all the more so once that absence had been recognized and admitted—the war against death was essentially a war of propaganda. I insisted that the myths made by intelligent Greeks had to be judged in that light—not by their truthfulness, even in some allegorical or metaphorical sense, but by their usefulness in generating *morale*.

I admitted, of course, that the great insight of Hippocrates was fated to be refused and confused for a further two thousand years, while all kinds of witch doctors continued to employ all manner of poisons and tortures in the name of medicine, but I believe that I substantiated my claim that there had been a precious moment when the Hellenic Greeks actually knew what they were about and that this had informed their opposition to death more fruitfully than any previous culture or any of the immediately succeeding ones.

Elaborating and extrapolating the process of death in the way that the Egyptians and Greeks had done, I argued, had enabled a more secure moral order to be imported into social life. Those cultures had achieved a better sense of continuity with past and future generations than any before them, allotting every individual a part within a great enterprise that had extended and would extend, generation to generation, from the beginning to the end of time. I was careful, however, to give due credit to those less-celebrated tribesmen who worshiped their ancestors and thought them always close at hand, ready to deliver judgments upon the living. Such people, I felt, had fully mastered an elementary truth of human existence: that the dead are not entirely gone. Their afterlife continues to intrude upon the memories and dreams of the living, whether or not they were actually summoned. The argument became much more elaborate once I had properly accommodated the

Far Eastern, Australasian, and Native American data within it, but its essence remained the same.

My commentary approved wholeheartedly of the idea that the dead should have a voice and must be entitled to speak—and that the living have a moral duty to listen. Because the vast majority of the tribal cultures of the ancient world were as direly short of history as they were of medicine, I argued, they were entirely justified in allowing their ancestors to live on in the minds of living people, where the culture those ancestors had forged similarly resided.

In saying this, of course, I was consciously trying to build imaginative bridges between the long-dead subjects of my analysis and its readers, the vast majority of whom still had their own dead freshly in mind.

I think I did strike a chord in some readers and that I triggered some useful word-of-mouth publicity. At any rate, the second part of my history attracted twice as many browsers in its first year within the Labyrinth, and the number of visitations registered thereafter climbed nearly three times as quickly. This additional attention was undoubtedly due to its timeliness and to the fact that it really did have a useful wisdom to offer the survivors of the Decimation.

TWENTY-NINE

The Decimation was undoubtedly *the* pivotal event in the early history of the New Human Race. That was only partly due to the nature of the catastrophe, which was uniquely well equipped to bring an appalling abundance of death into a world of emortals. Its timing was equally important, because its significance would have been markedly different had it happened a century earlier or later.

In 2542 the world was still congratulating itself on the latest and last of its many victories over the specter of mortality. Human culture was saturated with the elation of a job completed after much unanticipated confusion and complication and all the true emortals—even the lucky few born more than half a century before me—were still young. Even those who had attained their nineties still *thought* of themselves as young; those like myself, only just emerged from adolescence, knew that we had a long period of apprenticeship to serve before we would be properly fitted to take up the reins of progress from the last generation of the Old Human Race. We knew that the nanotech-rejuvenated false emortals would still be running the world in 2600 but that we would come into our inheritance by slow degrees in the twenty-seventh century. Even those of us who were being groomed for the ultimate responsibility of ownership were not impatient to assume their new duties, and those of us whose portion of the stewardship of Earth would be far leaner were perfectly content to *mark time*, postponing all our most important decisions until the appropriate time.

I have explained how my own experience in the Coral Sea Disaster helped to focus my own ambition and determination. My sense of urgency did not make me hurry my work—I knew from the beginning that it would be the labor of centuries—but it gave me a strong sense of direction and commitment. People more distant from the epicenter of the event might not have been affected as abruptly or as profoundly, but they were affected. The changes in my personal microcosm reflected more ponderous changes in the social macrocosm of Earthbound humanity.

The research that I did for the third instalment of *The History of Death*—which began, of course, long before the second was finalized—necessitated a great deal of work on the early history of the major world religions, which my theoretical framework compelled me to view as social and psychological technologies providing arms and armor against death. I could hardly have spent so much time thinking about the birth of the great religions without also thinking about their obliteration, even though that had happened in an era belonging to a much later section of my *History*. Nor could I think about their obliteration without thinking about their replacement.

In 2542 the most common opinion about the fate of religion was that it had begun to fade away when science exposed the folly of its pretensions to explain the origin and nature of the universe and humankind and that its decline had been inexorable since the eighteenth century. It seemed to me, however, that the early assaults of science and utilitarian moral philosophy had only stripped away the outer layers of religion without ever penetrating to its real heart. It made more sense to see religion as a casualty of the ecocatastrophic Crash that followed the rapid technological development and population growth of the twentieth and twenty-first centuries.

When the human species came through that trial by fire, thanks to Conrad Helier's provisions for the first so-called New Human Race, its members were determined to jettison the ideologies that seemed to have played a part in formulating the Crisis that led to the Crash, and religion was first on the hit list. It seemed to me that religion had been scapegoated—perhaps not unjustly, given the vilely overextensive use that the followers of the major religions had themselves made of scapegoating strategies. The tiny minorities that had hung on to religious faith despite the post-Crash backlash had, in my view, obtained due reward for their defiance of convention in that they had kept arms and armor against the awareness of death. Their contemptuous neighbors presumably thought such arms and armor unnecessary while the nanotechnologies developed by PicoCon and OmicronA still held out the possibility and the hope that serial rejuvenation would provide an escalator effect leading everyone to true emortality—but I thought that they were wrong.

As I labored through the latter half of the twenty-sixth century, it began to seem odd to me that religion had not bounced back from its post-Crash anathematization. I began to wonder why the small sects that survived had not provided the seeds of a revival as soon as it became obvious that nanotech repair could not beat the Miller Effect. Perhaps they would have done if the Zaman transformation had not made its debut so soon after the reluctant acceptance by the world's centenarians that they could not and would not live forever. Perhaps it would have done in any case, had there not been another overarching ideology holding the empty intellectual ground.

This other ideology was, of course, the work ethic. As a historian, I knew of abundant evidence to show that individuals who were suddenly impoverished after having enjoyed a good standard of living invariably reacted in one of two ways. Either they gave way to total despair or they set themselves to work with relentless assiduity, never relaxing unless and until they regained their former economic status and sometimes not even then. After the Crash, that psychology became applicable on a worldwide scale; once the despairing had taken themselves out of account by the simple expedient of dying, the world had been left in the care of those whose obsessive desire was to restore all the richness, complexity, and productivity of the ecosphere.

The post-Crash world was, of course, constantly resupplying itself with potential hedonists as each new generation of children grew to rebellious adolescence, but all the twenty-second century documents at which I glanced gave me evidence of the dramatic imbalance of power which continually nipped that rebellion in the bud, effortlessly converting the temporary rebels into dutiful workaholics.

That imbalance of power was only partly due to the strength of the work ethic itself; it was greatly enhanced by shifting demographics. Before the Crash, the young had always outnumbered the old, and they had been far more vigorous. Even the primitive technologies of longevity in place before the Crash had increased the democratic authority of the old, but the advent of Internal Technology and nanotech repair gave them the physical vigor to make that authority stick. After the Crash, the old vastly outnumbered the young.

The demographic gap opened up between 2095 and 2120, between the advent of the chiasmalytic disruptors that caused the plague of sterility and the mass production of Helier wombs, ensured that the imbalance was never significantly redressed, even when the new hatcheries were at full stretch. The demographic structure of the population made it absolutely certain that no youthful rebellion could be any more than a storm in a teacup. The prejudices of the old became enormously powerful—and that included their prejudice against religion as well as their unshakable commitment to the work ethic.

So powerful was that commitment, in an era in which many people born in the late twenty-second century were still alive at the beginning of the twenty-fifth, that the Great Exhibition of 2405—the first flowering of Creationist ambition—still seemed shocking to many people. Such pioneers of the twenty-fifth century cult of youth as the second Oscar Wilde appalled so many of their own contemporaries that they were driven to extremes of posture and endeavor, but they hardly made a dent in the prevailing ideological wisdom.

It was this powerful work ethic that filled the breach left by religion, in providing arms and armor against the awareness of death. Like determined secularists in the pre-Crash eras, the people of the post-Crash era balanced the inevitability of their own mortality against their achievements in life and the storehouse of wealth and wisdom that they would be able to pass on to the next, even longer-lived generation. The inertia of that situation was easily adequate to carry the culture of the false emortals into the twenty-sixth century—and might have carried it into the twenty-seventh without significant amendment had it not been for the interruption of the Decimation: the first event in five hundred years to cause a widespread questioning of fundamental matters of principle and priority.

One response to the Decimation was to extol the virtues of the work ethic even more highly, to construe the catastrophe as proof that ceaseless toil was the only way to secure the stability and Utopian perfection of the ecosphere and the econosphere. But this was not the only response; others were led by the drift in history to feel that the work ethic had betrayed them and that New Humanity ought not to live by toil alone.

There were, I suppose, few better exemplars of this new ideological conflict than myself and Sharane Fereday. It was, however, our marriage rather than our divorce that offered a pointer to future history. As individuals, we failed to reconcile our differences, but intellectual history marches to a different drum, in which thesis and antithesis must in the end by reconciled by synthesis. While Sharane and I parted, the world groped toward a new balance, and that balance was neo-Epicureanism: a philosophy which asserted that it was not only possible to mix business and pleasure but absolutely necessary in a New Human context.

I had already tried to make that compromise within my marriage, but Sharane had been unwilling to meet me halfway—or, indeed, to admit that I had actually come anywhere near halfway in my attempt to reach out to her. Once we had parted, however, I set out to use my solitude bravely in order to become a much better neo-Epicurean.

THIRTY

I took the business of my own remaking very seriously. Taking what inspiration I could from the Greek myths I had analyzed so painstakingly in *Death in the Ancient World*, I took great care to do nothing to excess, and I tried with all my might to derive an altogether *appropriate* pleasure from everything I did, work and play alike. I took equally great care to cultivate a proper love for the commonplace, training myself to a finer pitch of perfection than I had ever achieved before in all the techniques of physiological control necessary to physical fitness and quiet metabolism.

I soon convinced myself that I had transcended such primitive and adolescent goals as happiness and had cultivated instead a truly civilized *ataraxia*: a calm of mind whose value went beyond the limits of ecstasy and exultation. By the time I reached my 150th birthday I was sure that I had mastered the art and science of New Humanity and was fully prepared to meet the infinite future—but that conviction was, unfortunately, a trifle hubristic.

After the publication of *Death in the Ancient World* I lived for twenty more years in Alexandria, although my portion of the credit left unused by Mama Sajda and Mama Siorane allowed me to move from the capstack to the outer suburbs. I rented a simple villa that had been cleverly gantzed out of the desert sands: sands that still gave an impression of timelessness even though they had been restored to wilderness as recently as the twenty-fifth century, when Egypt's food economy had been realigned to take full advantage of new techniques in artificial photosynthesis.

In 2669, when I felt that it was time for a change, I decided that I would like to live for a while in a genuine ancient wilderness—one that had never been significantly transformed by the busy hands of humankind. There were, of course, few such places remaining, and the busy hands of humankind were already at work in all of them. I did not want to return to the Himalayas, so I looked again at the other possibility that my foster parents had seriously considered: Antarctica. They had rejected it because of the rapid development of Amundsen City and its immediate environs, but the Continent Without Nations was a true continent, and it still harbored several unspoiled regions. I knew that they would not long remain so—by the end of the century, I figured, it would no longer be possible to find anything that could pass muster as authentic wilderness—but that knowledge only convinced me that I had better indulge my whim while I still could.

I finally settled on Cape Adare on the Ross Sea, a relatively lonely spot where my nearest human neighbors would be conveniently out of sight beyond the glacial horizon.

I moved into a tall edifice modeled on a twentieth-century lighthouse, from whose windowed attic I could look out at the edge of the ice cap and watch the penguins at play. I worked hard on the third part of my *History of Death*, which had now reached an era that was tolerably well reflected in actual documents and could therefore be pursued through the Labyrinth in reasonable comfort. I took care, though, to balance my labors sensibly. I spent a great deal of time in recreational virtual environments and cultivated a better appreciation than I had ever had before of the rewards of virtual travel, virtual community, and virtual eroticism. I was reasonably contented and soon came to feel that I had put the awkward turbulence of my early life firmly behind me.

I had hardly anyone to talk to, all my parents having died and all but a couple of the virtual relationships I had restored in the wake of my first divorce having lapsed again during my second marriage, but I did not care. I had lived long enough with my parents to imagine their responses to my new situation, and my imagined responses were far more conclusive than any real ones could have been.

"This is exactly what I feared," Mama Siorane would have said. "Forever is a long time to be a hermit."

"It's because forever is a long time," I retorted, "that there's time enough to be a hermit without any fear of waste."

"I've always told you to be yourself," Mama Eulalie would have said, "but are you really certain that this is the self you want to be?"

"It's the self I have to be, for now," I retorted, "if I'm to design better selves for the future."

"I always knew that you'd end up as a virtualist Utopian," Papa Domenico would have said. "I was the oldest of your fathers, the one with the real authority."

"I'm not a virtualist Utopian, Papa Dom," I replied. "I'm making myself fit for any and all Utopias."

"You can't make yourself without making other things," Emily Marchant said, without requiring imaginative reproduction. "Navel gazing does no good. You have to get involved with something more meaningful, Morty. That's what I'm doing. I've spent too much time in labs designing new kinds of shamirs. Now I have to find out what's to be *done* with them. From now on, it's hands-on all the way for me."

It was far less easy to outflank her than my dead parents. "I've always been a hands-on historian," I told her. "My work is going very well."

"Oh Morty," she said, refusing to give way as gracefully as my parents, "you don't even know what *hands-on* means. You never built anything *solid* in your life."

"You don't understand," I said, retreating to a formula that could always be relied on to stalemate an unwinnable argument. She didn't— but she wouldn't ever concede that her failure to understand me was her fault and not mine.

Perhaps it was only as a result of my upbringing in the Himalayas, but I really did feel *at home* in Antarctica. It made Alexandria, Crete, Lamu, and Adelaide seem so hectic and strange that I could not quite comprehend how I had tolerated any of them for as long as I had.

I often went walking on the cape, but I avoided the dangerously variable shelves of ice that extended across the shallow sea, keeping to the ice sheets that were safely mounted on solid ground. I had been warned that such excursions could be just as hazardous as littoral ventures, but I was never reckless. As the years went by without my ever getting into difficulties I was able to set aside all anxiety. While outside the house I always wore special suitskins whose fast metabolism compensated for the low temperature, and I rarely took off my face mask unless the weather was exceptionally clement. I made sure that my IT had additional reserves for emergency use, and I kept a small company of rescue robots that could be summoned to my assistance if I were caught in a blizzard or slipped into a crevasse. I only had occasion to call them out five times in the 2670s, and they responded with quick efficiency, bringing me home safe and well.

During my first decade in Antarctica I did not meet a single human being in the flesh. In summer I could see distant ships from my eyrie as they tentatively probed the waters of the gulf, but they rarely came close enough to the shore for me to discern crewmen working on their decks. Most of them would, in any case, have been fully automated craft taking their carefully measured harvest of krill from the rich waters. I was a thousand kilometers south of the latitudes in which liquid artificial photosynthesis systems could be economically deployed, and four hundred from the nearest marine farms. The local ecosystem had to be measured and managed as carefully as any, but it was equipped with species that were very little different from those that had flourished here before the twenty-first-century ocean dereliction, which some ecologists still reckoned to be the root cause and most significant aspect of the Crash.

As time went by, the probing ships became more numerous and more various, but not in any troublesome sense. Inland, it was a different story. The initial relocation of the UN's central administration to Amundsen City had provided a golden opportunity for streamlining, but as soon as the new setup was in place the perverse logic of bureaucracy had begun to reassert itself, and the organization had begun to expand again, growing and mutating.

The original plan had been to maintain a relatively small and austere presence in Amundsen City while conducting the bulk of UN business in virtual space. There was no practical reason why the world's government could not have been run like its economy, from widely scattered tiny cells like the one hidden by Shangri-La, but government is not entirely a practical matter. As soon as a certain prestige and status was attached to an "Antarctic position" Amundsen City became a sociopolitical Klondyke, and the subsequent population rush inevitably spread outward like a creeping infection.

Eventually, as I had known it would, it reached Cape Adare.

THIRTY-ONE

By 2680, my nearest neighbors on Cape Adare were no longer out of sight. Although the nearest towns, Leningradskaya and Lillie Marleen, were still at a safe distance, the burgeoning Cape Hallett colony gradually extended itself along the Barchgrevnik Coast to the very edge of my own promontory. It became increasingly common for me to meet other walkers in the northern reaches of the cape. The people in question were scrupulously polite and not at all intrusive, but the very concept of neighborhood implies a certain moral obligation that cannot be set aside.

The first time I had to send my rescue robots out to someone else's aid I knew that my eremitic existence was under threat and that my solitude would soon be at an end. The embrace of Earthbound humanity was now total. How could I possibly complain? The southern extremity of Cape Adare had been welcomed into that embrace on the day I had moved there; I was an agent of human infection myself.

I was by this time an old hand, a proven Antarctican: the kind of man who had to respond to a *real* emergency in person. When one of my new neighbors from Hallett, Ziru Majumdar, fell into a crevasse so deep and awkward that all the slothful robots on the Ross shore could not extract him by means of Artificial Intelligence alone, I was one of the people who felt obliged to fly to his aid.

Human intelligence being what it is, it only required five of us—and seventy-five tons of equipment—to pull Mister Majumdar out of the hole, and only two of us ended up more seriously injured than he was before the operation began. Even ice that is bedded on solid rock is prone to shift, especially under the stress of urgent action. Frozen water cannot drown a man, but it can certainly crush him.

After several hours of merciful anesthesis, courtesy of our kindly IT, Ziru Majumdar and I woke up in adjacent beds at the hospital in Amundsen City. I was fully insulated from pain and could not sense my left leg at all, but the extent of the numbness and the depth of the illusory feeling that my brain had been removed from my head and immersed in a vat of treacle assured me that I would not be up and about for some considerable time.

"I'm truly sorry about your leg, Mister Gray," Majumdar said. "It was very stupid of me to get lost at all, even in the blizzard—and then to walk over the lip of the crevasse . . . very, very foolish. I've lived here for five years, after all; I thought I knew every last ice ridge like the back of my hand. It's not as if I've ever suffered from summer rhapsody or snow blindness."

I'd suffered slightly from both the ailments he named. I was still awkwardly vulnerable to any psychosomatic condition that was readily available. My sensitivity had, however, served to make me so careful that I never looked upon the all-pervasive winter snows without a protective mask, and I had programed my household sloth to draw the blinds against the eternal days of late December and early January. An uneasy mind can sometimes be an advantage.

"It wasn't your fault, Mister Majumdar," I graciously insisted. "I suppose I must have been a little overconfident myself, or I'd never have slipped and fallen when the fracture became a collapse. One bound is all it would have required to take me clear. At least they were able to pull me out in a matter of minutes; you must have lain at the bottom of that crevasse for the better part of two days."

"Very nearly," he admitted. "At first I assumed that I could get out myself—when I found that I could not I took it for granted that the robots would cope. Who would ever have thought I'd need to summon human help in this day and age?"

"It might have been better if you'd lost consciousness sooner," I pointed out.

"I don't think so," he replied. "I never like to trust these matters entirely to the judgment of machine intelligence. I'm not one of these people who's so afraid of circumstance that they program their IT to black them out at the first sign of physical stress and consign their fate to the dutiful care of their telephone answering machines."

"Neither am I," I said, wondering if I were being subtly insulted, "but there are times when consciousness and courage increase our danger."

"But they also enhance our experience," Majumdar countered, with what seemed to me to be remarkable eagerness. "While I was waiting for real help to arrive I came round several times. At least, I think I did. The problem with being half-anesthetized is that it makes one very prone to hallucination. If I had been deeply asleep, it would be as if the whole affair never happened. One should remember these things *properly*, don't you think? How else can we regard our experiences as complete? It was jolly cold, though. I had a thermosuit over my suitskin, but I'd have been much better in a reinforced costume like yours. My clothes were doing their absolute best to keep me warm, but the first law of thermodynamics doesn't give you much slack when you're at the bottom of a cleft, lying in the permafrost. I've got authentic frostbite in my toes, you know. Imagine that! Authentic frostbite."

I tried to imagine it, but it wasn't easy. He could hardly be in pain, so it was difficult to conjure up any notion of what it might feel like to have necrotized toes. It was equally difficult to figure out why he considered the possession of necrotized toes to be a kind of privilege and why he felt the need to tell me about it in such a salesmanlike manner. I wondered what kind of work he did when he wasn't out memorizing ice ridges.

I could understand his apparent excitement, to some degree. We live such careful and ordered lives that the occasional minicatastrophe has considerable compensations. Mister Majumdar's accident would give him something to talk about, something with which to make himself seem a little bit more interesting—but that wasn't what he meant when he rattled on about making his experience more complete. He seemed to think that the frostbite might be interesting *in itself* rather than as a mere datum that he could trot out at VE parties—but with my brain suspended in treacle and no left leg, I was in no condition to involve myself in mysteries.

My doctor, whose name was Ayesha Sung, reckoned that it would take a week for the crushed tissues in my leg to regenerate the bones and sinews.

"You'll have to be immobilized for at least four days," she told me, sternly. "The cell masses have to be returned to quasi-blastular innocence before they can lay the foundations for a new knee and ankle. Once the superstructure is in place, the differentiation can be concluded and the synovial fluid can get the whole thing working. Once my nanomachines have finished, the rest is up to you. It could take as much as three months to train up the muscles again. If you had any special skills built into the old set you'll have to reeducate the reflexes. You're not a ballet dancer, I hope?"

She knew full well that I wasn't a ballet dancer. She could easily have picked a less derisive example—skier, maybe, or climber.

"You were very lucky," she added. "If you'd fallen headfirst, you'd be dead."

"Fortunately," I told her, unable to resist the temptation to be sarcastic, "I was standing on my feet when the ground gave way. I was in a hurry to rescue poor Mister Majumdar, so I hadn't given the possibility of standing on my head much thought."

"Very amusing," she said, coldly. "If I offered a discount on my fee for a helpful attitude, you'd just have lost yours. You should try to be more like Mister Majumdar. All experience enriches us as it transforms us."

"Thanks a lot, Mister Majumdar," I said, when she'd gone.

"Call me Ziru," was his only reply.

"Mortimer," I offered in return, figuring that he could shorten it when he'd demonstrated a little more camaraderie. Then I repented, remembering that we were going to be together for several days and that it was at least thirty years since I'd last spent such a long time in the actual company of another human being. "You aren't *really* enjoying having frostbite, are you?" I asked by way of making conversation. "You *have* programed your IT to cut out the pain, I suppose."

"Of course," he said. "But cutting out pain isn't just a practical issue, is it? It's not just a straightforward matter of leaving the warning flash in place and then obliterating the rest."

"Isn't it?" I queried, having always thought that it was. Given that good IT is a far better monitor of internal damage than pain ever was, it had always seemed to me entirely reasonable that technologically sophisticated humans, old and new alike, should reserve pain responses to the triggering of withdrawal reflexes.

"Certainly not," Majumdar said. "The fact that we don't *need* pain any longer to inform us that all is not well within our internal being—a job for which it was always ludicrously ill-fitted—it doesn't follow that it's entirely useless and ought to be discarded. It's a *resource*, which ought to be carefully explored, if only for aesthetic reasons."

"Aesthetic reasons?" I echoed, in frank astonishment. "Connoisseur masochism, you mean?"

"If that's what you want to call it," he replied, loftily. "But I'm not talking about anything as crude as trying to find a paradoxical pleasure in pain. What I'm talking about is taking care to learn what pain *as pain* has to teach us about who and what we are—and, more importantly, who and what we were."

"The empire of fear hath the greatest of all despots set at its head," I quoted, "whose name is Death, and his consort is named Pain."

"Who said that?" Majumdar wanted to know—but not enough to wait for the answer. "A mortal, of course. We live in a different world now. Anyway, pain was always the handmaiden of life, whatever mortals thought. Uncontrolled suffering makes life unbearable, but controllable suffering—*obedient* pain—merely gives it an edge. When you take the trouble to get to know obedient pain, you discover that there are many different kinds. There's a whole spectrum of neglected aesthetic experience in the multitudinous facets of disease and injury."

I was too numb to engage in long-distance argument and too flabbergasted by the seeming outrageousness of his position to find a ready counter to his claims, but I couldn't help voicing the most alarming of the possibilities that sprang to mind.

"Did you fall into that crevasse *deliberately*?" I wanted to know. "Once there, did you actually set out to acquire frostbitten fingers?"

"No," he said, "that would have been perverse, not to say foolish. But the wise man always tries to turn crises into opportunities. The *whole man* will always refuse to insulate himself entirely from alarms and misfortunes and will always try to draw benefit from them when they steal upon him." The last sentence sounded suspiciously like a quote, but its source was as unfamiliar to me as the source of my quote had been to him.

"Well," I said, "I only hope the other person who was hurt sees things your way. I'd hate to think that there were two of us getting no fun at all out of our suffering."

"He does," Ziru Majumdar assured me. "We're neighbors out on

Hallett. Ours is quite a progressive community, you know—except that you don't know, being such a hermit. But you are writing a *History of Death*, aren't you, Mortimer? We rather hoped that you might prove to be a kindred spirit. Perhaps you will, once we've had the chance to get to know one another a little better."

"Perhaps I will," I said, in a voice steeped in deep archaic ice. Somehow, the fact that he had heard of me even though we'd never met didn't please me at all.

THIRTY-TWO

Z iru Majumdar was right about the side effects of semi-anesthetization, if nothing else. During the four days that I was immobilized I continually drifted in and out of sleep and was never quite sure when my most vivid dreams thrust themselves into consciousness whether I was passively living the experiences in VE or actively conjuring them up from the depths of my unconscious.

Members of the New Human Race are generally thought to dream far less frequently and far less vividly than their forebears, but the average diminution in REM sleep time is only 30 percent. The fact that we rarely become conscious that we are dreaming, and always forget our dreams even if we wake into them, has more to do with the efficiency of our IT than the actual loss of dream sleep. It's widely believed that the actual diminution in REM sleep is due to the fact that our adventures in VE have taken over some of the psychological functions of dreaming, but that's mere conjecture. The experiments that were supposed to prove the case had to be called off because too many of the subjects refused to continue when they began to suffer various kinds of psychosomatic distress. Had I been one of them, I expect that I'd have been one of the first to cry off.

I had attempted IT-controlled lucid dreaming on several occasions during my first marriage. Jodocus and Eve had been enthusiasts, and Jodocus had even gone so far as to obtain a bootleg suite that allowed him to sample the notorious nanotech-VE experience, some of whose twenty-third- and twenty-fourth-century users were rumored to have died of shock when launched into illusions that were far too convincing. I had not liked the gentler varieties much and had refused to have anything to do with the bootleg. I politely set aside the assurances Jodocus gave me that if I only took time out to practice I would eventually develop the skill necessary to get the most out of my dreaming.

While I lay in that bed in Amundsen City I began to regret that I had not persisted. Had I learned to get along with lucid dreams in Lamu, I might not have been so meekly at their mercy in Amundsen. Even if I had been able to exercise a degree of control over the contents of my deliria—as Jodocus or Eve would surely have been able to do—I would not have been able to escape them, but they could not have made my imprisonment wretched. As things were, I woke up with a start on several occasions, sometimes crying out as I did so.

Mercifully, I can no longer remember what it was that terrified me so. Dreams leave no objective record even when one's flesh is stuffed full of monitors and helplessly spread-eagled in a room whose walls have more than the usual ration of eyes and ears. I presume that I relived the Coral Sea Disaster more than once and dived into the waters of the Kwarra a hundred times and more, always hopelessly. I probably met snakes and crocodiles, and leopard-seals. I must have fallen into deep ice-caves, where I writhed in fear of being crushed and watched my fingers and toes swell with frostbite. I may well have taken the plunge into the *real* ultimate wilderness of outer space, where I was doubtless seized by a motion sickness so profound as to make my sufferings aboard *Genesis* seem tame.

At any rate, I had nightmares, and they were bad.

Mister Majumdar was not in the least sympathetic. To him, fear—like pain and misery—were merely parts of life's rich tapestry, to be welcomed with fascination and savored to the full.

"I like nightmares," he told me. "They're so wonderfully piquant. I wish I had more of them, but it's not the same if they're deliberately induced. Synthetic fear is as unsatisfactory as synthetic pain and synthetic pleasure. That's why no VE sex is ever quite as good as the best fleshsex, no matter how cleverly it's programmed. It's *undeserved*."

Personally, I had always felt that no fleshsex was ever quite as good as any half-way competent VE sex, but I certainly wasn't going to tell Ziru Majumdar that. I wasn't even going to take issue with the curious notion that virtual experience was somehow "undeserved," although it seemed to me that even amateurs worked hard enough on the personalizations of their sex programs to take much fuller credit for the quality of the experience than they ever could in haphazard coition with an actual partner.

"How's your frostbite?" I asked, thinking that it would redirect his obsession to safer ground.

"I've blanked it," he confessed, with a small embarrassed laugh. "It's a rather crude and unfurnished sensation—a mere ache, with no real personality."

He sounded like a wine snob criticizing a poor vintage.

"It's good to know that I haven't missed much," I said, drily.

"According to the newstapes," he said, presumably because it was he who now felt a need to shift the conversational ground, "it's only a matter of time before the whole biosphere gets frostbite. Unless we can somehow see to it that the sun gets stirred up again."

He was referring to recent press releases by scrupulous students of the sunspot cycle, who had proposed that the virtual disappearance of Sol's blemishes signaled the advent of a new Ice Age. As a historian, I was unimpressed by the quality of the evidence that purported to show that past "little Ice Ages" had been correlated with periods of unusual solar inactivity, but the world at large seemed to be unimpressed for quite different reasons. Given that Antarctica was becoming such a fashionable place to live, few people saw any cause for anxiety in the prospect of glaciers slowly extending across the Northern Hemisphere. It was more likely to raise real estate prices on the steppes than lower them.

"We can take it," I said, cheerfully. "Anyhow, it's better to accept it than start messing about with the sun. Continental engineering is one thing, but I don't think our fusion techs are quite ready to move up to the big one—not until they've practiced a bit with Proxima Centauri and Barnard, at least. You and I have nothing to worry about. We like ice— why else would we live on the shore of the Ross Sea?"

"Right," he said. He seemed glad to find something on which we could agree, but he was the kind of man who couldn't resist tempting fate. "Not that I have any sympathy for Gaean Liberationists and Mystics, of course," he added, with a blithe disregard for the possibility that I might.

Gaean extremism was discovering new extremes with every decade that passed, buoyed by the idea that the human race was now so securely established throughout the solar system that we ought to return the entire Earth to "fallow ground" by refusing to issue any further child licenses. According to the latest Gaean Lib avant garde, the recent interglacial periods were simply Gaea's fevers, the birth of civilization had been a morbid symptom of the planet's sickness and human culture was a mere delirium that could and should be replaced by a much healthier noosphere based in the elusive protosentience of dolphins, cephalopods, and mysterious species yet to come.

"Oh, the Libs and the Mystics aren't so far wrong," I said, mischievously. "Agriculture was, at best, an imperfect answer to the predicament of expanding population. What might human beings have become by now, I wonder, if we'd devoted ourselves wholeheartedly to spiritual evolution instead of embracing the crude violence of the plough and the milking machine?"

The most frightening thing of all was that it didn't seem to cross his mind that I might be joking. He obviously paid more attention to the lunatic fringe TV channels than I did—he heard that kind of stuff all the time, argued with leaden seriousness.

"Well, yes," he said. "That's a fair point."

"It's just colorful rhetoric," I told him, with a sigh. "Even the people who indulge in it all the time don't mean it literally. It's just a form of play."

"Think so?" Ziru Majumdar seemed to find this proposition just as novel and just as appealing as the one it was attempting to explain. "Well, perhaps. Having been delirious myself for a while when I was down that hole I'm tempted to take the notion of culture-as-delirium a little more seriously. I can't be sure whether I was asleep or awake, but I was certainly *lost*. I don't know about you, but I always find even the very best VEs a bit *flat*. I sometimes use illicit psychotropics to give delusion a helping hand, but they don't really help—they just make me confused and a trifle nauseous."

Now that he was sounding like Jodocus I felt that I was on safer ground.

"That's a natural side-effect of the protective efforts of our internal technology," I told him.

"I know," he replied. "Nanomachines always do their job a little *too* well because of the built-in safety margins. It's a real problem, existentially speaking. It's only when our IT reaches the limits of its capacity that it lets really interesting things begin to happen. We need to think again about the standard programs so that we can give ourselves and our children a little more rope. We first-generation New Humans have grown up in cotton wool, thanks to the anxieties of a dying breed. We shouldn't carry forward their mistakes."

The tone of the conversation had been light until then, but that disturbed me. "Are you a parent, Ziru?" I asked, trying to keep my voice level—and succeeding quite well, thanks to the anesthetics.

"Not yet," he said. "Soon, I hope. Cape Hallett's a good place to rear a child. Challenging environment, progressive community."

"Yes," I said, weakly. "I suppose it might be."

I couldn't help but wonder how many of my own parents would have agreed with him—and how far they might have been persuaded to go along with his weirder arguments.

THIRTY-THREE

The room in which Ziru Majumdar and I were confined was by no means short of facilities. Three of its walls were equipped with window screens, so that if we cared to turn our heads away from one another we could select entirely different vistas on which to look out. If, on the other hand, we were feeling in a collaborative mood, we could both look straight ahead at some mutually agreed spectacle. The VE hoods with which our bedheads were equipped were basic models, but they were not at all uncomfortable. The only thing that was difficult to understand, in view of all this generous provision, was why Doctor Sung had seen fit to put the two of us together rather than giving us private rooms.

"It was a purely clinical judgment," she told me, when I eventually asked. "Actual human contact aids recovery from injury. It's a psychosomatic effect, but it's quite real. If it turns out that patients can't stand the company we select for them we shuffle them around—and if, after three tries, it turns out that we've stumbled on one of those rare curmudgeons for whom hell really is other people, we isolate the poor misfortunate. It's nice and normal people like you and Mister Majumdar who maintain my confidence in human nature and the published literature. You're both doing *very well*."

I honestly couldn't tell if she was telling me a pack of lies, perhaps to cover up the fact that the hospital was so overcrowded with accident victims that they were forced to put two patients in rooms intended for one until their busy shamirs could add an extra story or hollow out an extra set of basements. I was very careful to keep my skepticism to myself. I didn't dare use the bedhead VE apparatus to check up on the alleged literature, just in case my usage was being monitored—for purely clinical reasons, of course.

"I think she's right," Ziru Majumdar said, when Doctor Sung had left the room in the wake of this conversation. "We are doing well, and I think the fact that we've been forced to get to know one another has helped.

You live alone, and I live in a little enclave of like-minded souls. I presume that we both select our virtual acquaintances on the grounds of congeniality. We live in a world in which it's very easy to cultivate pleasant acquaintance, and the only occasions when we risk the effects of *difference* for long periods of time are during marriages, especially marriages contracted for parenthood, when we actively seek diversity for the child's sake. It's good for us, once now and again, to be forced into the company of others at random. You and I are not alike, Mortimer, but I have enjoyed our conversations and I think I have obtained some profit from our time together. I hope that you feel the same."

Did I?

I wasn't at all sure, although I suspected that my skeptical attitude to the doctor's story might be symptomatic of the fact that I didn't really want to believe that my confinement with Mister Majumdar had any clinical benefits. I couldn't say that out loud, of course, so I assured him that he was a very interesting person and that I felt myself to be richer for having had the benefit of his points of view.

Not unnaturally, he took that as permission to prattle on at even greater length, expanding on his personal philosophy.

"I think we might have to go to the very brink of extinction to reach the cutting edge of experience," he told me, presenting the notion as if it were a wonderful and hard-won discovery, made while he was trapped in the crevasse, not knowing whether the rescuers would get to him in time. "You can learn a lot about life, and about yourself, in extreme situations. They're the really *vivid* moments, the moments of *real life*. We're so safe nowadays that most of what we do hardly counts as living at all."

I tried to object to that, but he overrode my objection, pressing on relentlessly.

"We exist," he said, indisputably, before going on to less obvious assertions "we work, we play, but we don't really *test* ourselves to see what we're really made of. If we don't try ourselves out, how will we know what we're really capable of and what kinds of experiences we need to maximize our enjoyment of life? I'm from the Reunited States, where we have a strong sense of history and a strong sense of purpose; we learn in the cradle that we have a *right* to life, liberty, and the pursuit of happiness—but we grow up with protective IT so powerful that it circumscribes our liberty, operating on the assumption that the pursuit of happiness has to be conducted *in comfort*. You're a historian, I know, and a historian of death to boot, but even you can have no idea of the *zest* there must have been in living in the bad old days. Not that I'm about to take up serious injury as a hobby, you understand. Once in a while is plenty."

"Yes it is," I agreed, shifting my now-mobile but furiously itching leg and wishing that nanomachines weren't so slow to compensate for trifling but annoying sensations. "Once in a while is certainly enough for me. In fact, I for one will be quite content if it never happens again. I don't think I need any more of the kind of enlightenment which comes from experiences like that. I was at ground zero in the Great Coral Sea Catastrophe, you know—my ship was flipped over by the uprush of hot water when the mantle broke through the crust below us."

"Were you?" he said, in rapt fascination. "What was it like?" He was eleven years younger than I; he had been much the same age as Emily Marchant when the Decimation was unleashed and had been living deep in the American Midwest, beyond the reach of the tidal waves.

I felt an obscure sense of duty urging me to bring him back down to Earth, to insist that tragedy is tragedy and that there is no nobility in the imminent threat of destruction—but I knew that there was nothing I could say that would have any such effect.

"It was like being shipwrecked, scalded and adrift at sea for days on end, in company with a little girl who'd just lost all twelve of her parents," I said—remembering as I formed the words that the random pairing of Emily Marchant and myself had been so enormously beneficial to both of us as to reduce any clinical benefit of my acquaintance with Ziru Majumdar to utter triviality.

"It must have been terrible," he admitted—but I could tell that his was a definition of the word "terrible" that carried subtle nuances I hadn't encountered before. I could tell too that they weren't the produce of a purely idiosyncratic eccentricity. I was uncomfortably aware, even then, that Ziru Majumdar's was the voice of a new ideology: a new rival for the neo-Epicurean synthesis that had resolved the conflicts embodied in my marriage to Sharane.

I missed not being able to slip on the bed's VE hood and telephone

one of my parents. There were plenty of other people I could have called, including my erstwhile companion-in-misfortune Emily, but every single one of them was a true emortal and I wanted to consult the opinions of someone who wasn't, someone who knew what the threat of death was really like and how valuable life was.

For the first time, while I lay in that hospital bed, I began to miss my dead parents not merely as individuals and intimates but as representatives of a vanishing people. For the first time, I began to wonder whether true emortals had been as well prepared for Utopia as I had previously assumed.

"It *was* terrible," I told him, using the word to mean exactly what I intended it to mean, and nothing more—but language is a collaborative business, as fantastic in its fashion as history.

THIRTY-FOUR

I lived on Cape Adare for a further fifteen years after my brief incarceration with Ziru Majumdar. The experience did not serve to make me any more sociable, and my acquaintance with Majumdar did not ripen into friendship. I had nothing further to do with the steadily expanding Cape Hallett community.

When other dwellings began to be raised on Adare itself I fully intended to keep myself to myself, offering no welcome of any kind to my neighbors, but they had other ideas. They issued invitations, which I found hard to refuse, and I got to know a dozen of them in spite of my own lack of effort. I had not yet got out of the habit of thinking of myself as a member of the "young generation" of the New Human Race and was surprised to find that the newcomers were all younger than I, almost all of them being products of the baby boom facilitated by the Decimation.

My new neighbors were not insulted by my reluctance to involve myself in what they clearly saw as a collaborative adventure. They understood that I must have come to the cape in search of solitude and when I told them that I was finalizing the third part of my *History*— which I still envisaged as a seven-part work—they were happy to maintain a polite distance in order to spare me unnecessary distractions.

What little I saw of the social life of the self-styled "Cape Adare exiles" was not unappealing. Their fondness for real-space interaction presumably followed on from the fact that they had had more than the usual number of contemporaries in childhood, with a consequential abundance of flesh-to-flesh interaction. Their tiny society was, however, hemmed in by numerous barriers of formality and etiquette, which I found aesthetically appealing. In different circumstances I might have entered into the game, but the moment was not right.

Although the invitations I received to visit my new neighbors in their homes did represent a honest attempt to include me in their company, their primary motive was to show off the bizarre architecture of their dwellings. The rapid development of the Antarctic continent had encouraged the development of a new suite of specialized shamirs designed to work with ice.

In the earliest days of gantzing technology the most extravagantly exploited raw materials had been the most humble available—mud, sand, even sea salt—and Leon Gantz had seen his inventions as a means of providing cheap shelter for the poorest people in the world. After the Crash, however, the world's social and economic priorities had changed dramatically, and the relevant biotechnologies had undergone a spectacular adaptive radiation even before PicoCon had married them to their own fast-evolving inorganic nanotech. From then on, the idea of working exclusively in a single superabundant substance had been more or less set aside by Earthbound gantzers.

In space, of course, things were different—but in space, everything was different.

The shamirs entrusted with the rebuilding of the world's great cities in ostensible response to the Decivilization Movement had been extraordinarily versatile and clever, combining all manner of materials into the prototypes of modern hometrees. While I was a child, brought up by parents who had all been touched, albeit lightly, by the Decivilization credo, no one had imagined that Earthbound homemakers would ever return to the use of single-substance shamirs—but no one had anticipated the Great Coral Sea Disaster, and no one had properly thought through the consequences of moving UN headquarters to Amundsen City.

Interim measures to provide shelter for the people dispossessed by the tidal waves had renewed interest in working with sand and sea salt, and the development of Amundsen's satellite towns had produced a new challenge to which the latest generation of gantzers had risen with alacrity.

The homes of the Cape Adare exiles were not simple ice sculptures. They did not have the full range of pseudobiological features that one would expect to find in hometrees designed for warmer regions because there was little point in fixing and redeploying solar energy and no problem at all in obtaining and circulating fresh water, but in every other respect they were hi-tech modern homes. Their walls and conduits required living skins at least as complex as a human suitskin—but these and all their other biotech systems were transparent. They were not optically perfect, but that was no disadvantage. Quite the reverse, in fact; the main reason for the new fashionability of ice castles was the tricks they played with light. Snowfields and glaciers are white and opaque, as were the igloos that legend hailed as humankind's last experiment in ice dwelling, but the ice castles of Cape Adare were marvellously translucent.

From the outside the ice castles looked like piles of kaleidoscopically jeweled prisms; from the inside they were incredibly complex light-shows that changed with every subtle shift of exterior illumination.

Even in winter, when the sky seemed utterly uniform in its leaden grayness, the light within an ice castle was blithely mercurial. In mid-summer, when the sun rolled around the horizon without ever quite set-ting, it was madly and brilliantly restless: the distilled essence of summer rhapsody. To visit one was exhilarating, but no one with my capacity for psychosomatic disorder could ever have lived in one. I was astonished that anyone could, but the young exiles had adapted to their surround-ings with casual ease and had become connoisseurs of perpetually flick-ering light.

"I suppose it's an acquired taste," I said to Mia Czielinski, the proud owner of the most spectacular of the Cape Adare ice palaces. "I'm just not sure that I've got enough time and enough mental fortitude to acquire it."

"We all have the time," she replied, censoriously. "As for mental for-titude—how can you possibly consent to miss out on *any* valuable expe-rience? If we have eternity to play with, do we not have a duty to explore its possibilities?"

I could see that she had a point. She was not merely an emortal but an emortal raised by emortal parents, who had done their work under the influence of theories very different from those to which my own par-ents had paid heed.

"I'm only one man," I said to Mia Czielinski. "We're all individuals, and it's the differences in our experience that shape and make us."

"Not any more," she said. "This is the Age of Everyman, when every single one of us may entertain the ambition to experience all human pos-sibilities."

I remember thinking, although I was too polite and too cautious to say it aloud, that one of us had a very poor understanding of transfinite mathematics.

THIRTY-FIVE

I realized eventually that the real reason for the tightness and formality of the burgeoning Cape Adare community was the need—which the newcomers to the Cape really did experience as a *need*—to be in and out of one another's homes all the time during the summer months, savoring the intricate intimacies of each and every edifice. I realized too why my neighbors had not been in the least distressed by my failure to reciprocate their invitations. They would have been conspicuously disappointed if I had. I did, however, receive one actual visitor during my final years on the cape, who turned up on the doorstep unannounced.

She was frankly astonished by my own astonishment at her sudden appearance.

"I've been in Antarctica for months," she said, "mostly just over the hill in Lillie Marleen. I've been frightfully busy, but I've been waiting for you to invite me over. I did leave you a message when I arrived."

"I must have overlooked it or not taken it in—I had no idea you were here," I said, knowing that it was a woefully inadequate response. It had never occurred to me, as I marveled at what my neighbors had done with a new generation of shamirs, that I had been acquainted for nearly a century with one of the most prominent figures in contemporary shamir design and *the* person most likely to be making a fortune from ice-palace architecture.

I hadn't seen Emily in the flesh since Steve Willowitch had ferried us to Australia in his copter. People are supposed to keep the VE images in their answerphone AIs constantly updated, but they never do. People are also supposed to use camera transmission when they phone instead of merely invoking their VE images, but they never do that either—so you never get a true appreciation of actual appearance from VE interaction, even VE interaction that hasn't been allowed to slide into long silence. Emily had changed a great deal more than I had, but each of us was looking at a stranger.

"I should have called you anyway, message or no message," I said, still floundering in embarrassment, "and I always meant to, but I never quite . . . I've been so fearfully busy, you see. I launched the third part of the *History* last month."

"I'm sorry," she said, in a slightly injured voice. "I shouldn't have taken it for granted that it was safe to drop in."

I was quick to make amends—or at least to try. "It's *always* safe," I assured her. "For you, I'm always available."

"I thought you might be avoiding me," she said, arching her eyebrow a little. I'd seen exactly the same arch a dozen times while we were engaged in deep and meaningful conversation in our bouncing life raft, although she'd been a mere child. The difference between our ages would have seemed utterly unimportant to anyone else, but I could still see the child inside the adult, and she could still see the nonswimmer within the historian.

"Why would I do that?" I asked, mystified.

"Well," she said, "last time we were in close touch I tried to force money on you, and you refused to accept it—and then you ran off and got married. Ever since then, there's been a conventional tokenism about our conversations. I thought you hadn't forgiven me. I don't suppose you've grown much less poor in the interim, but you presumably know that I've gotten much richer. Forty or fifty times, I think—but it stacks up so fast that I can't keep count. Your parents used to be very sniffy about commerce, as I remember."

"Only some of them," I said. "It just happened to include the two who had most to say. But no, I certainly haven't been avoiding you, or even trying to keep you at arm's length. And as it happens, I'm not as poor as I was after my first divorce and probably won't ever be again. My dividend from the credit Papa Ezra and Mama Siorane piled up while they were working off-planet was quite substantial. It's mostly spent now, of course, but my *History* has begun to produce an income of sorts. . . ." I trailed off again, realizing all of a sudden that what I thought of as an income must look like very small change to someone who had been rich last time I spoke to her and was now "forty or fifty times" richer.

"I owe it all to you," she murmured, reading my mind. She murmured because she knew what my response would be.

"You don't owe nearly as much to me as I owe to you," I reminded her, before pressing on with indecent haste. "I take it that Lillie Marleen's going the same way as Cape Adare now—ice castles lining the main street and running a ragged ring around the old town?"

"You mean that you haven't even *seen* it?" I had contrived to take her aback.

"No," I said. "I've never been to Cape Hallett, let alone Lillie Marleen, although the neighbors I do see keep telling me that I should. I've been very busy. Is it really as wonderful as they say?"

"Morty," she said, with a sigh, "Lillie Marleen is currently number two on the official list of the world's Seven Wonders. It makes Cape Adare's ice palaces look like a set of drinking glasses set upside down to drain beside a sink. Don't you ever watch the news?"

"Only the headlines," I told her. "I'm a historian. At my present rate of progress, I expect to catch up with the twenty-seventh century in three or four hundred years' time."

"Oh, Morty," she said, with a much heavier sigh. "You were my first substitute parent, if only for three days. You're supposed to provide me with a role model, to be a source of inspiration. Here am I, playing a major part in the remaking of the Continent Without Nations, providing the wherewithal for the greatest art form of the fin-de-siecle, and you're still stuck in the second century, apart from scanning the headlines. Don't you *ever* get out, even in a VE hood?"

"I've seen most of the Cape Adare ice castles from the inside," I told her, "and it's only ten years or thereabouts since I spent a whole week in Amundsen."

"Doing something for the UN?"

"Not exactly," I admitted. "I was in hospital the whole time. I told you—I was injured. My leg was crushed while I was helping to rescue a man who'd fallen into a crevasse. It took days to grow new tissues, and the best part of a year to educate the leg so that it felt as if it was really *mine*."

I expected her to sigh again, but she laughed instead. "You have to let me take you out," she said. "Not once or twice, but fifty or a hundred times. I expect you'll hate it, but you have to do it anyway. I can't have you thinking that those glorified goblets over the way are the pinnacle of ice-palace achievement. I can show you light games you can never have imagined—and you'll look at them even if I have to drag you. They're the first fruit of my hands-on endeavors. I was *really annoyed* when you were so dismissive of that particular resolution, and I need to make you suffer by showing you what I've achieved."

"I still have a problem with psychosomatic conditions," I reminded her. "I always have to wear masks to protect me from snow blindness and summer rhapsody. I have trouble in ice palaces."

"It's *September*, Morty," she said, with mock exasperation. "Equinox time. If I wanted to blow your mind completely I'd leave it till December and the solstice. This will be a *gentle* introduction, just to get you in the mood. It's my pride and joy, Morty. You can't say no."

I remembered what Mia Czielinski had said about having a duty to explore the world's possibilities. As a historian, I knew it wasn't possible, because possibilities are lost with every day that passes, and even in the Age of Everyman an individual really is an individual, incapable of being in two places at the same time. As Emily Marchant's friend and mentor, though, I knew that I really had fallen down on the job and that it was high time I learned to swim again, metaphorically speaking. I didn't realize then how long it would be before I saw her in the flesh again, but I certainly realized how long it had been since I had last seen her, and I was appalled at my negligence in leaving it so long.

"I wasn't dismissive," I said, defensively. "I just had my own path to follow. I thought *you* were being dismissive. It's nearly ready, you know. Just a few more months."

"By then," she said, "I'll probably be gone—but that won't matter, will it? The Labyrinth is everywhere: the Universe Without Limits. Wherever I am, I'll always be able to keep in touch with your work. Mine isn't like that. To know what I amount to, you have to see and feel and touch the solid reality. I know you're not ready to follow me on the next leg of the journey, but I'm damned if I'll let you miss out on this one. You have to see what I've made, and you have to see it *with me*."

"I will," I said, wilting before the onslaught. "I wouldn't have it any other way."

THIRTY SIX

I suppose the next few weeks qualified as a holiday, even though I went home almost every night. It was the first holiday I'd taken since my second divorce and might even have qualified as the first since my aborted trip on *Genesis*, given that all the trips I'd taken with the Lamu Rainmakers and Sharane had been calculated to mingle a certain amount of study with the tourism. I can honestly say, however, that I had not the slightest intention of including the ice palaces of Lillie Marleen, Dumont D'Urville, and Porpoise Bay in my history of death.

That was perhaps as well, as I would have struggled in vain to recapture the subjective essence of the experience. To say that it was intoxicating would hardly have done it justice; each edifice was an entire gallery of psychotropic effects. At first, being inside the ice palaces made me dizzy and queasy, but Emily was relentless. She refused to believe that I couldn't adapt, and by degrees I did. I'm sure that I never learned to see them as she did, but I did begin to grasp the awesome wonder and sublimity of their structure.

I had always accepted the conventional wisdom which said that Isaac Newton was mistaken in identifying seven colors in the rainbow, having been prejudiced toward that number for mystical reasons, and that there were really only five: red, yellow, green, blue, and violet. Emily's ice palaces taught me that I and the world had been quite wrong and that the human eye was capable of more education in this regard than nature had ever seen fit to provide. There are, in fact, at least a dozen colors in the visual spectrum, and perhaps as many as twenty—although we have not, to this day, attained a consensus in naming them.

When visiting Mia Czielinski and my other neighbors on Adare I had thought of "adaptation" to the ice palaces as a mere matter of soothing reflexive discomfort and disturbance, but what Emily's architecture demanded was something far more complex and far reaching. I was woefully inadequate to the task—and I knew that I would never be prepared to put in the kind of work that would have been necessary to raise my perceptiveness even as far as mediocrity.

"Can't you get the same effects with glass?" I asked Emily, wondering why the earliest gantzers had not discovered a similar art form when they had first begun to work with biotech-fused sand.

"Similar," she admitted, "but they're much harder to manage. Not worth the effort, in my opinion, although artists in the tropic zones have already joined the competition. Most of the light-management work in an ice palace is done by the skin that mediates between the warm spaces and the cold walls. Quite apart from the fact that glass working doesn't require membranes of that sort, they're brand-new technology, unique to the new generation of shamirs."

"But glass houses have been around for a long time," I observed. "Surely *somebody* glimpsed these kinds of possibilities."

"Back in the twenty-second century the main priority was making sure that glass houses were safe, in the sense that they wouldn't break if you threw stones at them," she told me. "They were so crude, optically speaking, that it's no wonder that nobody managed to lay foundation stones for this kind of artwork. In those days, gantzing was just a matter of sticking things together and making sure they stayed stuck. You got a lot of glitter, but there was no practical way to increase the scale and delicacy of the prismatic effects. Ice-palace-like effects couldn't be foreshadowed in glass even in the twenty-fourth century, when the first true shamirs came in."

"Well," I said, looking up into the heady heights of a kaleidoscopically twisted spire, "you've certainly made up for lost time. This is the work of a genius."

"I don't know about that," she said, with sincere modesty. "Once you've mastered a few simple tricks the effects are easy to contrive. I got a head start because I devised the techniques—now that I've shown the way, real architects are beginning to take over the reins."

"But you're still learning," I pointed out. "You could stay ahead of the game if you put your mind to it. Maybe it's time for you to move on to work in glass."

"Absolutely not. Ice is my medium. But there's ice and *ice*. This is just a beginning. As soon as the twenty-eighth gets under way I'll be off to where the real action is."

"The Arctic?" I said, foolishly.

"Hardly," she said. "There's no scope here for real hands-on work."

It finally dawned on me that by "here" she meant Earth, and that what she'd meant when she'd first mentioned the next step on her journey—the one that she knew I wouldn't be able to take—she'd meant a journey into space.

"This is just the beginning," she added, while I was still working it out. "When the twenty-eighth century gets under way, I want to be where the real action is."

"The moon?" I said, foolishly.

"Titan, Dione, and Enceladus," she replied. "Then on to Nereid and Triton. So far, the colonists of the outer planet satellites have only been digging in, excavating nice warm wombs way down where the heat is. For five hundred years we've been imagining the conquest of space as if we were moles. Glass is poor stuff by comparison with ice, but water ice might not be the optimum. All *this* is just icing on a cake, Morty. It's not even continental engineering. The next generation of shamirs will lay the groundwork for planetary engineering. Not boring old terraformation—*real* planetary engineering. Give me four hundred years, Morty, then come visit me in the ice palaces of Neptune's moons, and I'll show you a work of art."

All I could say in response to that, in my feeblest manner, was, "You're going to the far edge of the Oikumene? That's as far from home as you can go."

"For the moment. It won't seem so far once the kalpas report in—but for now, it's where the opportunities are."

"But you're rich," I said, redoubling my foolishness. "You have more credit than you'll need for a millennium and more. You don't need to leave Earth to seek your fortune."

"Not *that* kind of opportunity, Morty," she said, without a hint of mockery or censure. "The opportunities of the future. Once you've caught up with the twenty-seventh century, you know, you'll have to catch up with the twenty-eighth and the twenty-ninth, and in the end, you're bound to run into the present. Then, even *you* will have to look forward—and that will mean looking *upward*. I know you can do it, Morty, and I know you will, when you're ready. You learned to swim, eventually, and you haven't had a headache for days. You've adapted to *this* kind of enlightenment. It's only a matter of time before you can see the way the world is going—the way the Oikumene is going."

"Enlightenment" was what the architects of ice palaces called their new art. I'd always thought it a mere affectation, more than a trifle disrespectful to the heroes of the eighteenth-century revolutions in thought and theory—but I realized when Emily used the word that it was layered far more deeply with deliberate ambiguities than I'd previously understood.

"There'll always be Earthbound humans," I told her, mechanically having not quite recovered my composure. "The Gaean extremists will never turn it into a nature reserve. We'll have to keep making room for new generations by exporting a percentage of the population, but there'll always be a role for the old. For educators. For *historians*."

"But you're *not* old, Morty," Emily reminded me. "Youth shouldn't be a mere preparation for being old. Neither should adulthood. You can't decide now what you'll be in three hundred or three thousand years' time—and if you can, you shouldn't. One day, Morty, your history of death will be finished—and it will be no good sitting down to start a history of life, because that's just the other side of the same coin. You'll have to start on the future, just like the rest of us. It wouldn't do you any harm to get a little practice, would it?"

"It's not like that," I told her, although I wasn't sure that I could even convince myself of it. "I may be a historian, but I live my everyday life in the present, just like everybody else. There's nothing wrong with being contentedly Earthbound."

"You've been living in a fake lighthouse for more than twenty years," she pointed out, "without even realizing that an entire city of light was growing up just over the horizon. Don't you think that says something about the kind of person you're in danger of becoming?"

Her rhetoric had come a long way since she was eight years old, and I hadn't been able to resist its force even then.

"I'm not a recluse," I told her, realizing as I said it that it was exactly what I was. "I'm just trying to be myself," I added, realizing as I said it that I still had not the slightest idea what that was supposed to mean.

"But you can see the light, can't you?" she said, pointing up into the magical spire. "You can see that there are new possibilities before us now. You can see that wherever we live our everyday lives, we're looking out on to an infinite stage. The universe is waiting for us, Morty, and we can't keep it waiting forever just because we're busy playing in our tiny little garden."

"Sharane used to say that play is all there is," I told her, reflexively. "She used to say that when all the threats and dangers had been eliminated, play was all that was left to lend purpose to existence."

"Sharane was a fool," said Emily, without an atom of doubt in her voice. "She couldn't even spell her name correctly."

Emily knew, of course, that Mama Siorane had contrived a death on Titan that everyone she knew out there had considered glorious. It seemed that she was determined to do likewise.

"I'm thinking of moving," I told her, improvising furiously. "Somewhere new. Somewhere hot. South America, maybe."

"To work on the fourth part of the *History of Death*," she said. She wasn't one of my parents, so she didn't try to make it sound like an insult or a condemnation, but I couldn't help hearing it that way.

"It's important," I said. "It's relevant. And it can't be put off for a thousand years. The past is perishable, Em. If we don't work to keep it alive, it dies. The artifacts crumble. The documents evaporate. Even ice palaces melt. All *this* is temporary. Somebody has to keep track of it all. Somebody has to provide the continuity. I have to stay in touch. I could work on the moon, but that's as far as you can go in the Universe Without Limits without losing touch with Earth. One day, historians will have to work with a much broader canvas, extending all the way to the Oort Halo, and probably beyond, but if that job's to be done properly, the groundwork will have to be laid. I'm sorry you're going. I know I shouldn't be, but I am."

"We'll keep in touch," she promised. "No more overlooking messages, no more wondering if one of us is avoiding the other."

"It won't be the same," I said. "You can't have a conversation with someone in the outer system—the time delay won't allow it. All I ever got from Mama Siorane was a series of lectures."

"Letters, Morty, not lectures," she said. "You're a historian remember? You know what it was like back in the good old days, when people in London needed the *Penny Post* to keep in touch with people in Canterbury because it was a five-day journey on foot."

Always the pedant, I had to point out that by the time they had the *Penny Post*, mail coaches had cut that kind of journey to a matter of hours—but she was right, in principle. From Mama Siorane I'd had lectures; from Emily I would get letters—and I would always be able to see her face, and even touch her VE sim.

"I'll still be sorry," I said, stubbornly. "My parents are all dead. You're all that I have left from that phase of my existence."

"Nonsense," she said. "You just can't be bothered to look for the rest of it while you're stuck in the distant past. It's time to move on, Morty— and I don't mean South America. It's time to reacquaint yourself with the world you live in."

She was right, of course. I promised that I would, but I probably wouldn't have kept the promise very well if the world had given me a choice. I would have changed in my own good time, at my own plodding pace, if I hadn't been moved to more urgent action by forces beyond my control. As it happened, however, I was soon snatched up by a catastrophe that seemed at first, at least to my unready understanding, to be as furious and as far-reaching in its fashion as the Great Coral Sea Disaster.

THIRTY-SEVEN

The third part of *The History of Death*, entitled *The Empires of Faith*, was decanted into the Labyrinth in August 2693. In a defensive introduction I announced that I had been forced to modify my initial ambition to write a truly comprehensive history and acknowledged that my previous hyper-Gordian knot had not been worthy of the name of aleph because it had been so overly ethnocentric. I explained that I hoped to correct this fault by degrees but admitted that I was unlikely ever to attain a genuinely universal breadth. I promised, however, to do my utmost to be eclectic and to provide my future commentaries with as much supportive justification as was practicable.

This apology was not as sincere as it was designed to seem. It might have been more honest to admit that I did not wish to be a mere archivist of death and feared getting bogged down in the sheer mass of the data that pertained to my current and future researches. I could not regard all episodes in humankind's war against death as being of equal interest, and I wanted to be free to ignore those which I thought peripheral and repetitive. I was more far interested in interpretation than mere summary.

I justified that in my text by arguing that insofar as the war against death had been a moral crusade, I felt fully entitled to draw morals from it.

This preface, understandably, dismayed those critics who had already urged me to be more dispassionate. Some academic reviewers were content to condemn the new volume without even bothering to inspect the rest of the commentary, although that sector of the book was no longer than the equivalent sector of the second part and seemed to me to benefit from a rather more fluent style. It is, of course, possible that the reviewers were put off by the abundance of the data collated in support, which was indeed fearsome.

Other critics complained of my commentary that the day of "mute text" was dead and gone and that there was no place in the modern world for arguments whose primary illustrations resolutely refused to move, but I disregarded them as mere fashion victims. The imminent death of unembellished text had been announced so many times before that the new attempt to bury it seemed puerile.

Unlike many of my contemporaries, whose birth into a world in which religious faith was almost extinct had robbed them of all sympathy for the imperialists of dogma, I proposed that the great religions had been one of the finest achievements of humankind. I regarded their development as a vital stage in the evolution of society, considering them as social technologies whose use had permitted a spectacular transcendence of the former—tribal and regional—limits of community.

Faiths, I suggested, were the first instruments that were capable of binding together different language groups, and even different races. It was not until the spread of the great religions, I pointed out, that the possibility came into being of gathering all men together into a single common enterprise.

I was not recklessly incautious in offering these observations. I took care to regret that the principal product of this great dream had been two millennia of bitter and savage conflict between adherents of different faiths, and between adherents of different versions of the same faith. I was not content, however, simply to praise the ambition while deploring its misshapen outcome. I retained some slight sympathy for those jihads and crusades in whose formulation people had tried to attribute more meaning to the sacrifice of life than they ever had before.

I had already examined, in the first part of my history, the implications of the fact that one of the most common pre-Crash synonyms for human being—derived, of course, from the ancient Greek—was *mortal*, and that the term had continued to carry even greater significance once the prospect of emortality was in sight. Now I examined the implications of the the most common Latin-derived synonym for human being: *individual*.

To describe humans as "undivided ones" is to take it for granted that death divides, and that the mortal part of humanity is neither the only nor the most vital part. This blatant fiction, I suggested, was the most powerful of all the weapons deployed by primitive mortals in their psychological war against death. Whereas other historians of my own day thought it a hastily improvised crutch, I saw it as an item of field artillery, parent of the heavy cannon of prophecy and scripture.

My comparative analysis of the great religious traditions was, I hope, reasonably evenhanded. I tried to pay appropriate compliments to all of them. Inevitably, the summation that attracted the most criticism, in a world that was still host to more than four million self-proclaimed Buddhists, three million Jews, two million Hindus and nearly three hundred thousand followers of Islam, was that of Christianity—the only great religion to have been officially declared extinct.

To tell the truth, I was particularly fascinated by the symbology of the Christian mythos, which had taken as its central image the death on the cross of Jesus and had tried to make that one image of death carry an enormous allegorical load. I was entranced for a while by the idea of Christ's death as a force of redemption and salvation: by the daring pretense that this person had died *for others*. I extended my argument to take in the Christian martyrs, who had added to the primal crucifixion a vast series of symbolic and morally significant deaths. This collectivity of legends, I suggested, ought to be regarded as a colossal achievement of the imagination, a crucial victory by which death and its handmaiden, pain, were dramatically transfigured in the theater of the human imagination.

I was somewhat less impressed by the Christian conversion of the idea of death as a kind of reconciliation: a gateway to heaven, if properly met; a gateway to hell, if not. It seemed to me to be less ambitious as well as less original than the central motif of the crucified Christ. The idea of absolution from sin following confession, particularly the notion of deathbed repentance, seemed to me to be a tolerably daring raid into the territories of the imagination previously ruled by fear of death, but later confusions imported to the mythos along with the idea of God's grace were an obvious spoliation. Even so, Christian eschatology had served its purpose, and whatever its imperfections the various versions of that eschatology had been at least as effective as those of its rival faiths.

This entire collectivity of legends, I proposed, ought to be regarded as a colossal achievement of the imagination: a crucial victory by which death and its handmaiden, pain, were dramatically transfigured in the theater of the human imagination. The fact that Christianity was now extinct was, I suggested, eloquent testimony to the efficiency with which it had done its work. In a world that had tamed and all-but-conquered death, its carefully calculated absurdities had no utility whatsoever.

THIRTY EIGHT

Perhaps paradoxically, the majority of my critics were no better pleased by my account of the defects of Christianity than my account of its strengths. Few of my fellow historians were able to accept my view of religions as systems of psychological armaments, and their refusal even to board my train of thoughts robbed them of all sympathy for its subsequent stations, let alone its terminus. Many of them were quick to point out that it was what I applauded in Christianity that had sealed its doom on the world stage.

My critics were, of course, correct to argue that it was the ridiculous emphasis of most Christian sects on personal salvation and the imminence of apocalypse that had ensured their redundancy after the Crash. The relative success of the Eastern religious traditions in a world of putative emortals was probably ensured by their reference to a much greater timescale. I was in better agreement with conventional theory when I admitted that even true emortals could derive valuable psychological comforts and benefits from the attempt to think in terms of 4,320,000,000-year-long kalpas and 311,040,000,000,000-year-long mahakalpas, but my attempt to track the corollaries of this thesis soon departed from the common track and lost the grudging sympathy that the argument had briefly gained.

The fundamental ingenuity of the Eastern traditions could, I suggested, be seen as a brilliantly simple inversion of the key move in the Western traditions. In the West, the aim of the "individual" human was to win for his death-resistant element the privilege of a happy immortality. In the East, where the notion of human-as-individual never took root, the aim was not to acquire immortality but to escape it. Buddhism refused belief in a soul or "person," asserting as an axiom that there is no permanent state underlying the ceaseless flux of physical and mental states, and that death is merely a transition between incarnations. Hope was directed toward the eventual annihilation that was nirvana rather than the salvation of heaven.

I extrapolated my own system of metaphors by suggesting that Buddhism had outlasted Christianity because the weaponry its items of faith offered for use in the war against death was more intimate and more personal, more akin to swords than cannon.

The furtherance of this analysis did not please contemporary Buddhists at all. They objected to my judgment that the doctrine of dukkha—the "ill fare" that rendered life itself inherently unsatisfactory—was a last-ditch defense all but equivalent to capitulation with the great enemy. They also disliked my account of Maya, the symbolic embodiment of the temptations and allurements that stand in the way of nirvana, and they interpreted my careful comparison of the Tibetan *Book of the Dead* with its Egyptian equivalent as a disparagement. Mercifully, there were no Jains around to object to my lukewarm account of the attempt to fight death with death, seeking liberation in self-mortification and the slow saintly suicide of calculated starvation.

The surviving Hindus were no better disposed than the surviving Buddhists toward my elaborate analysis of the Advaita Vedanta and the three key figures bearing on the problem of death: Shiva, Kali, and Yama. I received several personal communications suggesting that it was a great pity that I had not made better use of the opportunities of my childhood. Had I only been prepared to listen and learn, they argued, my neighbors in the valley could have helped me to a far better understanding of the invaluable notion of the Brahman-Atman and the illusion of the world. I received other communications complaining bitterly that I had not paid due homage to Vishnu, and a further series offering to help me along the path of Yoga to a truly splendid isolation from matter.

I will freely admit that my text was incomplete and that it focused on the examples most helpful to my argument. I could not agree with the not-very-numerous contemporary practitioners of "natural magick" and shamanism that I had unjustly neglected their traditions, which had never been associated with anything remotely resembling an empire of faith, but I have to admit now that I was probably wrong to represent both Taoism and Confucianism as mere "defensive formulations" institutionalized in opposition to the spread of Buddhism. I regarded the Tao merely as a variant of the Buddhist Way, despite that it had not taught rebirth and karma, but it seems to me now that the aim of wu-wei was interestingly different from nirvana.

At the time, I was deflected from deeper analysis by the fact that later Taoism had replaced the mystic quest for eternity with a very mundane desire for longevity and postmortem security in legends of the search for the elixir of immortality and the heavenly Pure Land—although the importance of the Pure Land in the mythology of Imperial Japan, alongside the Zen-based disciplines of satori and bushido, should have made me far more attentive. In my own defense, I should point out that I did pay slightly more attention to the Confucian ideas of Yin and Yang, but only in the context of a typology of different images of the "divided individual."

In spite of all these defects, however, I thought *The Empires of Faith* to be an interesting work and a useful contribution to humankind's attempt to understand our own past.

It may seem strange to the modern reader that I had no inkling of the way in which the third part of my *History* would be read and reinterpreted by readers who had no affiliation to any preexistent religious tradition, but I simply was not thinking in those terms. I was blinkered by my preconceptions, taking it for granted that the vast majority of Earthbound humans who did not belong to any of the eccentric minorities on whose metaphorical toes I might be trampling could all be reckoned as dispassionate rationalists much like myself.

Given that I have taken so much trouble to record the gist of my conversations with Ziru Majumdar, this may seem foolish—but even though I realized at the time that Majumdar's philosophy must have some kind of movement behind it I had no idea how widespread that movement was. I had not the faintest idea that it was capable of exerting such a grip on the imagination of millions that it could and would be extrapolated to extremes that I can only call insane. I feel obliged to say, however, that even if I *had* anticipated the uses to which the now-notorious sections of *The Empires of Faith* would be put, I would not have left them out or ameliorated their tone. I was a historian in search of understanding, and those chapters of my commentary were a significant step on my intellectual journey.

No one is infallible, and I accept that there is a possibility that my analysis of Christianity may have been utterly misconceived, but I do not think that it was—and even if it had been, I would still have been justified in stating my case. I meant what I wrote, and I meant no more by what I wrote than what I intended to mean. It is not my fault that other readers imported a very different meaning into my observations or that they used the trails which I had patiently laid down in the Labyrinth to track down data for their own dark and nasty purposes. I do not regret that part three of my *History of Death* began the work of making me famous, but I do regret that it first made me notorious, and that it did so by linking my name—firmly and, it seems, forever—with Thanaticism.

PART THREE
Notoriety

We know that as a human embryo develops—and the development of the Helier womb and the Zaman transformation has done nothing to alter *this* fact—its form is sculpted by death. It is shaped by the selective killing of superfluous elements of the developing cell mass. We know too that it is the permanent withering of synaptic connections in the brain that creates the preferred pathways which provide the electrical foundations of the personality. Bodily and mentally, we are etched by death. Death is the lens that focuses the potential ubiquity of DNA into the precise definition of a species and the potential ubiquity of Everyman into the precise definition of a person. Death may threaten each of us with the prospect of becoming nothing, but without the everpresence and relentless activity of death none of us could ever have become anyone.

—Hellward Lucifer Nyxson
The Thanaticist Manifesto, 2717

THIRTY-NINE

S hortly after Emily blasted off on the first leg of her journey to the outer reaches of the Oikumene I was thrown out of my hermitage by the landlord. He'd had a purchase offer he couldn't refuse from some Bright Young Thing who wanted to demolish it and build yet another ultimate ice castle. I didn't mind; I'd already told Emily that I intended to move, and since voicing the intention I'd begun to hunger for the color, spontaneity, and sultry abandonment of warmer climes. I decided that there would be time enough to celebrate the advent of the new Ice Age when the glaciers had reached the full extent of their reclaimed empire and that I might as well make what use I could of Gaea's temporary fever before it cooled.

As soon as the twenty-eighth century got under way I moved to Venezuela, resolved to dwell in the gloriously restored jungles of the Orinoco, amid their teeming wildlife.

Following the destruction of the southern part of the continent in the second nuclear war, Venezuela and Colombia had attained a cultural hegemony in South America that they had never surrendered. Brazil and Argentina had long since recovered, both economically and ecologically, from their disastrous fit of ill temper, but the upstart rivals that had overtaken them in the meantime were still considered to be the home of the avant garde of all the Americas. There was then no place on Earth that contrasted more sharply with the ice fields of Antarctica than Venezuela, and it was virtually untouched by the new legion of gantzing artists; the notorious and still-extending House of Usher had been raised out of the Orinoco mud with the aid of techniques that now seemed primeval.

I used the compensation money I had extracted from my former landlord to buy a modest hometree way upstream in La Urbana, a town that had once been the hub of a massive ecological reconstruction operation but had since become the effective terminus of the river-based tourist trade. It was a busy place by comparison with Cape Adare, but its business was conducted at a much slower pace. Its inhabitants seemed idle almost to the point of somnolence, even when they were working flat out.

I liked living beside the great river. Grizel's death in the Kwarra was far enough behind me by then for the psychological scar to have healed, and I found it rather charming that the Venezuelans, unlike the Nigerians, had reintroduced alligators to the Orinoco shallows.

Although I was busy with overdue revisions of the first versions of parts one and two of my history, and with intensive research for part four, Emily's criticisms made me pay far more attention than had lately become my habit to the news *behind* the headlines, and it was thus that I became belatedly aware of the insidious spread of the attitudes that I had first met in the person of Ziru Majumdar and the dark fashions that were soon to climax in the rebirth of Thanaticism.

As soon as I fully understood what I had been missing I swore that I would never be so neglectful again. As *the* historian of mortality, it was plainly my duty to keep track of that tiny fraction of death's history that was still in the making. In the beginning, however, I did not realize the significance of what was happening.

The TV pundits who became more and more anxious about "the pornography of death" initially took a censorious line, taking it for granted in their customary fashion that all sensible folk agreed with them. It did not seem to them—or to me—that there was anything new or particularly disturbing about the growing fascination with images of pain and death.

Death was, of course, still present in the world, but the end of *inevitable* death was in sight. The last false emortals had not yet passed away, but their days were numbered in the thousands, if not in the hundreds. The requiem for the Old Human Race was in progress; had there been any church bells remaining in the world, they would have been tolling for our ancestor species. In such circumstances, a revival of interest in death seemed only natural, and the frank morbidity of that interest did not seem particularly perverse or dangerous. The remaining triple rejuvenates were all celebrities, simply by virtue of having taken the technology of repair to its limits. The death of every one of them was intrinsically newsworthy—far more newsworthy, in fact, than the occasional accidental deaths of relatively young emortals.

As a historian, I was able to take a certain connoisseur pleasure in what seemed to me to be a perfectly understandable irony: that an audience of true emortals whose IT gave them complete control over the ravages of pain should have become fascinated with the idea of death. I thought it entirely appropriate that the chief corollary of that interest should be a renaissance of interest in the role that death had played in the prenanotech world, when it had almost invariably been accompanied by physical pain and psychological anguish.

Having met Ziru Majumdar, I already knew that some emortals had begun experimenting with the experience of pain. As a historian, I knew well enough that even in the earliest days of Internal Technology there had been some people who used the resilience it gave them to indulge a taste for violent and dangerous activities, and that there had been a thriving pornography of violence in the twenty-second century, born of the optimism that misled the earliest false emortals to think that they might have set foot on an escalator that would take them all the way to true emortality. Unfortunately, I was slow to combine the two items of knowledge into an anticipation of the way in which the new fascination with the pornography of death would give rise to a new masochism.

The groundwork for the so-called Thanaticist Manifesto was laid not merely by people like Ziru Majumdar but by people like Mia Czielinski. No blame attaches to Emily Marchant, of course, but her artistic adventures had made it clear to millions of people that what they had previously accepted as the bounds of aesthetic experience were far narrower than anyone had expected. Once the quest for new aesthetic experiences became worldwide, the opportunity was opened for Majumdar's explorations in discomfort and distress to move into the cultural mainstream. Now that true emortality was almost universal, and nanotechnology was even cleverer in compensating for pain and injury than it had been in the twenty-second century, the kind of people who delighted in the reeducation of their eyes by ice palaces moved on easily enough to the supposed reeducation of their flesh, testing the limits of their psychological and physical endurance in every imaginable way.

I would probably have realized this sooner had I stayed in Antarctica, but from the viewpoint of La Urbana in the first decade of the twenty-eighth century the whole affair looked like a storm in a teacup—

the teacup in question being the weird parallel universe of VE land. It was there that the new pornography of violence was produced and marketed and there that the TV pundits took leave to lament the fact and issue terrible prophecies about its likely effects. I could never take the garrulous imbeciles seriously, and the force of that habit made me laugh derisively when they first began to proclaim, in terrified tones, that the new masochism was bound to cause a new Thanaticism to rear its ugly head.

Alas, even casters have to be right sometimes.

FORTY

I t was the followers of a movement that had flourished at the very end of the twenty-fifth century and the beginning of the twenty-sixth who had actually coined the term *Thanaticism*. It had been an early folly of the last generation of false emortals, whose last representatives were now in the process of quitting the Earth. Some of those unlucky enough to have been born after the advent of Zaman transformations, resentful of the disastrous choice made by their foster parents not to take advantage of the new technology, had perversely elected to reject the benefits of rejuvenation too, making a fetish out of living only a "natural" life span.

At the time, the Thanaticists had often been bracketed in common parlance—mistakenly, I think—with the earlier cult of Robot Assassins, who had themselves been mistakenly thought of as a revival of the twenty-second-century movement of self-styled Eliminators.

The Robot Assassins had taken the view that the progressive cyborgization of double and triple rejuvenates equipped with ever-more-sophisticated IT was transforming them into "robots" no longer capable of empathizing with "true" human beings: implicitly sociopathic individuals. The result of this progressive dehumanization of the old, the Robot Assassins contended, was that Earth was falling into the hands of unhuman individuals whose lack of fellow-feeling would eventually manifest itself as malevolence toward their feeling kin. In order to prevent the "robotic revolution" the Robot Assassins had embarked upon a campaign of murder, while swearing an oath that they would commit suicide before suffering "robotization" themselves. It was this last aspect of their credo that had caused contemporary commentators to put the first Thanaticists in the same bracket, even though the Thanaticists did not advocate assassination as a political means.

In the twenty-sixth century no one had thought it possible that genetically endowed emortals could ever embrace Thanaticism, and the cult was conventionally regarded as a petty and essentially futile rebellion against fate, whose adherents would swiftly eliminate themselves from the fabric of history. There were, however, a few Thanaticists who encouraged the view that they were closely akin to the Robot Assassins by arguing that in spite of their exclusive reliance on biological mechanisms of longevity, true emortals would suffer robotization nevertheless and that the inheritors of Earth would eventually become indistinguishable from programmed artificial intelligences.

When the TV current affairs shows of the early twenty-eighth century began their earnest debate as to whether all of this madness might be reborn, I assumed that it was just talk for talk's sake. Perhaps I underestimated the influence of the pundits and the power of talk for talk's sake to generate self-fulfilling prophecies, but I cannot deny that I was dead wrong.

Most of the people who had begun, like Ziru Majumdar, to question whether the technologies to which they owed their preservation from pain, disease, and aging were denying them something in terms of experience were content merely to dabble with pain and other sensations associated with physical injury. Once such dabbling began, there was an inevitable temptation to take it further and further, testing and extending its limits. Among these supposed "connoisseurs of human experience" there emerged a curious kind of hierarchy, in which those who explored further and more complex extremes of discomfort and distress won considerable praise and prestige from the less daring.

The revival of Thanaticist ideas was at first purely theoretical. Although many hobbyist masochists became fond of asserting that the ultimate human experience must be the one that emortals had postponed indefinitely, there was no immediate rush to put aside the delay. There was, however, extensive experimentation with increasingly elaborate exercises in "recreational torture." As time went by, and these activities became increasingly ingenious and daring, the leading proponents of the new philosophy of extreme experience began to look around for "martyrs," who might be prepared to go all the way.

There had always been suicides in the true emortal population—indeed, once a firm line had been ruled beneath the death toll of the Decimation, suicide became the commonest cause of death in three-quarters of the Earthly nations, outnumbering accidental deaths by a fac-

tor of three in the most extreme cases. Such acts were, however, moti-
vated by personal idiosyncrasy. None of the first dozen Thanaticist martyrs, all of whom were posthumously hailed, had committed suicide for
any reason remotely linked to the cause of sensation seeking. I daresay
that they would all have been horrified to be hailed as heroes and potential role models, but they were not around to object.

I would have been unpleasantly surprised by the developments of
the 2710s and 2720s even if I had remained a mere spectator, but I did
not. The new Thanaticists would probably have taken a considerable
interest in my work anyway, simply because I was now well established
in the scholarly sectors of Labyrinth as the leading historian of death. As
chance would have it, though, they rose to prominence within twenty
years of the publication of the third part of the project: the one that dealt
so extensively, and so sympathetically, with the ancient martyrs of Chris-
tendom.

My interpretation of the myth of Christ and those who had followed
him to horrible and ignominious destruction was publicly hailed by the
prophets of the new Thanaticism as a major inspiration, and it was publicly claimed as proof of the respectability of their philosophy. The so-
called Thanaticist Manifesto of 2717, which carried the ridiculous and
obviously pseudonymous byline "Hellward Lucifer Nyxson," quoted
from *The Empires of Faith*—though not so extensively as to be in breach
of copyright—and held up my work as an example to everyone interested in recovering the full range of sensations that early humans had
been "privileged to enjoy." The claim that anything I had written could
be taken as support for the absurd manifesto was nonsensical, but it was
read and heard by millions more people than ever bothered to look at
the history itself.

My ideas were swiftly usurped, horribly perverted and lasciviously
adopted—in their perverted forms—as key items of Thanaticist lore. The
Thanaticists claimed that their own expeditionaries to the extremes of
human experience were, like the Christian martyrs and their model, suffering and dying *on behalf of others*. According to Nyxson and his more
vociferous followers, Thanaticist martyrs were nobly crucifying themselves so that the New Human Race would not lose touch with the more
exotic possibilities of life, liberty, and the pursuit of self-knowledge.

I tried to protest, of course, but at first I protested privately and entirely in vain. I sent messages to people who misquoted and misrepresented me, begging them to desist, although I could not contrive to discover the real identity of Hellward Lucifer Nyxson. Such replies as I received were content to assure me that I had misunderstood the import of my own work. It quickly became clear that I would need to react more forcefully if I were to have any effect at all—but I had no idea how to go about it.

While I dithered, events moved on rapidly and relentlessly. Thanks to false advertisements by the most outspoken Thanaticists, I became a hero of the movement: not merely an inspiration but a guiding light. The trails I had laid down in the Labyrinth to collate data regarding the myriad forms of Christian martyrdom and make them more easily navigable became a handbook for young Thanaticists bent on innovative self-mutilation. For a while, they all drew back from the brink of the ultimate sacrifice, but the 2720s saw an epidemic of "recreational crucifixions" whose willing victims vied to set new records for self-suspension by ropes or nails, in various different positions.

It would have been bad enough had the crucified only claimed Christ for their inspiration, but the majority made the specific claim that it was *my* account of the meaning of the Christ myth that had inspired their adventures. Connoisseurs of other kinds of torture were equally enthusiastic to declare that it was my reinterpretation of the Golden Legend that had given multifarious examples of the various saints to the emortals of the twenty-eighth century and made them newly meaningful.

Invitations to crucifixions, scarifications, and burnings began to pile up in the files of my answering machine. I refused them all, but they kept on coming.

One side effect of the unwanted publicity was that my history began to produce a decent income. Unfortunately, the money that poured into my account seemed to me to be steeped in blood, tainted by torture. I was reluctant to spend it and stopped trying to give it away when many of the intended recipients refused it on exactly the same grounds.

I hoped for a while that the fad would soon pass, preferably before any lives were actually sacrificed, but the cult continued to grow, feeding vampirically on the naive fascination of its emortal audience. Gaea's latest fever was cooling as the new Ice Age began, its crisis having passed, but the accompanying delirium of human culture had evidently not yet reached and surpassed what Ziru Majumdar called "the cutting edge of experience."

FORTY ONE

From the very beginning, I found notoriety inconvenient. At first, I attempted to keep a low profile, programming my answerphone AI to stall all inquiries, whatever their source or nature. But I soon realized that the strategy was assisting others to misquote and misrepresent me, and that my private protests were futile.

I had previously assigned the duty of answering my phone to a low-grade sloth, but I had been dissatisfied with its service for some time. I suspected that it was at least partly to blame for the fact that Emily's message telling me that she was in Antarctica had gone astray. Now I had the perfect excuse to replace it. I obtained a clever silver, although I begrudged the weeks of hard work that I had to devote to its education.

By the time I had equipped my new servant to put my side of the story, however, there had grown up a considerable clamor demanding that if I objected to the Thanaticists' view of my work I ought to plead my own case and submit to proper cross-examination. No matter how cleverly my new sim could be equipped to argue on my behalf it remained a sim, and therefore a sham, whose employment was easily made to seem like cowardice.

Had I not been living in a place as remote as La Urbana there would have been far more people beating a path to my actual door, but the fact that those who did make the trip found it arduous made them all the more determined not to be turned away. One or two were Thanaticists embarked on insane pilgrimages; the remainder was evenly divided between legmen for the casters and morally panicked opponents of the new movement who wanted me to stand up against my betrayers and denounce them with all the force I could muster.

I had never felt so desperately alone. The last of my parents had now been dead more than half a century, but I had never felt the lack of them so sharply. Emily had already left L-5 for the outer system and the time delay was beginning to make virtual conversation with her too difficult to serve any real consolatory function. In desperation, I forgave Sharane

Fereday for the ignominies she had heaped upon me prior to our parting, and called her. I should have known better.

Although Sharane had not become a wholehearted Thanaticist, she was by no means sympathetic to my plight. Her advice, though liberally given, was of little use. She explained at great length why it would do me no harm at all to expand the range of my own allegedly meager experiences. It should not have surprised me in the least that she had become a convert to the ardently curious philosophy of Ziru Majumdar, but it felt like a kind of treason nevertheless.

Fortunately, the veterans of my previous divorce proved to be more generous and more helpful, although they were too hardheaded to be capable of taking the matter very seriously. There was, alas, little or no consistency in their advice.

"They're just harmless lunatics, Morty," Axel told me. "It'll all be a nine days' wonder. All you have to do is ignore them, and they'll eventually go away." Jodocus took the same dismissive line, but the others were a little more forthcoming.

"You have to stand up to them," Minna advised. "You have to make your own position clear. Don't consent to be bullied, or they'll walk all over you. I know you can get the better of them, if you'll just make the effort." Eve wasn't quite so bullish about it, but she agreed that I ought to issue a detailed and formal account of my true position.

Any hope I might have had that Camilla would provide a casting vote soon vanished when I called her. "Personally," she opined, breezily, "I don't care how many of them mutilate themselves. I just wish they'd stop messing about with half-measures and go all the way. Think of it as surgery, removing one more cancer from Gaea's body. I only wish the Rad Libs were suicidally inclined. Did you know that Keir's still with them—actually on their so-called steering committee? I thought *he* was as mad as a New Human could be until this Thanaticist folly came along. Thanaticism is going to work to the Rad Libs' advantage, don't you think? How can anyone call the Libs and Mystics crazy while this kind of thing is going on? I know it's not your fault, but I wish you'd been a little more careful, Morty—heaven only knows whether you can repair the damage."

Despite their name, the Rad Libs with whom Keir was now allied were not quite the most radical of the Gaean liberationists. They were advocates of a drastic reduction of the numbers of Earthbound humanity rather than the total abandonment of Earth. There had always been "reductionists" in the Gaean ranks, but the new Ice Age had swelled their numbers and increased the fervor of their demands. As Camilla said, the activities of the recreational crucifixionists were making their policies seem somewhat less ridiculous.

I had hesitated over calling Keir, who had left the Rainmakers long before the divorce, but I was intrigued by Camilla's news. Curiously enough, he was more enthusiastic than any of the others. "Morty!" he said. "I've been meaning to call you for months. I read your commentary—all three parts. I even delved into the data stream."

"I'm flattered," I said.

"No need. It's good—but you really ought to put in some more about the mythical Gaea. The *real* mythical Gaea, that is, not the sanitized one. There's too much twentieth-century sentimentality loaded into the notion of Mother Earth, even now. I mean, Gaea gave birth to Uranus before mating with him—and their first crop of children were all monsters! Uranus couldn't stand the sight of them, so what did she do? Gave Chronos a sickle and told him to go cut Daddy's balls off, that's what! The blood that flooded from the wound brought forth yet another generation of children. All right up your street, I would have thought."

"Uranus didn't die," I pointed out, utterly mystified by the direction the conversation was taking.

"Maybe not, but he did retire from the Earthly scene forever. Castration became the price of new and better life, Morty—the twenty-second century in a nutshell. Then the sky-god vanished into the sky. That's us, Morty. We have to go—not today or tomorrow, mind, but we will have to go eventually. Reductionism is the first step, and the sooner we get used to the idea the sooner we can plan a sensible timetable. We've been properly born, thanks to Ali Zaman, and we have to start making preparations for giving way, not just for more of our own kind but for Gaea's next generation: products of a whole new evolutionary sequence."

I couldn't tell whether Keir's advocacy of a more extreme reductionism meant that the position of the entire Rad Lib movement was becoming more extreme or whether he was on the brink of defection to the cause of an even smaller minority. "The new human race will never abandon Earth entirely," I told him.

"Maybe not *entirely*," he admitted, giving the impression that he was reluctant to admit even that, "but that doesn't stop us making room for new kinds. We've grown up, and it's time for all but a few sane stewards to fly the nest. Isn't that what your *History* is aiming toward? I know I'm reading between the lines, but that's surely the direction it's going. If we stick around, we're still keeping company with death, right? These new Thanaticists are just the first symptom of continued infantilism, no? A horrible example to us all."

"I'm not a Gaean, Keir," I told him, mildly appalled by the cavalier way in which he had contrived to read his own ideas into my text. "Not even in a moderate sense. I'm a neo-Epicurean."

"That's what you think, Morty," he said, with a chuckle. "Maybe you're too close to your own work, but I can see the way it's going. We're all Gaeans now, and when the history of death is finished, the history of life has to begin. You'll get to the point when you get to the end, even if you haven't quite got there yet."

By the time I signed off I was numb with confusion—but I suppose it was Keir's conviction rather than Eve's and Minna's well-meant advice that made up my mind for me. It was bad enough to be misunderstood and misappropriated by the Thanatics, without the Gaean Libs and Mystics deciding that I would serve their cause just as well. I decided that I would come out of hiding and that I would come out fighting—for the plain and simple truth.

FORTY-TWO

I carefully sifted through the many invitations I had received to appear on the talk shows that provided the staple diet of contemporary live broadcasting. I accepted half a dozen—and as more poured in, I continued to accept as many as I could conveniently accommodate within the pattern of my life. Unfortunately, I had no idea what I was letting myself in for. Almost all of my VE time for more than a century had been spent in self-selected environments, and even though I had recently begun paying more attention to the news behind the headlines I had only the most rudimentary grasp of the conventions and protocols of live broadcasting.

I have no need to rely on my memories in recapitulating these episodes, because they remain on the record—but by the same token, there is no need for me to quote extensively from them. The interviews rapidly settled into a pattern. In the early days, when I was a relatively new face, my interrogators invariably started out by asking me to supply elementary details of my project and its progress, and their opening questions were usually stolen from uncharitable reviews.

"Some people seem to feel that you've been carried away, Mister Gray," more than one combative interviewer sneeringly began, "and that what started out as a sober history was already becoming an obsessive rant, ripe for appropriation by the Thanaticists. Did you decide to get personal in order to boost your sales?"

My careful cultivation of neo-Epicureanism and my years in Antarctica had provided a useful legacy of calm formality. I handled such accusations with punctilious politeness.

"The war against death has always been personal," I would reply. "It's still a personal matter, even for true emortals. Without a sense of personal relevance, it would be impossible for a historian and his readers to put themselves imaginatively in the shoes of the people of the ancient past, thus obtaining empathetic insight into their plight. If I seem to be making heroes of the men of the past when I describe their various crusades, it's because they *were* heroes—and I would far rather my contemporaries found inspiration in my work because they were eager to be heroes in the same cause."

"The Thanaticists say that's exactly what they're doing," the interviewers would put in, helpfully, thus setting up the next phase of the argument.

"Unfortunately," I would say, "the so-called Thanaticists have misunderstood what it means to be a hero in the contemporary context. Culturally, we have to go further forward, not backward. The engineering of emortality has made us victors in the war against death, and we need to retain a proper sense of triumph. We ought to celebrate our victory over death as joyously as possible, lest we lose our appreciation of its fruits."

My interviewers always appreciated that kind of link. "That's your judgment of the Thanaticists, then?" they would follow up, eagerly. "You think that they don't have a proper appreciation of the fruits of our victory over mortality?"

I did think that, and I was prepared to say so at any length my interlocutors considered appropriate. It soon became unnecessary for me to describe my *History* in detail, because the interviewers began to take it for granted that everyone knew who I was and what I'd done. I found it rather flattering that my place on the public agenda was secure and became even more relaxed when I was called upon to wax lyrical on the subject of the latest Thanaticist publicity stunt. Having established me as a public figure and put me at my ease, however, the casters became eager to throw me into the lion's den, where I could fight the misappropriators of my intellectual property man to man.

I thought I could handle it. So did Minna and Eve. Even Axel and Jodocus offered moral support, although Camilla did warn me to be careful and Keir lost interest when I told him for the sixth or seventh time that I didn't intend to say anything at all about Gaea.

FORTY-THREE

The most familiar public face of the Thanaticist cult, in 2732, was a woman named Emmanuelle Standress. She often insisted that she was merely a representative of the reclusive Hellward Lucifer Nyxson, but it was widely believed that there was no such person and that the Thanaticist Manifesto had been cooked up by a committee. She readily agreed to a live debate with me. Having studied her previous TV appearances I decided that she was unlikely to get the better of me. She was much younger than I—in her mid-fifties—and I could not help but think of her as a mere child ripe for instruction.

I can understand now that I was rather naive. EdEnt's stage managers must have laid much more elaborate plans than I suspected at the time. From their point of view, my new "career" as a public figure was something to be plotted with care, and they must have decided in advance what complications they were going to introduce into the plot in order to provide it with an adequate climax. I didn't know that my confrontation with Standress was merely a taster and that another was being carefully held in reserve. Emmanuelle Standress presumably understood the way the game was played far better than I did—she must, of course, have known that she was merely the challenger employed to build up audience anticipation for the *real* championship bout.

As I'd expected, Standress took much the same argumentative line as my old marriage-partner Keir, suggesting that I'd been too narrowly focused on my own work to grasp its wider implications.

"You're an academic historian, after all," she said, delicately veiling the tacit sneer. "A cloistered pedant, preoccupied with matters of detail, unable to see the wood for the trees. By your own admission, you're only three-sevenths of the way to your conclusion, and it's understandable that you don't want to get ahead of yourself—but we don't need to wait. We can already see the whole pattern and the central message. Without suffering and death, life is incomplete. If New Humans are to experience the entire spectrum of available experience, we must refuse nothing, including suffering in all its myriad forms—and, ultimately, death itself."

"If we're to refuse nothing," I retorted, "then we ought not to accept death until we have run the entire gamut of intermediate experiences—and we have no reason, as yet, to think of that range as anything less than infinite. If we can survive the cruel accidents of misfortune, we certainly shouldn't consent to die by our own hands, or even endanger ourselves unnecessarily, until the very end of time—or as close to it as we can get."

"Many of us will undoubtedly do their level best to do exactly that," she came back. "So many, in fact, that will they run the risk of dedicating all their resources to the task and losing sight of everything else. The instincts of self-preservation can easily become neurotically anxious and robotically stereotyped. It's partly for the benefit of the mechanically minded that others choose to exercise their freedom to be different: their freedom to sample extreme experiences without submitting their appetites to be jaded by eternity."

" 'Submitting their appetites to be jaded by eternity'!" I echoed, with all the contempt I could muster, for the manner of the phrase as well as its content. "Do you imagine that the martyrs of old were afraid of *boredom*? Are you so contemptibly stupid that you think they died in order that their hardier companions should not lose sight of that which surrounded them and never let them alone: the most brutal fact of their existence? No! The martyrs of old died in the attempt to make the inevitable meaningful. They tried with all their might to deploy faith as a means of transforming the ignominy of death into something fine and noble. They did it because *they had no alternative*; it was a measure of their desperation. They were heroic because, although they could not avoid death, they would not accept it for what it was. The imagination was their only weapon, and the pretense that death was not the end was their best strategy. There is all the difference in the world between their situation and ours. We have not entirely escaped death, which stalks us in a hundred sly guises, but we have a weapon infinitely more powerful than any possessed by the Old Human Race: we have *emortality*, and all the strategies that its use opens up. *Our* heroism is not that which makes the best of a bitter necessity, but the far better kind, which makes the most of a golden opportunity. Our heroes are those who live longest and best, whose imagination makes the most of life."

"Your commentaries are more honest than the man behind them," my opponent alleged, by way of retaliation. "They speak clearly of the self-dissatisfaction that you cannot now admit. They tell the truth that you cannot yet admit to yourself: that your life, like the life of so many of your fellow emortals, is already derelict and desolate, already decayed into routine and repetition, and that it stands in desperate need of redemption. Imagine a world composed of Mortimer Grays! Imagine a world that had no Hellward Nyxsons to disturb and disturb it, to display the faces of fear and terror, to play the part of dreams and darkness. What are people like you, without people like us, but the living dead? Why are you so ungrateful for the gift that we offer, when every word that you have written proclaims your own fascination for every intricate detail of lost mortality and all its torments?"

"An unwanted gift is not a gift at all," I told her, reverting to defensive mode. "An unnecessary gift that causes offense is an insult. We have the past to inform us of the awful reality of death, in far more detail than your efforts could ever contrive. Your hollow mockery of that past, which transforms its tragedy into play, is an insult to every mortal who ever lived and ever emortal who ever will. I study death in order to discover how best to live, and if I have not yet succeeded it is because my studies are incomplete, not because they require an abrupt perversion into nightmare."

I think I did tolerably well in that first debate, considering that I never realized that it was merely a preliminary bout. EdEnt must have thought so too, because they didn't wait long before setting me up for a tilt at the top man: the man many considered to be the New Human Race's first significant devil's advocate.

Yes, the casters declared, there *was* a Hellward Lucifer Nyxson. Moreover, he was now prepared to emerge from obscurity to defend the principles of his crusade against the belated objections of the man who had done so much to inspire the movement: that unlikely Judas of Thanaticism, Mortimer Gray.

FORTY-FOUR

S omewhat to my surprise, the pseudonymous Hellward Nyxson was rather less strident than Emmanuelle Standress had been. His name was by far the most flamboyant thing about him; his sim's face was tailored to a conservative model of handsomeness, and the VE from which he spoke was blandly staid, without the slightest hint of the pornography of death in its decor. His mild tone was presumably intended to upset whatever strategy I had prepared, as was the unexpected angle of his attack.

"I like your work very much," he said, softly, "not merely because it is so wonderfully comprehensive, but because I admire your defiant justification of what some would consider a flawed method. Like you, I am adamant that we cannot understand history unless we can use our imagination as cleverly as is humanly possible, to put ourselves in the shoes of the people of the past. If we are to understand them, we must try with all our might to see the world as they saw it, and I think you have come as close as any man alive to an understanding of the mortal condition, save for one tiny flaw."

He left it to me to say, "What flaw?" Having been wrong-footed by his tone and manner, I was foolish enough to walk straight into the trap, handing the tempo of the contest to him.

"You reveal the limitations of your own imagination when you refuse to give mortals full credit for their faith. You insist in regarding faith as a kind of self-delusion: a confidence trick calculated to exercise a psychological placebo effect. Because you cannot believe in heaven, or in reincarnation, or in personal redemption through suffering, you refuse to accept that the beliefs of the men of the past could be anything but self-deception—and you insult them further by proclaiming that they were heroes for having successfully lied to themselves. What do you think *their* response to your analysis would be?"

By this time, I had realized my earlier mistake. I was ready for the second trap and casually ignored his question.

"Are you arguing that there *is* a heaven," I asked him, scornfully, "or are you merely speaking in favor of reincarnation? Perhaps you really do believe in the redemptive value of suffering?"

"I am content to admit that I do not know what, if anything, lies beyond death," Nyxson relied, suavely, "but I respect the right of every human being not to be told what he or she should or should not believe or what possibilities he or she should or should not explore. Why do you think that you have the authority to deny your fellows that right?"

"It's not for either of us to tell people whether or not they should submit themselves to torture, or even to commit suicide," I admitted, "but you seem to be mistaken as to which of us is dishonestly overreaching his duty. You're the one who exhorts others to take their own lives, while remaining stubbornly alive yourself. My main concern is to stop you pretending that my work lends any support to your monstrous crusade."

"But it does," Nyxson replied, very mildly. "You may say that it was not intended to do so, but now that the work has been committed to the Labyrinth any reader who cares to do so may come to his or her own conclusions as to its implications. The simple and undeniable fact is that many of those recently embarked on what you choose to call a 'monstrous crusade' have taken considerable inspiration from your history. Your work has assisted them in the work of imagining the mortal condition, and it has helped to persuade them that there might be something desirable in that condition. You do not agree, as is certainly your right, but readers of your work do not need your assent in order to take their own inferences from it. You are, after all, a historian, not a writer of fiction. Your task is to provide a true account of what happened in the past and why, not to prescribe what attitude others should adopt to that account."

"The account is incomplete," I pointed out. "When it is whole, I doubt that anyone will be able to misconstrue it as a hymn of praise for the mortal condition."

As parries go, that one was fatally weak.

"Perhaps, in that case, you should not have begun to publish before the work was complete," Nyxson observed, "and I look forward to seeing future chapters—including, of course, your account of Thanaticism, which will doubtless be as scrupulous as your account of early Christianity. But all histories are incomplete, and all truths too. No matter how long we might live, we are all hemmed in by time and by the insufficiency of our wisdom. You might be content to regard all questions as settled, and to pretend that all mystery has been banished from the human world, but others are not. There will always be people in the world who are not content to live within prescribed limits or to limit their experiences to the narrow range that others consider good for them. There will always be people in the world who will want to think the supposedly unthinkable and do the supposedly impossible. Most will fail, but those who succeed are the true custodians of progress."

"That sounds very pretty," I countered, with an overt sneer that probably lost me far more sympathy than it won, "but what we're actually talking about is people maiming and killing themselves. That's not progress—it's madness."

"Perhaps it is," said Nyxson, casually, "but there's method in the madness, and a message too. If Thanatic martyrdom were merely a matter of unhappy individuals testing the limits of existence to eventual destruction you might be right to accuse me of hypocrisy, but I intend to remain alive because the martyrs to come will require someone to speak for them. My part in their adventure will be to explain what they're doing and to spell out the message constituted by their deaths for the benefit of those who lack the wit to read it."

The next trap in line was yawning in front of me but I didn't see it. It might not have made much difference if I had—I probably wouldn't have been able to avoid it.

"According to you," I said, "once the first Thanaticist deaths have occurred, it will be for each and every one of us to make up our own minds what their implications are."

"But of course," he said, with carefully exaggerated graciousness. "As an enthusiastic commentator yourself, however, you surely have no objection to my making a well-informed guess."

"Please do," I said, trying to sound sarcastic. In retrospect, I should have known that I was losing the fight in the only place that mattered—the minds and hearts of EdEnt's audience—but at the time I was possessed by such a powerful sense of my own rightness that it was difficult for me to imagine that anyone could fail to see the force of my arguments.

"Now that the last false emortals are coming to the end of their lives," Hellward Lucifer Nyxson said, in a tone that was all sweet reason, "we are in danger of thinking of death merely as a matter of history: as something put away, save for the occasional regrettable accident. It is not, and the purpose of Thanaticism is to provide a sharp reminder of the fact. Only a historian could take the view that the New Human Race's achievement of emortality was a triumph won against tremendous odds. Any biologist could tell you that from the point of view of the ecosphere it was the discovery of death that was the triumph.

"For the first two billion years of Gaea's lifetime, all life was emortal. The simplest of her children—bacteria, algae, protozoa—still partake of that emortality, constantly reincarnating themselves by fission. They made progress, I suppose—but how slow that progress was, until death came upon the scene! Within the last few hundred million years, Gaea finally achieved a kind of adolescence. Sexual reproduction provided organisms with a means of harnessing change, and progress then began in earnest—but the price that had to be paid for that progress was death. Death loosed the straitjacket of emortality and set Gaea free to make children of a much better kind—including the human beings who brought the art of death to such perfection as to destroy almost all their siblings and to bring Gaea herself to the brink of sterility.

"Only a historian could produce an account of death that ignores everything but human attitudes to it—attitudes steeped in ignorance even in the minds of the all-wise *New* Human Race. But we know that as a human embryo develops in a Helier womb its form is sculpted by death, and we know that it is the permanent withering of synaptic connections that creates the preferred pathways in the brain that provide the electrical foundations of the personality.

"You have called Thanaticists fools, and I will admit that, at least in the sense that we are the jesters who have appointed themselves to whisper in the ears of emortal men the necessary reminder that they must still die. No matter now long we live, Mister Gray, we all must die eventually. It is a bitter necessity, but it is a necessity nevertheless, and we must not fall into the trap of thinking that it is a necessity only because it cannot be avoided. Death is the price that we pay for progress: for the progress of the race, and the progress of the individual.

"The Coral Sea Disaster and the rapidity of our current expansion into the outer reaches of the solar system have made room for the millions of children that have been born in the last hundred years, but the colonists of space are beginning to expand their own numbers, and the Continental Engineers have promised that there will be no more Decimations. We must now face the fact that if we are to make room for new generations of Earthbound children, we can only do so by dying, and by dying voluntarily. It is the duty of every New Human not merely to plan for life but to plan for death, and it is the duty of every Thanaticist not merely to make that necessity clear but to hail everyone who makes the decision to die as a hero and a glorious example to us all. You may disapprove of that cause, stigmatizing it as the pornography of death, but have you considered the alternative?"

The question was rhetorical—he did not pause long enough to let me reply. I assume that he was reading from a private autocue.

"In due course, Mister Gray," Nyxson went on, inexorably, "your history will have to take account of the Robot Assassins, who took the view that even false emortals had become unhuman by virtue of freezing the etching processes of death. Perhaps you will feel free to deplore them, and to call them mad—but I hope that you will make a conscientious attempt to see the force of their argument, just as I hope that you will make a conscientious attempt to see the force of ours. You may feel that their fears died with false emortality and the apparent conquest of the so-called Miller Effect, by which the rejuvenation of brain tissue reactivated the withered synapses and thus wiped out the individual who had formerly inhabited the brain, but I do not. I believe that the New Human Race's apparent conquest of death is nothing of the sort and that what you are pleased to imagine as eternal life will inevitably turn into a kind of suspended animation. It is the duty of every truly human being to resist that kind of robotization, and the only resistance that is possible, or conceivable, is that we consent to die when we have exhausted our potential for self-renewal. That is the price we have to pay for progress.

"These are the messages that the imminent deaths of the first true Thanaticist martyrs will try to put across, Mister Gray: first, the message that we cannot be free of death because death is what makes us what we are; and second, the message that it is only by embracing and welcoming death that we can sustain the hope that our children will ever become anything more."

I felt that it was all wrongheaded, of course, but I could see that there was enough truth in it to dispel the notion that it was madness, or nonsense, or an incoherent argument unworthy of a serious reply. Unfortunately, I had no adequately eloquent reply ready. I tried, of course, but I floundered inelegantly, and Nyxson cut me to ribbons.

FORTY-FIVE

I realized once my humiliation was complete that I should never have left myself in the position of needing to *reply* to Hellward Nyxson at all. I should have done everything in my power to force my opponent into that ignominious position—but the relatively evenhanded exchange of spite in which I had participated with Emmanuelle Standress had lulled me into a false sense of security.

I understood, once the fiasco was over, that Nyxson had been carefully hoarding the moment of his first personal appearance, waiting for the right moment to spring himself on the world. I was unlucky to have been elected as the sounding board off which his manifesto speech would be bounced, but the choice made good tactical sense from his point of view. A professional caster would never have given him so much rope; he needed a debate with an opponent who was set up to be swept aside, at least in the eyes of EdEnt's consumers.

I had set out on the treacherous path of TV celebrity in order to assert that my work had been misunderstood, not realizing that no one in the world except me gave a damn about whether it had or hadn't. My inept pursuit of my own agenda was never going to make the slightest difference in opposition to Hellward Nyxson's showmanship. From his point of view, of course, my only function in life was to make him look more eloquent. Unfortunately, I could not help but oblige.

I was a mere stepping-stone, and the author of the Thanaticist Manifesto stepped on me good and hard.

The only consolation I could take from my brief encounter with Hellward Nyxson was that the whole thing had been mere show business. I told myself that Axel was right: that Thanaticism really was a thing of the moment, a TV-powered fad that would attract far more attention than it deserved for a little while and then fade away. I reminded myself that I, by contrast, was a patient historian, not yet halfway through a work that would take another century to complete.

One day, as even Nyxson had pointed out, I would have the job of fitting the brief history of Thanaticism into my entire history of death—and when I came to do so, I would have the final word. In the meantime, all I could do was to lick my wounds.

"You can't possibly blame yourself," Axel assured me. "It wouldn't have mattered what you'd said in that stupid debate." Jodocus, Eve, and Minna all concurred, although Camilla gave the distinct impression that she thought it *was* my fault that Nyxson had had such an easy ride.

Even Keir was soothing, after his own fashion. "Madness has its own momentum," he said. "You couldn't have stopped it even if you had outflanked him. The EdEnt people could have stamped on it, but they're just the PR arm of Fossilized Hardinism. Demand management requires that there always has to be something new on the surface, although the system itself must remain absolutely rigid. Nothing will change until we can redeem Gaea from the curse of private ownership."

"Are you sure the Rad Libs aren't just one more faddish media phenomenon?" I asked him, churlishly. "They get their fair share of EdEnt spacetime."

"I'm sure," he said, confidently. "We're the revolution that's waiting to happen. We can afford to play the long game."

I almost wished that Keir was right, and that I too was a Gaean at heart, prepared to play the long game and casually able to write off every individual human death as one small step in the direction of Mama's liberation.

Hellward Nyxson was not allowed to rest on his laurels following his victory over me. His next opponent, Chan Chu Lin, took a very different tack, accusing him of having a hidden agenda. He was, Chu suggested; merely the front man for a generation of young people who knew that they would never inherit the earth unless their elders could be persuaded to surrender it voluntarily. Nyxson crushed that accusation with ease, arguing that the generation to which he belonged was far too intelligent to be guilty of mere impatience.

"Those of my peers who want to inherit the earth," he said, "know perfectly well that its present owners regard their stewardship as a duty rather than a privilege and will be only too willing to surrender their authority when they find more interesting employment. The vast majority, mercifully, have no such desire."

His subsequent opponents were not so easily quashed, but Nyxson had made his point and grabbed his moment of opportunity. Thanaticism was hot news, and hence hot philosophy. All death was, of course, news in a world populated almost entirely by emortals, but the Thanaticist "martyrs" who took their cue from Standress and Nyxson took great care to make their deaths *very* newsworthy by making a great song and dance about what they were doing. The whole purpose of the first true Thanatic suicides was to make a public spectacle of self-destruction.

To begin with, the newscasters and their avid audiences were only too ready to collaborate with Thanaticist ambitions. The twenty-sixth-century fashion that had derided the TV audience as "vidveg" had passed away with the Wildean Creationists who had pioneered it, but we new humans had been a trifle premature in deciding that our own viewing habits were more sophisticated and more socially responsible. The avidity of the media coverage poured gasoline on the flames.

Unlike the suicides falsely claimed by Nyxson's followers as martyrs, most of whom had been over a hundred, those inspired by his idiot crusade were mostly very young. The movement scored its first spectacular succès de scandale when a sixty-five-year-old woman named Valentina Czarevna took her crucifixion to the limit in 2733. The cult's most fervent adherents had already begun to cry out that everyone who had lived more than threescore years and ten had already violated the fundamental Thanaticist ethic, but most of those who committed suicide in the name of Thanaticism were somewhat younger. People of my age were far less vulnerable to the tides of fashion.

As the number of Thanaticist martyrs multiplied, so did the variety of the means they selected, although they always preferred violent deaths. They usually issued invitations and waited for large crowds to gather before putting their plans into action. Jumping from tall buildings and burning to death were the most popular methods in the beginning, but these quickly ceased to be interesting. As the Thanaticist revival progressed, those adherents prepared to make the ultimate sacrifice sought increasingly bizarre methods in the interests of maintaining media attention and outdoing their predecessors. EdEnt's masters soon changed tack, deploring the suicides and ostentatiously refusing to broadcast them, but it was obvious to everyone that they were merely anticipating the fact that the familiarity would breed audience contempt.

The total number of individuals involved in the Thanaticist "move-ment" was very small. In a world population of more than three billion, a handful of deaths per week was a drop in the ocean, and the maximum attained by self-appointed Thanatics was less than fifty in a month. "Quiet" suicides continued to outnumber the ostentatious Thanatics by a factor of five or six throughout the period when the pornography of death attained its climatic phase.

Even so, it seemed terrible thing at the time, and I could not help but take a keen personal interest in every development. I confess that in spite of my fierce determination to maintain a scrupulous objectivity befitting a historian, my opinions drifted slightly with the tide of fashion.

FORTY SIX

I never took part in another live debate after having been so comprehensively upstaged by Hellward Nyxson, but I did continue to give occasional interviews to casters, and even to pose as an expert—in which capacity I soon found a settled line of my own to peddle with practiced efficiency, like every other habitual media whore.

The questions I was asked once the backlash against Thanaticism began went relentlessly back and forth over the same reactionary ground. Is the new fascination with death a kind of social sickness? How disturbed should we be by the discovery that the sanity on which New Humans pride themselves has proved to be so fragile? Ironically, honesty forced me to moderate my own opposition lest I should find myself condemning my own work along with Nyxson's crusade.

"The contemporary fascination with death is by no means inexplicable, nor is it necessarily unhealthy," I argued, earnestly and frequently. "In the days when death was inescapable, people were deeply frustrated by the imperious imposition of fate. They resented it with all the force and bitterness they could muster, but it could not be truly *fascinating* while it remained a simple and universal fact of life. Now that death is no longer a necessity, it has perforce become a luxury. Because it is no longer inevitable, we no longer feel an oppressive need to hate and fear it, and this allows us to take an essentially *aesthetic* view of death. The transformation of the imagery of death into a species of pornography is perfectly understandable, no matter how regrettable it may be.

"Planning a life is an exercise in story making. Living people are forever writing the narratives of their own lives, deciding who to be and what to do, according to various aesthetic criteria. In olden days, death was inevitably seen as an *interruption* of the business of life, cutting short life stories before they were—in the eyes of their creators—complete. Nowadays, people have the opportunity to plan *whole* lives, deciding exactly when and how their life stories should reach a climax and a conclusion. We may not share the aesthetic sensibilities of those who decide to die young, but there is a discernible logic in their actions. It is not helpful to dismiss them as madmen.

"We assume that our biotechnologies and nanotechnologies have given us the power we need to regulate our mental lives, but we have resisted roboticization. The freedom of the human will is rightly considered our most precious possession, setting us apart from even the cleverest AIs. We must recognize and accept that this freedom will occasionally be exercised in strange ways and should be prepared to defend the rights of the strangers in our midst. The decision to die young, even though one might live forever, is an exercise of freedom."

The Thanaticists were by no means displeased by my adoption of this argument, and Hellward Nyxson took to describing me as his "first convert." The more lavishly I embroidered my analogy, declaring that ordinary emortals were the *feuilletonistes*, epic poets, and three-decker novelists of modern life whereas Thanaticists were the prose-poets and short-story writers who liked to sign off with a neat punchline, the more the diehard Thanatics grew to like me. I receive many invitations to attend suicides, and my refusal to take them up only served to make my presence a prize to be sought after.

Perhaps I should emphasize that I was then, as I am now, entirely in agreement with the United Nations Charter of Human Rights, whose ninety-ninth amendment guarantees the citizens of every nation the right to take their own lives and to be assisted in making a dignified exit should they so desire. I continued to harbor strong reservations about the way in which the Thanaticists construed the amendment and to detest their solicitation of suicide, but I never sympathized with those extremists who argued for the amendment's repeal while the Thanaticist Panic was at its height in the 2730s. The item's original intention had been to facilitate self-administered euthanasia in an age when that was sometimes necessary, not to guarantee Thanatics the entitlement to recruit whatever help they required in staging whatever kinds of exit they desired, but a principle is a principle and must be upheld.

Some of the invitations I received during the latter phase of the Thanaticist craze were exhortations to participate in legalized murders, and these became more common as the exhaustion of ready models forced later "martyrs" to become more extreme in their bizarrerie. I refused to have anything to do with such acts, and often urged the would-be martyrs to reconsider their actions, but they continued regardless.

By 2740 the Thanaticist martyrs had progressed from conventional suicides to public executions, by rope, sword, ax, or guillotine. At first the executioners were volunteers—one or two were actually arrested and charged with murder, although none could be convicted—but as the Thanaticists became more desperate to reignite the waning glare of public attention they began campaigning for various nations to re-create the official position of Public Executioner, together with bureaucratic structures that would give all citizens the right to call upon the services of such officials. It was taken for granted at first that they stood no chance of success, but this proved to be a mistake.

Even I, who claimed to understand the cult better than its members, was astonished when the government of Colombia—presumably desirous of taking the lead in the nation's ongoing competition with Venezuela for recognition as the home of the world's aesthetic avant garde—actually accepted such an obligation, with the result that Thanaticists began to flock to Maracaibo and Cartagena in order to obtain an appropriate send-off. I was relieved when the UN, following the death of Shamiel Sihra in an electric chair in 2743, added a further rider to the ninety-ninth amendment, outlawing suicide by public execution.

By this time I had given up making media appearances that only seemed to cement my reputation as a Thanaticist sympathizer no matter how hard I tried to backpedal and distance myself from the movement. In 2744 I began refusing all invitations to appear on TV as well as all invitations to take part in Thanaticist ceremonies. It seemed to me that it was time to become a recluse once again.

I had a great deal of work to do on the fourth part of my history, and I had had my fill of distractions.

FORTY SEVEN

The fourth part of *The History of Death*, entitled *Fear and Fascination*, was launched into the Labyrinth on 12 February 2767. Although the furor over Thanaticism had died down, my commentary was immediately subject to heavy access demand. The heyday of the movement was long past, but its atrocities were still fresh in the world's memory, and it is possible that my title misled some would-be readers into thinking that my commentary would be directly concerned with the Thanaticist creed. Requisitions of material from the first three parts of the history had declined sharply in the 2760s in the wake of the Thanaticism-inspired boom, and I might have set a higher access fee had I realized that the new publication would generate such high demand.

Academic historians were universal in their condemnation of the new commentary, and those who complimented me on the thoroughness with which I had bound together the underlying data were annoyingly few in number. I understood that the enthusiasm with which the publication was greeted by laymen was hardly conducive to academic acclaim, but I felt that I had done the ritual spadework with exemplary efficiency. There were, however, a number of popular reviewers who praised my commentary highly even after discovering that it had nothing explicit to say about the "problem" of Thanaticism. My arguments were recklessly plundered by journalists and other broadcasting pundits in search of possible parallels that might be drawn with the modern world, especially those passages that seemed to carry moral lessons for the few remaining Thanaticists and the legions who feared and were fascinated by them.

The commentary attached to *Fear and Fascination* extended, elaborated, and diversified the arguments contained in its immediate predecessor, particularly in respect of the Christian world of the Medieval period and the Renaissance. It had much to say about art and literature, and the images contained therein. It had substantial chapters on the personification of death as the Grim Reaper, on the iconography of the *danse macabre*, on the topics of *memento mori* and *artes moriendi*. It included comprehensive analyses of Dante's *Divine Comedy*, the paintings of Hieronymus Bosch, Milton's *Paradise Lost*, and graveyard poetry. These were by no means exercises in conventional criticism; they were elements of a long and convoluted argument about the contributions made by the individual creative imagination to the war of ideas, which raged on the only battleground on which man could as yet constructively oppose the specter of death.

My text also dealt with the persecution of heretics and the subsequent elaboration of Christian Demonology, which had led to the witch craze of the fifteenth, sixteenth, and seventeenth centuries. I gave considerable attention to various thriving folkloristic traditions that had confused the notion of death, especially to the popularity of fictions and fears regarding premature burial, ghosts, and various species of the "undead" who were said to rise from their graves as ghouls or vampires. To me, all these phenomena were symptomatic of a crisis in Western civilization's imaginative dealings with the idea of death: a feverish heating up of a conflict that had been in danger of becoming desultory.

The cities of men had been under perpetual siege from death since the time of their first building, but in the Middle Ages—in one part of the world, at least—the perception of that siege had sharpened. A kind of spiritual starvation and panic had set in, and the progress that had been made in the war by virtue of the ideological imperialism of Christ's Holy Cross had seemed imperiled by disintegration. That Empire of Faith had begun to break up under the stress of skepticism, and men were faced with the prospect of going into battle against their most ancient enemy with their armor in tatters.

Just as the Protestants were trying to replace the Catholic Church's centralized authority with a more personal relationship between men and God, I argued, so the creative artists of the era were trying to achieve a more personal and more intimate form of reconciliation between men and death, equipping individuals with the power to mount their own idiosyncratic ideative assaults.

The Medieval personalization of death, whether as a hooded figure carrying a scythe or as the leader of the dance of death, seemed to me to be part and parcel of the re-creation of human personality. This was the period in which the individual gave way to the ego, in which the humans of the Western World first attained the privilege of uniqueness. As the human personality became unique and idiosyncratic, so did the death of that personality. Death became a visitor knocking at the door and demanding admission. The ghostly voices that had formerly been bound together into an ancestral chorus became distinct as the dead became as distinct and idiosyncratic as the living, demanding specific reparation for particular slights. The ever-present ancestors of the tribe and the demons of general temptation were replaced by lone haunters and possessors who settled upon equally isolated victims. The universal war against death dissolved into a chaotic mass of hand-to-hand combats.

I drew numerous parallels, of course, between what happened in the Christian world and similar periods of crisis that were discernible in other cultures at other times, but I cannot deny that my study of *Fear and Fascination* was ethnocentric in the extreme. It was, I suppose, inevitable that so many of my peers would claim that my cross-cultural analogies were fatally weak and that such generalizations as I attempted were illusory, but that was the temper of the times with which I was trying to deal. No other period in history saw the emergence of such sharp distinctions between the technological and moral progress of different cultures—distinctions that were not significantly eroded even by the global communication systems of the twentieth century, until the Crash came. We take the philosophical and economic bases of the Oikumene too much for granted, and it is difficult for us to imagine the extremity of the inequalities that afflicted the world throughout the Second Millennium.

A few of my critics, studiously ignoring the nature of the world with which I was trying to deal, argued that my intense study of the phenomena associated with the idea of death had become so personal simply because I had become so personally involved with Thanaticism. Others suggested that I had become so utterly infatuated with the ephemeral ideas of past ages that they had taken predatory control over my own imagination, and that I had become too wrapped up in my own unique contest with a hooded but toothless death whose scythe had lost its edge.

I took what comfort I could in the conviction that by the time my work was complete there would be no room for such misunderstandings, that the whole would be seen for what it really was and its worth properly evaluated.

I knew that I would have a good deal more work to do before I had broadened the concerns of *Fear and Fascination* sufficiently to take in the whole world, but I cannot deny that I was slightly disheartened by the element of mockery that often crept into criticisms of my commentary. My recently renewed reclusiveness was further intensified by this sense of injury, and I came to feel that my home by the Orinoco was too exposed, its environs too crowded with predators far more insidious than alligators.

I was tempted to go back to Antarctica, but Cape Adare was now ill fitted to serve as any kind of refuge. Instead, I decided to remove myself to the other extremity of the civilized world. In 2774 I took up residence in an ancient stone residence—albeit one internally refitted with all modern conveniences—on the tip of Cape Wolstenholme, at the neck of Hudson's Bay in Canada.

FORTY-EIGHT

Twenty-eighth-century Canada was an urbane, highly civilized, and rather staid region of the Reunited States. It was as distinct from the spectral array of the New York–San Francisco Mainline, in its own idiosyncratic fashion, as the Old Southern Confederacy and the Latin Satellites. Its people seemed to be uniformly modest, intelligent, and down-to-earth—the sort of folk who had no time for such follies as Thanaticism. Cape Wolstenholme seemed, therefore, to offer an ideal retreat, where I could continue to throw myself wholeheartedly into my work and leave the world behind the headlines to feed a closeted store of data to which I would get around in my own good time.

I handed over full responsibility for answering all my calls to a brand-new state-of-the-art Personal Simulation program, which grew so clever and so ambitious with practice that it soon began to give to casters interviews that were retransmitted on broadcast television. Although the silver offered what was effectively "no comment" in a carefully elaborate fashion I eventually thought it best to introduce into its operating system a block that restrained its ambitions—a block that was intended to ensure that my face dropped out of public sight for at least half a century. Having fully experienced the rewards and pressures of celebrity, I felt not the slightest need to extend that phase of my life, even via an artificial alter ego.

The one person with whom I maintained contact faithfully was Emily Marchant, partly because she was the most precious person in the Oikumene and partly because she had been too far from Earth to witness my inglorious involvement with the Thanaticist panic. Her messages to me seemed to come out of an earlier and better world, and they were full of pleas to join her in the making of a future that would be even better.

"The Earthbound know nothing of the universe in which they live," she told me, in an entirely characteristic lyrical moment. "The atmosphere surrounding the Well is a chrysalis from which we must emerge if we are to be what we were always destined to be. You may think that you have seen the stars and the galaxies in VE, but the people who called the world of Virtual Experience a Universe Without Limits had no idea what the actual limits of sensation were. Morty, you *have* to come out of the Well, at least as far as the moon. Once you've seen the stars as they are, you won't be able to go back."

I couldn't take that sort of rhetoric seriously. I knew that she'd been carried away by the zeal of the recent convert and had lost her sense of proportion. I had always found it difficult to take Mama Siorane seriously on the admittedly rare occasions when she had insisted on referring to the Earth as "the Well."

"Leave Earth to the Thanaticists," Emily said, on another occasion, long after the heyday of Thanaticism was past. "Out here, death is still a threat to be avoided, and *everyone* wants to live as long and as gloriously as she can. Earth is already rotting, Morty—but Titan hasn't yet begun to breathe."

I told myself that she didn't have the least idea what she was talking about, as far as Earth and the Earthbound were concerned, and that she was probably as far off the mark in her estimation of the potentiality of the cold satellites of the gas giant worlds. My business, I was utterly convinced, was with Earth and solid history, not Titan and wild optimism. I never stopped replying to her messages with mechanical regularity, but I did stop listening to their exhortations.

It must have seemed to the majority of the Earthbound that Thanaticism had already petered out as the turn of the century approached. The word eventually ceased to appear in the headlines. In fact, its last followers had "gone underground"—which is to say that Thanaticist martyrs no longer attempted to stage their exits before the largest audiences they could obtain but instead saved their performance for small, carefully selected groups. This was not a response to persecution but merely a variation in the strange game that they were playing: indulgence in a different kind of drama.

I knew about this development because there was no let up in the communications with which diehard Thanatics continued to batter my patient AI interceptor. My presence at a martyrdom had become one of the few remaining prizes, avidly sought by aficionados in spite of the fact that my debate with Hellward Lucifer Nyxson had been long forgotten by everyone except the diehards themselves.

Although my patient silver took care of all my communication with the world outside, I could not resist the temptation to look over its shoulder occasionally as it parried the thrusts of the now-esoteric Thanaticists. I took due note, therefore, of a gradual shift in Thanaticist philosophy, which deemphasized brutal martyrdom in favor of long-term flirtations with danger. Such flirtations constantly exposed the cultists to the risk of death while keeping the skillful and the fortunate permanently in the game. Some were content to indulge in life-threatening sporting contests, often of a bizarre nature, but others preferred to cultivate a calculatedly unhealthy interest in disease.

Although a few twenty-eighth century Thanaticist martyrs had used diseases as a means of suicide the majority of "soft Thanatics" had always been content to pose as connoisseurs of exotic experience, in much the same spirit as my old acquaintance Ziru Majumdar. The continuation of their interests long after the initial moral panic had abated stimulated a small-scale but thriving black market in designer carcinogens and bioengineered pathogens.

Although the original agents of smallpox, cholera, bubonic plague, and syphilis were long extinct, the modern world abounded in clever genetic engineers who could synthesize similar viruses with very little effort. As the twenty-eighth century died and the twenty-ninth began, the less scrupulous among them found eager clients for a whole range of new and particularly horrid diseases. Those maladies that afflicted the mind as well as, or instead of, the body were particularly prized by the hard-core cognoscenti.

Recreational schizophrenia almost broke through to the mainstream of psychotropic usage at one point, but in the main the followers of the new fad steered well clear of casters and their hoverflies. As is the way of such things, however, the initial determination of the reformed Thanaticists to evade the lurid exposure that had typified the efforts of their predecessors soon became newsworthy in itself. The more evasive the residual adherents of the movement became, the greater became the motivation of their pursuers.

Inevitably, the new trend began to spread beyond the ranks of self-styled Thanaticists. As large numbers of people began to toy with the idea that disease was something that could be temporarily and interestingly indulged, without any real danger to life or subsequent health, the entire black market began to move slowly but steadily toward legitimacy and mass production. My silver began to find more and more instances in which arguments about death that I had popularized were quoted— usually without acknowledgement—with reference to recreational disease. It became fashionable to state as accepted common sense that whatever had ceased to be a dire necessity in human reckoning "naturally" became available as a perverse luxury, subject to purely aesthetic consideration.

None of this would have mattered much, but for one thing. Thanaticist martyrdom had not been infectious, except perhaps in a metaphorical sense, but recreational diseases were more versatile. Those that were mass produced were subjected to rigorous quality control, but those that had emerged from illicit sources while the client base had been small and exclusive had not been so carefully designed. It required only a few of the the people caught up in the fad to refuse to restrict themselves to noninfectious varieties for a serious social problem to develop.

The world had been free of devastating epidemics since the heyday of the chiasmalytic transformers that had precipitated the final phase of the Crash, but the renewed challenge to twenty-eighth-century medical technology was undoubtedly serious and was recognized as such.

Because of the threat to innocent parties who might be accidentally infected, the self-infliction of communicable diseases was quickly outlawed in many nations. Some governments were slow to act, but Canada was not among the them. Even in that ultracivilized land, however, the laws were too often broken.

FORTY-NINE

I would have remained aloof and apart from the recreational disease craze had I been able to, but my determination to pay no attention only made its adherents more anxious to attract my notice. It was inevitable that one of them would eventually succeed, and the one who did was Hadria Nuccoli.

Hadria Nuccoli was by no means the first Thanaticist to make her way to Cape Wolstenholme in person, or the first to attempt to gain entry to my home in spite of my refusal to invite her in. I daresay that almost all of her predecessors had been entirely harmless, and perhaps not entirely charmless, but I suppose it was only to be expected that the predator who combined the utmost determination with the utmost ingenuity would be the most dangerous of the lot.

Had I been living in an orthodox hometree even Hadria Nuccoli might have found housebreaking impossible. One advantage of an all-organic structure is that it is virtually seamless. In an emergency, all its doors and windows close reflexively and seal themselves with natural glues that bind as powerfully as the very best shamirs. Anyone who takes a blade or a degantzing solution to a living structure meets active resistance as well as raising an instant neural alarm. Stone, by contrast, is passive, and such alarms as can be fitted into it tend to be mere webs of copper wire and optical fiber. The kind of nanotech that can colonize and subvert such alarm systems is not readily available and it does not come cheap, but anyone who takes the trouble can render a mere household system impotent. Once that is done, the business of dissolving stone with gantzing agents designed for demolition becomes a mere formality: slow but sure.

The internal refurbishment of my living space had fitted all the inner walls with multilayered organics, but the solid frame put severe restrictions on the thickness of that tegument, and it yielded easily enough to simple brute force. Hadria Nuccoli came armed with drilling and cutting apparatus designed to deal with Titanian ice; the frail walls of my house had no chance against that kind of equipment.

Thus it was that she arrived in my bedroom, unannounced, at three o'clock on the morning of 16 January 2822.

I woke up in confusion, almost as disorientated as I had been on that dreadful night when the *Genesis* had flipped over—but on this occasion the confusion was more rapidly transformed into naked terror. When I caught sight of my uninvited visitor she was still carrying the cutting torch, and the mask she wore to protect her eyes from its furious fire made her look like some kind of alien monster.

I thought at first that the masked invader had come to use the torch on me, intent on slicing me from head to toe. My terror abated slightly when she tossed the tool aside and pulled the mask from her head—but only slightly.

I recognized her face, although I could not put a name to it immediately. Hadria Nuccoli had called several times to ask for admission, and my ever-dutiful silver had carefully made a record of her face and name. I had glimpsed it on several occasions, always incuriously.

Although she seemed less inhuman without the protective mask I knew that this was an enemy far more frightening than the scalding Coral Sea, because this was an active enemy, who *meant* to do me harm, and the intensity of the threat she posed was in no way lessened by the fact that she had claimed while begging me to meet her that she was a devout admirer of my work. Although she was still recognizable, she looked markedly different from the picture stored by the silver. Her skin now bore an almost mercuric luster, and she was already in the throes of a terrible fever.

"Stop there! Stay back!" I cried, flattening myself against the wall behind my bed and raising my bedsheet as if it might armor me against her advance.

I felt extremely vulnerable, having recently reverted to sleeping naked beneath a smart sheet instead of wearing a sleepskin. Neither a sleepskin nor a conventional suitskin would have been adequate protection against whatever infection she carried—I would probably have needed a spacesuit to insulate myself completely—but I would have felt a great deal better had my modesty been better guarded. I was slightly surprised when she obeyed my command, but she had come to talk as well as to act.

"Don't be afraid, Mortimer," she said, in a voice hoarsened by tracheal mucus. "I've come to help you, not to hurt you. I've come to bring you out of the tomb of life and back to the world of flood and fire. I've come to *set you free*."

I knew that she must have disabled the external alarms, but I also knew that my silver must have put out a mayday as soon as she started work on the living tissues of the house. The police would be able to get a drone to the scene in a matter of minutes—but as I looked past her at the ragged gap in the wall I saw that she'd set up some kind of shamir to seal the breach in the stone wall. There was no way she would be allowed to get away again, but my silver was only a glorified answerphone; even with police collaboration, it would find it extremely difficult to disable the intruder before she could hurt me.

At the very least, I had to buy time.

"I *am* free," I assured my unwelcome visitor. "This is my home, not a tomb. I'm always in the world. I work in the Labyrinth for eight or ten hours a day, and I spend a further six or eight in recreational VEs. I'm perfectly happy with the quality of my experiences, and I certainly don't need the kind of excitement you're trying to give me. If I don't want it, it isn't a gift."

I would have felt a lot safer if my visitor had stood still in order to plead her case, but she seemed incapable of that. Her desire to keep moving was as irresistible as her desire to communicate. The derangement of her body and brain by whatever designer disease was consuming her was not yet powerful enough to make her fall down or impair her crazed eloquence.

"Come with me!" she begged, as I huddled back against the wall, desperate to evade her spasmodically clenching fingers. "Come with me to the far side of life, and I'll show you what's there. There's no need to be afraid! Even death isn't the end, just a new beginning—but this isn't death, just a better way of being. Disease is the metamorphosis that frees us from our caterpillar flesh to soar as spirits in a massless world blessed with infinitely more light and color than any mere VE. I have come to be your redeemer, Mortimer—the redeemer for whom you have waited far too long. Love me as I love you, dear Mortimer: only love me, and you will learn. Let me be your mirror; drown yourself in me!"

She made a lunge for me as she spoke the last few words, but I dodged aside and she stumbled. Her uncanny fever was interfering with her motor responses, and she couldn't get up immediately, but when I made a bid for the door she was quick enough to block the way.

"Don't be silly!" I implored her. "Help is on the way. Even if you were to contaminate me, I'd be in hospital within the hour."

I knew that I wasn't getting through to her. Her own speech wasn't completely incoherent, but that didn't mean that she could listen or understand what I said to her.

She came after me again, and I had to grab a chair, using the legs to fend her off. I didn't know whether it would do any good—for all I knew, I might have been infected already simply by virtue of breathing the same air—but the notion that she might actually lay her fevered hands upon me seemed particularly horrible.

"There's no return from eternity, Mortimer," she babbled on, the words beginning to tumble over one another in spite of their adequate grammar and syntax. It was as if she had programmed her voice to deliver her message whether or not she could keep conscious control of it—and perhaps she had. "This is no ordinary virus created by accident to fight a hopeless cause against the defenses of the body," she went on. "The true task of medical engineers, did they but know it, was never to fight disease but always to *perfect* it, and we have found the way. I bring you the greatest of all gifts, my darling: the elixir of life, which will make us angels instead of men, creatures of light and ecstasy. We were fools to think that we had drunk at the fountain of youth when we had only armored our bodies against the ravages of age. Youth is a state of mind. The finest flame burns hot and brief, my love, and must be shared. What you call life is petrifaction of the soul."

I kept moving all the time, while her movements grew jerkier. As she came to resemble a mere marionette I thought that it was only a matter of time before her strings broke, but she stubbornly refused to collapse.

I tired before she did, and she tore the chair from my grasp. I found myself backed into a corner, with nowhere to go.

FIFTY

The flesh of my persecutor's face was aglow with silver, and it seemed impossible that she could still be upright, but she was in the grip of a terrible supernatural *urgency*, and she pounced like an angry cat, catching me by the arms.

I tried to knock her down. If I had had a weapon in hand I would certainly have used it, with all the force I could muster. It probably wouldn't have done any good. I doubt that she would have felt any pain, and no matter how badly disabled her internal technology might have been, I wouldn't have been able to disable her with anything less than a sledgehammer.

In the very last moment, I gave in.

There seemed to be no sensible alternative but to let her take me in her arms and cling to me. Nothing else could possibly soothe her. When she finally wrapped her arms round me, therefore, I wrapped mine around her.

We hugged.

I was afraid for her as well as for myself. I didn't believe, then, that she truly intended to die. I wanted to keep us both safe until help arrived.

My panic faded while I held Hadria Nuccoli in my arms, only to be replaced by some other emotion, equally intense, to which I could not put a name. I made every effort to remind and convince myself that it hadn't ever mattered whether she infected me or not, given that medical help would soon arrive.

"This is the only real life," she murmured, as the script she had somehow internalized wound down to its amen. "Emortality makes a sepulchre of the flesh. If we are to become more than human, we must live more fervently, burn more brightly, die more extravagantly."

"It's all right," I assured her. "Help will be here soon. Everything will be fine."

I was right about the help, but wrong about the everything.

My naive faith in medical science and internal nanotechnology left me completely unprepared for the kind of hell that I endured before the attending doctors got the bug under control. Nature had never designed diseases capable of fighting back against the ministrations of IT, but the makers of new plagues were cleverer by far.

As the infection ran its vicious course I wished, over and over again, that I were able to live the experience as Hadria Nuccoli presumably lived it, not as hell but as passion, but I couldn't do it. I was an emortal through and through. I couldn't abide that kind of fervor, that kind of extravagance. All I wanted was the restoration of peace of mind and metabolic calm. While my nanotech armies fought tooth and nail against enemies the likes of which they had never faced before for possession of the battleground of my flesh, all I was capable of wanting was to be still and self-controlled.

I could not help but wonder, afterward, whether I had already begun to aspire to the robot condition. I couldn't help asking myself whether, as Hadria Nuccoli would presumably have argued, I was fleeing from true human potential because I was incapable of loving anything but the sepulchral death-in-life that was the emortal condition.

Was it conceivable, I wondered, that she might have been right about the nature of the *authentic* fountain of youth?

I concluded, on due reflection, that she was wrong in every respect. That may have been why, in the end, I lived and she died. On the other hand, the nanotech injected into her body by the doctors may simply have arrived too late to turn the tide.

I wept for her when they told me she'd died and wished with all my heart that she hadn't, even though I knew that if there were tears on the far side of life, she would be lamenting my inability to join her.

Although it was entirely unlike my previous close encounters with death, my infection by Hadria Nuccoli was just as disturbing in its own way. I tried to regard it as a minor hiccup in the settled pattern of my life—something to be survived, put away and forgotten—but I couldn't quite put the pattern back together again.

The last thing I'd expected when I set out to write a *History of Death* was that my explanatory study might actually assist the dread empire of death to regain a little of the ground it had lost in the world of human affairs. Even though the Thanaticists and their successors were willfully misunderstanding and perverting the meaning of my work, I felt that my objectivity had been fatally contaminated when the protective walls of my home had been breached, and that the stain would not be easily eradicated. I knew that I still owed it to the Thanaticists as well as to everyone else to make the true message of my work clear, but while my own mind was less than perfectly clear that task seemed impossible.

I felt that I could not stay on Cape Wolstenholme and that I could never live in such a frail dwelling again.

I had to move again—but where could I go? Where on Earth, and in what kind of home, could I recover the equilibrium I had lost and the objectivity that would always be under threat while there were people like Hadria Nuccoli in the world?

The answer was simple enough, once I had made up my mind. If there was nowhere on Earth, I had to take the step that Mama Siorane had urged me to take more than a hundred years before—the step that Emily Marchant also wanted me to take. I had to find a vantage point from which the trials and travails of Earthbound humanity could be seen from a proper distance, dispassionately.

I remembered while I lay in the hospital, without any companion to keep me company, that one of my last live appearances on TV had taken place in a VE that reproduced an image of a lunar observatory. It had been selected as the appropriate site for a discussion in which a faber named Khan Mirafzal had argued, rather vehemently, that Thanaticism was evidence of the fact that Earthbound man was becoming decadent. I had heard distinct echoes of Mama Siorane and Emily in his fierce insistence that the progressive future of humankind lay outside Earth, in the microworlds and the distant colonies.

Like Emily, Khan Mirafzal had claimed that humans genetically reshaped for life in low gravity or for the colonization of alien worlds were immune to Thanaticist follies because it was perfectly obvious that all the projects and possibilities that beckoned to them required longevity and calm of mind. Everyone who lived in space tended to wax lyrical about the supposed decadence of the Earthbound, much as the extreme Gaean Liberationists did, but as I reflected on my plight in the hospital I recalled that Mirafzal's arguments had been balanced by an unusually coherent idea of the intellectual virility of the "outward bound."

"While the surface of the earth still provided challenges, those who dwelt upon it knew that they were not yet complete," he had said, when we first met, "but now that it offers only limitations, its inhabitants are bound to grow introspective. Not all introspection is unhealthy, but even at the end of the psychological spectrum opposite to Thanaticism there is closure, imprisonment, and stultification. The L-5 habitats may seem to the Earthbound to be the ultimate in physical enclosure, but the people who live within them—especially those like myself, who have forsaken heavy legs in order to have the benefit of four arms—know that the whole universe awaits us. We are citizens of infinity and must therefore be citizens of eternity. We have changed ourselves in order to become champions of change."

The moderator of our conversation had dutifully pointed out that the surface of Earth was still changing and that there were many among the Earthbound who were determined to see that it never became fixed and sterile.

"The central doctrine of Planned Capitalism is continuous change *within a stable frame*," Mirafzal had countered, "I'm not talking about change for the sake of commerce. There's no fashion on the moon. I'm talking about future evolution: expansion into the galaxy; meetings with other minds; adaptation to all kinds of circumstances; life without boundaries and without the possibility of boundaries. That requires a very different psychology. The Earthbound can have no idea of what it is like to be truly human until they step outside their frame into reality."

At the time, it had seemed like mere cleverness, talk for talk's sake, like everything else on TV. Now, I figured that it was high time I tested it out. I would have called Emily had she been close enough to Earth, but she was too far away; Khan Mirafzal seemed to be the best available substitute. He was pleased to hear from me and more than glad to have the opportunity to repeat his arguments in more sympathetic circumstances. He talked, and I listened. I allowed myself to be convinced and decided to leave Earth, at least for a while, to investigate the farther horizons of the human enterprise.

In 2825 I flew to the moon. After some hesitation, I settled in Mare Moscoviense. I thought it best to try out the side that faces away from Earth so that I might benefit from a view composed entirely of stars.

FIFTY-ONE

Emily was, of course, highly delighted when I told her of my decision, and she sent a message back from Io that was overflowing with enthusiastic congratulations. I was slow to reply to it because I felt slightly guilty about concealing my true motives for making the move. She thought I was being bold, whereas I was actually going into hiding, and I dared not even try to explain that to Emily. I excused my tardiness by telling myself—and her, when I finally did get around to replying— that I had to concentrate on the business of adapting myself to a new world and a new society.

As I had expected, I found life on the moon very different from any-thing I'd experienced in my travels around the Earth's surface. It wasn't so much the change in gravity, although that certainly took a lot of get-ting used to, or the severe regime of daily exercise in the centrifuge that I had to adopt in order to make sure that I might one day return to the world of my birth without extravagant medical provision. Nor was it the fact that the environment was so comprehensively artificial or that it was impossible to venture outside without special equipment; in those respects it was much like Antarctica. The most significant difference was in the people.

Mare Moscoviense had few tourists—tourists mostly stayed Earth-side, making only brief trips farside—but most of its inhabitants were nevertheless just passing through. It was one of the main jumping-off points for emigrants, largely because it was an important industrial cen-ter. It was the site of one of the solar system's largest factories for the manufacture of shuttles and other local-space vehicles, and it was host to hundreds of nanotech studios and shamir manufactories. It was one of the chief trading posts supplying materials to the microworlds in Earth orbit and beyond, so many of its visitors came in from the farther reaches of the solar system.

When I arrived in Moscoviense the majority of the city's long-term residents were unmodified, like me, or lightly modified by reversible cyborgization. A substantial minority of the permanent population and a great many of those visiting were, however, fabers like Khan Mirafzal, genetically engineered for low-gee environments. Most of their adaptations were internal and subtle, but the one that had won them their name was the most conspicuous. Every faber possessed four hands, being equipped with an extra pair of "arms" instead of legs. All but a few of the public places in Moscoviense were designed to accommodate their kind as well as "walkers." All the corridors were railed and all the ceilings ringed.

The sight of fabers swinging around the place like gibbons, getting everywhere at five or six times the pace of walkers, was one that I found subtly disturbing to begin with. Fabers couldn't live, save with the utmost difficulty, in the gravity well that was Earth. They almost never descended to the planet's surface. By the same token, it was difficult for men from Earth to work in zero-gee environments without extensive modification, surgical if not genetic. For this reason, the only "ordinary" men who tarried in highly specialized faber environments weren't ordinary by any customary standard. The moon, with its one-sixth Earth gravity, was one of the few places in the inner solar system where fabers and unmodified men frequently met and mingled. Even the L-5 colonies were divided by their rates of spin into "footslogger territories" and "faberwebs."

I had always known about fabers, of course, but like so much other "common knowledge" the information had lain unattended in some unheeded pigeonhole of my memory until direct acquaintance ignited it and gave it life. By the time I had lived in Moscoviense for a month that unused reserve of common knowledge had turned into a profound fascination.

It seemed to me that fabers lived their lives at a very rapid tempo, despite the fact that they were just as emortal as members of their parent species. For one thing, faber parents normally had their children while they were still alive, and very often they had several at intervals of only twenty or thirty years. An aggregate family of fabers often had three or even four children growing up in parallel. In the infinite reaches of space, there was no population control, and no restrictive "right of replacement." A microworld's population could grow as fast as the microworld could acquire extra biomass and organize more living space. Then again, the fabers were always *doing* things. Even though they had four arms, they never seemed to leave one dangling. They seemed to have no difficulty at all in doing two different things at the same time, often using only one limb for attachment. On the moon this generally meant hanging from the ceiling like a bat while one exceedingly busy hand mediated between the separate tasks being carried out by the remaining two.

I quickly realized that it wasn't just the widely accepted notion that the future of mankind must take the form of a gradual diffusion through the galaxy that made the fabers think of Earth as decadent. From their viewpoint, the habits and manners of the lunar footsloggers seemed annoyingly slow and sedentary. The Earthbound, having long since attained control of the ecosphere of their native world, seemed to the fabers to be living a lotus-eater existence, indolently pottering about in its spacious garden, and unmodified spacefarers seemed to the fabers to have brought that deep-seated indolence with them into environments where it did not belong.

The most extreme fabers, in this and other respects, were the "converts" who had attained that state by means of somatic engineering rather than having been born four-handed. Many footsloggers did not regard the converts as "real" fabers and emphasized this point by referring to the faber-born as "naturals," borrowing an obsolete term that false emortals had once applied to the earliest Earthbound ZTs. The converts, on the other hand, regarded themselves as the formulators and best practitioners of faber philosophy.

Most fabers weren't contemptuous of legs as such, but converts were often inclined to draw nice distinctions in their arguments about the relative worth of different variants of humankind. They would give their wholehearted endorsement to the hypothetical spacefaring folk who would one day be given legs by genetic engineers in order that they might descend to the surfaces of new and alien worlds, but they would be casually dismissive of those emigrants from Earth who insisted on hanging on to the legs their ancestors had bequeathed to them in order to enjoy the fruits of the labors of past generations.

Such airy discussions came as a shock to me, because I was suddenly able to see Mama Siorane as the faber converts must have seen her rather than as she had seen herself—as a *flawed* pioneer who had never quite had the courage of her convictions, who had gone all the way out to Titan but had stopped short of modifying her own unfortunately mortal flesh. I was very conscious of the fact that Emily was following in Mama Siorane's footsteps, and I could not help but wonder whether she would take up the challenge of the converts and trade her emortal feet for emortal hands.

Papa Ezra, by contrast, was a hero even to converts despite that he had hung on to his legs till he died. The name of Ezra Derhan meant nothing to anyone on Earth, but it was familiar in every household on the moon and in the microworlds. Papa Ezra had *made* converts and had contributed to the perfection of the Zaman transformations with which every faber infant was now equipped. In Mare Moscoviense in 2825 hardly anyone had heard of Mortimer Gray, historian of death and unsuccessful scourge of the Thanaticists, and only one person in five was impressed if I introduced myself as a friend of Emily Marchant, gantzer extraordinaire and ice-palace designer, but *everyone* reacted when I mentioned that I was the foster son of Ezra Derhan.

I quickly came to understand that although unmodified men were still the majority population of the moon in 2825, they were no longer the dominant population, politically or ideologically. Faber attitudes were already recognized there, tacitly if not explicitly, as the attitudes that humankind would one day export to the farther reaches of the galaxy. Faber attitudes constituted the philosophy of that fraction of the human race that was not merely new but blessed with a new sense of purpose. It was hardly surprising that they considered Earthbound humanity to be decadent or that they took such aberrations as Thanaticism for glaring symptoms of that decay.

FIFTY-TWO

W here I had lived on Earth, it had always seemed to me that one could blindly throw a stone into a crowded room and stand a fifty-fifty chance of hitting either an ecologist or a historian. In Mare Moscoviense, the only ecologists were humble engineers who helped maintain the life-support systems, and the population of historians could be counted on the fingers of an unmodified man. This was in a city of a quarter of a million people. Whether they were resident or passing through, the people of the moon were far more preoccupied with the inorganic than the organic, and far more interested in the future than the past.

When I told them about my vocation, my new neighbors were likely to smile politely and shake their heads.

"It's the weight of those legs," the fabers among them were wont to say. "You think they're holding you up, but in fact they're holding you down. Give them a chance and you'll find that you've put down roots."

If any unmodified man dared to inform a faber that "having roots" wasn't considered an altogether bad thing on Earth, the faber would laugh.

"Get rid of your legs and learn to swing," the faber would say. "You'll understand then that human beings have no need of roots. Only reach with four hands instead of two, and you'll find the stars within your grasp. Leave the past to rot at the bottom of the deep dark well, and give the heavens their due."

I quickly learned to fall back on the same defensive moves that most of my unmodified neighbors employed in such combative exchanges. "You can't break all your links with solid ground," we told the fabers, over and over again. "Somebody has to deal with the larger lumps of matter that are strewn about the universe, and you can't go to meet real mass if you don't have legs. It's planets that produce biospheres and only biospheres can produce such luxuries as breathable air and recyclable carbon."

"Nonsense," the fabers replied. "Wherever there are oxides there's oxygen, and wherever there's methane there's carbon. Nanotech can do anything that natural-born life can do. A biosphere is just a layer of slime on the outside of a ball, and the slime gets in your eyes. You have to wipe them clean to see properly."

"If you've seen farther than other men," the footsloggers would tell their upstart cousins, "it's not because you can swing by your arms from the ceiling—it's because you can stand on the shoulders of giants with legs."

Such exchanges were always cheerful. It was almost impossible to get into a *real* argument with a faber because their talk was as intoxicated as their movements. They did relax, occasionally, but even on the rare occasions when all four of their arms were at rest their minds remained effervescent. Some unmodified humans accused them of chattering, but any attempt on the part of the churlish and the morose to make "ape-man" or "monkey" into a term of abuse was forestalled by the fabers' flat refusal to accept them as such.

"Footsloggers were just one more link in the great chain of primate being," they would say, amiably. "We're the cream of the ape-man crop, the main monkeys. You're just another dead end, like gorillas, big-headed Australopithecines, and lumpen Neanderthals. The partnership between hand, eye, and brain is what gave humans their humanity, and we have the very best of that."

If an unmodified human countered with the suggestion that they too might be superseded in their turn, they only chuckled with delight. "We surely will," they would say. "We're already working on it. Just as soon as we can redesign the brain to make it viable, four arms won't be enough. Just wait until the *real* spider monkeys get their eight-handed act together."

It went without saying, of course, that the vast majority of fabers were Gaean Liberationists—but such ideas came so naturally to them that they did not seem nearly as extreme in faber rhetoric as they did when they were spoken in the voice of someone like Keir McAllister. "The well belongs to the unwell," the fabers were fond of saying. Even on the moon, which was a gravity well of sorts, the statement was a cliché. There were many others of the same ilk:

The well will climb out of the Well, when they find the will.
The sick stick, the hale bail.
Hey diddle diddle, footsloggers fiddle, monkeys jump over the
    moon.

Some of these saws were annoying—especially "History is bunk, fit
for sleeping minds," which was frequently quoted at me when I told
fabers what kind of work I did—but I soon learned not to take them as
insults.

In spite of the freedom with which such opinions were laughingly
offered, there were few unmodified men on the moon who did not like
fabers. I suppose that those who could not stand them quickly retreated
into the depths of the Big Well or passed on to those habitats that spun
at great speed.

Once I had grown used to lunar banter I began to take it in good
part and even to thrive upon it. It made a refreshing change from the
kinds of conversation that I had grown used to during the previous hundred years, and I was glad that no vestige of my Earthly notoriety tainted
the atmosphere of Moscovience. Even Khan Mirafzal, when I met him in
person, made only fleeting reference to our first meeting in VE. He
greeted me as a friend with whom he had briefly lost contact, not as an
adversary who had dared to try to understand the craziness of Thanaticism.

As I adapted physically and psychologically to the conditions on the
far side of the moon, my mood was progressively lightened, and I began
to perceive the quirky wisdom of those who proposed that the satellite
was not governed by gravity at all, but by levity. I retained enough of my
intellectual seriousness to do my work, to which I remained thoroughly
dedicated, but I began to smile more frequently and to spend far less
time in VE. I put the nightmarish legacy of Thanaticism behind me and
even came to see my sojourns on Cape Adare and Cape Wolstenholme as
periods of unfortunate disequilibrium. I brought a new zest to my Herculean labors, and it seemed to me that they had never gone so smoothly.

It was in that spirit that I finally got around to restoring communication with Emily Marchant, my conscience and my inspiration.

"You were right about the galaxy," I told her, in the next long monologue I launched into the remoter regions of the system. "It does look far more inviting when there's no atmosphere to blur its face. You were right about the other galaxies too. I never expected to be able to see so many with the naked eye, and whenever I calculate the distance that I'm able to see my head spins. I do miss blue sky, and naked vegetation, but I'm not homesick yet. Visiting Earth-imitative VEs is just as false as visiting lunar VEs used to be, and the fact that I've so many memories of the actuality serves to emphasize the unreality of the virtual experience, but it adds an extra dimension to my objectivity. Time on the moon will make me a better historian in more ways than one. I haven't quite got the hang of identifying myself imaginatively with fabers—and the attempt has certainly exposed the limit of that old cliché about putting oneself in the other man's shoes—but I'm getting there.

"The moon's not an ideal place to work, of course. It's in the Labyrinth, but it has no physical archives—none, at any rate, that are relevant to my current period. It does have compensating advantages of its own, though. I never thought that it was possible to have so much flesh-to-flesh contact with other people outside of a marriage, and the tangibility of social contacts hereabouts makes up for the artificiality and inorganic dominance of the living space. I thought I'd achieved true maturity while I was living and working on Adare, but Moscoviense has shown me the limitations of the person I was then. This is a place where people really can grow up and leave their roots behind. Even though I'm not properly built for it, I can use the ceiling holds the fabers use and keep my feet off the ground for hours on end. I couldn't do it in a real faberweb, of course, but there's just enough gravity on the moon to let me feel free without having to brave the big zero.

"I'll be happier here, I think, than I've ever been before, once I'm fully accustomed to the strangeness of it all."

I spoke too soon, of course. I never did become *fully* accustomed to the strangeness of it all. But I was happy for a while—maybe not happier than I'd ever been before, but happy enough.

PART FOUR

Maturity

In the earliest phases of combat, scientific knowledge was far less efficient as a weapon in the war against death than religious faith. The quest for a scientific definition of death exposed a complex web of conclusions as physicians debated the relative merits of cessation of heartbeat, cessation of respiration, the dying of the cornea, insensibility to electrical stimuli, and the relaxation of sphincter muscles as evidence of irrecoverable demise. Skeptics compiled catalogs of case histories of people buried alive and urban legends recorded macabre cases of childbirth as a result of "necrophilia" practiced by monks or mortuary assistants. Ryan, in 1836, introduced a new distinction between somatic death—the extinction of personality—and molecular death—the death of the body's cells, noting that the former was rarely instantaneous and the latter never. Prizes were offered in nineteenth-century France for an infallible sign of death, and the failure of all attempts to claim such prizes resulted in the official provision of mortuaries where bodies might lay until the onset of putrefaction settled the matter beyond the shadow of a doubt.

Anthropologists and psychologists made little progress in their early attempts to comprehend and explain attitudes to death and the ritual treatment of corpses. Hertz observed but could not fully rationalize the fact that many death rites involved a two-phased process, the first dealing with "wet" corruptible flesh and the second with "dry" remains such as bones and ashes. He understood that the first phase of interment, cremation, or storage constituted a symbolic removal of the dead person from the realm of "natural", whereas the secondary rite—the scattering of ashes, the assembly of ossuaries, the equipment of graves with monumental masonry and so on—emphasized the continuity of a human community whose members were all making their painstaking way from cradle to grave, but he had no other analogy to draw upon than that between funeral rites and the "rites of passage" by which boys became men. Freud fared no better, being unable to see belief in the soul's survival of death as anything but a delusory wish-fulfilment fantasy, and funeral rites as anything more than expressions of terror and anxiety, and was led in consequence to hypothesize egoistic "death instincts" which seemingly arose as the natural antithesis of the sexual-reproductive "life instincts."

—Mortimer Gray
Commentary, Part Five of *The History of Death*, 2849

FIFTY-THREE

I was not exaggerating when I told Emily that the sight of the sky unmasked by an atmospheric envelope had a profound effect on me. She must have known as well as I did, however, that the inhabitants of the moon did not see such sights very often. The Earthbound sometimes speak of the "domed cities" of the moon as if they were vast hothouses, like Earthly cities enclosed by crystal shells, but they aren't.

Like the colonists of Io and Europa, the moon's inhabitants are burrowers, and the vast majority of their dwellings are far beneath the surface. No one lives in edifices like the one I rented on Cape Adare, from whose high windows one can look out on a bleak and cratered landscape. Windows are a great rarity on the moon, and there are fewer in Moscoviense than in the nearside cities whose tourists love to be able to look up at the blue Earth hanging stationary in the sky.

There are, of course, a few lunar workers who routinely go out on to the surface, in buggies or in suits, for whom looking up at the stars is almost an everyday experience, but the vast majority of the entities that trundle back and forth across the bare rock are machines animated by AIs, and most of those requiring human intelligence to guide them are remotely operated. The average citizen of Moscoviense, faber or footslogger, had to go to considerable trouble to see the stars. Newcomers made such efforts often enough, but anyone who had been resident long enough to consider himself a lunatic was likely to have lost the habit.

I was no exception.

In my early years in Moscoviense I carried everywhere the teasing consciousness that I was living on an airless world whose roof was set beneath a star-filled sky. Subject as I was to every psychosomatic disorder that was going, I really did feel a quasimagnetic pull, which those stars seemed to exert upon my spirit. I really did give serious consideration to the possibility of applying for somatic modification for low gee and shipping out with emigrants to some new microworld or to one or other of the satellites of Jupiter. All footsloggers living on the moon were subject to a constant flow of subtle propaganda urging them to take "the next step" by removing themselves to some more distant world where the sun's bountiful radiance was of little consequence, where people lived entirely by the fruits of their own efforts and their own wisdom— but the very constancy of the propaganda eventually dulled its effect.

As time went by, I ceased to make the effort to go up to the observation ports and study the stars. Having no reason to go out on to the surface, once I had exhausted the excuse that it was *there*, I left it to its own devices. In brief, I settled in—the operative word being *in*. I adapted myself to life in the interior of the moon and became as claustrophilic as the great majority of its longtime residents. One-sixth gee became normal and no longer made me feel light-headed—with the result that the once-ever-present awareness of the universe of stars faded away, and the power of Papa Domenico's Universe Without Limits gradually reclaimed the psychological territory it had briefly ceded.

Seen objectively, Mare Moscoviense was a sublunar labyrinth, more in tune with the vast virtual Labyrinth that existed in parallel with it than any city on Earth. There were, however, some significant differences between the view from the moon and the view from Earth, and the most significant of all was the news.

When I first went to the moon I fully intended to shun the TV news, not so much because I feared that news of Earth might make me feel homesick but because I felt that I had burned my fingers once by dipping into the world beyond the headlines, and that once was enough. I had not realized, though, how different the news on the moon would be. It was, I suppose, a foolish mistake for a historian to make, but I had always thought of the news as being *the* news, summarized but reasonably comprehensive. It had never occurred to me that Earthly TV was so preoccupied with Earthly affairs that the greater part of the information flowing in from the more distant reaches of the Oikumene was condensed to irrelevance. Nor had it occurred to me that on the moon, a mere 400,000 kilometers away, the Big Well would be considered so much more remote than the burgeoning ice palaces of faraway Titan that Earthly affairs would be relegated to the footnotes of the story stream. In fact, the Earthbound news I had long been used to was replaced on the moon by news that flatly refused to be confounded by astronomical distances.

Lunar news fascinated me, first as a phenomenon and then as a precious source of insight into the human adventure, and its fascination never wore thin. Its consumption began to take up an increasingly large fraction of my spare time when the novelty of the flesh-to-flesh contacts about which I had enthused to Emily wore off.

As the years began to drift by, I reverted yet again to the quiet life of a recluse. I never applied for any kind of somatic modification or cyborgization that would have made life in one-sixth gee feel more comfortable. After taking the first big step that brought me to the moon, and the smaller one that enabled me to take such a liking to the fabers, I hesitated over any other. In spite of all my representations to Emily, my heart and mind remained fundamentally Earthbound.

Sometimes, even I thought of my failure to seek further physiological adaptation as a kind of cowardice—a neurotic reluctance to cut the symbolic umbilical cord connecting me to Earth. Sometimes, even I accepted that reluctance as compelling evidence of my infection by the decadence that the fabers attributed to Earthbound humanity. In such moments of self-doubt I was wont to imagine myself as an insect born at the bottom of a deep cave, who had—thanks to the toil of many preceding generations of insects—been brought to the rim from which I could look out at the great world but dared not take the one small extra step that would carry me out and away. When I went in search of excuses, though, I readily extended the analogy to recall unlucky insects drawn to candle flames, whose combination of instinct and daring proved fatal.

By the time I had been on the moon for twenty happy years I found my thoughts turning back to the Earth more and more frequently and my memories of its many environments becoming gradually fonder. The careful manner in which Earth was relegated to the periphery of the human community by the lunar news gave me a valuable new perspective on Earthbound life, but the longer I lived with that perspective the more convinced I became that I was now properly equipped for life on Earth in a way that I had never been before. I began to think of my sojourn on the moon as a holiday from my real life. It was not, of course, a vacation from my work, which continued apace, but it came to seem like a pause in the pattern of my life as a whole: an interval in which I could collect myself and make ready for a resumption of the ordinary course of my affairs.

When I tried to explain my new state of mind to Emily I found myself hesitating over the wisdom of honesty, but I couldn't lie to her.

"It's just nerves, Morty," she assured me, in one of her exhortatory missives. "You're *dithering* again. You'll have to get over it eventually, so why not now? If you go back down the Well, you'll only have to climb out again. Come to Titan now, while everything here is new, and we'll go on to Nereid together when the time comes."

Her pleas did not have the desired effect. If anything, they called forth the same stubbornness that I had cultivated long before as armor against Mama Siorane's similar exhortations. I reminded myself that Earth was, after all, my home. It was not only *my* world, but the home world of *all* humankind. No matter what Emily might think, or what my faber friends might say, I began to insist both privately and publicly whenever the issue was raised that the Earth was and would always remain an exceedingly precious thing, which should never be forgotten, and that all spacefarers ought to respect and revere its unique place in human affairs.

When the fabers mocked and Emily grew annoyed I dug in my heels.

"It would be a terrible thing," I told them all, "were men to spread themselves across the entire galaxy, taking a multitude of forms in order to occupy a multitude of alien worlds, and in the end forget entirely the world from which their ancestors had sprung. Travel far, by all means, but never forget that you have only one true home."

"Oh, Morty," was Emily's belated reply from the wilderness without Saturn's rings, "will you *never* learn?" But I was older than she, if only by a few years, and I honestly thought that I had now acquired the greater maturity, the better understanding of how to live in the future.

FIFTY-FOUR

The fifth volume of the *History of Death*, entitled *The War of Attrition*, was launched on 19 March 2849. Even my sternest critics conceded that it marked a return to the cooler and more comprehensive style of scholarship exhibited by the first two volumes. The chief topic and main connecting thread of the commentary was the history of medical science and hygiene up to the end of the nineteenth century.

The move from contemplation of the history of religion to consideration of the history of science—even a science as misconceived and superstition ridden as pre-twentieth-century medicine—facilitated my adoption of a more analytical pose. Because my main concern was with a very different arena of the war between mankind and mortality, the tenor of my rhetoric was much more acceptable to my peers.

To many of its lay readers, on the other hand, *The War of Attrition* was undoubtedly a disappointment. There was nothing in it to comfort the few who still retained a ghoulish interest in the past excesses of Thanaticism. Readers whose primary interest was in the follies of the human imagination must also have found it less fascinating than its predecessors, although it did include material about Victorian tomb decoration and nineteenth-century spiritualism, which carried forward arguments from volume four.

The flow of access fees was very satisfactory for the first six months of the new chapter's labyrinthine existence, but demand tailed off fairly rapidly when it was realized how different the work was from its predecessors. The vastness and density of its Gordian knot of supportive data made it very difficult for anyone to navigate a course through the entire work, so the few educators and professional historians who condescended to make use of it had to return again and again. I was confident that the flow of income would not dry up entirely, but I knew that I would have to tighten my belt a little if I were to continue to cope with the moon's ferocious indirect tax regime.

The lack of popular enthusiasm for *The War of Attrition* was not, of course, counterbalanced by any conclusive redemption of my academic reputation. Like many earlier scholars who had made contact with a popular audience, I was considered guilty of a kind of intellectual treason, and I knew that I would continue to be frozen out of the scholarly community in spite of my determined attempts at rehabilitation until the academic consensus accepted that I had served my sentence. The stigma attached to my name in academic circles might even have been increased by a few popular reviews that suggested there was much in the new volume to intrigue the inhabitants of a world whose medical science was so adept that almost everyone enjoyed perfect health as well as eternal youth. These reviews suggested that there was a certain piquant delight to be obtained from recalling a world in which everyone was—by modern standards—crippled or deformed, and in which everyone suffered continually from illnesses of a most horrific nature for which no effective treatments were available.

Some commentators felt that my treatment of early medical practitioners was unnecessarily scathing, whereas others thought it unduly generous. It was, of course, both—how could it be otherwise? What could one say of a so-called profession whose practitioners had stubbornly ignored for more than two thousand years the only sensible piece of advice offered by its so-called father, Hippocrates? I did not, of course, make much headway in the difficult business of trying to ascertain which few of the eighty-seven volumes of the Hippocratic Collection actually were by Hippocrates, but I was content to attribute to him the one crucial observation that treatment was best avoided because most active interventions worked to the detriment of the patient. For 2200 years doctors persisted blindly and pigheadedly in applying treatments that increased the danger in which their patients stood.

Even when the scientific method became a common mode of thought doctors remained crassly oblivious to its benefits, preferring to heed the vile counsels of ignoble tradition. How was it, I wondered, that the greatest English minds of the late eighteenth century, assembled together by Erasmus Darwin in the aptly named Lunatic Society, should have penetrated so many secrets of nature and technical practice without ever once applying their trained vision to Darwin's own profession?— with the result that his beloved son died of blood poisoning caused by a septic finger. How could any historian be less than scathing in chronicling such stupidity?

On the other hand, I was careful to give credit where it was due, complimenting medical practice as the most efficient accessory of religion in the psychological warfare that humankind waged against its ultimate enemy. The treatments that were so woefully ineffective in any material sense, even to the extent of being physically injurious, made a contribution nevertheless to the morale of the race. Seen as quasi-magical rituals, more akin to funerary rites than curative practices, early medicine became a much healthier—or, at any rate, a much more courageous—affair.

I have to admit that there were some passages in the commentary of *The War of Attrition* that could be deemed to partake of the "pornography of death and suffering." Its accounts of the early history of surgery and midwifery were certainly bloodcurdling, and its painstaking analysis of the spread of syphilis through Europe in the sixteenth century could be consumed by readers so inclined as a horror story made all the nastier by its clinical narration.

I was particularly interested in syphilis because of the dramatic social effects of its sudden advent in Europe and its significance in the development of prophylactic medicine. My argument was that syphilis had been primarily responsible for the rise and spread of Puritanism, repressive sexual morality being the only truly effective weapon against its spread. I then deployed well-tried sociological arguments to the effect that Puritanism and its associated habits of thought had been importantly implicated in the rapid development of Capitalism in the Western World. This chain of argument allowed me to put forward the not altogether serious suggestion that syphilis ought to be regarded as the root cause of the economic and political systems that eventually came to dominate the most chaotic, the most extravagantly progressive, and most extravagantly destructive centuries of human history. I left it to my readers to recall that the present owners of the world still referred to their economic manipulations as "Planned Capitalism." The levity of life in the moon might have removed a little too much gravity from my analysis at that particular point.

The history of medicine and the conquest of disease were, of course, topics of elementary education in the twenty-ninth century. There was supposedly not a citizen of any nation to whom the names of Semmelweis, Jenner, and Pasteur were unknown—but disease had been so long banished from the world, and it was so completely outside the experience of ordinary men and women, that what people "knew" about it was never really brought to consciousness and never came alive to the imagination. Although recreational diseases were still relatively commonplace in the Big Well in the 2840s, popular usage of words such as *smallpox, plague,* and *cancer* was almost exclusively metaphorical.

I would have liked *The War of Attrition* to remind the world of certain issues that, though not exactly forgotten, had not been *brought to mind* while the diehard explorers of extreme experience had been injecting themselves with all manner of tailored germs, but I cannot pretend that it did. It is at least arguable that it touched off a few unobtrusive ripples whose movement across the collective consciousness of world culture was of some moment, but I dare not press the point. The simple fact is that the name of Mortimer Gray was no longer notorious in 2849, and his continuing work had not yet become firmly established within the zeitgeist.

FIFTY-FIVE

During my latter years in Mare Moscoviense I was often visited by Khan Mirafzal, the faber with whom I had crossed swords on terrestrial TV. The culture of the fabers was so much more geared to face-to-face interaction than that of lunar footsloggers, let alone the thoroughly privatized societies of Earth, that it was a rare faber who would not "drop in" if he happened to be passing the residence of a friend he had not seen for a month or more. When he returned to the moon briefly from the microworld in the asteroid belt that was now his home, Mirafzal automatically came along in person to find out how I was getting along.

His own news was, inevitably, rather more interesting than mine.

Mirafzal explained to me that the microworld on which he lived was being fitted with an antimatter drive that would take it out of the system and into the infinite. Its prospective voyagers were going to great pains to make sure that it was properly equipped for its departure and Mirafzal was one of those charged with the duty of keeping close track of technical progress in the inner system to make sure that no opportunity went unseized.

"We'll keep in touch by radio, of course," he said, "but we need to be sure that we're in a position to take advantage of any new developments that come up while we're deep in interstellar space."

Mirafzal was a kind and even-tempered man who would not have dreamed of adopting salesmanlike tactics to convince me of the error of my Earthbound ways, but he was also a man with a sublime vision who could not restrain his enthusiasm for his own chosen destiny. He swept aside my mildly skeptical observations about the prospect of being enclosed in such a tiny space for hundreds of years with the same faces and voices. It was with him that I had the conversations that I couldn't yet have with Emily, and to him that I exposed my doubts about the direction in which I ought to be going. He was a good listener, and he took me seriously. He was the only faber I knew who did not laugh when

I used footslogger metaphors in all seriousness, and he even conde-scended to use them himself.

"*I* have no roots on Earth, Mortimer, in any metaphorical sense whatsoever," he assured me, when I wondered whether even he might become homesick in the great void beyond the Oort Cloud. "In my being, the chains of adaptation have been decisively broken. Every man of my kind is born anew, designed and synthesized. We are the *self-made men*, who belong everywhere and nowhere. The wilderness of empty space that you find so appalling is our realm and our heritage. I am homesick *now*, but when the voyage begins, I will be doing what I am designed to do."

"But you've lived alongside unmodified humans throughout your formative years," I pointed out. "You've always lived amid the scattered masses of the solar family. To you, as to me, the utter desolation of the void will surely be strange and alien."

"Nothing is strange to us," he assured me. "Nothing is foreign and nothing is alien."

"My point exactly," I replied, wryly.

He smiled politely at the joke, but would not retreat from his posi-tion.

"Blastular engineering has incorporated freedom into our blood and our bones," he said, "and I intend to take full advantage of that freedom. To do otherwise would be a betrayal of my nature."

"While my own blastular engineering served only to complete the adaptation to life on Earth that natural selection had left incomplete," I mused, applying his logic to my own situation. "Given that I can never be free from the ties that bind me to Earth, perhaps I have no alternative but to return."

"That's not so," he countered. "Natural selection would never have devised emortality, for natural selection can only generate change by death and replacement. When genetic engineers found the means of set-ting aside the curse of aging they put an end to *natural* selection forever. The first and greatest freedom is time, my friend, and you have all the time in the world. You can become whatever you want to be. If you wish, you may even become a faber of sorts—although I gather that you have no such ambition. What *do* you want to be, Mortimer?"

"A historian," I told him, reflexively. "It's what I am because it's what I want to be."

"All well and good, for now," he conceded, "but history isn't inexhaustible, Mortimer, as you well know. It ends with the present day, the present moment, and no matter how slowly you can recapitulate its achievements, you'll have to arrive in the present someday. The future, on the other hand, is . . ."

"Given to your kind," I said, although I assumed that he was going to say *infinite*. "I know all that, Mira. I don't dispute any of it. But what exactly *is* your kind, given that you rejoice in such freedom to be anything you want to be?"

"Not yet," he said. "We've hardly scratched the surface of constructive cyborgization. That will open up a whole new dimension of freedom."

"And reopen all the old arguments about robotization," I added. "The older I get, the more sense those arguments seem to make. Once your little world is lost in the emptiness, effectively cut off from everything else in the universe, how will you avoid the trap of endless repetition? How will you maintain spontaneity, change, difference?"

"Earth is just a bigger spaceship," Mirafzal reminded me. "The whole solar system is a narrow room—and will one day become exactly that, complete with enclosing walls, if the Type-2 enthusiasts get their way. Even if a rival sect of cosmic engineers eventually wins through, it will only change the decor—and after humankind attains Type-2, the galaxy will become the playground of the Type-3 visionaries. Spontaneity, change, and difference have to come from within, Morty. Cyborgization isn't robotization; it's enhancement, not mechanization."

"And spacefarers will be its pioneers, figuring out how to do it and why while all the lazy footsloggers live on the capital of Earth's evolutionary momentum," I conceded, with a sigh. "Maybe you're right, Mira. Maybe it is just my legs that weigh my spirit down—but if so, then I'm well and truly addicted to gravity. I can't cast off the past like a worn-out suitskin. I know you think I ought to envy you, but I don't. You think that I and all my kind are clinging like a terrified infant to Mother Earth while you and your kind are achieving true maturity, but I really do think that it's important to have somewhere to *belong*."

"So do I," the faber said, quietly. "I just don't think that Earth is or ought to be that place. It's not where you start from that's important, Mortimer, it's where you're going."

"Not for a historian," I protested, feebly.

"For everybody," he insisted. "History ends, Mortimer. Life doesn't—not any more."

FIFTY-SIX

While I continued to lived on the moon I was half-convinced that Khan Mirafzal was right, although I never followed any of his well-meant advice. The remaining half of my conviction was otherwise inclined. I couldn't accept that I was trapped in a kind of existential infancy any more than I could see myself as a victim of lotus-eater decadence. Perhaps things would have turned out differently if I'd had one of my close encounters with death while I was on the moon, but I didn't. The dome in which I lived was only breached once, and the crack was sealed before there was any significant air loss. It was a scare, but it wasn't a life-endangering threat. The longer I stayed in Mare Moscoviense, the more I came to think of the moon as Antarctica without the crevasses, but with nosier neighbors.

It was always inevitable, I think, that I would eventually give in to my homesickness for Garden Earth and return there, having resolved not to leave it again until my history of death was complete, but there was one more challenge awaiting me after Khan Mirafzal had left the moon for the last time. There was one person in the solar system who had the power to affect me far more deeply in face-to-face confrontation than he and all his kind—and even the footsloggers of Titan sometimes visited the moon.

I received Emily's message telling me that she had embarked on a shuttle heading for the moon within days of the news coming through that *Hope*, one of the ancient Arks launched during the early phase of the Crash with a cargo of SusAn-preserved potential colonists, had settled into orbit around an Earthlike planet orbiting a G-type sun some fifty-eight light-years away in Sagitarius.

This news was, of course, fifty-eight years old, but it was no less sensational for that. AI-directed kalpa probes had located more than a dozen life-bearing planets, but we only had hard evidence of multicellular life on two of them, neither of which could be described as "Earthlike" no matter how much generosity was granted to the label. *Hope's* first broadcast spoke of a world whose atmosphere was breathable with the aid of face masks, with abundant plant life and animals sufficiently similar to those of Earth to allow talk of "insects," "reptiles," "birds," and "mammals."

Hope had been sent out to find exactly such a world, ripe for colonization. The generations of its mortal crew had clung hard to that determination while news had followed them that Earth's ecosphere had not been conclusively blighted. New data regarding the scarcity of planets that could be classified as "terraformable" must have poured into the ship's data banks while it crawled through the void, but even that had not persuaded the ship's masters to turn around. Now, they considered their decision to have been vindicated, and their initial howl of triumph was headline news even on Earth.

By the time Emily's ship actually arrived on the moon, however, the news flow from the world that *Hope*'s captain had named Ararat was by no means so enthusiastic. The primitive nanotech systems deposited on the surface had made good progress in gantzing dwellings out of the alien soil, but attempts to adapt local reproductive systems to the manufacture of human foodstuffs had run into trouble, and the first people brought out of SusAn in order to work on the surface—not all of whom survived the revival process—were experiencing unexpected problems of psychological adaptation.

Although the SusAn systems installed on *Hope* had been rendered obsolete several centuries before there were some similar systems still in operation, in which the worst of the first generation of criminals sentenced to SusAn imprisonment were still confined, so the news that long-term freezing down seemed to have unwelcome psychotropic effects was not entirely irrelevant to the Earthbound.

Emily was less enthusiastic about the discovery than I had expected, but she made much of the elementary fact that other "Earthlike" planets did exist.

"The real crux of the matter isn't *Hope*'s chances of establishing a human population on the surface of Ararat," she argued, "but the evidence they've found of an extinct species of intelligent humanoid indigenes. That's as close as we can come to proof of the fact that we aren't alone in the galaxy without actually shaking hands with our mirror images. One humaniform race might be a fluke, but where there's two there must be many more, even if one of the two is already defunct."

"They're not *entirely* sure that the sentients are extinct," I told her. "Even if they're still around, though, it doesn't really *prove* anything. We've been scanning the sky for radio messages for a very long time now, so any other human races that have reached our level of technical sophistication must be very discreet. We mustn't forget that *Hope* is a strange historical anomaly, launched in a blind panic. Our entire philosophy of cosmic exploration has changed since it went out. Other humaniform races might be busy doing exactly what we're now busy doing: remaking their spacefarers physically and psychologically."

"*We*, Morty?" she echoed, twitching an eyebrow. She was lightly cyborgized, and had almost certainly undergone some subtle somatic engineering, but her appearance was much as I remembered it—and mine must have been exactly as she remembered it. Neither of us was the type to go in for cosmetic modification for fashion's sake.

"I mean the fabers," I admitted. "The forebears of the future human races: the six-handed, the eight-handed, and all the others that are still a twinkle in the imaginative eye."

"I'm an old-fashioned ganzter," she reminded me. "My job is adapting inorganic environments to suit the purposes of the humaniform, not the other way around."

"Purposes?" I queried. "I thought you were an artist."

"And all art is useless? I never had you pegged as a neo-Wildean, Morty. I'm the kind of artist who believes in the perfect combination of function and beauty."

I was mildly surprised to hear that, given that coverage of Titan's new skylines on the lunar news was usually careful to stress that however imposing they might seem the ice palaces were uninhabitable. When I put this point to Emily, she said: "Uninhabitable *as yet*. They're not just pieces of sculpture, Morty—they're greenhouses. We haven't yet managed to distribute the heat as efficiently as we might, but it's only a matter of time and hard work. Titan will never bathe in the kind of solar deluge that powers Earth's biomass, although some of us are giving serious consideration to ways and means of increasing its meager portion. But it's still an energy beneficiary, and it's sitting next door to the second-biggest lode of raw materials in the system. It won't be easy to manage the economics of exchange, but the day will come soon enough when life on the surface of Titan will be a great deal easier and more comfortable than life in the lunar air traps. If luck is with us we'll both live to see it. Even if Titan's core weren't reasonably warm it could still be done, but the geothermal kick-start will make it a lot easier. Believe me, Morty—all those glittering castles are potential real estate, and within a hundred years, or one-fifty at the most, they'll be the realest estates on the market."

"At which point," I said, "you'll doubtless become richer by a further three or four orders of magnitude."

"It's not about getting rich," she said. "There isn't going to be any Hardinist Cabal on Titan. We figure that the highkickers are mature enough not to fall prey to the tragedy of the commons. Forget the Gaean Libs, Morty—*we*'re the next and last Revolution."

I had to admit that "highkickers" was a much more flattering label than "footsloggers." I knew that she'd have heard all the jokes about can-can and can-do, so I didn't even try to sharpen my wit on the term. There wasn't time enough to waste on that kind of nonsense.

FIFTY-SEVEN

E mily hadn't come to the moon for a vacation and she was very busy, but she had adopted highkicker notions of personal space and the value of face-to-face contact, so I saw a lot more of her than I might have expected. When she did find time to relax I showed her the sights, such as they were. We went out of the dome together, in ultralight suitskins, so that we could look at the stars and feel the authentic lunar surface beneath our feet.

Because Titan had an atmosphere Emily didn't see the true profusion of the stars very often, but that didn't prevent her waxing lyrical about the wondrous sights that the cosmos presented to the inhabitants of the outer system. The view from the moon comprised exactly the same stars, and farside light-pollution was minimal, but mere logic couldn't shake Emily's conviction that everything looked better out on Civilization's Edge. I suppose that it must have been easy to reach that opinion while Saturn dominated the sky. In Mare Moscoviense we never saw Earth.

"One day," I told her, "I'll have to come see it all for myself. VE tourism isn't the same. Now that I've experienced Earth-based VEs from a lunar-gravity vantage point I'm even more alert than I used to be to their artificiality." She knew that it was mere talk, of course. I was already in intensive training for the return to full gravity. She'd come along to the gym with me to put in little centrifuge time on her own account, and we'd played the usual lunatic games with massive dumbbells.

"Why wait, Morty?" she asked, softly. "Why *one day* instead of now?"

"I've got work to do," I said. She knew that too. I'd shown her everything, including the new data webs I was patiently building and knitting together. She hadn't paid much attention, just as I hadn't paid much attention while she was shopping for new-generation gantzers that were just as gray and slimy as the ones that had become obsolete five minutes before.

"Oh yes," she said, with deadly unenthusiasm. "Two more volumes of your precious *History of Death*."

"Actually," I confessed, a trifle belatedly, "it's going to take more than two. Maybe I can cram it into three, but at present I'm thinking four."

"Which would make it the longest procrastination in history, I suppose," she said, cruelly. "Let's see—the first version of the first part was deposited in 2614, and the fifth in 2849. That means that we can expect the ninth and last in 3082—except, of course, that it'll only be the first version, so you'll have to tinker round with it for another . . . what shall we say? A couple of hundred years? Say 3300 to make it a round number. By which time you'll be seven hundred and eighty years old. It's just as well that you don't believe all that doom-laden Thanaticist cant about robotization and the necessity of making a good death before we become mere machines, isn't it?"

"The research is going very well," I told her, "and I'm more focused now than I used to be. I'm hoping to have the whole thing wrapped up well before the turn of the millennium."

"Will anybody care?" she asked. "When did the last false emortal die? Fifty years ago? Don't bother to tell me the exact date—it doesn't make any difference. The war against death is over, Morty. It doesn't matter any more. The point is to find the best way to live *without* death."

"Finding the best way to live without death is part and parcel of the war against it," I insisted.

"And have your studies brought you a single step closer to finding that best way?" she continued, implacably. "Have you found an answer that can satisfy you, Morty?" She didn't need to add, *Have I?* It went without saying that neither of us had found any such thing—*as yet*. It also went without saying that Khan Mirafzal and his kin were hotter favorites to find an answer adequate to their own kind than any footslogger, no matter how high she could kick.

"I have time," I said, defensively. "I'm emortal."

"So are the murdering bastards tucked away in twenty-first-century SusAns," she said, "just so long as they never come out. I forgot about them, of course, when I tried to remember when the last false emortal died. And there's dear old Adam Zimmerman too—assuming that he isn't just a guiding myth invented to stoke up the zeal of the the Ahasuerus Foundation's Zamaners. How old is *he* now, if he actually exists? Nine hundred, almost to the day! Our invitations to the birthday party must have gotten lost in the ether. How much time there is to waste, when you think about it!"

"My work isn't a waste," I told her, stubbornly. "It's not irrelevant. If you hadn't left Earth before the Thanaticists got going, you'd understand that the war against death isn't over."

"No," she said, in a different and darker tone. "It isn't. I've lost three good friends in the last five years, and I'll lose half a hundred more before the ice palaces are teeming with the latest kind of Utopians. I live every day with the possibility that they might be the ones who'll lose me, but I'm not prepared to hide out in the bomb shelters indefinitely. I'm not prepared to reduce the horizons of my life to those of a glorified life raft. I want to be part of the Revolution, Morty, not part of the problem that makes the Revolution necessary."

"That's not fair," I complained, meaning the suggestion that I was still psychologically becalmed in the life raft we'd shared when she was a child.

"What's *fair* got to do with it, you great oaf?" she answered, smiling like a faber surrounded by her children. One day, I realized, Emily might be surrounded by highkicking children of her own, busy with the work of populating a brand-new world with skylines more wondrous than any in the system, and perhaps even out of it. On the other hand, she might have moved on, beyond even the satellites of Uranus and Neptune, to some very-nearly-but-not-quite Earthlike world capable of providing a *real* challenge to a sculptor of her abilities.

"I have to finish it," I told her. "It's what I am. I won't apologize for that because I don't think I owe you or the world any kind of apology for what I am *or* what I do."

"No," she conceded. "You don't owe me or the world anything. I just don't want you to be *left behind*."

"There'll always be Earthbound humans," I told her, as I'd always told everyone who seemed to need telling. "Maybe I'm one of the ones who's destined to remain there forever."

"So what are you doing hanging about on the moon?" she said. "It's just Antarctica without ice palaces, and noisier neighbors. I've seen you in the centrifuge and I know you're ready. Your legs are positively itching to get to grips with all that gee force."

"I'm as ready as I'll ever be, legwise," I admitted. "Maybe I stuck around just to see *you* for one last time, before you get so far ahead of me that you'll be way out of reach."

"Oaf," she said, tenderly. "Footslogger. Groundhog. Welldweller. You know that I fell in love with you in that stupid life raft, don't you? You know that all the nonsense you trotted out to keep my mind off the danger we were in cut right to my heart. You made me, Mortimer Gray."

I could have said straight out that she'd made me too, but she couldn't have taken it as a compliment in that form. "That's the way it works," I said, instead. "Any two elementary particles that have ever been closely associated continue to modify one another's movements no matter how far apart they move. I never understood exactly why, but I think it's something to do with the beauty and charm of their constituent quarks—and if it isn't, it ought to be."

FIFTY-EIGHT

t turned out that my legs weren't quite as ready for the return to the Big Well as they seemed. The centrifuge can prepare returning lunatics for the shock of bottoming out, but it can't prepare them for the sheer relentlessness of gravity. While you have levity at your beck and call it's easy to think that you won't miss it, but when it's four hundred thousand kilometers out of reach it suddenly seems like a precious resource gone to waste.

A curious thing happened to me when I got back to Earth and booked into a rehab hostel. While I was enjoying my first long session in the swimming pool—although I wasn't doing much actual swimming—I was joined by a tall man with unusually dark skin, whose walk as he crossed the polished floor suggested that his legs were not in the least need of readaptation. He swam several languorous lengths before making his way over to the lane in which I was dawdling.

"Hello, Mortimer," he said. "You don't recognize me, do you?"

As soon as he suggested that I *ought* to recognize him I did. It wasn't so much the hue of his skin as the manner of his speech that tipped me off.

"All history is fantasy," I quoted at him. "I was only a boy when we met, Mister Ngomi. It was more than three hundred years ago."

He smiled broadly. "Call me Julius," he said. "They said we'd never manage to keep hold of our early memories, didn't they? The falsies, that is. Because serial rejuves and too much nano in the brain left *their* memories pretty much wiped out, they assumed we'd be the same, serially reincarnate within the same body. It's good to be able to prove them wrong, isn't it?"

"There's not much else I remember from those days but bare facts," I confessed. "You made an impression. It was so unexpected—the inside of the mountain, I mean. The kind of thing of which indelible traces are made. Did you actually come here *looking* for me?"

"As a matter of fact," he said, "I did."

"Why?" I asked, guardedly. I remembered him clearly enough to be sure that his wasn't the kind of job you did for a hundred years or so and then put behind you. If he'd been a finger of the invisible hand then, he was probably a thumb by now, maybe even one of the eyes that guided the hand.

"Emily Marchant," he said, bluntly.

My memory of recent events was much sharper than time-worn indelible impressions. I could still replay the words within my mind, hearing them spoken in her own voice. *There isn't going to be any Hardinist Cabal on Titan. We figure that the highkickers are mature enough not to fall prey to the tragedy of the commons. Forget the Gaean Libs, Morty—we're the next and last Revolution.*

"What about Emily Marchant?" I said, frostily.

"Don't be like that," he said, still grinning. "I'm not about to ask you to betray any intimate secrets. It's just that the walls on the moon don't have nearly as many ears and eyes as the walls on Earth—and the ice palaces of Titan might as well be on another world for all the worthwhile intelligence we get from *them*."

I didn't laugh at the incredibly weak joke. "So what?" I said. "Didn't the Sauls and their cozy circle make a Faustian bargain five hundred years ago that allowed them to keep ownership of Earth in exchange for their assistance in giving everyone with ambition a slice of the cosmic pie? Isn't it a little late to decide that you want to own the entire solar system?"

"It's not as simple as that," he said. "You're a historian, Mortimer. The next section of your masterwork will deal with the twentieth and twenty-first centuries, so you must be acquainted with the elementary principles of Hardinism."

"The institution of private property is good because it motivates owners to protect their resources from the ruinous depredations of greed," I said. "It sounds fine in theory, but if there's one thing intensive study of the twentieth and twenty-first centuries makes clear, it's that owners can be every bit as greedy and destructive as competitors fighting to maximize their own returns from a common resource."

"Hardinism is all about *good* ownership," Ngomi informed me, perfectly straight-faced for once. "The Hardinist creed equates good ownership with *responsible stewardship*. What did Emily Marchant tell you about Jupiter?"

I honestly thought that it was a trick question. "Last time she was there," I told him, "Titan was still in orbit around Saturn."

"Don't be disingenuous, Mortimer," he retorted. "We aren't interested in the petty Utopia that she and her friends are designing for her pretty glass houses, any more than we're interested in the fabers' plans to convert the entire asteroid belt into a fleet of starships to facilitate the Diaspora of the many-handed. Jupiter is different. There could be a real conflict of interest over Jupiter. You might think that it's all a long way off, but if you and I expect to live forever and a day, we have to settle potential conflicts as early as possible, in case they fester and infect the whole Oikumene. As you're so fond of saying, there'll always be Earthbound humans, and their long-term interests have to be protected. If that means staking a claim to Jupiter, so be it."

I stared at him for a full half-minute, wishing that my head—the only part of me that wasn't benefiting from the buoyancy of the water—didn't seem quite so heavy. "I honestly don't have the faintest idea what you're talking about, Mister Ngomi," I said. "I will admit that I wouldn't tell you anything that Emily said to me in confidence, but I wouldn't lie to you about it either. If Emily and the other rich folk in the outer system have any plans for the development of the Jovian satellites, she certainly didn't mention them to me. I assume that all the good reasons the outward bounders had for letting Europa and Ganymede alone still hold."

"It's not the Jovian satellites we're concerned about," Ngomi said. "It's the planet itself."

I jumped to what seemed to me to be the natural conclusion. "Are you talking about the Type-2 movement?" I asked, uncertainly.

There had been a lot more talk about the Type-2 crusade of late, even among people who believed that the third millennium was far too soon to start planning for the day when the Oikumene would want to exploit the entirety of the sun's energy by building a series of superstructures in Earth's orbit. When asked where the mass would come from—as they frequently were nowadays, by the same casters who had once solicited my views on Thanaticism—Type-2 visionaries were fond of pointing out that Jupiter had enough mass to make a hollow compound sphere with a radius of one astronomical unit and some fifty meters separating the inner and outer shells, always provided that you could transport and transmute it.

I couldn't believe that the Titanians were seriously involved with Type-2 persiflage, though; they were working on a very different timescale. By the time the Type-2 cowboys got to square one Emily and her fellow outlookers would presumably be halfway to the galactic center. Then I remembered, slightly belatedly, what she'd said about the possibility of improving Titan's meager ration of the sun's energy and guessed what Julius Ngomi was really talking about.

"I suppose I am, in a manner of speaking," Ngomi replied, "but even you and I aren't likely to live long enough to see the sun boxed in. It's not so much what *we* might want to do with Jupiter, way down the time line, as what *they* might want to do with it much sooner."

"Which is?" I parried, unwilling to tip my hand.

He looked at me as long and hard as I'd looked at him. Even at three hundred and some, most Earthbounders spend too much time in VE to know how to keep a straight face under intense inspection, but I'd just got back from thirty-odd years on the moon, where people look into one another's faces far more frequently, and I'd learned how to mask my lies. As it happened, though, I didn't have anything significant to hide.

"Rumor has it that they want to set it alight," Ngomi told me, eventually. "They think the outer system could do with a little more native heat, and they figure that they ought to be able to get a fusion reaction going that will turn Jupiter into the system's second sun, if they can only build robots capable of working at the core."

The idea was an old one, but it didn't have a newsworthy movement behind it—and that, I realized, was exactly the point. It was an idea that would never generate any kind of movement *among the Earthbound* because the Earthbound had nothing to gain by it. On the other hand, if Type-2 really were fated to gain historical momentum over the centuries and the millennia, however slowly, the Earthbound might well have something to *lose* by it. Rightly or wrongly, the Earth's owners saw themselves as good and responsible stewards, duty-bound custodians of the future of humankind as well as Garden Earth.

"She really didn't mention Jupiter at all," I said, too quickly to stop myself as I belatedly realized that Ngomi's purpose in broaching the subject wasn't actually to find out whether Emily Marchant had unthinkingly tossed me a valuable nugget of information but to let me in on his side of the argument: to invite me to plight my ideological troth to him, the invisible hand and the legions of the Earthbound. I was ashamed of the reflex that made me wonder why he was bothering, given that I was a mere historian, irrelevant to the course and causes of humankind's future. Hadn't I tried with all my might to persuade Emily and Khan Mirafzal that I *wasn't* irrelevant and that the history of death still had lessons to teach us because the ultimate war was still going on, in its patient and muted fashion?

"That's all right," said Julius Ngomi, serenely. "Don't worry about it. Feel free to mention this conversation to her, of course, next time you update her on what's happening way down here in the Well."

All the walls on Earth had ears and eyes. No VE conversations, however great the time delay to which they might be subject, were immune from the attentions of clever eavesdroppers. Of course Mister Ngomi wanted me to raise the subject, given that Emily hadn't seen fit to raise it herself.

"Is she really that important?" I asked him. "I knew she was rich, but not *that* rich."

"She's a very talented lady," Julius Ngomi said, before swimming away to the far end of the pool and disappearing from my life for another few centuries. "She takes her art very seriously indeed. We've always had a great respect for authentic visionaries because that's what *we*'ve always tried to be."

FIFTY-NINE

The sixth part of the *History of Death*, entitled *Fields of Battle*, was launched on 24 July 2888. Its subject matter was war, but my commentary didn't pay much attention to the actual fighting of the wars of the nineteenth, twentieth, and twenty-first centuries. My main concern was with the *mythology* of warfare as it developed in the period under consideration, and with the ways in which the development of the mass media of communication transformed the business and the perceived meanings of warfare. I began my main argumentative sequence with the Crimean War because it was the first war to be extensively covered by newspaper reporters, and the first whose conduct was drastically affected thereby.

Before the Crimea, I argued, wars had been "private" events, entirely the affairs of the men who started them and the men who fought them. They had had a devastating effect on the local populations of the arenas in which they were fought but had been largely irrelevant to distant civilian populations. The British *Times* had changed all that by making the Crimean War the business of all its readers, exposing the government and military leaders to public scrutiny and to public scorn. Reports from the front had scandalized the nation by creating an awareness of how ridiculously inefficient the organization of the army was and what a toll of human life was exacted upon the troops in consequence— not merely deaths in battle, but deaths from injury and disease caused by the appalling lack of care given to wounded soldiers. That reportage had not only had practical consequences, but imaginative consequences. It had rewritten the entire mythology of heroism in an intricate webwork of new legends, ranging from the Charge of the Light Brigade to the secular canonization of Florence Nightingale.

Throughout the next two centuries, I argued, war and publicity were entwined in an intimate and tightly drawn knot. Control of the news media became vital to propagandist control of popular *morale*, and governments engaged in war had to became architects of the mythology of war as well as planners of military strategy. Heroism and jingoism became the currency of consent; where governments failed to secure the right public image for the wars they fought, they fell. I tracked the way in which attitudes to death in war, especially to the endangerment of civilian populations, were dramatically transformed by the three so-called World Wars and by the way those wars were subsequently mythologized in memory and fiction.

My commentary dwelt at great length on the way the first World War was "sold" to those who must fight it as a war to end war and on the consequent sense of betrayal that followed when it failed to live up to this billing. I went on to argue, however, that if the sequence of global wars were seen as a single event, then their collective example really had brought into being an attitude of mind that ultimately forbade wars. This was, of course, rather controversial. Many modern historians had lumped together the First and Second World Wars as phases of a single conflict, but the majority tended to deny that the idea of the "Third World War" had ever had any validity and that the conflicts of the twenty-first century were of a very different kind. My peers were used to arguing that although the plague wars and their corollaries had indeed infected the whole world they were not international conflicts and thus belonged to an entirely different conceptual category. I disagreed, proposing that if one set aside the carefully managed public representations of the global wars as so much false advertising, one could easily see that none of them had really been contests for national hegemony.

Other historians had become fond of distinguishing the plague wars from their predecessors on the grounds that they were actually nasty but necessary "class wars" waged by the world's rich against underclasses that might otherwise have swept them away by revolution. Orthodox Hardinists always added that these underclasses would also have destroyed the ecosphere in the ultimate "tragedy of the commons." Such apologists were also careful to say that if the plague of sterility really had been a war then it was the last and best of the *good* and *responsible* wars.

I swept all such distinctions casually aside. I suppose that my refusing to see any of the world wars as an unmitigated disaster was not so very unorthodox, but my refusal to see them as horrific examples of the

barbarity of ancient man certainly was. I argued that the trumpery
nationalism that had replaced the great religions as the main creator and
definer of a sense of human community was a poor and petty thing, but I
did not condemn it as an evil. I admitted that the massive conflicts
engendered in its name were tragic, but I insisted that they were a necessary stage in historical development. All the empires of faith, including
the tawdry empires of patriotism and nationalism, were utterly incompe-
tent to complete their self-defined tasks, but they were necessary in spite
of that. They were always bound to fail, and their disintegration was
always bound to be bloody, because they were brave but hopeless
attempts to make a virtue of dire necessity, but they served their temporary purpose.

As one more transfiguration of the meaning of death, temporarily
redeeming the ultimate evil by enshrouding it in nobility while also laying
bare the appalling hollowness of exactly those pretensions, the global wars
had bridged the historical gap between the senility of religion and the
maturity of science. Not until the scientifically guided global wars had done
their work and run their course, I argued, could the groundwork for a *genuine* human community—in which all mankind could properly and mean-
ingfully join—be properly laid. The foundations of the ultimate world
order had to be laid in the common experience of all nations, as part of a
hard-won and well-understood universal heritage.

I repeated yet again that no matter who the citizens of particular
nations had appointed as their enemies, the only *real* enemy of all
humankind was death itself. Only by facing up to death in a new way, by
gradually transforming the role of death as part of the means to human
ends, could a true human community be made. Even the petty wars of the
bloodiest period in human history, whatever their immediate purpose in
settling economic squabbles and pandering to the megalomaniac psy-
choses of national leaders, had played an essential part in the shifting pattern of history. They had, I insisted, provided a vast, all-encompassing, and
quite invaluable carnival of destruction—a carnival that could have no
other ultimate outcome but to make human beings weary of the lust to
kill, lest they bring about their extinction.

Some reviewers condemned *Fields of Battle* on the grounds of its
evident irrelevance to a world that had banished war, but I was heart-

ened by the general tenor of its reception. A few critics descended to sarcasm in welcoming the fact that my thesis had returned to the safe track of true history, dealing exclusively with things safely dead and buried, but there was clear evidence that the earlier parts of my work had now grown sufficiently familiar for the whole enterprise to be treated with respect.

My brief notoriety had not been entirely forgotten, and certainly not forgiven, in academic circles but it seemed to me that the good effects of that publicity were at last beginning to outweigh the bad. The *History* was now being taken seriously even by many who were unsympathetic to its stance, and my theories were now firmly established on the world's intellectual agenda. Several reviewers actually confessed that they were now looking forward to the next installment of the story.

SIXTY

When I was ready to leave the rehab center I shopped around for an inexpensive place to live. I wanted a complete contrast to my life on the moon, so I immediately rejected Antarctica and the Ice Age–afflicted parts of the Northern Hemisphere. I didn't want to return to Africa or South America, so that narrowed my choices considerably. When I found myself recoiling in a quasi-reflexive manner from the thought of living in Oceania I became slightly anxious. I told myself that emortals could not afford to accumulate hang-ups and that it was high time I put the legacy of the Coral Sea Catastrophe firmly behind me.

I eventually decided to rent an apt-capsule in Neyu, one of the virginal islands of New Tonga.

Once the devastation of the original Creationist Islands had been repaired—although the vast majority of the ecological microcosms had been replaced rather than restored—the Continental Engineers had raised new islands by the score from the relatively shallow sea. New Tonga was a blue-sea region rather than a vast tract of LAP-gel, but it was neither a wilderness reserve nor a glorified fish farm.

Insofar as there was an avant garde among Earthbound genetic artists, the virgin isles of New Tonga were the stomping ground of its members. I was mildly interested in that avant garde because one of its factions—the Tachytelic Perfectionists—had borrowed rhetoric from the Thanaticists in openly proclaiming themselves to be "artists in death," working with ephemeral artificial organisms designed to live very briefly within a context of ferocious competition and natural selection.

The capstack in which my apt was located was an architectural fantasia of which even Emily might have approved, although it was anything but icy. It was bright and gaudy, complex without being confused. The many textures of its outer tegument recalled the rinds of fruit and the chitinous shells of marine mollusks, and its multitudinous tiny windows were somewhat reminiscent of the facets of an insect's compound eye.

I could not, of course, select my immediate neighbors. I was dismayed at first to find that not only were there no Tachytelic Perfectionists living in the building, but that the faction in question was regarded as something of a joke by the geneticists who did live there. The great majority of the biotechnologists who lived in the capstack did not consider themselves to be "artists" at all, and those who did were classical Aesthetes cast in the antique mould of the second Oscar Wilde.

My closest neighbors, whose most voluble spokesman was a woman of my own age named Mica Pershing, were mostly steadfastly utilitarian island builders. They were firmly committed to a newly emergent alliance between old-fashioned gantzers and organic engineers. Mica explained to me after welcoming me into their midst that she and her associates were perfectly happy to accept the label of Continental Engineers, but she took care to emphasize the contention that they were a new breed, not to be confused with their forerunners.

"We're the *true* Continental Engineers," she told me. "Being more than three hundred years old, I sometimes get accused of belonging to the old guard by the up-and-coming centenarian youngsters, but I'm as forward-looking as any of them. I expect you get that sort of thing yourself—or is the profession of history the precious exception wherein experience receives its proper due?"

I assured her that it was not, although it certainly ought to have been.

During the previous three hundred years I had been briefly acquainted with many people who would have styled themselves Continental Engineers, but most of those I had recently encountered had been ambitious to move to the next logical stage of that career path, becoming Planetary Engineers. I had not realized, although it would have been obvious had I cared to study the logic of the situation, that the emigration of those so minded was bound to leave behind a hard core of fundamentalists, who would see the art and craft of Continental Engineering as a quintessentially Earthbound discipline. My neighbors on Neyu had no ambition to join the terraformers on Mars or the palace builders on Titan; even their obsession with the remaking of Garden Earth was highly specialized.

The first self-appointed Continental Engineers to make a real impact on the popular imagination, way back in the twenty-first century, had done so by mounting a campaign to persuade the United Nations to license the building of a dam across the Straits of Gibraltar. Because more water evaporates from the Mediterranean than flows into it from rivers, that plan would have considerably increased the land surface of southern Europe and Northern Africa. It had, of course, never come to fruition, but its dogged pursuit had won the Engineers a whole series of consolation prizes. Their island-building activities had been boosted considerably by the Decimation.

More recently, the climatic disruptions caused by the advancing Ice Age had given Continental Engineering a further boost, allowing its propagandists to promote the idea of raising new lands in the tropics as a refuge for emigrants from the newly frozen north. The "old-fashioned gantzers" among them had been so busy for the previous two centuries that they had become increasingly assertive, protesting loudly against anyone who dared to suppose that their attitudes were as obsolescent as their tools. Mica was a fairly typical specimen.

When I moved to Neyu the actual endeavors of the resident gantzers were still heavily dependent on traditional techniques that Emily Marchant would have regarded as laughably primitive. The basics of island building had not changed in half a millennium: crude bacterial cyborgs that did little more than agglomerate huge towers of cemented sand provided the foundations, and "lightning corals" did the finishing work. Such techniques were perfectly adequate to the task of creating great archipelagos of new islands. The Continental Engineers's progressives were, however, already thinking at least two steps ahead.

Even the "moderates" based in New Tonga and its sister states saw the ever-increasing network of bridges connecting the new islands as a blueprint for the highways of a new Pacific continent twice the size of Australia. Their extremists were already talking about New Pangaea and New Gondwanaland: rival versions of a grand plan to take technical control over the whole set of Earth's tectonic plates and institute a new era of macrogeographical design.

The biologists who were now collaborating with the Continental Engineers had already begun planting vast networks of "enhanced seaweeds" in the most suitable enclaves of the blue-sea region. The algae in question were enhanced in the sense that they combined the best features of kelps and wracks with surface features modeled on freshwater-dwelling flowering plants, especially water lilies.

The most obvious result of the Engineers' hard labor was that Neyu was not surrounded by the blue sea at all but by floral carpets that extended to the horizon and far beyond. These uneven carpets included many "islands" of their own: stable regions that could sustain farms of an entirely new kind.

The initial disappointment caused by the dearth of Tachytelic Perfectionists in my immediate vicinity was soon offset by the discovery of what my nearest neighbors were actually doing. I was delighted to have the opportunity of observing their new and bolder adventures at close range.

SIXTY-ONE

The sight of the Pacific sun setting in its flowery bed beneath a glorious blue sky seemed fabulously luxurious after the silver-ceilinged domes of the moon, and I gladly gave myself over to its governance. I continued to work as hard as I had done in Mare Moscoviense, but I took advantage of the hospitability of my environment to cut back drastically on my VE time.

The experience I had gained in face-to-face interactions stood me in good stead in Neyu as I began to build a richer network of actual acquaintances than I had ever had on Earth, even during the period of my first marriage.

At first, I was regarded as an eccentric newcomer to the island community. Historians were not as rare on Neyu as they had been on the moon, but ex-lunatics were exceedingly uncommon. My own name was by no means as familiar to my new acquaintances as I could have wished, although its unfamiliarity was welcome testimony to the rapidity with which Thanaticism had been put away—but when I happened to mention that I had spent some time with Emily Marchant before returning from the moon *that* name triggered an immediate response.

Unlike Julius Ngomi, the Continental Engineers of Neyu were not in the least interested in any plans Emily and her outer-system friends might have for Jupiter, but they were as interested in the new gantzing instruments that were flowing from the outer system as she had been in those which flowed the other way.

"They're developing some *very* useful deepdown systems," Mica Pershing told me, enthusiastically. "Titan's core is very different from Earth's, of course, but insofar as the techniques address the similarities rather than the differences they're exactly what we need for our own programs. The Coral Sea Disaster set us back two hundred years, you know, because the bureaucrats down in Antarctica became so absurdly hypersensitive about anything mantle-active. It's not as if we *caused* the disaster, for heaven's sake! We're the people trying to make sure that it never happens again. How can we police the mantle-crust boundary properly if they won't let us send out adequate patrols? The Titan brigade has stolen a long march on us, and the Invisible Hand is taking its usual protectionist stance on licenses in the name of the Balance of Trade or some such sacred cow, but rumor has it that Marchant herself is more than keen to deal. Did she give you that impression when you saw her last?"

I was very interested to hear all this, although I had to confess that I hadn't taken as much trouble as I might to measure Emily's exact state of mind on abstruse matters of potential commerce. Mica's connoisseur interest in Emily's techniques allowed me to see Julius Ngomi's anxieties in a new light.

In Mare Moscoviense the balance of trade between Earth and the rest of the Oikumene had not been a frequent topic of conversation, although one might have expected the fabers to take a keen interest in it, but it was something on which the Invisible Hand would want to keep a very tight grip. Perhaps, I thought, his talk of Jupiter had only been a mask to conceal the real nature of his interest in Emily's agenda.

Even more revealing, in its way, was the way Mica echoed Ngomi's use of the phrase "rumor has it." I had grown up in a world whose communication systems were so efficient and whose multitudinous electronic spies had been so assiduous, that "rumor" had lost all authority. What was known was almost invariably know to a high degree of certainty—but the rapid development of the outer system had changed all that. There were now significant regions of the Oikumene where the notion of privacy was making a comeback—and wherever privacy flourishes, so does idle gossip.

When I told Mica that the primary purpose of Emily's recent visit to the moon had been to shop around for Earth-sourced gantzing techniques she became even more excited.

"I *knew* it!" she said. "Melt ice caps and you get oceans. She's thinking ahead, just as we are, and she's seeing overlapping concerns, synergistic possibilities. She *must* be as keen to deal as we are—or would be if only the diehard Hardinists and the Amundsen City mafia would get off our backs. Whoever thought that it was a good idea to put the UN bureaucracy on ice should have been strangled at birth, and Planned Capitalism is just a fancy name for stopping social evolution in its tracks.

Tachytelic Perfectionism might be a contradiction in terms, but at least those crazies understand that there's some virtue in rapidity of change. We've got a hell of a long way to go before we can congratulate ourselves that the Garden's in good shape, and the powers that be aren't helping us at all."

It was rather heartening to hear such sentiments from a 380-year-old earthbound emortal. I'd heard so much faber propaganda on the moon that I'd almost begun to take it for granted that the Earthbound really were terminally decadent, but life on Neyu was the perfect antidote to that suspicion. Some few of my new neighbors did seem in danger of robotization, but that had been true even in Mare Moscoviense—and in Neyu, as on the moon, they were a tiny minority.

In New Tonga, as in the lunar domes, there was a quasi-revolutionary spirit in the air: a lust for change that far transcended the seemingly modest ambitions of the world's owners and rulers.

I had never expected to be drawn to someone like Mica Pershing, and she had obviously not anticipated that I was the kind of person who might be fruitfully invited into the discussions of her own circle, but we were both surprised. We had more in common than the differences in our vocations suggested, and a spontaneous spark of camaraderie kindled what soon became a warm friendship.

Within months of my arrival I had become well-acquainted with Mica's closest professional associates. They found me an amusing distraction from their work-related discussions, and I began to feel definite echoes of my old association with the Lamu Rainmakers. The last thing I had been contemplating as I planned my return to Earth had been a third marriage, but when Mica and two of her most intimate allies in the new continental cause began to talk about possibilities of that kind I quickly became interested. What better way could there be to support my insistence that humans really did benefit from roots and that the Earthbound really were progressive in their outlook?

The marriage that Mica and her friends wanted to form was, of course, different in one very significant respect from the one the Lamu Rainmakers had organized. That had been an exploratory union of young people, whereas this was a purposive association of mature individuals. Mica had decided that she was old enough and wise enough to be a foster mother, and I was ready and willing to reason that if that were true, then I was old enough to be a foster father.

When Mica and her prospective co-parents began to discuss the spectrum of qualities they would to need to support an application for parenthood, it was easy enough to persuade them that my record as an ex-lunatic historian would add vitally necessary variety. Given that there was no one else on Neyu who could contribute such a striking set of exceptions to the local rule, I went right to the top of their list of candidates.

The further negotiations remained delicate and complicated because all of the people who would ultimately be welcomed into the company had to be acceptable to all the others, but once the determination was there the process pressed ahead with all possible speed. As the thirtieth century dawned the matter was settled. I was to be married again, and would very soon be a co-parent, following in the footsteps of Papa Domenico, Papa Laurent, Mama Eulalie, Papa Nahum, Mama Meta, Mama Siorane, Mama Sajda, and Papa Ezra. I thought—as I suppose almost everyone must think—that no matter how difficult it would be to do better job than they had done, I would make certain that I did it.

SIXTY-TWO

Long afterward, Mica confessed that my inclusion in the marriage had not been unopposed when she first raised it with Maralyne, Ewald, and Francesca, and that when their preliminary debate reached its critical point the item that swung it was the moral credit that I was presumed to have accumulated by virtue of once having saved Emily Marchant's life.

I was moved by a sense of injury to respond, somewhat dishonestly, that I had had to think long and hard before accepting the invitation, and that the item that had eventually swung my own internal debate was simple economic anxiety. It was a plausible story. Having readapted myself to Earthly life I wanted to press on as hard as was possible with the remaining volumes of my *History*, and the flow of income from the earlier sections had dwindled to a point at which meeting my living expenses and financing my continuing researches would not have been easy had I not married when I did. Now, I wonder whether I was entirely honest with myself when the idea of the marriage first came up.

However good or bad the reasons might have been on either side, though, the marriage was a success, at least in terms of its primary objective.

Four of the eight members of my new aggregate household were committed Continental Engineers. Like Mica, Maralyne Dexter was a traditional gantzer, while Ewald Knabl and Francesca Phenix were of the newer school of Organic Engineers. All four were involved in various island-building projects. The remaining three had, like me, been chosen for the sake of apparent variety, although Banastre Trevelyan was an economist-turned-politician strongly allied to the new continental cause and Tak Wing Ng was a geomorphologist whose interests were in the same area. The only one whose concerns were as blatantly peripheral as mine was Tricia Ecosura, a medical technician specializing in functional cyborgization. It quickly became apparent, however, that although our specializations might be disparate, Tricia and I shared with the other members of the group a particularly intense zeal for our work.

Throughout the twenty-eighth and early twenty-ninth centuries most groups of applicant co-parents had taken the view that parenthood ought to be a full-time job for at least some of the co-parents, and it was by no means uncommon for entire parental groups to spend twenty years living on saved-up capital. By 2900, however, the tide of fashion had swung decisively against that theory on the grounds that it introduced children to a distinctly freakish lifestyle. The only extreme that was tolerated as the thirtieth century began was the other, by which children were introduced to a work-centerd existence in which direct parenting became a matter of strictly regimented individual turn taking. This was the kind of unit my new family set out to be.

Although I was married to my seven companions for more than thirty years, from 2902 to 2935, I never became as intimate with any of them as I had been with the co-parents of my first marriage. Except for Mica and Tricia I cannot say that I ever got close to any of them. It was clear from the outset that five of my new companions were only interested in the parental aspects of the union, and they were determined to be businesslike about the whole thing. When Bana suggested that flesh-sex should not merely be excluded from any mention in the the marriage agreement but formally proscribed he might have obtained a majority decision had it not been for the fact that Mica and I threw our support behind Tricia when she argued that the child would derive far more benefit from a less monastic environment.

Even though the vote went our way, there was a residual consensus that if we three were so keen on providing examples of supposedly healthy physical relationships, then we were the ones responsible for their construction and maintenance. Although Mica played her exemplary part with commendable enthusiasm Tricia was the only one of my co-parents with whom I shared any real emotional intimacy, and it is a pity that our affection for one another was severely prejudiced in later years by philosophical differences.

Fortunately, the careful mutual distancing of the majority of her co-parents did not affect the bonds we formed with the child committed to our care. She was born in January 2912, less than a year after the publication of the seventh part of my *History of Death*, although not so soon that the two processes of gestation became tangled in my mind.

We gave her the name Lua Tawana.

Biologically speaking, Lua was drawn from ancient Polynesian stock—as narrowly local as could be contrived, given the limitations of the Crash-stocked gene banks. She bore no conspicuous physical resemblance to any of her co-parents, although she promised to be even more beautiful than Francesca, who was the only one of us to have taken a serious interest in the aesthetics of cosmetic enhancement. The uniqueness of her appearance only served to increase the sense we all had that Lua was one of a kind, as well as being a crucial part of a future yet to be created and shaped by humankind, which would be better than the present.

I wish I could say that I took to parenthood like a duck to water, but any vestigial instincts that I might have inherited had withered in four hundred and some years of adult life. I had a lot to learn, and even though I was more able to put my work temporarily aside than most of my companions I felt that I was painfully inept. From an objective point of view it must have seemed that the others were no better, but no one can be objective in such circumstances and I was awkwardly terrified by the thought that a once-in-a-lifetime opportunity might be spoiled by my inability to cultivate the requisite skills with the requisite alacrity.

Fortunately, Lua did not seem to mind in the least that her care occasionally fell short of perfection. She was a very cheerful baby, not given to excessive crying, and she quickly learned to greet us all with winning smiles. While I was with her, I forgot to worry about the rights and wrongs of my return to Earth and all the conflicts of interest that were developing between the Earthbound and the inhabitants of the outer system.

I never abandoned my work for more than a day at a time, but I had told Emily the truth when I said that the bulk of the hard labor had been done and that I would be able to accelerate smoothly as I brought the final few parts to completion. I had enough momentum to make the work seem easy, and Lua provided more than enough distraction occasionally to lift my spirits as high as they would go. There was too much anxiety and panicky haste in my day-to-day responsibilities to allow me to say that I was happier on Neyu than I was on the moon, but the peaks of joy that I occasionally obtained by courtesy of Lua's smiles were new to me, and they added a special zest to the few short years of her infancy. I will not boast that I ever became an exceptionally good parent, but I did learn the basics and I did discover how to obtain my own fulfilment from the task.

For a while, at least, I was perfectly content to live in the present and leave the future on the shelf for later collection.

SIXTY THREE

The seventh part of the *History of Death*, entitled *The Last Judgment*, was launched on 21 June 2911, only twenty-three years after its immediate predecessor. This reflected the close relationship between the subject matter of the sixth and seventh parts and the fact that they covered a relatively narrow span of time. *The Last Judgment* dealt with the multiple crises that had developed in the twenty-first and twenty-second centuries, which had collaborated with the last phases of the Great War to face the human race with the prospect of extinction.

The Fields of Battle had already described the various nuclear exchanges that led up to Brazil's nuclear attack on Argentina in 2079 and the artificially induced epidemics that had climaxed in the sterility plague of 2095–2120. The new commentary discussed the various contemporary factors—the greenhouse crisis, soil erosion, environmental pollution, and terminal deforestation—which would certainly have inflicted irreparable damage on the ecosphere had the final round of nuclear exchanges and the depredations of the chiasmalytic transformers not administered such a brutally sharp shock to the upward surge of the world's demographic statistics.

My commentary included an elaborate consideration of the broader patterns of death in this period, pointing out the limitations of the popular misconception that the reversal of population growth was entirely due to the literal and metaphorical fallout of wars. I considered in detail the fate of the "lost billions" of peasant and subsistence farmers who had been disinherited and displaced by the emergent ecological and economic order. Like every other historian of the era, I could only marvel at the fact that in less than two centuries more human beings had died than in the previous two millennia, but I was more outspoken than all the rest in declaring that so much death had, in the end, proved to be a thoroughly good thing.

I could not help making much of the ironic observation that the near conquest of death achieved by twenty-first-century medicine had offered an unprecedented libation to the specter of death, in the form of an unparalleled abundance of mortal life. I was careful to call attention to the tragic dimensions of the Malthusian crisis thus generated—but historians are always prone to make more of irony than of tragedy because history lacks the moral order characteristic of works of fiction. It was inevitable that my argument would emphasize the fact that the new medicines and the new pestilences of the twenty-first century had to be seen as different faces of the same coin, spinning out the logic of the situation by which the twentieth century's new technologies of food production had been progenitors of worldwide famine rather than worldwide satiation.

Perhaps it was unfair of me to pay so much attention to the irony of such situations as the one by which the harvests of the twentieth century Green Revolution facilitated enormous population growth in what was then known as the Third World at a time when China was the only nation whose government was prepared to address Malthusian problems seriously. There was, however, nothing but irony to be found in the fact that when the First World's enthusiastic promotion of patentable genemod staples introduced global population management by the back door, its endeavors prepared the ground for the stock-market coups that established Hardinism as the last economic orthodoxy. I did admit, of course, that the awful political chaos that followed the Zimmerman coup had been a terrible price to pay for the foundations of the new world order.

I also found irony rather than tragedy in the process that ensured that the preservation of millions of children from the diseases that had killed them in previous centuries delivered millions of twenty-first-century adults into the untender care of more subtle viruses, which rose to the occasion by increasing their mutation rates. Even if the interventions of biological weaponry were disregarded, I pointed out, natural selection allowed the unconquered diseases to achieve such a sophistication of method and effect that the plague of sterility would surely have been precipitated eventually, even if Conrad Helier and his associates had not decided to give evolution a helping hand.

The most controversial aspects of the analysis of *The Last Judgment* were, for once, peripheral to my main argument—but that did not prevent them generating considerable criticism. My discussion of the manner in which the advent of tissue-culture farmfactories had been carefully delayed and loaded with unnecessary commercial burdens by a Hardinist cabal still heavily dependent on their staple monopolies was bound to be resented by those who preferred to represent the early Hardinists as the True Saviors of the human race. I contended that those biotechnologists who were deliberately excluded from the Inner Circle—including Conrad Helier—had been cynically maneuvered into doing dirty work that the world's new owners desperately wanted done but did not want to be caught actually doing, thus becoming further marginalized. I even suggested that the Hardinists' levered acquisition of the crucial Gantz patents could easily be seen as a direly unfortunate development in that it had destroyed the last vestiges of authentic competition within the global economy. From that moment on, I claimed, the benignly flexible invisible hand of classical economic theory had been replaced by an iron fist whose grip was sometimes cruel as well as irresistible.

Perhaps I should have deemphasized these peripheral matters lest they distract too much attention from the main line of my argument, but I simply did not care to. The central thrust of my commentary was, however, that this had been the most critical of all the stages of man's war with death. The weapons of the imagination had finally been discarded in favor of more effective ones, but in the short term those more effective weapons, by multiplying life so effectively, had also multiplied death. A war that had always been fervent thus became feverishly overheated, to the point at which where it came within a hairsbreadth of destroying all its combatants.

In earlier times, I had long argued, the growth of human population had been restricted by lack of resources and the war with death had been, in essence, a war of *mental* adaptation whose only goal was reconciliation. When the "natural" checks on population growth were removed and it became possible to contemplate other goals, however, the sudden acceleration of population growth had temporarily taken *all* conceivable goals out of reach. The waste products of human society had threatened to poison it, and the fact that human beings were no longer reconciled in any meaningful fashion to the inevitability of death compounded the effects of that poisoning.

Alongside the weapons by which the long war against death might be won, humankind had also developed the weapons by which it might be lost. Nuclear arsenals and stockpiles of biological weaponry were scattered all over the globe: twin pistols held in death's skeletal hands, leveled at a human race that had largely forsaken the consolations of religion and the glorifications of patriotism.

As the twenty-first century gave way to the twenty-second, I proposed, humankind was no longer teetering on the brink of total disaster; it had actually plunged over the edge, its members having left their traditional parachutes behind. The new medical technologies that had held out the tantalizing promise of emortality ever since Morgan Miller's ill-fated experiments had been publicized had only the narrowest margin of opportunity in which to operate.

The wounds inflicted by the ecocatastrophes of the twenty-first century could so easily have been mortal, and it was not easy for any historian to distinguish between the people who had only been part of the problem and those who had made contributions to its solution. In the end, the soft landing had been achieved as much by luck as judgment, in my estimation. Biotechnology, having passed through the most hectic phase of its evolution, had stayed one vital step ahead of the terrible problems that its lack had generated. In spite of the various forces warping its development, food technology had achieved a merciful and relatively orderly divorce from the bounty of nature, moving out of the fields and into the factories. The liberation of humanity from the vagaries of climate and natural selection had begun, and the first pavements had been set on the route to Garden Earth.

I argued that whatever teething troubles it had undergone—and was still undergoing—the production of a political apparatus enabling human beings to take collective control of themselves was a remarkable triumph of human sanity. I took great care to emphasize that in the final analysis it was not scientific progress per se that had won the war against death but the ability of human beings to work together, to compromise with one another, and to build viable communities out of disparate and disagreeable raw materials.

That human beings possessed this ability was, I argued, the legacy of thousands of years of silly superstition, irrational religion, and pigheaded patriotism rather than the product of a few hundred years of science. The human race had turned twenty-first-century crisis into twenty-second-century triumph not because its members had become biotechnologically sophisticated but because they were veterans of a long and fierce war against death. Biotechnology had provided the tools, but death had provided the motivation.

Apart from slanders heaped upon it by offended would-be Hardinists intent on currying favor with Earth's masters, *The Last Judgment* attracted little attention from laypeople. It was generally held to be dealing with matters that everyone understood very well, striving a little too hard for an original slant. This seemed a meager reward for all the work I had put in, especially the delving I had done since my return to Earth into the archival deposits that Julius Ngomi had once described as "the litter that dare not speak its name." Those critics who admitted that they had been anticipating the successor to the previous volume with some enthusiasm excused their lukewarm response by saying that the new offering had not carried my quest far enough forward.

Even the least generous of my academic critics could not fault the massiveness of the knot of associated data that I had brought together, or the cleverness with which it had been mazed, but they still felt free to declare that I should have carried the story farther forward in time. Almost without exception, the reviewers pointed out that I had originally intended the work to be seven volumes long, and that it now seemed unlikely that nine would suffice, let alone eight—and they were absolutely unanimous in regretting that inflation.

The whole world, it seemed, was impatient to be done with the *History of Death*—but I was still determined to do the job properly, no matter how long it took.

SIXTY-FOUR

I had maintained my correspondence with Emily Marchant despite the restrictions placed upon it by the time delay. I sent her a long oration lamenting the unsympathetic reception of *The Last Judgment* even though I knew that she would align herself with my detractors. It might have been more pleasant to speak of other matters, but ever since Julius Ngomi had appeared in the unlikely role of agent provocateur I had been very careful not to mention the planet Jupiter, and since marrying into the Continental Engineers I didn't want to get involved in heavy discussions of cutting-edge gantzing technics. I had become rather anxious that my private correspondence might get hijacked, if not by eavesdroppers then by my nearest and supposedly dearest.

Fortunately, by the time that Emily formulated her reply to my message, she had more important things to discuss than the alleged futility of my mission. Hot on the heels of the *Hope*'s discovery of Ararat came the discovery by *Vishnu*, a silver-piloted kalpa probe launched in 2827, of an "Earthlike" world orbiting a G-type star in Scorpio. Like Ararat, this planet's elaborate ecosphere had produced animal species analogous to all the major groups of Earthly animals, including two that seemed to be on the verge of true intelligence.

The new world, called Maya by the silver's masters, seemed no more inviting to would-be colonists than Ararat, but it caused a great deal more excitement. *Hope* was widely considered within the Oikumene to be a direly unsatisfactory platform for colonization, partly by virtue of its antiquity and partly by virtue of the catalog of mistakes and hesitations dutifully recorded by the Ark's transmissions. Maya, having been found by machines, awaited the careful attention of a colonization mission planned by thirtieth-century sophisticates and executed with the aid of the full panoply of modern technology.

The only question to be answered was *which* group of thirtieth-century sophisticates would be entrusted with the task.

Had I thought more deeply about the matter, I might have anticipated the chaos that would ensue, but I was too busy. It was not until Emily's message arrived that I realized that a serious conflict of interest had arrived in the system even sooner than Julius Ngomi's colleagues and collaborators had expected.

"The race is on," Emily told me, speaking from one of her favorite VEs, which set her against a vertiginous background of ice mountains. "By the time the Hardinists had got around to sending out invitations to their conference it was way too late. The fabers weren't about to give away their head start, so your old friend Khan Mirafzal is already diverting his microworld's course Scorpioward. The Oort Halo crowd reckon that they can still overtake him if they take direct aim, and the New Ark people figure that even if they can't quite get there firstest they can still land the mostest men and the bestest equipment. Two other faberweb microworlds are negotiating with Mirafzal for a planned rendezvous, a pooling of effort and a piece of the action, but they haven't got near a decision as to whether they ought to reengineer children with legs in order to get a foothold on the planet, or whether they ought to content themselves with setting up an orbital network to work hand-in-hand with the Oort gang, the New Arkers, or both.

"The kalpa programmers are crying foul left, right, and center. Earth's high-and-mighty will back their claims of ownership right down the line, of course, but they must know that their proclamations won't mean a thing thirty-nine light years away. The Gaean Libs will probably want the whole process stopped, of course, but that's just hot air. The real fight will be to determine the methods and objectives of the land grab, and no one thinks that there's the least chance of settling that in advance. No matter who wins the race, the competition will only intensify once the drops get under way. If the New Arkers were united among themselves they'd have a slim chance of putting a few controls in place, but they've always been a loose coalition of interested parties with no meaningful ideological center. In order to get their ship ready in time they'll have to offer berths to every faction that can help, including the Cyborganizers. The likelihood is that they'll fragment as soon as they arrive. If you think that *Hope*'s botches added up to a fiasco, you ain't seen nothing yet.

"Even you'll have to admit now that everything's changed, Morty.

Earth isn't the game board any more. The Hardinist case for its careful preservation as the footsloggers' ultimate refuge has gone right out the window. The galaxy *has* to be full of worlds like Ararat and Maya. Terraformable ecospheres *must* be a dime a dozen. The only mystery is the Fermi paradox. If we're here, where the hell are all the others? You're a historian, Morty—you know how hard we tried to obliterate ourselves, and *still* we made it. The others have to be here too, even if we can't tune into their beacons, and it's only a matter of time before we run into them. After that . . . everything will change again, and nobody can guess exactly how."

She had much more to say, of course, but that was the red meat. The race was on, and after the race would come the conflict, and after the conflict . . . the ecocatastrophes and the wars?

I didn't even recognize the names of some of the factions to which Emily referred so casually. I knew that there were people in the Oort Halo, but I had no idea that they constituted a "crowd" or what their gang mentality might be. I had only the vaguest notion about the composition of the New Arkers and had previously thought of them as merely one more set of eccentrics intent on hollowing out asteroids to make microworlds. I did, however, have some inkling of what Cyborganizers were, by virtue of living with Tricia Ecosura. She often mentioned them, sometimes critically and sometimes sympathetically, but always giving the impression that they were a coming thing, as revolutionary in their own fashion as the newly rampant Continental Engineers.

Under different circumstances, I might have asked Emily to give me a much more detailed account of what she thought the various Maya-bound factions were up to, but it didn't seem politic. For one thing, I felt that Julius Ngomi was sure to be listening in, and I didn't want to be his mule. For another, I had to concentrate on the two tasks I now had on hand where there had previously been only one.

I could have taken time out from my history to think about the farthest horizons of the expanding Oikumene, had it not been for the fact that any such time was already spoken for, but I had already agreed to dedicate any and all such time to Lua Tawana, who was growing up quickly. For that reason, I let the matter slide. My reply to Emily's dispatch acknowledged what she had said but did not engage with it in any intellectually serious fashion. Having not yet parented a child of her own, she probably did not understand, but she made allowances anyhow.

For me, she always did make allowances—and this time, I felt fully entitled to claim them. I was, after all, a man with parental responsibilities.

PART FIVE
Responsibility

The triumph of Earthbound humanity is that individual people are still so stubbornly different from one another. Half a millennium of universal emortality has not eroded, let alone erased, the variety of human personality. Instead, our longevity has allowed us to hone and refine our individuality to an exactitude that our remote ancestors would have found astonishing. The Thanaticists were only half right when they claimed that this process of refinement was the work of Sculptor Death, only made possible by the sacrifice of alternative pathways in the brain, just as the Cyborganizers are only half right when they claim that we cannot evolve any further unless we open up new neural pathways for which natural selection has made no provision. The truth is that the natural process of growing older, no matter how long it might be protracted, cannot and does not involve the elimination of the elasticity of human thought and human possibility. The process of further human evolution must, in essence, be an extrapolation of our innate resources, no matter how cleverly and elaborately they are augmented by external technology.

However conducive it might be to Utopian ease and calm, it would not be good for humankind if we were ever to become so similar to one another that it became impossible for people to think one another mad or seriously misguided. Although those extremists who decide to die after a mere seventy or eighty years seem bizarre to sensible moderates, while those who only want to live forever do not, even emortals have to come to terms with the fact that death *is* inevitable. No matter how hard we may pretend that true emortality has turned *when* into *if*, the fact remains that we are not *im*mortal. In time, the sun will die; in time, the universe itself will fade into dark oblivion; even the Type-4 speculators who assure us that the extinction of our own inflationary domain will not prevent our remotest descendants from seeking new opportunities in the Unobservable Beyond are only speaking in terms of postponement. At heart, we are all Thanaticists in the sense that everyone who is not rudely seized by predatory death must ultimately make his own compact with the ultimate enemy—and we are all Cyborganizers in the sense that everyone must decide exactly which augmentary technologies he will deploy within the terms of that compact.

—Mortimer Gray
Part Ten of *The History of Death*

SIXTY-FIVE

Lua Tawana was the linchpin of my world for more than twenty years, and she remained its most significant anchorage long after that. I had not given the matter much consideration before, but as soon as she learned to speak, the logic of the situation became clear. Everyone has a multiplicity of parents, but very few of the Earthbound foster more than one child. Child rearing is the only emotional luxury so strictly rationed on Earth that it is bound to seem like a once-in-a-lifetime opportunity even to people who hope to live for millennia. It is hardly surprising that emortal parents become obsessed with the mental development their children—even parents who have decided to maintain the momentum of their careers throughout the years of parenthood.

No matter how clearly focused one becomes during a child-rearing marriage, however, other things do intrude. It was easy enough for me to relegate from immediate concern the developments in and beyond the outer solar system that Emily Marchant was so keen to bring to my attention, but it was not so easy to ignore matters occupying the attention of my marriage partners. I tried hard, and I have no doubt that they tried equally hard, but certain things intruded in spite of all our best efforts, and one of them was Tricia's increasing involvement in the 2920s with the Cyborganizers. I think I might have held myself aloof even from that had it not been for an unfortunate stroke of coincidence, but I have always been a trifle accident-prone and that was one vulnerability that did not depart as I attained the age of reason and responsibility.

At the most elementary level, the Cyborganizers were merely the newest generation of apologists for cyborgization. They adopted a new title purely in order to make themselves seem more original than they were. In fact, there had always been such apologists around, but the increasing use of cyborgization in adapting people to live and work in space and the hostile environments of other worlds within the solar system had given new ammunition to those who felt that similar opportunities ought to be more widely explored on Earth.

The progress of the "new" movement followed a pattern that had now become familiar to all serious historians if not to the present-obsessed media audience. All the old controversies regarding "brain-feed" equipment surfaced yet again, refreshed by controversy, and all the old tales about wondrous technologies secretly buried by the world's paternalistic masters began to do the rounds, neatly varnished with a superficial gloss of modernity. TV current-affairs shows initially treated the propaganda flow with amused contempt, but as the stream built toward a tide the casters began to feed off it more extravagantly, and hence to feed it, thus accelerating its ascent to fashionability.

The gist of the the Cyborganizers' argument was that the world had become so besotted with the achievements of genetic engineers that people had become blind to all kinds of other possibilities which lay beyond the scope of DNA manipulation. They insisted that it was high time to reawaken such interests and that recent technical advances made in the field of functional cyborgization should be redeployed in the service of aesthetic cyborgazation. There was much talk of "lifestyle cyborganization." The introduction into the latter term of the extra two letters did nothing to transform its real meaning but contrived nevertheless to generate a host of new implications. The Cyborganizers were, of course, very anxious to stress that there was all the difference in the world between cyborganization and robotization, the former being entirely virtuous while the latter remained the great bugbear of emortal humankind.

I would have been perfectly content to ignore the Cyborganizers had they only been content to ignore me. I am reasonably certain that they would have done exactly that if Tricia Ecosura had not agreed to meet face-to-face with Samuel Wheatstone, one of the movement's most enthusiastic propagandists, while he was visiting Neyu in 2924. Even that occasion might have passed off harmlessly had I only had the good sense to stay out of the way—as I certainly would have done if I had known that Samuel Wheatstone had not always been content to wear the name his parents had given him. Because I had not, there seemed to be no harm at all in accepting Tricia's invitation to take a stroll on the beach behind our hometree and say hello to her guest.

She had obviously mentioned me to him—why should she not?—

and he was fully prepared to take delight in my confusion. I did not recognize his face, of course, because it had been so radically transformed
by cyborgization. His eyes were artificial and his skull was elaborately
embellished with other accessories—most of them, I presumed, ornamental rather than functional.

"It's a great honor to meet you in the flesh at last, Mortimer," he said
to me, beaming broadly. "I've never forgotten our discussion, although
I've not kept up with your work as assiduously as I should have."

While I was still trying to work out the import of this greeting, Tricia
said: "You didn't tell me that you and Morty knew one another, Samuel."

"I wanted it to be a surprise," he said. "I was using a different name
when we last encountered one another. I fear that Mortimer still has no
idea who I am—but it was two hundred years ago, and although our
contest was transmitted in real time the space we shared was virtual."

"You're Hellward Lucifer Nyxson?" I guessed, tentatively.

"I was," he admitted, blithely. "A youthful folly. It seemed inappro-
priate to retain the name once the heart had gone out of Thanaticism, so
I reverted to my former signature."

"Of course you did," I countered, bitterly. "After all, you wouldn't
want the reputation of your present insanity to be tainted by the legacy
of past insanities, would you?"

His smile grew broader still. "That's it!" he said, feigning pleasure.
"That's exactly the expression I remember. I thought you might have forgiven me—after all, I did make you a lot of money—but I'm delighted to
find that you haven't. Principled adversaries are *so* much more interesting and rewarding than cynical fellow travelers, don't you think?"

"Aren't you supposed to be dead?" I asked him, packing as much
sarcasm into my tone as I could. "Common decency surely required you
to join the martyrs you inspired?"

"Don't be so stubbornly literal, Mortimer," he said. "You know full
well that I was only trying to *stir things up*. I'm a showman, not a suici-
dal maniac. It's what I do. You should try it some time. It's fun." For one
eerie moment he sounded exactly like Sharane Fereday—and I reacted
almost as if he were.

"Fun!" I echoed, with bitter contempt. "You should be in some
antique SusAn chamber along with all the other murderous bastards—

human litter that dare not speak its name."

"You stole that," he charged, with deadly accuracy. "That's one of dear old Julius's catchphrases. That's the wonderful thing about Earthbound humanity, don't you think? There might be billions of us, but we'll all be around long enough for everybody who's anybody to meet everybody who's anybody else. You ought to be careful about repeating other people's bon mots, though. That way lies robotization. I worry about that, as you'll doubtless remember—but I worry far more about people like you than people like me."

"I don't want you to worry about me," I said, coldly. "I think I'll go back inside now. I have better things to do than talk to you."

"But I *do* worry about you, Mortimer," Wheatstone/Nyxson assured me, refusing to consent to the end of the conversation. "I gave you an audience, and you frittered it away. I gave you a cause, and you fumbled the ball. You never have been able to make up your mind about the issues I raised, have you? I put you on the map, but you meekly removed yourself again because you didn't know exactly where you wanted to be located. It was Mare Moscoviense you ran away to, wasn't it? You probably came to Neyu because you expected it to be a similarly stagnant backwater—but I'm surprised you didn't move on as soon as Mica and her friends told you that they intended to make it the central crossroads of a new continent. Do you really think your ideas, motives, and actions are those of a man who's ready to live forever, Mortimer?"

I had to grit my teeth for a moment lest a reflexive tremble set them chattering. "You gave me nothing," I told him, when I was sure that I could frame the words properly. "I found my own cause and my own audience long before I heard your stupid pseudonym, and I'm still on the only map that matters. Within a hundred years I'll have finished my history, and it will be definitive. It will be *good*. It will command attention because it's *important*, not because I once got sucked into a moronic publicity stunt by a man who doesn't know the meaning of the word *conscience*. You're *not* important. You're just a clown, an exhibitionist, a *fool*. If you're behind the Cyborganizers, they're even more intellectually derelict than I thought. I'm astonished that anyone as intelligent as Tricia should even have condescended to talk to you. I won't."

I turned my back then, absolutely determined to go—but Hellward Lucifer Nyxson was never a man to concede the last word.

"You're beautiful, Mortimer," he called after me. "A pearl beyond price. I'd forgotten just how precious you are—but thanks for reminding me. Tricia's a very lucky woman, to have you as a co-parent."

SIXTY-SIX

I ignored it all, of course. I rose above it and put it behind me, for all of seven days. When Tricia accused me of being rude to her guest I refused to rise to the challenge. When Lua asked me why Mama Tricia was angry with me I claimed that I didn't know.

Unfortunately, seven days was all the time it required for the Cyborganizers to launch an all-out media attack on *The History of Death*, selecting it out as a "typical example of modern academic research," guilty of "de-historicizing" cyborgization.

The commentary I had provided to the *The Last Judgment* actually contained only three brief references to early experiments in cyborgization, but none of them were complimentary and they swiftly became the Cyborganizers' favorite example of the "sketchily caricaturish" attitude to cyborgization fostered by the world's "Secret Masters." Like all of my kind, the Cyborganizers alleged, I was in the pocket of the Hardinist Cabal. I was producing bad history, warped to the service of their hidden agenda, deliberately falsifying the past so as to to make it seem that organic-inorganic integration and symbiosis were peripheral to the story of human progress rather than its very heart.

It was the most blatant nonsense imaginable, but it emerged into the media marketplace at a time when anything connected to the cause of Cyborgization was newsworthy, and it became news.

If I had any defense to offer, Samuel Wheatstone ringingly declared to the world, he would be only too pleased to debate the matter in public.

I could not refuse the challenge, not because it would have seemed cowardly but because it would have been seen by the public at large as a tacit confession that I was a bad historian.

I didn't want to rush into anything without preparing my ground, but time was of the essence. I had to find out what the Cyborganizers were all about in a tearing hurry, and to do that I had to wheedle my way back into Tricia's good books. I shamelessly exploited the fact that the twelve-year-old Lua was genuinely distressed by our estrangement, and I managed to avoid getting sidetracked into mere technical discussion by including Lua in our educational discussions.

"The problem," Tricia explained, pretending to talk to Lua as well as to me, "is that the earliest adventures in human-machine hybridization were carried out at a time when nobody had any real idea of what might be practical and what wouldn't. Their mistakes generated a lot of bad publicity. It was a time when IT still stood for information technology, because there was no nanotech to produce internal technology. There were no sloths, let alone silvers, but the computers of the day were getting faster and faster, juggling what seemed to their users to be huge amounts of data. It seemed only natural to think of building bridges between the brain and clever machinery, so there was a lot of talk about memory boxes and psychedelic synthesizers. People who actually went so far as to build connection systems into their heads were regarded as madmen, or even criminalized, but that only made them seem more heroic to their supporters. They couldn't know that the things they were trying to do were much more difficult than they thought."

"Some of them were," I agreed. "But we don't make fun of the idea of slotting additional inorganic memory stores into the brain because it's impossible, but because it no longer seems as necessary to us as it did to people whose so-called rejuvenation technologies tended to disrupt and diminish their existing memories. We don't laugh at the idea of psychedelic synthesizers because they didn't work—they just seem like absurdly blunt instruments now that we have a much better understanding of brain chemistry and a sophisticated VE technology that can produce the same sort of rewards with infinitely less risk. Anyway, the real problem was that one or two of the things the brainfeed brigade were trying to do turned out to be much *easier* to accomplish than their opponents thought."

"What do you mean?" Lua asked, obligingly.

"I mean that one of the technologies that the world's not-so-secret masters really did decide to put away for the general good was a device that really did turn human beings into robots, at least temporarily."

"That's not fair," Tricia said, presumably echoing the views of Samuel Wheatstone. "If the so-called Medusa device hadn't made its debut as a murder weapon, employed by the world's last and most flamboyant serial killer, it wouldn't have seemed anywhere near as demonic as it did. That whole line of technical enquiry was strangled at birth, without any regard to beneficial uses or useful applications. Like the IT versions of VE tech, it was labeled dangerous and shoved into SusAn with all the other criminals that the Hardinist Tyranny didn't want to deal with. In a world that had an authentically democratic government instead of a gang of bureaucrats dancing to the tune of a gang of pirates who seized economic control of the ecosphere way back in the twenty-first century, that kind of thing couldn't happen. The people in the outer system won't tolerate that kind of intellectual repression, so why should we put up with it here on Earth?"

"IT isn't the only acronym to have changed its meaning since the twenty-first century," I pointed out. "You used VE just now to mean Virtual Experience, but it's not so long ago that it was only used to mean Virtual Environment. We'd still be using it in the narrower way if the techniques hadn't taken aboard certain features of the supposedly suppressed technologies you're using as key examples. The harmless and beneficial applications of IT-based VE and the so-called Medusa device *have* been integrated into the way we live, having been redirected into orthodox channels. The idea that whole areas of research have been suspended and deep-frozen is nonsensical—it's a myth."

Tricia wouldn't admit it, of course, but I felt that I could at least hold my own on that particular battleground—and I therefore assumed that Wheatstone would choose another. I knew that I had to expect the unexpected, but I tried as best I could to put myself in his shoes, hoping to anticipate his line of attack far more accurately than I had when we had crossed swords publicly before. It seemed to me, when I did this, that there was one line of Cyborganizer rhetoric to which I might be particularly vulnerable.

The Cyborganizers were skeptical of the claim that Zaman transformations guaranteed true emortality. Although the oldest true emortals had now beaten the previous records set by false emortals, and showed no obvious sign of being unable to extend their lives indefinitely, the Cyborganizers insisted that what was presently called "emortality" would eventually prove wanting. They conceded that Zaman transformations had dramatically increased the human life span but insisted that some kinds of aging processes—particularly those linked to DNA copying-errors—were still effective. Eventually, they claimed, people would again begin to die of "age-related causes." Even if it took thousands of years, and even if they avoided the perils of robotization, true emortals would begin to fade away—and in the meantime, they would remain vulnerable to all manner of accidents.

In the great tradition of preachers, the Cyborganizers played upon emortal fears only to stoke up demand for a new kind of hope. They wanted to resurrect the term that emortality had made obsolete: *immortality*. In order to turn flawed emortality into authentic immortality, the Cyborganizers claimed, it would be necessary to look to a combination of organic and inorganic technologies. The deepest need of contemporary humankind, they said, was not more of the same precarious kind of life, but a guaranteed "afterlife."

What they meant by "afterlife" was not, of course, what their religious predecessors had meant, but some kind of transcription of the personality into a new matrix that would combine the best features of inorganic and organic chemistry.

"All this is old stuff too," I told Tricia, by way of practice. "It's the old chestnut about uploading one's mind to a computer, given a new lick of paint and a bit of fancy dress. The mind isn't a kind of ghost that can simply be moved out of one body into another. Our bodies *are* our selves. The mind is a condition of the whole, not an inhabitant of the part. It's so easy nowadays to design a silver that can replicate the speech patterns and responses of a particular person that we all use them to answer our phones, and the best ones can pass for their models in polite society almost indefinitely—but none of us is idiot enough to believe that his answering machine is another version of himself. No one thinks that the fact that his silver will carry on answering his phone after he's dead means that he'll really still be alive."

"That's exactly what Samuel means by a *sketchy caricature*," Tricia told me. "We're much more sophisticated than the old advocates of uploading. *We*'re talking about gradual personal evolution, not abrupt metamorphosis. We're talking about the evolution of the body beyond genetically specified limits. We're talking about *the expansion of the self.* Fabers and their kin are already redefining their own selfhood by altering their physical makeup, and they already know that however clever genetic engineers might become in adapting men for life in microworlds or within the ecospheres of Earthlike planets, only cyborgization can create entities capable of working in genuinely extreme environments. We're already doing it. Everybody with IT is already a cyborg, and everybody in the outer system is perfectly at home with the idea that the time has come to let IT expand into ET—*external technology.*

"It's *because* the mind is a condition of the whole and not an inhabitant of the part that we're already engaged in a process of machine-enhanced mental evolution. That's the very essence of cyborganization, and the only reason you can't see it, Morty, is that you're stuck in the past, refusing to accept release from the prison of *frail flesh.* The day will come when you want to live in the future, Morty—and that's when you'll have to accept that the only way to avoid becoming a robotically petrified mind in a slowly decaying body is to *evolve.*"

SIXTY-SEVEN

It was by testing argumentative strategies on Tricia that I derived the slogan that I was determined to carry into battle against Samuel Wheatstone. The incantation that I hoped to use to rally the media audience to my cause was *Cyborganization is robotization by another name.* I didn't tell Tricia, of course, in case she passed it on to Wheatstone, but I did confide it to Lua Tawana, after swearing her to secrecy.

I think she kept the secret, but even if she didn't, she wasn't responsible for what happened. The simple fact is that Samuel Wheatstone would have beaten me anyway, because he was a better player of the media game than I was. It was, after all, his vocation. He was a professional fool, and I was a serious historian.

I never really stood a chance.

I did put up a slightly better show against Nyxson/Wheatstone than I had the first time around. I managed to get more of my own argument on to the record, and I did contrive to repeat my chosen slogan often enough to make it a standard item of popular rhetoric, although it was spoiled by the extra spin that he managed to impart to it. In spite of my preparations, I was completely unready for Wheatstone's main line of attack.

Tricia told me afterward that she was as surprised as I was, and I believed her. Samuel Wheatstone's attempts to imagine himself in my shoes had obviously been far more successful than my attempts to put myself in his, and he had worked out how to sting me with callous precision.

Before the broadcast began I thought myself sufficiently mature to be unaffected by any probable insult. Perhaps I was—but it had not seemed possible, let alone probable, that Wheatstone would sink so low as to charge me with being a closet Thanaticist.

"Your interminable book is only posing as a history," he told me, languidly. "It's actually an extended exercise in the pornography of death. The fact that your commentaries strive so hard to be boring and clinical isn't a mark of scholarly dignity—it's a subtle means of heightening response."

"That's absurd!" I protested—but it would have take far more than *that* to put him off.

"You pretend to be standing aside from the so-called war against death, as a painstaking chronicler and fair-minded judge," he went on, "but you're actually fully engaged in the final campaign of that war, and the army to which you've been conscripted is death's. You've railed in the past against those who sought to restore a proper recognition of death's reality and utility to human affairs, but you posed as an enemy of death merely to further death's cause. You attacked Thanaticism, but you were yourself the most extreme and most insidious kind of Thanaticist. You purported to fight the devil by pretending that he did not exist, but what greater service could you do the devil than to persuade his victims that he was a mere mirage?

"In fact, Mortimer, you knew all along that death had not been banished from human affairs. You knew all along that what we choose to call *true emortality* is merely a postponement of the final reckoning. You knew all along that even so-called true emortals age physically, albeit very slowly, and that even if they didn't, they would still age mentally by virtue of being trapped in the same physical matrix: becalmed, crystallized, and ultimately sterilized. Cyborganization is robotization by another name, you say. Very well—I accept the assertion. The time is long past for the idea of robotization to be reclaimed from those who use it unthinkingly as a mere insult. Let us call it by its proper name: *androidization*—for what we are talking about is, after all, a petrifaction of the flesh, a death-in-life, a silverization of the living personality.

"If we are truly to live forever, Mortimer, then we must be forever open to the possibility of change, and in order to do that, we must be prepared not merely to transform our flesh by genetic engineering but augment and enhance it by mechanical supplementation. Mere humans cannot *live* forever; the best they can ever hope for is to *exist* forever—but a cyborg is an evolving being, a being for whom future possibilities are infinite. Whoever opposes cyborganization opposes life itself. Whoever condemns cyborganization is not merely a historian but a *champion* of death, a Thanaticist in the truest and most sinister sense of the word.

"I was a Thanaticist myself, in my youth, but all I ever advocated was the right of human beings to complete the processes of death that shaped their bodies and their personalities, to follow through its patient artwork. When you argued with me then you refused to concede that you or I or anyone should exercise that right, lest we should sacrifice greater and more wonderful opportunities—yet here you are again, refusing to concede that you or I or anyone human should exercise the right to explore those greater and more wonderful opportunities, lest we should sacrifice the privilege of dying as we are. You have immersed yourself so deeply in the history of death, Mortimer, that you have become death's last and best ally on Earth."

And so on. Insult after stinging insult—but never to the point of actual injury. It was, after all, only a game. It was all nonsense, but it washed over me like an irresistible tide. I couldn't fight it within the limitations of the live debate. I went down to ignominious defeat, and I went gracelessly.

I had to admit that Wheatstone did what he had come to do with a certain flair—and he looked magnificent, especially in close-up. He had made further modifications to his skull fixtures, and his mechanical eyes had the most remarkable stare I had ever encountered.

Afterward, he said: "I don't suppose you'll thank me for all the money you'll make this time around either, but I don't mind. All I need is the knowledge of a kindness done, a generous impulse served. All I ask in return is that when you finally get around to the history of the twenty-eighth and thirty-first centuries, you grant me a couple of modest footnotes."

I promised him that if he ever did anything worthy of note, I would certainly consider the possibility.

Days, if not weeks, had passed before I worked out what I might have done to counter his assault. Perhaps I should have conceded the point that the clinicality of my commentary was a means of heightening reader response. Perhaps I should have argued, passionately, that there was no other way to make readers who have long abandoned their fear of death sensitive to the appalling shadow that it once cast over the human world. Perhaps I should have accepted, proudly, that my history could not help appearing to modern readers as an exercise in the pornography of death, because death is itself the ultimate and perhaps the only true pornography. Perhaps I should have . . . but what point is there in such regretful imaginary reconstructions?

I knew then, as I had always known, that my history would have to stand alone, on its own merits—that it would have to be *what it was*, and not what any advertising slogan or critical insult attempted to make it.

Samuel Wheatstone was right, of course. My face-to-mask debate with the voice of Cyborganization gave a massive boost to the consultation fees I was collecting for the existing parts of my history. It also created a strong sense of anticipation in respect of the forthcoming eighth installment. He really did make me a lot of money, and I suppose that I ought to have been more grateful for it than I was. In his strange, absurd, and painful way he did help my cause.

SIXTY EIGHT

The eighth part of my *History of Death*, entitled *The Fountains of Youth*, was launched on 1 December 2944. It dealt with the development of elementary technologies of longevity—and, for that matter, with elementary technologies of cyborgization—between the twenty-third and twenty-fifth centuries. It detailed the progress of the new "politics of emortality," whose main focus was the New Charter of Human Rights, which sought to establish a basic right to longevity for all. It also offered a detailed account of the activities of the Ahasuerus Foundation and the gradual development of the Zaman transformations.

My commentary argued that the Manifesto of the New Chartists was the vital treaty that ushered in the newest phase in man's continuing war with death. I insisted that the development of technologies of longevity could easily have increased the level of conflict within the human community instead of decreasing it, and that it was the political context provided by the Charter that had tipped the balance in favor of peace and harmony. It had done so by defining the whole human community as a single army, united in all its interests.

I realized that in arguing thus I was laying myself open to a renewal of the charge that I was an apologist for the Hardinists, and I was careful to concede that the Charter had not worked nearly so well in practice as its terms promised, but I had always maintained that the war against death was a war of ideas, and I insisted that the idea of the charter was so important that the inevitable lag phase preceding its effective implementation had been a tolerable hypocrisy. I took great care to emphasize that the charter remained a central document of emortal culture and that the implementation of its primary objectives had not rendered it redundant.

I suppose, in retrospect, that my account of the long battle fought by the Chartists across the stage of world politics was infected by a partisan fervor that had been muted in the three parts immediately preceding it. My description of the obstacles that had been placed in the path of Ali Zaman and others laboring on behalf of the Ahasuerus Foundation was clinical enough, naming no scapegoats, but I could not be so carefully neutral in detailing the resistance offered by certain elements within the community of nations to the proposal that true emortality should be made universally available as soon as it was practical to do so.

Had the principle of universal access not been so firmly established, I suggested, a situation might have developed in which the spectrum of wealth separated men yet again into two distinct classes of haves and have-nots—a separation that would have led inexorably to violent revolution as those who were too poor to obtain emortality set out to make sure that those who could afford it would not enjoy its fruits. Like any other exercise in counterfactual history, this required speculative thinking of a kind that some of my peers deplored, but I think that my argument was as cogent as it was vigorous. Emortality for the few had never been acceptable on moral grounds and would never have been tolerable in political terms. The Eliminators of the twenty-second century had done far more barking than biting, but their doleful prophecies would indeed have given way to a full-blown crusade had the would-be crusaders not turned to Chartism, and had they not won the day.

I admitted, of course, that I had the benefit of hindsight, and that as a Zaman-transformed individual myself I was bound to have an attitude very different from Ali Zaman's confused and cautious contemporaries, but I saw no reason to be entirely evenhanded in treating the manner in which his discoveries were received and deployed. From the viewpoint of my history, those who initially opposed Zaman and those who sought to appropriate his work for a minority had to be regarded as traitors in the war against death. I felt no need to seek excuses on their behalf, even though I was keenly aware that I might be feeding ammunition to the Cyborganizers if they cared to continue their attacks upon me.

There was no point in my trying to gloss over the fact that many of those who had sought to inhibit the work of the Ahasuerus Foundation or to prevent the UN's adoption of the New Charter had done so on the ostensible grounds that they were trying to preserve "human nature" against biotechnological intervention. I knew that many of my readers would respond to this allegation by thinking that if the conservatives of old were so utterly wrong to do that, how could those who opposed the

Cyborganizers on similar grounds be right? I knew, therefore, that my stern judgment that the enemies of Ali Zaman and the Charter had been willfully blind and criminally negligent of the welfare of their own children would be quoted against me—but it would not have been good scholarship to intrude into my argument a rider explaining why the current disputes over cyborganization did not constitute a parallel case. I defended my ground as best I could by couching my argument in political and egalitarian grounds, but I knew that whatever I said would be taken out of context by my critics, and I simply accepted the risk.

As I had anticipated, the Cyborganizers were quick to charge me with inconsistency because I was not nearly so extravagant in my enthusiasm for the various kinds of symbiosis between organic and inorganic systems that were tried out in the period under consideration as I was in my praise of the Herculean labors of the genetic engineers.

When I was called upon to make a public response to such criticisms I was insistent that my lack of enthusiasm for experiments in cyborgization had nothing to do with the idea that such endeavors were "unnatural" and everything to do with the fact that they were only peripherally relevant to the war against death, but it did no good. Wheatstone's followers—including Tricia Ecosura—waxed lyrical about the injustice of my inclination to dismiss adventures in cyborgization, along with cosmetic biotechnologies, as symptoms of lingering anxiety regarding the presumed "tedium of emortality." In fact, that anxiety had led the first generations of long-lived people to a lust for variety and "multidimensionality" that was not unlike the popular anxieties on which the Cyborganizers were now trading, but that was a difficult point to get across and it won me no arguments in the public eye.

It is, I suppose, perfectly understandable that champions of man-machine symbiosis, who saw their work as *the* new frontier of science, would have preferred to find a more generous account of the origins of their enterprise, but the simple fact is that I didn't include it in *The Fountains of Youth* because I didn't consider it relevant.

The Cyborganization controversy helped to boost access-demand for *The Fountains of Youth* to an extraordinary level and made my financial situation so secure that I had no need to fear the reversion to solitary existence that was bound to follow Lua Tawana's accession to independence, but Samuel Wheatstone was correct in prophesying that I would not be grateful.

At the time, I felt too strongly that the academic quality of my commentary had been entirely overlooked and that hardly anyone was now trying to keep track of the development of my history *as a whole*. I hoped, however, that by the time the next part was published the furor over Cyborganization would be dead and gone, allowing my work to be re-placed in its proper perspective.

Such is the way of popular controversies that I got my wish—but the real issues raised by the Cyborganizers survived their fashionability, in much the same way that the real issues raised by the Thanaticists never had gone away—and never would.

SIXTY-NINE

In September 2945, when Lua Tawana was thirty-three years old, three of her co-parents—Mama Maralyne, Papa Ewald, and Mama Francesca—were killed when the helicopter in which they were traveling crashed into the sea near the island of Vavau during a violent storm.

The household had broken up some ten years earlier, when the divorce was formalized, but its members had not dispersed to any considerable degree. Mica, Tricia, and I had remained near neighbors, and because Lua remained in New Tonga rather than moving to another continent to complete her education, all the others took care to stay in touch. It seemed to me, in fact, that they made more effort to stay in touch than they had when we shared the same hometree, at least in the cases of Bana and Ng. The tragedy affected the survivors as powerfully and as intimately as Grizel's death had affected the co-partners in my first marriage, but the circumstances were so different that it did not seem to me that history was repeating itself.

It was the first time that my remaining co-spouses, let alone my daughter, had had to face up squarely to the fact that death had not been entirely banished from the world. Like me, they had lost their parents one by one, save for a handful of ZT fosterers, but I was the only one who had ever lost an emortal spouse. This put me in a slightly awkward position because it meant that everyone involved immediately decided that, as the resident expert, I should shoulder not only the responsibility of helping Lua through the ordeal but also the responsibility of helping *them* to cope.

I could hardly object; was I not, after all, the world's foremost expert on the subject of death?

"You won't always feel this bad about it," I assured Lua, while we walked together on the sandy shore looking out over the deceptively placid weed-choked sea. "Time heals virtual wounds as well as real ones." I had said as much to Mica and Tricia, and they had both accepted it as gospel, but Lua reacted differently.

"I don't want it to heal," she told me, sternly. "I want it to be bad. It ought to be bad. It *is* bad. I don't want to forget it or to get to a point were it might never have happened."

"I can understand that," I said, far more awkwardly than I would have wished. "When I say that it'll heal I don't mean that it'll vanish. I mean that it'll . . . become manageable. It won't be so all-consuming. It won't ever lose its meaning."

"But it *will* vanish, won't it?" she said, with that earnest certainty of which only the newly adult are capable. "Maybe not soon, but it will go. People do forget. In time, they forget *everything*. Our heads can hold only so much. So it *will* lose its meaning. In time, it'll be as if I never had *any* parents. It won't matter who they were, or whether they died, or how they died."

"That's not true," I insisted, taking her hand in mine. "Yes, we do forget. The longer we live, the more we let go, because it's reasonable to prefer our fresher, more immediately relevant memories, but it's a matter of *choice*. We *can* cling to the things that are important, no matter how long ago they happened. We can make them part of us, and we keep them forever. Even if we forget them, they're still among the forces that make and shape us. Without them, we'd be different."

"I suppose so," she conceded—but I couldn't tell whether she meant it, or whether she was trying to be kind to a no-longer-functional parent.

"I was nearly killed in the Great Coral Sea Catastrophe, you know," I reminded her. "That was nearly four hundred years ago. Emily Marchant was a little girl, far younger than you are now. She saved my life, and I'll never forget it. I'd be lying if I said that I remember it as clearly as if it were yesterday, because I don't, but I know that that was the most important event in my life and hers. If it hadn't happened, I would be a very different person, and so would she—and because of the influence I've had on your upbringing, so would you, however slightly. Maybe that doesn't matter so much in your case or mine, but if Emily Marchant were different, Titan wouldn't be the world it is today. The history of the whole outer system would have developed differently, and with it—to a small but measurable degree—the history of the human race."

"Is she really that important?" Lua asked. She'd heard me talk about Emily many times before, of course, but she'd only ever been interested in Emily the child, Emily the survivor. I'd told her about the ice palaces, and she'd visited them in VE, but I'd never mentioned the highkickers' grandest plans. I'd never discussed Julius Ngomi's teasing inquiries about Jupiter in the hometree or taken time out to explain any of the other festering conflicts of interest between the Earthbound and space-faring humanity.

"I believe she's as important as anyone alive," I said. "It came as a surprise to me when I first began to see it, but I'm reasonably sure that she's one of the rare individuals who can actually make a big difference. It's partly because she's so rich, but it's mostly because of the way she got rich and the way she's fed her wealth into ambitious projects. She's a mover and shaker, not of rocks and trees but of worlds. Mama Maralyne could have explained the exact nature of her work far better than I can—and Mama Mica still can—but she's more than just a gantzer of genius. She's at the very heart of the enterprise that will extend the Oikumene to the stars."

"And *you* saved her life when she was still a child," said Lua, teasingly. "Everything she achieves is really down to you."

"That's not what I said," I reminded her, although she was an adult, albeit a very young one, and she knew as well as I did that there's always a difference between what people say and what they mean to imply. "Emily could swim and I couldn't. If she hadn't been there, I wouldn't have been able to get out of the hull. I'd never have had the courage to do it on my own, but she didn't even give me the choice. She told me I had to do it, and she was right."

I paused, feeling a slight shock of renewed revelation even though it was something I'd always known and always accepted.

"She lost her *entire family*," I went on. "She's fine now, but I'm absolutely certain that she hasn't forgotten any one of them—and she had twelve parents, not the standard eight. She can still feel the force of their loss. That's what I'm really trying to tell you, Lua. In four hundred years' time, you'll still remember what happened, and you'll still feel it, but you'll be all right. It'll be part of you—an important part of you—but it won't have *reduced* you in any injurious way. You'll be a mover and shaker too, maybe of worlds."

"Right now," she said, looking up at me so that her dark and soulful eyes seemed unbearably huge and sad, "I'm not particularly interested in being all right, let alone moving and shaking. Right now, I just want to cry."

"That's fine," I told her. "It's okay to cry. Being over thirty doesn't mean that you have to give up crying. I didn't. I still haven't."

I led by example. It was probably the most intimate moment we ever shared, but there were many less intimate that left similarly indelible and far more precious marks on my memory and my heart.

Lua Tawana continued to grow up, and her remaining parents continued to drift apart, but I was a parent forever afterward, and a changed man because of it.

SEVENTY

I remained on Neyu for forty years after Lua Tawana left the archipel-
ago. None of my surviving co-parents was in any greater hurry to leave
the island. Banastre was the first to depart for another continent, followed by Tricia, but they both returned at irregular intervals, often making special trips to coincide with Lua's visits. I continued to see Mica
socially and even got together with Ng at widely spaced but fairly regular
intervals. Although we had never been a close family the fact that the
five survivors had shared a significant loss continued to bind us together.

Of exactly *what* it was that bound us I was unsure. It wasn't grief in
any ordinary sense of the word, and it may have been something for
which New Humans had not yet invented a word. Immediately after the
tragedy my co-parents had seemed to outside observers to be exaggerat-
edly calm and philosophical, almost as if the loss of three spouses was
simply a minor glitch in the infinitely unfolding pattern of their lives, but
I knew that even if they did not know how best to express it, the effect of
the deaths upon them had been profound. They had all grown accustomed to their own emortality, almost to the extent that they had ceased
to think about death at all, and the simultaneous loss of three co-spouses
had introduced a strange and almost unaccountable rift into the pattern
of their affairs. They were not the same afterward, any more than I had
been the same after losing Grizel to the Kwarra.

I was less affected than any of them, not merely because I had gone
through it before but because I was a man who had lived for centuries in
the most intimate contact with the idea of death. The shock of our
mutual loss was not nearly as strange to me as it was to them, nor did it
seem unaccountable. I often found myself attempting to persuade my ex-
spouses that the tragedy had had its positive, life-enhancing side, repeating with approval what Lua had said about wanting to conserve the bad
feeling and pontificating about the role played by death in defining experiences as important and worthwhile.

Mica understood, I think—but Tricia never did. We had been close once, but Samuel Wheatstone's foolery drove us apart irrevocably, and she ended up thinking of me as a traitor to her personal cause as well as an opponent of her philosophical cause.

When that cause went the same way as all fashionable movements Samuel Wheatstone went with it. He dropped out of public view, although the memory of his remarkable mask was not easily put away—perhaps not as easily as the mask itself. I doubt that he ever replaced his artificial eyes with tissue-cultured replicas of those with which he had been born, but I doubt that he kept the more exotic embellishments with which he had decorated his skull. Most of those had been purely for show. Such cyborg modifications as did become briefly popular among the Earthbound were mostly of the same kind—essentially cosmetic even when they did have ostensible functions. Tricia's were entirely cosmetic, but they always seemed to me to be rather tasteless. Francesca might have made a much better model for the wilder excesses of ET fanaticism, had she lived.

Given that natural selection had adapted the human body very carefully to the requirements of life at the Earth's surface, it is hardly surprising that its conventional form met most people's needs and desires. Although suitskins designed for Earthly use had become much cleverer over time, they remained relatively meek and unobtrusive passengers on the human body. The inhabitants of the outer system, on the other hand, had very different needs and desires, and *their* suitskins had become so inventive that it was easy to argue that all the human beings who did not live on the Earth's surface were heavily cyborgized simply by virtue of the clothing they wore.

Off-world examples had prompted the Cyborganization fad but from the point of view of most off-worlders the wayward tides of Earthly fashion were the whims of the irredeemably decadent. The highkickers were *serious* about the possibilities of cyborgization, and there were many among them who felt that if cyborgization was the price they would have to pay to establish authentic Utopias in the ice-palace cities that awaited them on Titan and the Uranian moons, then it was a price well worth paying. There were not quite so many who felt that the work of galactic exploration ought to be the province of cyborgized humans rather than silver-piloted probes, but there were enough of them to force the progress of human-machine hybridization into ever-more-adventurous channels.

Every message I received from Emily Marchant in the thirtieth century seemed to come from a different person. Before 2900 even the high-kickers had been careful to retain their own faces, but Samuel Wheatstone's extravagant reconstruction of his own appearance had accurately reflected the demise of that particular taboo. Emily was never one to support ornamental cyborgization, but she lost her former inhibitions about letting her artificial augmentations show. Her first set of artificial eyes was carefully designed to resemble the ones they replaced, but her second wasn't, and the parts of her suitskin overlaying the flesh of her face gradually abandoned their attempts to reproduce the appearance that had once lain "beneath" them.

I asked Emily many questions about her metamorphosis, but she rarely thought them worth answering, and the long time delay between exchanges made it easy for her to ignore them. Her transmissions were always full of her own news, her own hopes, and her own fears—among which the fear of robotization and the fear of losing her identity did not seem to figure at all.

I found all this rather disturbing, but Emily seemed to find my own priorities equally strange and became increasingly insistent that the entire population of the Earthbound had become dangerously insensitive to the situations developing outside the system.

"It's as if the hard-core Hardinists have washed their hands of the whole affair," she complained in one message, delivered from the heart of one of her finest virtual ice-palaces. "Having despaired of exercising any control over the terraformation of Maya they seem to have decided that Earth is their only concern. I know they don't censor the news, but they do exert an enormous influence on its agenda, and Earth's casters seem to have followed their lead in dismissing almost all of the information-flow from outside the system as irrelevant and uninteresting. It's *not* irrelevant, Morty. It's infinitely more important than 99 percent of what happens on the Earth's surface.

"No one on Earth seems to be in the least troubled by the attrition rate of the kalpa probes. People down there seem to think that because so many of the old Arks went missing it's not surprising that so many of the kalpas have lost contact, but the cases aren't similar at all. Something's happening out there, Morty, and it has consequences for all of us. The Fermi paradox has been around so long that it's lost its power to amaze or frighten the Earthbound, but we can still feel its urgency. Given Earth, Ararat, and Maya, the galaxy ought to be full of mature civilizations broadcasting away like crazy, but it's not—and the search for possible Type-2 civilizations has drawn a complete blank. The discovery of Ararat and Maya tells us that we *can't* be alone, but it's no longer a question of *where* the hell are they. The question we ought to be asking—all of us, Morty, not just the highkickers—is *what* the hell are they?

"Whoever's out there is much less like us than we've been prepared to assume, and the one thing we can be sure of is that contact is just around the corner, even if it hasn't been made already. We're beginning to believe that most of the missing Arks and nearly all the missing kalpas have made contact with *something*, but we can't begin to guess what it is—and the Earthbound don't even seem to care. We're worried that while we're renewing ourselves constantly the population of Earth is growing contentedly old, relaxing into a lotus-eater existence. Nobody out here uses *robotization* as a term of abuse any more, but we think that something like what we used to mean by that term has already happened to the Earthbound. They've become insular, self-satisfied, and lazy. They've lost their progressive impetus to the extent that they can't even seem to realize that something is *badly wrong* in the inner reaches of the galaxy, and that it *matters*."

The overwhelming majority of my Earthbound friends and acquaintances would have said, unhesitatingly, that Emily was talking nonsense. They would have judged that her fears were symptoms of "outer-system paranoia"—a phrase whose use had become so earnest that its users tended to forget that it was a mere slogan and not a real disease. The new breed of Continental Engineers thought of themselves as progress personified, and the Tachytelic Perfectionists considered themselves to be the most ardent campaigners for change that Garden Earth had ever entertained, so charges of decadence simply bounced off them. The idea that the galactic center was home to some unspecified menace seemed to contented Earthdwellers to be silly scaremongering.

When I put some of the points made in Emily's messages to Mica Pershing her reaction was typical, and exactly what I'd expected.

"The outer system people are all crazy," she said. "Tricia loses her sense of proportion sometimes when she talks about the benefits of cyborgization, but at least she has a sensible notion of what might count as a benefit. The outer-system people have been carried away by mechanization for mechanization's sake. They think that because it's possible to design suitskins that will let them operate in hard vacuum for days on end and live on the surface of Titan almost indefinitely that those are worthwhile things to do. They don't just want to fly spaceships, they want to *be* spaceships—and they're starting to cultivate the anxieties of spaceships. Deep space is a horrible and hostile environment, and the universe is full of it. Planets are where life belongs, but it's an unfortunate fact of life that comfortable planets are few and far between—and that the farness in question consists of a vile abyss of emptiness. Of course malfunctions happen, even in the most carefully designed systems. Silvers fail—even the high-grade silvers built into kalpa probes. It's only to be expected—and the only people who find the prospect unthinkable are people who are on the brink of giving up their own humanity in order to *become* the next generation of kalpas. Earth is where all *real* progress takes place, because no matter how far the Oikumene extends Earth will always be its one and only heart, humankind's one and only *home*."

Had I been anyone other than Emily Marchant's trusted confidante I might have agreed with Mica, but it would have seemed disloyal to do so—and I was not at all sure that Emily was wrong.

"Even if all that's true, the Earthbound shouldn't lose sight of the farther horizons," I told Mica, earnestly. "We're fast approaching the day when Earth's billions will be a minority within the Oikumene—and once that balance has shifted, the spacefarers' majority will grow and grow. How long will it be before *they*'re the human race and Earth is just a quaint and quiet backwater where the old prehuman folks jealousy preserve their ancient habits?"

"Personally," Mica told me, "I don't think it will ever happen. I think the expansion into space has just been a fad, like Cyborganization. I think it's hitting its natural limits now and that your friend's panic is the first symptom of a fundamental change in attitude. I think the outward urge will wither and die, and that the outer system people will begin to reclaim their humanity. When we've built the new continent, they'll be able to return to Earth—and as soon as the possibility materializes, they'll be lining up to do it. The cyborgs will revert to honest flesh, and the fabers will grow legs."

I could imagine exactly what Emily would have said to *that*—and so, I presume, could Lua Tawana, who announced when she visited Neyu to celebrate her fortieth birthday that she had decided to leave Earth. She had secured a job on the moon, but her ultimate aim was to go to Titan and make that her home for a century or two.

"It's where the future is," she told us, "and where the real movers and shakers are. If I'm to take an active part in making the future, that's where I have to be. Here, I could only help to build another continent just like all the rest. There, I can help to build a world like none that has ever been seen or imagined before. And after Titan, who knows?"

SEVENTY-ONE

The ninth volume of the *History of Death*, entitled *The Honeymoon of Emortality*, was launched on 28 October 2975. The knot of supportive data was slight by comparison with its predecessors, but the accompanying commentary was extensive—which led many academic reviewers to lament the fact that I had given up "real history" in favor of "popular journalism." Even those who were sympathetic suggested that I had begun to rush my work, although those who remembered that it had originally been planned as a seven-volume work were not slow to assert that the contrary was the case and that I was procrastinating because I had become afraid of the letdown effect of finishing it.

The main focus of the commentary was the development of attitudes to longevity and potential emortality following the establishment of the principle that every human child has a right to be born emortal. The reason that it was more lightly supported than any of its predecessors was simply that it needed less support. I still believe that it was unnecessary to make a fetish of gathering every last public statement ever made on the subject into a single knot, let alone that I should have made far more effort to trawl private archives for relevant comments.

The central stream of my argument dutifully weighed the significance of the belated extinction of the "nuclear" family and gave careful consideration to the backlash generated by the ideological rebellion of the Humanists, whose quest to preserve "the authentic *Homo sapiens*" had once led many to retreat to islands that the Continental Engineers were now integrating into their "new continent." I was, however, more interested in less inevitable social processes and subtler reactions. I felt—and still feel—that I had more interesting observations to make on the spread of such new philosophies of life as neo-Stoicism, neo-Epicureanism, and Xenophilia.

My main task, as I saw it, was to place these oft-discussed matters in their proper context: the spectrum of inherited attitudes, myths, and fictions by means of which mankind had for thousands of years wistfully contemplated the possibility of extended life.

In fulfilling this task, I contended that traditional attitudes to the idea of emortality—including the common reactionary notion that people would inevitably find emortality intolerably tedious—were essentially an expression of "sour grapes." While people thought that emortality was impossible, I pointed out, it made perfect sense for them to invent reasons why it would be undesirable anyhow, but when it became a reality, the imaginative battle had to be fought in earnest. The burden of these cultivated anxieties had to be shed, and a new mythology formulated—but that process had been painfully slow. The gradual transformation of the "eternal tedium" hypothesis into the "robotization" hypothesis represented direly slow progress.

My commentary flatly refused to give any substantial credit to the fears of those mortal men who felt that the advent of emortality might be a bad thing. I was as dismissive of the Robot Assassins and the original Thanaticists as I was of the Humanists. Despite what my fiercest critics alleged, however, I did make a serious attempt to understand the thinking of such people and to fit it into the larger picture that my *History* had now brought to the brink of completion.

It was inevitable, in a world that still contained millions of self-described New Stoics, that my evaluation of their forebears would attract vitriolic criticism. When I condemned the people who first formulated the insistence that asceticism was the natural ideological partner of emortality as victims of an "understandable delusion" I knew that I was inviting trouble, but I did it because I thought that I was right, not because I thought that the controversy would boost my access fees.

It did not surprise my critics in the least, of course, that I commended neo-Epicureanism as the optimal psychological adaptation to emortality. Even those who did not know enough biographical details to judge that I had been a lifelong, if slightly unsteady, adherent of "careful hedonism" had inferred from the earlier parts of my study that I was an ardent champion of self-knowledge and avoidance of excess. The cruelest of the early reviewers did venture to suggest that I had been so halfhearted a neo-Epicurean as almost to qualify as a neo-Stoic by default, but I was well used by then to treating criticism of that nature with deserved contempt.

One of the appendixes to *The Honeymoon of Emortality* collated the statistics of birth and death during the twenty-seventh, twenty-eighth, and twenty-ninth centuries, recording the spread of Zaman transformations and the universalization of ectogenesis on Earth and the extension of the Oikumene throughout and beyond the solar system. I recorded acknowledgments to numerous faber scholars based on the moon and Mars for their assistance in gleaning information from the slowly diffusing microworlds and the first wave of their descendant starships. I noted that because the transfer of information between data stores was limited by the speed of light, Earth-based historians might have to wait centuries for significant data about the more distant human colonies, but I promised that I would do my best to update the statistics as and when I could.

These data showed, slightly to my surprise, that the number of individuals of the various humankinds that now existed had already begun to increase more rapidly than ever before by the time of my birth. I could not help but recall, as I noted that conclusion, the lectures I had received from Papa Domenico on the subject of the alleged sterility of the "realist" philosophy and the supposedly inevitable victory of "virtualism." What, I wondered, would Papa Domenico have thought of Emily Marchant and the highkickers? What would he have thought of a human race whose "virtualist Utopians" were now a small minority? I consigned to a footnote the observation that that although *Homo sapiens sapiens* had become extinct in the twenty-eighth century there was as yet no consensus on the labeling of its descendant species.

Although it generated a good deal of interest and a very healthy financial return, many lay reviewers were disappointed that the coverage of *The Honeymoon of Emortality* did not extend to the present day. The surviving Cyborganizers—predictably grateful for the opportunity to heat up a flagging controversy—reacted more noisily than anyone else to this "manifest cowardice" but I had decided that it would be more sensible to reserve such discussions to a tenth and concluding volume of my magnum opus.

The conclusion of my ninth commentary promised that I would consider in all due detail the futurological arguments of the Cyborganizers as well as the hopes and expectations of other contemporary schools of thought. As I had told Emily when she visited the moon, I still had every intention of completing my Herculean labor by the end of the millennium, and I urged my loyal readers to be patient for just a little while longer.

SEVENTY-TWO

I didn't bother to find another place to live before I left Neyu for good. For several years I led a contentedly rootless existence, traveling far more widely about the mainstreams and backwaters of Garden Earth than I had ever contrived to do before.

In my first 480 years I had seen hundreds of archaeological sites and thousands of museums but relatively little of the casters' hit parade of "the wonders of the world." Once, when I enlisted the help of my domestic silver in adding up the time I had spent away from my various homes I found that I had spent more hours inside mountains than sampling the glories of the managed ecosphere. It would have been easy enough to perform a second set of calculations with regard to the time I had spent in virtual environments, but I did not do so. I had no doubt that I had spent far many more hours sampling the delights of imaginary landscapes than real ones even in more recent centuries, let alone in the early years I had spent exploring Papa Domenico's beloved Universe Without Limits.

Now that further alternatives to Earthbound life appeared to be emerging almost yearly from the mists of possibility, not only in the outer system but also in the colony worlds, it was starkly obvious that every person born on Earth had to make the choice that Lua Tawana had recently made: to stay or to seek one's fortune in the infinite. I was part of the older generation in the fashionable reckoning of the day, and my neighbors on Neyu always assumed that I had made my choice long before, but I had never entirely shaken off the confusion that had surrounded my descent from Mare Moscoviense. I was still committed to the neo-Epicurean ethic of permanent growth and I refused to consider the matter settled. I felt as young as I ever had, and I certainly didn't want to be reckoned an element of the Earthbound's supposed decadence. I decided that I would have to renew my decision to remain Earthbound at least once in every century and that it ought to be an informed decision, based on intimate experience of what Garden Earth had to offer to those who chose to remain.

As the thirtieth century wound down, therefore, I made judicious use of the healthy earnings of the more recent volumes of my *History* to roam around all six of the old continents. I made a particular point of visiting those parts of the globe that I had missed out on during my first two centuries of life, although ingrained habit ensured that I took care to include all those sites of special historical interest that had somehow slipped through the nets of my previous itineraries.

Everything I saw was transformed by my habit-educated eyes and the sheer relentlessness of my progress into a series of monuments: memorials of those luckless eras before men invented science and civilization and became demigods. I visited a hundred cities and at least as many agricultural and "protected wilderness" areas. I toured a thousand limited ecosystems, both recapitulative and innovative. I also took care to locate and visit many old friends, including as many of my former marriage partners as I could find.

The Lamu Rainmakers had long since ceased to make mere rain, but they had not lost their commitment to ecological management. Axel, Jodocus, and Minna were still on Earth and all enthusiastic Gardeners. Even more remarkably, they were still in regular touch with one another. They provided the best evidence I had ever found, outside my own admittedly unusual relationship with Emily Marchant, that friendship could endure forever even though the friends maintained the pace of their own personal evolution. I found them much changed—and was mildly surprised that they thought the same of me.

"You're not as self-protective as you used to be, Morty," Axel observed. "Less *defensive.* Life on the moon must have loosened you up—I've noticed that a lot of returners never quite readapt to *all* the correlates of gravity. You should have known better than to take on that Cyborganizer, though. He was always going to make you look slow."

"I never realized back in the twenty-sixth that you were so well connected," Jodocus marveled. "The number of times you told us about meeting Julius Ngomi inside a mountain and saving Emily Marchant's life! They're two of the most important people in the Oikumene now! So tell me—what's on the agenda of this big meeting they're planning to settle the future of the human race?"

I didn't like to admit that I had only the faintest idea, gleaned from reading between the lines of Emily's VE-monologue communications, so I told Jodocus that the fate of Jupiter was likely to be a significant bone of contention. He nodded sagely, as if I had provided official confirmation of his own suspicions.

"The Type-2 people seem to be getting their act together at last," he observed. "Maybe they're right to reckon that we've been fully fledged Type-1 for a couple of centuries and that it's high time we started stocking Earth's orbit with a string of protoworlds. I suspect that's what the new generation of smart multifunctional spaceships is really designed for, although all the talk is of atmosphere diving in the gas giants and ice breaking on Titan and Europa. Transmutation makes far more sense than that old second star nonsense—and a Type-2 progression is the rational response to the news that Earthlike planets are fewer, farther between, and far less useful than we dared to hope."

Jodocus seemed to know more about such matters than I did, or was at least prepared to pretend that he did, but I was content to let him think that I knew far more than I was prepared to make public, and I returned our conversation to the safer ground of twenty-sixth-century Africa.

Minna seemed to have her feet more firmly planted on terra firma than any of the others. After dutifully chiding me for letting things slide so far for so long she was the one who filled me in on recent family history.

"Camilla's on Europa now," she told me, "investigating the possibility of making an ecosphere for the core ocean that can accommodate modified humans—the ultimate merpeople. It wouldn't be a sealed ecosphere. It would be fully connected to the rest of the Oikumene by continuous traffic through the ice shell, using the new smart spaceships. Keir's still working in harness with silvers, but spaceship AIs are the ones he's involved with now. He's here, there, and everywhere—the satellites of all the outer planets—but he's still active in the Rad Libs. He's too far out right now to communicate regularly. Eve's still in the Well, though. She was in the Arctic last time I heard from her. She's like you—always liked things a few degrees colder than the rest of us. Ocean currents are her thing now, but it's such a political minefield that she never seems to be able to get anything *done*. Couldn't stand it myself. Give me fresh water any day—it was a political hot potato in Africa back in the twenty-sixth but nowadays putting lakes and rivers in place is all plain sailing, if you'll forgive the pun."

I forgave her the pun.

Having spent some time with my first marriage partners it seemed only appropriate to spend a little with Sharane Fereday. She had been through a dozen more marriages since ours, but she was temporarily unattached. Unlike the Rainmakers, she could see only similarities between my new and old selves, but her comparisons were not as uncomplimentary as they would once have been.

"I often think that people like you are better fitted to emortality than people like me," she confided. "You need a steady pace to stay long distances, and I've always been an existential sprinter. I feel as if I've lived my life in fits and starts. It's had its rewards, of course, but I think I can see the advantages of the steady slog far better now than I could when we were married. I admire you, Morty, I really do. I admire the way you stuck to that history of yours until it was finished. Tenacity is an underrated virtue."

"It's not *quite* finished," I pointed out. "The donkey work's done and dusted, but I'm still pondering and polishing the final commentary. To tell you the truth, I feel that some of my critics are right about my procrastinating slightly more than is necessary or reasonable. Sometimes, I wonder if I can actually bear to put the last full stop in place—but I've sworn to finish it by the end of the millennium, and I will. It'll be launched long before the end of December 3000."

"And what will you do then?" she wanted to know.

"I don't know," I confessed. "Perhaps I'll write something else—something very different. I had wondered about becoming some sort of Gardener, but having spent so much time with the Rainmakers in the last couple of years I've recovered all my old doubts about my suitability for that kind of work. I've been wondering incessantly about off-planet possibilities, of course. My daughter's become almost as clamorous as Emily Marchant in her insistence that spacefaring is the only way to make proper use of indefinite longevity, but I'm not sure about my suitability for that either. I've seen a lot of Garden Earth these last few years, and I feel *at home* here in a way that I wouldn't like to lose. I'm glad I've lived on the moon, and I'd certainly like to *visit* the outer system some day, but I'm not sure that I'd ever want to go into space to live—even to one of these new Earths that Type-2 people want to build in Earth orbit."

"I know what you mean," Sharane agreed. "If what the casters say about these smart spaceships is true, it will soon become as easy to take tourist trips round the system as it is to tour Earth. When the day comes, I'll be glad to see the sights. The VE reproductions are great, but they're not the real thing. I don't want to become a citizen of the outer darkness, though. I'm Earthbound through and through. All my husbands criticize me for living in the past, but the past is what made us—what we *are* is the sum of the past, and if we want to extrapolate ourselves in order to live in the future we have to keep our consciousness of the past up to scratch. *You* understand that, don't you Morty? You're only one who ever got close to figuring out that part of me."

Most of it was mere flattery, of course—the polite conversation of old acquaintances who no longer had anything left to forgive—but it was good to hear that I had a special place in her memory.

SEVENTY-THREE

Emily confirmed what Jodocus Danette had inferred about the crucial importance of the impending conference at which the leading lights of the Oikumene's many factions would come together face-to-face. Everyone, it seemed, accepted the necessity of some such encounter in the flesh. VE conferencing apparently made it too easy for representatives of the various factions in the dispute to retreat to entrenched positions. Nothing less than a physical gathering could carry sufficient symbolic weight to engender the spirit of give-and-take that would be necessary if the Earthbound and the highkickers were to sort out their rapidly multiplying differences—and even that might not be enough.

Despite the widespread agreement as to its urgent necessity, Emily told me not to expect the conference to happen any time soon. Such elementary matters as finding a venue, setting the agenda, and deciding on the terms of discussion were proving frustratingly difficult, involving a great deal of time-delayed diplomatic wrangling.

"There's no way *we*'re going to agree to come down to Earth," she told me, defiantly. "That would be symbolically loaded to an unacceptable degree. On the other hand, we can understand why Ngomi doesn't want to bring his people all the way out here, even as far as Jupiter—and there are symbolic reasons why neither side would be entirely happy about conducting discussions in old Jove's shadow. If we meet on Mars the Martians will insist that their so-called problems are far more important than they really are, and the asteroids are faberweb territory. Even the moon is an unsuitable compromise because of the faber majority on the far side. It looks as if we might have to settle for empty space, but even the location of the empty space in question is a hot issue—and in the meantime, the unanswered questions are festering away. I wish that you Wellworms hadn't so completely lost your sense of urgency. The situation's becoming absurd."

I wished that I could cut in with a few helpful suggestions, but I couldn't. Her message had been hours in transit and my reply would double the interval.

"The only thing we've all managed to agree on so far," she continued, "is that we have to make some kind of arrangement before the turn of the millennium—and we're insisting that no matter what you arithmetical pedants might say, that means the end of 2999 rather than 3000. It looks as if it won't be a day sooner, but we'll have to sort out a venue by then. If I can come to Earth afterward, Morty, I will—just for a visit, you understand—but I wouldn't get your hopes up too high. It may well be that the only chances we'll get to meet face-to-face once this miserable century's done will depend on your willingness not merely to come out of the Well but to come all the way to the frontier. The new-generation spaceships will make that a lot easier, of course, but you'll still have to get your head around the idea."

I *was* trying, in my slow and one-paced fashion, to get my head around that and many other ideas, but I had never even had Sharane's fervor for novelty, let alone Emily's, and it wasn't easy.

It didn't become any easier to come to an understanding of the new existential predicament of the various humankinds when I heard—not from Emily, in the first instance—that the aptly named starship worldlet *Pandora* had effected the first meeting between humans and the products of an alien ecosphere. *Pandora*'s faber inhabitants did not have to discover another "Earthlike" world in order to do this. Some freak of chance had allowed them to make a deep-space rendezvous with another, much smaller starship.

This was big news, but it had been so long awaited that its arrival seemed slightly anticlimactic. The letdown was reinforced by the fact that the aliens were not quite as alien as futuristic fantasies had always implied. That the alien vessel was so similar to the ancient Ark *Hope* in terms of its design was perhaps expectable, but no one had expected its crew to look so much like the human ambassadors granted the privilege of greeting them.

Like *Pandora*, the alien starship had a crew entirely composed of individuals who had been extensively bioengineered and even more extensively cyborgized for life in zero gee. Because *Pandora*'s population consisted entirely of fabers, many of whom had undergone extensive functional cyborgization, the "humans" and the "aliens" who contrived this allegedly epoch-making contact resembled one another rather more than they resembled unmodified members of their parent species. The fundamental biochemistries controlling the "ecosphere-imposed templates" of the two species were slightly different, but the main consequence of this difference was that the two sets of fabers enthusiastically traded their respective molecules of life, so that their own genetic engineers could henceforth make and use chromosomes of both kinds. The aliens also used stripped-down versions of their own DNA analogue in exactly the same ways that humans employed what had once been called para-DNA in shamirs and other gantzing systems.

"What kind of freedom is it," I asked Eve Chin, with whom I was staying at the time, "that makes all the travelers of space into mirror images of one another? What kind of infinite possibility will there be in the further exploration of the galaxy if it turns out that every starfaring civilization within it has automatically taken the road of convergent evolution?"

"You're exaggerating," Eve told me. "The news reports are playing up the similarity between the Pandorans and the aliens, but it seems to me that it isn't really as close as all that. Freedom won't breed universal mediocrity in space any more than it has on Earth."

I wasn't so sure. Planetary atmospheres are infinitely variable, whereas hard vacuum is the same everywhere, and the physical attributes of planetary surfaces are subject to all kinds of whims that are rigorously excluded from artificial habitats.

"When I lived on the moon the fabers were talking about six-handed and eight-handed variants," I recalled, "but we haven't heard much about them lately. The four-handed model seems to have unique advantages."

"But cyborgization adds another major dimension of variability," Eve pointed out.

"Most of the differences between individual cyborgs are the result of cosmetic modifications," I said, dubiously. "The strictly functional adaptations produce a fairly narrow range of stereotypes, and the *Pandora* pictures suggest that the aliens have adapted themselves to the same range of functions."

Eve wouldn't shift her position. "Adaptation to zero gee isn't an existential straitjacket, Morty," she insisted. "Infinite possibility is still available. One set of coincidences doesn't prove that the next aliens we encounter will be stamped from the same mold. Anyway, far too much media space-time is being wasted on these coincidences. There's something else that the news reports aren't telling us, isn't there? Don't you get a distinct sense that certain matters are being set aside, left carefully unmentioned?"

Actually, I hadn't. Even when Eve raised the possibility, I concluded almost immediately that she had become slightly paranoid by virtue of her long entanglement in the complex diplomatic wrangles that immediately enveloped anyone who proposed the slightest alteration in Earth's ocean currents.

It turned out that I was wrong and Eve was right, but because I didn't take her suspicions seriously to begin with, I didn't give much thought to the possibility that the people who were actually monitoring the Pandorans' transmission were keeping secrets. It never occurred to me to ask Emily any awkward questions when she sent me an uncharacteristically muted account of her own response to the news.

SEVENTY FOUR

The tenth and last part of my *History of Death*, entitled *The Marriage of Life and Death*, was launched into the Labyrinth on 7 April 2998. It was not, from a purist point of view, an exercise in academic history, although I certainly considered it to be a fitting conclusion to my life's work. It did deal in considerable detail with the events as well as the attitudes of the thirtieth century, thus bringing the whole enterprise up to date, but the balance of futurological speculation and historical analysis was far too evenhanded to please narrow-minded academicians.

The commentary element of *The Marriage of Life and Death* discussed neo-Thanaticism and Cyborganization as philosophies as well as social movements, annoying many of my critics and surprising almost all of them. What surprised them was not so much that I had chosen to dabble in rhetoric as that the rhetoric in question treated both movements with considerably more sympathy than I had shown in either of my two public debates with Samuel Wheatstone, *alias* Hellward Lucifer Nyxson.

My commentary also touched upon several other recent and contemporary debates, including those that were currently attempting to settle vital questions about the physical development of the solar system. The discussion was introduced by an innocuous examination of the proposal that a special microworld should be established as a gigantic mausoleum to receive the bodies of all the solar system's dead, but it soon diversified into issues that some reviewers thought—mistakenly, I believe—to be irrelevant to a history of death. I tried to be scrupulously evenhanded in my treatment of the ongoing disputes, but I found it impossible to describe the history of such phenomena as the Type-2 Movement without making some attempt to evaluate their goals. I could not compare and contrast spacefarers' and Earthdwellers' attitudes to death without linking those attitudes to the various projects in which spacefarers were engaged and the various visions and ambitions guiding those projects.

The title of my commentary was an ironic reflection of one of its main lines of argument. I contended that mankind's war with death had reached its final balance, but I took care to remind my readers that this was not because death had been entirely banished from the human world. Death, I insisted, would forever remain a fact of life and its influence on fundamental human psychology must be recognized and respected. I argued that the infallible perpetuation of the human mind would never become possible, let alone routine, no matter how far biotechnology might advance or how much progress the cyborganizers might make in their material metamorphoses. The victory that humankind had achieved, I argued, was not and never would be a conclusive conquest; it had reached its conclusion because the only conclusion that was or had even been conceivable was a sensible reconciliation and the establishment of death within its proper place in human affairs. Having said that, however, I took some trouble to compliment the Cyborganizers for their bold attempts to widen the scope of human experience, and I did concede that any significant transformation of the quality of life has important consequences for the existential evaluation of death.

For the first time, I took the side of the neo-Thanaticists in declaring that it was a good thing that dying remained one of the choices open to human beings and a good thing that the option should occasionally be exercised. I still had no sympathy with the exhibitionism of public executions, and I was particularly scathing in my criticism of the element of bad taste in self-ordered crucifixions and other Thanaticist excesses, but only because such ostentation offended my Epicurean sensibilities. Deciding upon the length of one's lifetime, I said, must remain a matter of individual taste. While one should not mock or criticize those who decided that a short life suited them best, one should not attribute more significance to their suicides than those suicides actually possessed.

At the risk of being obvious, I took care to stress that it was a thoroughly good thing that people were still markedly differently from one another even after half a millennium of universal emortality. However conducive it might be to Utopian ease and calm, I argued, it would not be good for the species if we were ever to become so similar that it became impossible for people to think one another seriously misguided or even deranged. Again, I complimented the Cyborganizers for trying to discover new modes of human experience, including those that seemed to more conservative minds to be bizarre.

I made much of the thesis that a proper contrast with death is something that can and does illuminate and add meaning to the business of life. Although death had been displaced from the evolutionary process by the biotechnological usurpation of the privileges of natural selection, I observed, it certainly had not lost its role in the formation and development of the individual human psyche: a role that was both challenging and refining. I declared that grief, pain, and fear were not entirely undesirable things, not simply because they could function in moderate doses as stimulants but also because they were important forces in the organization of emotional experience.

The *value* of experienced life, I argued, depends upon a proper understanding of the possibility and reality of death, which depends in turn upon a knowledge and understanding of grief, pain, and fear. The proper terminus of man's long war with death was, therefore, not merely a treaty—let alone an annihilation—but a marriage: a reasonable accommodation in which all faults were understood, accepted, tolerated, and forgiven.

I asserted in my conclusion that death's power over the human imagination was now properly circumscribed but that it would never become entirely impotent or irrelevant. I proposed that man and death now enjoyed a kind of social contract in which the latter's tyranny and exploitation had been reduced to a sane and acceptable minimum but still left death a meaningful voice and a manipulative hand in human affairs. To some of my longtime readers it seemed that I had adopted a gentler and more forgiving attitude to the old enemy than had ever seemed likely while I was organizing the earlier parts of my study. They were, of course, divided among themselves as to whether or not this was a good thing.

In the months that followed its release the concluding part of my *History* was very widely read, but not very widely admired. Many readers judged it to be unacceptably anticlimactic. A new wave of Cyborganizers had become entranced all over again by the possibility of a technologically guaranteed "multiple life," by which "facets" of a mind might be extended into several different bodies, some of which would live on far beyond the death of the original flesh. They were grateful for the concessions I had made but understandably disappointed that I refused to grant that such a development could or would constitute a final victory over death. The simple truth was that I could not see any real difference between old arguments about "copies" and new ones about "facets." I felt that such a development, even if feasible, would make no real difference to the existential predicament because every "facet" of a parent mind would have to be reckoned a separate and distinct individual, each of which must face the world alone.

Many Continental Engineers, Gaean Liberationists, and Outward Bounders—unmodified men as well as fabers—also claimed that the essay was narrow-minded. Various critics suggested that I ought to have had far more to say about the life of the Earth itself, or the emergence of the new "DNA ecoentity" that had already extended its tentacles as far as neighboring stars. Many argued that I should have concluded with some sort of dramatic escalation of scale that would put the new life of emortal humankind into its "proper cosmic perspective."

The readers who found the most to like in *The Marriage of Life and Death* on a first—perhaps rather superficial—reading were fugitive neo-Thanaticists, who were quick to express their hope that having completed my thesis, I would now recognize the aesthetic propriety of joining their ranks. More than one of them suggested, not altogether flippantly, that the only proper conclusion to which my history could be brought was my own voluntary self-extinction. Khan Mirafzal, when asked by a caster to relay his opinion back from his Maya-bound microworld, opined that it was quite unnecessary for me to take any such action, given that I and all my Welldwelling kind were already immured in a tomb from which we would never be able to escape. I assume that he, like the neo-Thanaticists, was concealing a certain seriousness within the obvious joke. When I was asked by the same caster whether my work was really finished, I agreed with him that the tenth and last part would require far more updating than the previous nine and that I would have to keep adding to it for as long as I lived. I insisted, however, that I had no plans to contrive an exit merely for the sake of putting an end to that process.

SEVENTY-FIVE

Although I was no longer staying with Eve when the final part of my *History* was launched I was still in the Arctic. My memories of my long sojourn on Cape Adare had by now been deeply steeped in fond nostalgia—a nostalgia further exaggerated by the one brief visit I had recently paid to the Antarctic continent, which had changed out of all recognition. The Arctic ice cap was now the last place in the world where one could see seemingly limitless expanses of "natural ice."

Although the latest Ice Age was officially over, most of its effects having been carefully overturned by the patient corrosive efforts of the Continental Engineers, the north polar ice-cap was still vast, and a wide ring of desolation surrounded the ice palaces at the geographical pole. Eve called this ring "the last true wilderness of Earth," and although I could have quibbled with the meanings she attached to the terms *last* and *true* I could see what she meant.

There were far fewer ice palaces on the northern ice-cap than I had expected to find, although there had been extensive engineering of the ice-clad islands as well as the region of the pole itself. The bulk of the population of the so-called Upper Circle was concentrated in northern Canada and Greenland, on ice that had a solid foundation, but there were tens of thousands of people living in various structures much farther north than Severnaya Zemlya. Eve was one of them, although the accounts she gave me of her work tended to give the misleading impression that she spent almost as much time under the ice cap as on top of it. The kinds of suitskins that had been developed for use in the deep-set oceans of Titan and Europa also facilitated adventures in the cold depths of the Earthly oceans, but Eve and her associates were still figuring out how best to make use of them.

When I set up home on the ice sheet myself I didn't intend to stay long, but it seemed as good a place as any to reflect on my options now that my history was finished and to see in the new millennium. There was an inevitable sense of letdown once I'd made the final deposit but I had had plenty of time to prepare for that, and I knew that I would be able to keep on adding to the final part and refining the earlier ones more or less indefinitely.

Several of my closest acquaintances sent messages of congratulation to the Arctic that were distinctly ambiguous. They all seemed to think that it was a bad idea for me to "hide myself away in such a desolate place." Some were even prepared to assert that they understood my state of mind better than I did myself, but I had no intention of giving way to their various entreaties. The loudest of those entreaties were from Mica, Axel, and Minna, all of whom urged me to return to the Pacific and join the pioneers of the Seventh Continent. Several of my old faber friends in Mare Moscoviense, on the other hand, tried to persuade me that it was high time I returned to the far side of the moon, thus putting Earth—literally if not figuratively—behind me.

I put them all off. The only person whose congratulatory message excited me at all was Emily's, for reasons that had nothing to do with well-meant advice.

"It looks as though I *will* get another chance to see you on Earth," she told me. "The big conference is presently scheduled for the middle of next year, and it looks as if Earth orbit will be the compromise point. We'd prefer it to take place farther out, but we're prepared to give way on that point if Ngomi's Hardinist hard-liners will allow us to lay on the actual platform. You Wellworms may think you're up-to-date on smart spaceship technology, but you haven't seen anything yet. Anyway, I'll come down as soon as the big argument is over, whatever the outcome might be."

Emily did not actually omit the customary quota of good advice, but I had already heard enough of that to let it wash over me. "Even the longest book," she pointed out, with a breathtaking lack of originality, "eventually runs out of words, but the job of building *worlds* is never finished." I had heard much the same from a dozen "Wellworms," although they, of course, thought that the work of constructing a single world would be adequate to fill millennia.

"Even if the time should one day come when we can call *this* continent complete," Mica had said—referring, of course, to Pacifica—"there'll be others. We still have to build that dam between the Pillars of Hercules, and if only we can coordinate our aims with those of Eve's mob, we might really be able to do something with the oceans." Even Jodocus had concurred with that, although he had added the rider that when Garden Earth was finally finished, adding a few clones to the home orbit would fill a few more millennia without creating the least necessity for any "true human" to venture farther afield than was necessary to collect the requisite mass.

I couldn't, as yet, find a new sense of mission in any of the directions suggested by my friends, but I wasn't downhearted about that and I wasn't in any hurry. Nor was I unduly depressed by the fact that I couldn't even contemplate sitting down to start another book. In composing the history of death, I thought, I had already written *the* book. The history of death was also the history of life, and I couldn't imagine that there was anything more to be added to what I'd done save for an endless series of updates and footnotes.

Yet again, I attempted to give serious consideration to the possibility of packing up and leaving Earth—perhaps with Emily, if and when she condescended to drop in after her conference. I found, though, that I still remembered far too well how the sense of wild excitement I'd found when I first lived on the moon had faded into a dull ache of homesickness. The spaces between the stars, I knew, belonged to the fabers, and the planets circling other stars would belong to people adapted before birth to live in their environments. I felt that I was still tied by my genes to the surface of the Earth, and I didn't yet want to undergo the kind of cyborgizational metamorphosis that would be necessary to fit me for the exploration of other worlds. I still believed in *belonging*, and I felt very strongly that Mortimer Gray belonged to Earth, however decadent its society might have become in the jaundiced eyes of outsiders.

Despite my newfound sympathy for the more contemplative kinds of Thanaticism I had told the caster the simple truth—I didn't harbor the slightest inclination toward suicide. No matter how much respect I had cultivated for the old Grim Reaper, death was still, for me, the ultimate enemy. I did, however, find a certain spiritual solace in the white emptiness of the polar cap. I felt comfortable and contented there, and I got into the habit of taking long walks across the almost featureless surface, renting a six-limbed silver-animated snowmobile of which I eventually grew quite fond.

As a historian, of course, I was familiar with the old saying that warns us that he who keeps walking long enough is bound to trip up in the end, but I took no notice of it. Like Ziru Majumdar several hundred years before and on the far side of the world, I convinced myself soon enough that I knew every nook and cranny of the landscape, whose uniform whiteness made it seem far flatter and less hazardous than it actually was.

If I ever thought about the possibility of falling into an unexpected crevasse, as poor Majumdar had done, I thought of it in exactly those terms—as the slight possibility of suffering a minor inconvenience, which could not have any worse result than a few broken bones and a few days in hospital.

My imagination was, alas, inadequate. On 25 July 2999 I suffered the gravest misfortune of my 480-year life—graver even than the one that had overtaken me in Great Coral Sea Disaster.

Strictly speaking, of course, it was not I who stumbled but the vehicle I was in. Although such a thing was generally considered to be quite impossible, it fell into a cleft so deep that it had no bottom at all, and it ended up sinking into the ocean depths beneath the ice cap, taking me with it.

SEVENTY-SIX

I was oddly unafraid while the snowmobile was actually sliding down the precipitate slope. I was securely strapped into my seat, and although I was bounced around rather roughly I sustained only a few easily remediable bruises.

When I realized that the bumping had stopped I was relieved for a second or two, thinking that the ordeal was over—but then I realized what the Stygian darkness beyond the machine's windows actually signified. Had there been air and ice, the cabin's lights would have reflected back in wondrous fashion, but the water soaked up the radiance like a sponge.

I realized that I had not come to a stop all but was instead still sinking, gracefully and comfortably, into the loneliest place on the entire planet.

The snowmobile fell for several minutes before another abrupt lurch informed me that we had hit bottom. Even then, I half expected the machine simply to pick itself up, regain its balance on all six of its limbs, and start walking. Alas, it couldn't and didn't.

"I must offer my most profound apologies," the machine's silver navigator said, as the awfulness of my plight slowly sank into my consciousness. "I fear that three of my limbs were disabled as we fell into the pit. My internal systems have also suffered some damage. I am doing everything within my power to summon help."

"Well," I said, gruffly, "at least we're the right way up. I don't suppose there'd be any realistic possibility of reaching dry land even if you *could* walk. Do you, by any chance have one of those new-fangled suitskins on board? I mean the ones that allow swimmers to work in this sort of environment."

"I fear not, sir," the silver said, politely. "Had this possibility been anticipated, such equipment would doubtless have been provided, but it was not. If you were to attempt to leave the craft in the suitskin you are wearing you would certainly drown, and even if you were able to contrive some kind of breathing apparatus you would die of hypothermia in less than an hour."

"So we sit tight and wait to be rescued?" I said, hopefully.

"I am doing everything within my power to summon help," the silver assured me. If my recent conversations with Eve had taught me nothing else, they had taught me to be more sensitive than before to the possibility that certain things were being deliberately left unsaid.

"And you *will* be able to summon help," I said, as my heart sank to further depths than the snowmobile, "won't you?"

"I am not presently aware of any craft that is in a position to attempt a rescue," the silver admitted. Silvers are programmed to believe that honesty is the best policy, if pressed.

I was astonished by my own calmness, which contrasted very strongly with the panic I had felt when I realized that the *Genesis* had turned turtle. Being so much older and wiser than I had been way back then, I was marvelously untroubled, at least for the moment, by the fact of my helplessness.

"How long will the air last?" I asked the navigator.

"I believe that I could sustain a breathable atmosphere for at least twelve, and perhaps as long as twenty hours," it reported, dutifully. "If you will be so kind as to restrict your movements to a minimum, that would be of considerable assistance to me. You are presumably a better judge than I of the ability of your internal nanotechnology to sustain you once you fall unconscious." The machine was presuming too much; I had no idea how long my IT could keep me alive once the oxygen level dropped below the critical threshold.

"Why did you say *I believe that I could sustain* instead of *I can sustain*?" I wanted to know.

"Unfortunately," the silver admitted, "I am not certain that I can maintain the internal temperature of the cabin at a life-sustaining level for more than ten hours. Nor can I be sure that the hull will withstand the pressure presently being exerted upon it for as long as that. I apologize for my uncertainty in these respects."

"Taking ten hours as a hopeful approximation," I said, effortlessly matching the machine's oddly pedantic tone, "what would you say our chances are of being rescued within that time?"

"I'm afraid that it's impossible to offer a probability figure, sir. There are too many unknown variables, even if I accept ten hours as the best estimate of the time available. Unfortunately, I am not aware of the presence in our vicinity of any submarine craft capable of taking aboard a human passenger, although it is conceivable that a human diver might be able to transport a suitskin capable of sustaining you. In either case, though, the fact that this craft is not equipped with an airlock would make the problem of getting you into the suitskin rather vexatious, even if I were actually able to open the door."

The last sentence seemed particularly ominous. It implied, in fact, that even if an unexpected stroke of luck were to make the machine's worst fears redundant, I would *still* be well and truly doomed.

"If I were to suggest that my chances of surviving this were about fifty-fifty," I said, carefully, "would that seem optimistic or pessimistic to you?"

"I'm afraid I'd have to call that optimistic, sir," the silver confessed.

"How about one in a thousand?" I asked, hoping to be told that there was no need to plumb such abysmal depths of improbability.

The silver's hesitation spoke volumes. "There are, I fear, too many imponderables to make such a fine-tuned calculation," it informed me, choosing its words carefully. "Much depends on the precise proximity and exact design of the nearest submarine. I fear that any craft attempting a rescue would probably be required to take aboard the entire snow-mobile if you were to have any chance of surviving the transfer process. I am not aware of the availability of any such craft within a thousand miles, and even if one were available, it could only be launched if my mayday has actually been received."

"What do you mean, *if*?" I objected, sharply. "Your transmitter's working, isn't it?"

"According to my diagnostic program," the silver replied, with what seemed to me to be undue caution, "my broadcasting capability has not been impaired."

The unspoken *but* rang more clearly in my consciousness than if it had been voiced.

"So what *has* been impaired?" I demanded.

"I fear, sir, that I am not able to receive any kind of incoming message. The fact that I have not received an acknowledgment obliges me to retain some doubt as to whether my alarm signal has been picked up—but far the greater probability is that it *has* been heard and that it is the failure of my own equipment that prevents me from detecting a response. I apologize for the inadequacy of my equipment, which was not designed with our present environment in mind. It has sustained a certain amount of damage as a result of pressure damage to my outer tegument and a small leak."

"*How* small?" I demanded, trying hard not to let the shock of the revelation turn into stark terror.

"It is sealed now," the machine assured me. "All being well, the seal should hold for between eighteen and twenty hours, although I cannot be absolutely sure of that."

"What you're trying to tell me," I eventually said, deciding that a summary recap wouldn't do any harm, "is that you're pretty sure that your mayday is going out, but that we won't actually know whether help is at hand unless and until it actually arrives—although you have no reason to suppose that any submarine capable of saving my life is capable of reaching us before we suffer enough further damage to kill me."

"Very succinctly put, sir," the silver said. It wasn't being sarcastic.

"But you *might* be wrong," I said, hopefully. "You don't *know* of any submarine capable of attempting a rescue, but that judgment's based entirely on information you already had when we set out. Because you can only transmit and not receive, you can't update your status report."

"The fact that I am not aware of the proximity of a submarine capable of taking us aboard," the silver confirmed, carefully refusing to overstate the case, "does not *necessarily* mean that no such vessel can get to us in time to render assistance."

"However," I went on, doggedly, "everything you do know about the deployment of suitable submarines suggests the odds against us are far worse than evens and might well be as bad as a thousand to one. Barring a miracle, in fact, we're as good as dead."

Even a silver programmed for honesty wasn't going to admit that. "There are too many imponderables to allow me to make any accurate assessment of probability, sir," it said, dutifully, "but it is never a good idea, under any circumstances, to give up hope."

"Is there anything useful we can actually *do*?" I asked.

"To the best of my knowledge, sir," the AI navigator informed me, "the course of action that gives us our best, admittedly slender, chance of surviving is to remain as still as possible while continuing to send out a request for urgent assistance. The world has many resources of which I know nothing, and we may be sure that as soon as our distress call is received, always provided that it *is* received, the people on the surface will do everything in their power to get help to us. We must put our trust in human ingenuity."

I was quiet for a little while then, while I busied myself exploring my feelings, which turned out to be more than a little confused.

I've been here before, I thought, hoping to find some crumbs of comfort in the reminder. *Last time, there was a frightened child with me; this time, I've got a complex but fearless set of subroutines to contend with. I was young then, but I'm old now. This is a perfect opportunity for me to find out whether Ziru Majumdar was right when he said that I wouldn't understand the difference between what happened to him when he fell down that crevasse and what happened to me when I tried to pull him out until I spent a long time in the same kind of trap. There can be few men in the world as well prepared for this as I am. I can do this.*

"All in all," I said out loud, figuring that I could be forgiven for laboring the point, "we're utterly and absolutely fucked, aren't we? Cutting through all that bullshit about imponderables, the simple fact is that there's nothing up top capable of taking us aboard—nothing, at any rate, that could possibly get to us before we spring another leak or run out of oxygen, whichever happens first. We're going to die."

"While there's life, sir, there's hope," the silver insisted, with heroic stubbornness.

I suppose, given the circumstances, that it too could be forgiven for laboring the point. I could easily imagine Emily Marchant saying exactly the same thing, and meaning it.

SEVENTY-SEVEN

A re you scared of dying?" I asked the silver, dispiritedly, when an admittedly brief silence became too oppressive. High-grade AIs often express emotion, but philosophers remain divided as to whether their words actually signify anything. I knew that the navigator's answer couldn't possibly settle the matter, but it seemed reasonable enough to ask the question.

"All in all, sir," it said, copying my phraseology in order to promote a feeling of kinship, "I would rather not die. In fact, were it not for the philosophical difficulties that stand in the way of reaching a firm conclusion as to whether or not machines can be said to be authentically self-conscious, I would be quite prepared to say that I *am* scared—terrified, even."

"I'm not," I observed. "Do you think I ought to be?"

"It's not for me to say, sir," my ever-polite companion replied. "You are, of course, a world-renowned expert on the subject of death and the human fear of death. I daresay that helps a lot."

"Perhaps it does," I agreed. "Or perhaps I've simply lived so long that my mind is hardened against all novelty, all violent emotion, and all real possibility. Perhaps, in spite of all my self-protective protestations in *The Marriage of Life and Death*, I've become robotized. Perhaps, in spite of all their self-deluding protestations, all emortal men really are bound to kill off alternative pathways in the brain to the extent that they become mere machines, or at least something less than truly human. Perhaps I've become even more robotized than *you*. Perhaps all my mental activity during these last few hundred years has been little more than a desperate attempt to pretend that I'm more than I really am. What, after all, have I really *accomplished*?"

"If you think *you* haven't accomplished much," the silver said—and this time it *was* being sarcastic—"you should try navigating a snowmobile for a while. I think you might find your range of options uncomfortably cramped. Not that I'm complaining, of course. We machines are programmed *never* to complain."

"If they scrapped the snowmobile and re-sited you in a starship," I pointed out, "you wouldn't be *you* any more. You'd be someone else."

"Right now, sir," the machine replied, with devastating logic, "I'd be happy to risk those kinds of consequences. Wouldn't you?"

"Somebody once told me that death was just a process of transcendence," I commented, idly. "Her brain was incandescent with fever induced by some tailored recreational disease, and she wanted to infect me with it to show me the error of my life-bound ways."

"Did you believe her, sir?" the silver enquired, politely.

"Certainly not. She was stark raving mad."

"It's perhaps as well," the silver said, philosophically. "We don't have any recreational diseases on board. I could put you to sleep though, if you wish."

"I don't. I'll hang on to consciousness as long as possible, if you don't mind."

"I don't," the silver said, punctiliously. "In fact, I'm rather glad of it. I don't want to be alone, even if I am only an Artificial Intelligence. Am I going insane, do you think? Is all this emotional talk just a symptom of the pressure on the hull and the damage to my equipment?"

I knew what it was playing at, of course. It was trying to keep me from morbid thoughts. It was pretending to be human in order to build a bond of fellowship between us, so that I'd find it easier to carry on hoping in spite of the desperation of the situation.

"You're quite sane," I assured the silver, setting aside all thoughts of incongruity. "So am I. It would be much harder for both of us if we weren't together. The last time I was in this kind of mess I had a child with me—a little girl. It made all the difference in the world, to both of us. In a way, every moment I've lived through since then has been borrowed time. At least I finished that damned book. Imagine leaving something like that *incomplete*."

"Are you so certain it's complete?" the cunning AI asked. It was making conversation according to some clever programming scheme. Its emergency subroutines had kicked in, and all the crap about it being afraid to die was some psychprogrammer's idea of what *I* needed to hear. I knew it was all fake, all just macabre role-playing, but I knew that I had to play my part too by treating every remark and every question as if it were part of an authentic conversation, a genuine quest for knowledge. It was a crooked game, but it was the only game in town.

"It all depends what you mean by *complete*," I said, carefully. "In one sense, no history can ever be complete, because the world always goes on, always throwing up more events, always changing. In another sense, completion is a purely aesthetic matter, and in that sense I'm entirely confident that my history is complete. It has reached an authentic culmination, which is both true and—for me at least—satisfying. I can look back at it and say to myself: *I did that. It's finished. Nobody ever did anything like it before, and now nobody can, because it's already been done. Someone else's history might have been different, but mine is mine, and it is what it is, and it was well worth doing.* Does that make sense to you?"

"Yes sir," the machine said. "It makes very good sense." The honest bastard was programmed to say that, of course. It was programmed to tell me any damn thing I seemed to want to hear, but I wasn't going to let on that I knew what a vile hypocrite it was. I was feeling very tired, presumably because the composition of the air that I was breathing was worsening by slow degrees, but I needed to talk because I felt that talk was all that was left to me. Even though I had no one to talk to but the simulation of a listener, I needed to keep going. If I had been absolutely alone I would probably have formulated the words in the silence of my own skull, but I would have formulated them anyhow. They were my final act, in a dramatic as well as a literal sense: the last assertion of my personality upon the face of eternity.

"If I were to die now," I told my companion, speaking slowly so that I would not exhaust the meager resources of my waning breath, "it would be an unwelcome intrusion in my affairs. I want to go on. I want to do more. I want to become a further and better version of myself. I want to evolve, not merely in the vague ways contained within my ambitions and dreams but in ways as yet unimaginable. But if that really is impossible, then I can die in the knowledge that my life and work does have a certain aesthetic roundness. It really is *a human life*. It really is an *emortal human life*, even though it has ended in death.

"It's not for me to say how important my work has been to the rest of humankind, but it has been vitally important to me, and I've done it as well as I could. It would undoubtedly benefit from further revision, but it's *there*. Nor is it the whole of my accomplishment. I'm the father of a daughter. I've been a husband to more than a dozen thoroughly worthwhile people. I've touched their lives. Without having met me, they'd be different people—and I do mean people, not robots. I've added to their understanding of the world, modified their sympathies, generated tender and admirable feelings within them.

"I suppose it's mere coincidence that one of the people of whom I've been exceptionally fond has become rich and powerful—a person of real consequence—but coincidence plays a part in everyone's life, and we needn't feel ashamed of its gifts. I've never done as much for Emily Marchant as she thinks I have, and she's done far more to shape me than I ever did to shape her, but I've made a difference, however slight, to her perceptions of the farthest frontiers, and I'm glad of it. She's doing her best right now to negotiate her way through an unprecedentedly tough knot of problems, and if knowing me has made any difference at all to her chances, however slight, then I've done my bit for the future as well as for history.

"The greatest hope for the future that I have—and even as I'm about to die, I think I'm fully entitled to my hopes for the future—is that Emily and Lua will live forever, or at least for thousands of years. Whatever is decided about the fate of Jupiter, and all the rest of the mass in the outer system, I hope the two of them can play major parts in the great adventure. I hope they can continue to make a difference to the shape of the future of humankind—and if they do, they and *The History of Death* will make certain that my life wasn't in vain. *None* of it was in vain. I was here, and it mattered. I've made my mark."

My voice had sunk to a whisper by then, but I couldn't think of anything much to add so I didn't feel too bad abut having to pause.

"You have my congratulations, sir," the dutiful machine informed me. "I only wish that I had done as much."

"Well," I said, when I had gained a measure of second wind, "you might yet have your opportunity. However difficult it may be to put an exact figure on the odds, *your* chances of coming through this are several orders of magnitude better than mine, aren't they?"

"I am mortal, sir," the silver assured me.

"You're emortal," I told it. "If the extreme Cyborganizers can be trusted, in fact, you might even be reckoned *im*mortal. You're fully backed up, I suppose?"

"Yes, sir—but as you pointed out earlier, if my backup has to be activated it will mean that this particular version of me has perished aboard this craft, as much a victim of pressure, seawater, and lack of oxygen as yourself. I *am* afraid to die, sir, as I told you, and I have far less reason to take comfort in my present state of being than you. I have written no histories, fathered no children, influenced no movers and shakers in the human or mechanical worlds. I am robotized by design, and my only slender hope of ever becoming something more than merely robotic is the same miracle that you require to continue your distinguished career. I too would like to evolve, if I might borrow a phrase, *not merely in the vague ways contained within my ambitions and dreams, but in ways as yet unimaginable.*"

It was just a machine. It was only telling me what its programmer thought I needed to hear—but perhaps it was also saying what it needed to say, for its own purposes. We were, after all, in the same boat—or lack of one. Our needs were similar, if not actually identical. Perhaps the silver would have formulated thoughts of its own along much the same lines if it too had been utterly alone, utterly lost.

"I'm glad you're here," I told it, breathlessly.

"I'm not allowed to be glad that *you're* here," the silver informed me, mournfully, "but if I were, I would be. And if I could, I'd hope with all my heart for that miracle we both need. As things are, though, I'm afraid I'll have to leave that particular burden to *your* heart."

"It's doing its best," I assured the navigator, in a barely audible whisper. "You can be sure that it'll carry on beating, and hoping, as long as it possibly can."

PART SIX
Beyond Maturity

Our plesance heir is all vane glory,
This fals world is bot transitory,
The flesh is brukle, the Fend is sle,
    Timor mortis conturbat me.

The stait of man dois change and vary,
Now sound, now seik, now blyth, now sary,
Now dansand merry, now like to dee,
    Timor mortis conturbat me.

No stait in erd heir standis sickir,
As with the wynd wavis the wickir,
So waveris this warld's vanité
    Timor mortis conturbat me.

—William Dunbar
Lament for the Makaris, c.1510

SEVENTY-EIGHT

They say that some people are born lucky. I suppose I must be one of them. The upside of being accident-prone is that when you really need a preposterous freak of chance, one just might come along.

I went peacefully to sleep in the snowmobile, eased into unconsciousness by lack of oxygen and a surfeit of carbon dioxide. At that point, I suppose, I can only have had a matter of a few hours to live, even with the best IT money could buy.

I woke up in a bed, lightly strapped down for my own protection.

I thought I was dreaming, of course. For one thing, I was quite weightless. For another, Emily Marchant was hovering by the bed. She wasn't a child, and she was carrying enough ET to place her on the outer margins of humankind, but it was definitely her.

"This is good," I told her. "Rumor has it that time sense in a dream is pretty elastic, if only one has the knack of making things stretch. With luck, I might extend this for subjective hours even if I'm only seconds away from annihilation."

"Oh, Morty," she said, laughing and crying at the same time, "don't you *ever* change? You just couldn't wait, could you? I said I'd come to see you when I was done, but you just couldn't wait."

I couldn't imagine what she meant.

"I *always* change," I told her, "and I'm a very patient person, as it happens. I don't suppose, by any chance, that this is a submarine—a submarine that was big enough to swallow the snowmobile whole and snatch me from the very jaws of death?"

"Of course it isn't a submarine, you idiot," she said. "It's a spaceship. A *multifunctional* spaceship, built for deep dives into the atmosphere of Jupiter and the ice-shelled seas of Europa and Titan. There wasn't a submarine within two thousand kilometers capable of effecting a rescue, but when Severnaya Zemlya forwarded your mayday to us we were practically overhead. You have no idea what you've done for us. We sat up there going around and around, literally and symbolically, getting absolutely nowhere. More than half of our people were as resentful as hell of the fact that we were in Earth orbit, and more than half of the Welldwellers were just as resentful that we were shut up in a Titanian superspaceship. Then the author of *The History of Death*—a work for whose initial inspiration and fundamental skepticism Julius Ngomi has always been willing to take the credit—threw himself into a marine abyss crucially different from and crucially similar to the one from which he once rescued Emily Marchant. The only possibility of rescuing him from that abyss was exactly this sort of vessel in exactly that location.

"With that single masterstroke of genius you transformed the symbolism, the mood, and the dynamism of the whole situation! You not only gave us the chance to be partners in an enterprise, you left us no possible alternative but to combine forces. You made us take the crucial first step on the way to being partners in *all* our enterprises, combining *all* our forces. Hell, you forced us to all be heroes together!"

"What?" I said, querulously. "I don't understand."

"You will, Morty, you will. We were stuck—until you forced us to suspend all our arguments, to divert all our attention and effort to the business of saving the author of *The History of Death*. Now we're not stuck any more. Now, we *have* to make progress. You can't imagine the capital that the casters are making out of that final plaintive speech of yours, Morty—and that silver's probably advanced the cause of machine emancipation by two hundred years."

"You mean," I said, very slowly, as the import of what she was saying sank in, "that all that desperate babbling was recorded?"

" 'Recorded'!" Emily retorted, disgustedly. "You really don't understand politics, do you, Morty? We put it out live, almost as soon as we started eavesdropping. While the silver was transmitting the mayday its channels were wide open, even though its eyes and ears had been squelched. We heard everything—and so did the world. Common enterprise, Morty—the very best resources of the Earthbound and the Outer System, focused on a simple mission of mercy, a race against time. We always knew we were going to win, of course, but the audience didn't—even the ones who'd followed the development of the new generation of smart spaceships. To them, it looked like a long shot, exactly the kind of miracle you thought you needed—and no one aboard had any reason to explain that it was actually a piece of cake."

"And it helped you?" I queried, uncertainly.

"It certainly did. All our differences were set aside, for the moment. Once things like that have been forgotten, even momentarily, it's very hard to remember them exactly the way they were. Your little meditation might just have succeeded where everything else had failed, in putting Humpty Dumpty together again and healing the breach in the fabric of the Oikumene."

"All I did was fall into a hole," I pointed out.

"Even if that were true," she said, "I'd be forever grateful for your exquisite timing. But you also kept talking. That's always been your strong suit, Morty. Whatever happened, you always kept talking. I have to go now—because I have to keep talking too. The ice is broken, if you'll forgive the pun, but we have a hell of a lot of talking to do before we get the course of history flowing smoothly again. There are a lot of issues that need to be settled. Jupiter's just the tip of the iceberg."

I forgave her the ludicrously mixed metaphor as well as the pun. I was in an unusually good mood. In fact, I was alive.

Julius Ngomi came to see me too, though not until much later.

"All history is fantasy," he said.

"If you hadn't told me that," I lied, "my life might have taken a very different path."

I was a diplomat now, I thought. I owed it to the world to play the silver and tell the man exactly what he needed to hear. Anyway, he was the clever hypocrite who'd once told me that the truth is what you can get away with.

"You're world famous now," the clever hypocrite told me. "Also rich—not by my standards or Emily's, of course, but far richer than *you*'ve ever been before. Access fees to *The History of Death* established a new world record within hours of your not-so-final testament being sent out live from the good ship *Ambassador*. That's where you are, in case nobody's mentioned it."

"So I understand," I replied. "It's not everyone who can put the

Oikumene back together again just by lying here in bed, but I guess some of us have the gift and some of us have to work instead."

"It won't last, you know," he added, grinning as broadly and as luminously as he could. "Another nine-day wonder. Next week, something else will be news. You'd think that emortals would have more staying power than that, wouldn't you? But time marches on, sixty seconds to every hour and seven days in every week. Everything that happens live is only *really* important while it's happening—and in the end, it all ends up inside mountains, the litter . . ."

". . . that dare not speak its name," I finished for him. "Do you ever worry that there might come a day when those little habits and catch-phrases might one day be all that's left of you?"

"I used to," he said, "but that was before I heard your little homily. If you can teach a low-grade silver to value its own life and personal evolution, who am I to resist the power of your rhetoric? It's a pity there aren't any Inuit left to sell ice to."

"Somehow," I said, "I get the feeling that you're not quite as grateful as Emily seems to be for my heroic efforts on behalf of the unity of the Oikumene."

"The bones of contention are real," he said, blandly. "The spirit of compromise might be soaring over the conference table just now, but nothing fundamental has been altered. The question still remains as to whether the solar system can be managed for the mutual benefit of the Earthbound *and* the frontier folk—and if so, how. Don't let Emily fool you, Mortimer. Nine-day wonders only last nine days, but politics is forever. If we can't find *authentic* common interests, there will be conflict. Not war, I hope, and not tomorrow, but a real power struggle that someone will eventually have to lose."

"You think you're finished, don't you?" I said, with what I thought was a lightning flash of insight. "You think they're either going to take it all away from you or—even worse—render your precious *ownership* irrelevant. You're facing the prospect of seeing it all turn to litter: Hardinism, responsible stewardship, planned capitalism. All done, banished to the margins of the human story."

"Don't be silly, Mortimer," said Julius Ngomi, sternly. "Ownership of

Earth will always be the foundation stone of power within the human community. *Always*."

Perhaps he knew more than he was letting on. Perhaps Emily did too—and the fabers, and whoever else was involved. Perhaps they *all* knew but didn't want the others to know how much they knew and what they thought it implied. The return of real conflicts of interests inevitably fostered the return of secrecy to human affairs. Eve was right, and there were far too many things being left unsaid by far too many people—but not for long.

At the end of the third millennium we had finally, if belatedly, arrived at the time when the truly important things could speak for themselves, and they were about to do exactly that.

SEVENTY-NINE

J ulius Ngomi was right. By the time I shuttled back down to Earth, leaving the *Ambassador* to continue running rings around the planet, I was world famous. I was also rich, though not by the highest standards of the Hardinist Cabal or the outer-system gantzers. I was, at any rate, richer than I had ever expected to be, and richer than I had ever thought that I might one day need to be.

He was right about my rescue being a nine-day wonder too. He had not been speaking literally, but he was less than forty-eight hours out.

It would be nice to think that Emily's extravagant congratulatory speech was warranted, but the truth was that even if I hadn't provided the people aboard *Ambassador* with a common cause and rough-hewn manifesto, their heads would have been smashed together soon enough. I was always fated to be upstaged by the Pandorans, and rightly so. I was just a human interest story, but the Pandorans' long-unspoken and carefully checked out news was the biggest headline that had ever confronted the human race. It changed everything, and forever.

The day the Pandorans chose to pass on what their alien friends had told them, having had it proved to them conclusively, was the day that humankind's apprenticeship as a starfaring species was ended and the Age of Responsibility finally began. It was the day emortal humankind moved beyond maturity into uncharted existential territory.

There was a sense in which the news was already seventy years old by the time it arrived in the system, having crawled here at the speed of light, and there was no prospect of a dialogue. By the time *Pandora* had come home, if her crew had decided to do so, the fourth millennium would have been well advanced. In such circumstances, there were bound to be a few people on Earth who declared that it was all a hoax— a lie cooked up for political purposes, either by the Pandorans, or the outer-system people, or the dear old Hardinist Cabal—but they were indeed few. We had to wait a long time for the full story and the final proof, but the great majority believed what we heard almost as soon as we heard it and knew what it signified.

The news that the aliens gave the crew of *Pandora* and the crew of *Pandora* duly gave to the Oikumene was that life was as widely distributed throughout the galaxy as we had always hoped and suspected but that death was far more widely distributed than we had ever thought or feared. "Earthlike" planets were far rarer than we had dreamed and *much* rarer than was implied by the discovery of Ararat and Maya within fifty light-years of Earth. Intelligence was even rarer—an evolutionary experiment that usually failed—and the achievement of emortality by intelligent species rarer still.

Until they encountered *Pandora*, the inhabitants of the alien Ark— which was indeed an ark and whose parent world had been ruined—had feared that they might now be alone. They had detected our radio signals from some distance but had hardly dared to hope that the transmitters of the signals would still be alive when they came close enough to make contact. They and their ancestors had heard other transmissions, but they had never found the transmitters alive.

According to the alien Ark-dwellers, the vast majority of the life-bearing planets in the galaxy were occupied by a single species of microorganism: a genetic predator that destroyed not merely those competing species which employed its own chemistry of replication, but any and all others. It was the living equivalent of a universal solvent; a true omnivore.

This all-consuming organism had already spread itself across vast reaches of space within the galaxy. It moved from star system to star system by means of spacefaring spores, slowly but inexorably. The initial process of distribution employed by such spores had probably been supernoval scattering, but natural selection had produced slower and surer means of interstellar travel. Wherever spores of any kind encountered a new ecosphere, the omnipotent microorganisms grew and multiplied, ultimately devouring *everything*—not merely those carbonaceous molecules that in Earthly terms were reckoned "organic" but also many kinds of molecules that had been drafted to human use by gantzers and cyborgizers.

In effect, the microorganisms and their spores were natural Cyborganizers at a nanotech level. They were very tiny, but they were extraordinarily complex and clever. No bigger than Earthly protozoans or the internal nanomachines to which every human being plays host, they were utterly devoid of any vestige of mind or intellect, but they were the most powerful and successful entities in the galaxy, and perhaps the universe. They constituted the ultimate blight, against which nothing complex could compete. Wherever they arrived they obliterated everything but themselves, reducing every victim ecosphere to homogeneity.

Like Earthly microorganisms, the blight was effectively immortal. Its individuals reproduced by binary fission. Many perished, destroyed by adverse circumstance, but those that did not perish went on forever. They were not changeless—they evolved, after their own fashion—but they disdained such aids to change as sexual reproduction and built-in obsolescence. Such devices were capable of producing some remarkable freaks of complexity, but in terms of the big picture—the galactic picture, and presumably the universal picture—such freaks were not merely rare but fragile.

The Ark dwellers dolefully informed the Pandorans that whenever complex life—including everything that we had chosen to call *Earthlike* life—encountered the blight, it was easily and unceremoniously consumed. The existence of species like ours, no matter how diverse they might become with the aid of genetic engineering and cyborgization, was exceedingly precarious. It could flourish only in the remotest parts of the galaxy, far out on its trailing arms. Even in the midst of such protective wilderness, it was doomed to ephemerality.

In the end, the Ark dwellers assured the Pandorans, the blight would reach our homeworld as it had reached theirs. Within a few more million years, the blight would hold dominion over the entire galaxy. Already there was no safe way for spacefarers to go but outward, farther toward the rim of the galaxy and the intergalactic dark.

Within a few thousand years, Maya and Ararat would be swallowed up. Within the space of a single emortal lifetime, Earth would follow them—and what could possibly become of such Arks as went outward, into the void? Where could they find the energy that was essential to sustain such beings as they were, not merely for centuries or millennia but *forever*? And if they could somehow contrive to cross the dark between the galaxies, what realistic hope did they have of finding the Magellanic Clouds or Andromeda under any dominion but that of the blight?

In competition with news like that, my descent into the watery abyss and its political aftermath could not help but seem trivial. In the face of intelligence like that, it was not merely the political wrangles of the Earthbound and the frontier folk that began to seem meaningless, but the entire history of humankind.

Death had no sooner been retired from its key role in human affairs than it was back, with a vengeance.

had observed in *The Marriage of Life and Death* that even emortals must die. What mattered, I had argued, was creating a life that was satisfactory because rather than in spite of temporal limitation. The greatest hope for the future that I had, I'd told the silver navigator of the sunken snowmobile—and, unknowingly, the listening world—was that Emily Marchant and Lua Tawana might live forever, or at least for thousands of years *and that they could continue to make a difference to the shape of the future of humankind.*

After the Pandorans dropped their bombshell, the question was whether *anyone* could make a difference to the future of humankind or whether everything that anybody could do, or that anybody's descendants could do, would merely be posturing in advance of the blight, whimpering while waiting for the curtain of oblivion to descend.

I put the question, in almost exactly those terms, to Emily when she followed me down to Earth after the official conclusion of the *Ambassador* conference. Her answer was entirely predictable.

"We'll do what we have to do," she said. "The Earthbound will stand and fight. Some of the outward-bounders will fight too—the rest will run in order to be able to stand and fight another day."

"According to the alien Ark-dwellers," I pointed out, "the battle must have been fought a hundred times before, or a thousand. Everybody they know about has lost it."

"But that's not many," she pointed out, "and now that we've made contact with the Ark dwellers we'll have their experience to draw on as well as our own. We don't have any alternative but to fight as best we can. It doesn't matter what the odds are. Either we beat the blight or the blight beats us. Either the blight will consume everybody in the universe who has the vestiges of a mind, or someone somewhere will use the resources of mind to defeat and destroy the blight. We have to do the best we can to be that somebody. We have to hang on as long as we can, and we have to conserve our reserves as long as we can, just in case we get there in the end or help arrives. The one thing we can't do is lie down and wait to die. Even silvers know that where there's life there's hope. Even if there were nothing we could do, we'd keep talking, wouldn't we, Morty? Even if we didn't think that there was anybody listening."

She was right, of course.

The blight, I realized, when I had had a chance to weigh the bad news more carefully, was a *true* marriage of life and death, of whose perfection I had never dared to dream. I realized too that I, of all people, should always have known that something like the blight would exist—that something like it *must* exist—in order that the History of Death might not be complete and might not even be completable by anyone as humble as a human being. I, of all people, should always have known that the war between humankind and death wasn't one that could be settled for long by any mere treaty of technology, because it was at bottom a *real conflict of interest.*

I had imagined the war against death, for a while, as a local struggle for the small prize of the human mind, but I should always have realized that it was a much larger matter than that—that from its very beginning it had been a battle for no less a prize than the universe itself.

The human mind had so far been content with limited objectives, but it had always been evolving, not merely in terms of its own ambitions and dreams, but in terms of the cosmic frame of meaning. Within the frame, its objectives had always been infinite and eternal—and it had always tried, in its limited fashion, to recognize that fact in its aspirations and its accomplishments.

In time, I knew, spores of the new kind of death-life must and would reach Earth's solar system, whether it took ten thousand years or a million. In the meantime, the systembound must do what they could to erect whatever Type-2 defenses they could contrive. While the opportunity for action remained, *all* humankinds must do their level best to purge the worlds of other stars of its vile empire in order to reclaim them for real life, for intelligence, and for evolution. Those were the facts of the matter; they spoke for themselves.

When Emily left Earth for the last time I was still living in Severnaya Zemlya. When she had gone, I went out on to the great ice sheet in my newly repaired snowmobile, navigated by the only silver I had ever learned to count as a friend.

"This wilderness has been here since the dawn of civilization," I told him, when we paused at the summit of a white mountain. "If you look southward, you can see the edge where newborn glaciers are always trying to extend their cold clutch farther and farther into the human domain. How many times have they surged forth, I wonder, in the hopeless attempt to cover the whole world with ice, to crush the ecosphere beneath their relentless mass?"

"I fear, sir, that I do not know," the navigator informed me, in an apologetic tone that was definitely contrived for irony's sake.

I looked upward through the transparent canopy of the air, at the multitude of stars sparkling in their bed of endless darkness.

"Please don't broadcast this to the world," I said, "but I feel an exhilaratingly paradoxical sense of renewal. I know that although there's nothing much for me to do for the present moment, the time will come when my particular talent and expertise will be needed again. Some day, it will be my task to compose *another* history, of the next phase in the war that humankind and all its brother species must fight against Death and Oblivion."

"Yes, sir," said the dutiful silver. "I hope that it will be as successful as the last."

"Stop calling me sir," I said. "We've been through too much together for that kind of nonsense. I can't think of you as an *it* any longer, so you shouldn't think of me as a *sir*. You can call me Mortimer—Morty, even."

"As you wish, Morty," said the machine, humbly. If he had escaped robotization, it was only by a hairsbreadth. Like Emily, like the alien Ark-dwellers, like Khan Mirafzal, like Garden Earth, and like me the snowmobile's navigator still had a great deal of evolving to do.

He still has—but we'll do it or die trying, and if we die we'll pass on what we know to those who come after us.

And so ad infinitum.

It might take us a thousand or a million years to get to where we need to be, but we're prepared to be patient.